TIGER PELT

TIGER PELT

PELT

a novel

Annabelle Kim

Leaf
Land

Published in the United States by Leaf~Land LLC
www.leaflandpress.com

ISBN 978-0-9976090-0-4 (print)
ISBN 978-0-9976090-1-1 (ebook)

Cover design by Teija Lammi / Grafemi
Photography by cacaroot and mari1408/Adobe Stock
eBook cover design by Kostis Pavlou
Interior design by wordzworth.com

For my parents

Fall seven times; get up eight.

—Korean Proverb

1

*A Young Soldier
Somewhere in South Korea
1957*

A young soldier muscled through the violence of the summer monsoon. He was a corporal in the Tiger Division of the Republic of Korea Army, stationed at the DMZ, the strip of no-man's land halving his country, crisscrossed with barbed wire, riddled with land mines. The soldier had been there in his youth, during the war. His child's eyes had witnessed the blood of Americans, Koreans, and Chinese consecrating the earth. The young soldier, his annual leave over, was bound back to that gash of land to report for duty. He knew the monsoon. In a matter of hours, roads would wash out, and buses would be stranded. Walking was his only recourse. It would take six hours to reach the train station from his mother's farm. He bent his slick dark head into the crashing columns of rain and chanted a Korean proverb like a marching jody.

Fall eight times; get up nine. Fall nine times; get up ten…

Outwardly, by all appearances, he was a man on the move, a sturdy figure of determination, slicing through sheets of rain at an inexorable pace. Inwardly, by his own reckoning, life was at a standstill. He was meant to be a student, not a soldier. He was meant to study, not march.

The mud sucked at his waterlogged combat boots. His heavily sodden knapsack weighed him down, and the relentless rain infiltrated his army issue raincoat. He abandoned his grip on the coat, letting the streaming fabric whip wildly about his body as he slogged on.

Fall one hundred times; get up one hundred and one.

He had made himself into a scholar, but the draft notice had unmade him. He had worked so long and so hard to reach a place of higher learning. He had quaffed every dram of knowledge his professors served. His devotion to his books could be waylaid by no distraction until the day he met *her*.

The firstborn daughter of the college founder and president. Her face was a drama. Her nose was aristocratic, her teeth gleaming, her skin pale as ivory. She stood a head taller than the women in the coterie over which she reigned. She strode down the corridor with a smart click of her saddle shoes and a swish of her flared skirt. Laughter echoed among the women when she was in their midst: not the obligatory chuckling at a superior's jokes, not the muffled twittering behind the modest hand of a Korean gentlewoman, but hilarity – great big blasts of pure joy. She spoke to him in a bold manner. When they sang a duet together, their voices blended perfectly.

Although he was the penniless son of an illiterate farm widow, the young man had dared to hope. After all, his genealogy documented a proud ancestry of *yangban* scholars, the highest caste in Korean society. He had the right to hope. But he was acutely aware that the longer a prospective suitor remains out of sight, the greater the chances an eligible young lady will meet another man. The soldier quickened his pace.

Fall one thousand times; get up one thousand and one.

To maintain his bearings, he was following along the banks of the Sap Kyo River. Muddy water roared past, excoriating the river bed. A tree hurtled by, wrong side up, its gnarled roots exposed. A wooden cart tumbled downstream, collided with the tree, and smashed to splinters.

As the sandy sediments washed away, slabs of unsupported soil calved off the banks and crashed into the boiling river. The exposed cross sections of mud bristled with worms, and the water was alive with eels feeding in a writhing frenzy. When conditions became safer, the villagers would be out in force, waist deep in the river, catching the fattened eels with nets and even bare hands. There would be eel stew on every table for supper. The soldier felt a rumble in his belly; he quelled the spasm of panic that invariably ensued from the first signs of hunger.

A desperate sound penetrated the rain, the cry of a drowning cow still tied to the stake uprooted from its grazing field. Only the cow's head was visible above the cauldron of brown current, its eyes goggling in terror. The river bent sharply, and the animal was flung toward the outer bank. Seizing its chance at survival, the cow plunged its hooves into the bank, arching its thick neck, hunching its back to heave up its bottom half.

The soldier silently rooted for the struggling beast. But the undermined soil suddenly gave way and plunged the braying animal back into the flood. Twisting with a startling agility, it battered its head against its own stake before going under. Farther downstream, the stake bobbed up, then the cow's head. The beast resumed its piteous bawling.

What a shame, mourned the soldier. The loss of so much meat depressed him. It would be tough, not like a younger cow, but it could have been marinated in soy sauce and enjoyed as a salty side dish.

A grid of rice paddies and a cluster of humble grass-roofed houses came into view. He recognized the village, and his spirits lifted. He was only an hour's walk from the train station. He resumed his mechanical marching chant.

Fall five thousand six hundred...

He lost count when he heard a woman's scream.

A flash of white, a woman's form in traditional dress, streaked through the rain. The young woman raced headlong away from her village. She was pursued by an old woman who screamed gibberish incomprehensible in the downpour. The distance between the two figures, one nimble and reckless, the other feeble and frantic, widened. Quickening his steps, the soldier came within earshot of the old woman.

She shrieked, "Help! Somebody stop her!"

The two women neared a group of farmers who were repairing the banks of the rice paddies. The woman ran past, unheeded by the menfolk, toward the swollen river. The soldier broke into a preparatory trot, instinctively, not knowing what would happen next. He looked toward the farmers hoping one of them would act, willing one of them to act. The men did not raise their heads, but appeared frozen in the rain, in exaggerated attitudes of work, like a ruined painting.

Anger rose in his breast. They were *her* people. He had a train to catch. This was frightfully inconvenient.

The soldier turned toward the woman. He ran to her, ditching his knapsack and ripping off his raincoat as he went. The woman reached the bank of the river and paused, looking over her shoulder. The soldier heartened, although he did not break his stride. Suddenly, the bank gave way under the woman's feet and, in an instant, the slim figure in white was engulfed in the muddy avalanche and plunged into the flood waters. The old woman collapsed on the bank of a rice paddy and wailed.

The soldier recalled the training in lifesaving he had received during army boot camp. For the practical unit, the trainees had paired up, and the "drowning" partners had been dropped into the ocean from motor boats while the "rescuing" partners dashed from the beach, stripping out of full uniform, boots flung to the rocks, buttons popped from jackets, to swim to the rescue of the drowning partners. As the soldier had breast-stroked to his partner, cutting the waves with the steady power of an ocean liner, he had been amused by his partner's dramatic thrashing and gulping and realistic expression of terror. As it happened, his partner's terror was not only realistic, it was real. A weak swimmer, panic-stricken in the rough waves, his partner had fought him, tried to scale him with scraping claws, and shoved his head over and over again under the frigid brine. The pair had nearly drowned in the struggle.

The young soldier summoned this recollection in a flash. There was no time to remove his army boots. They might just as well be a ball and chain if he tried to swim in them. He turned mid-stride and sprinted downstream, solidifying a strategy as he ran. He slid down the bank on his backside, planted his boots into the riverbed, and waded like a tightrope walker with a shifting riverbed for a wire. As the disorienting current rose to his chest, and floating debris lacerated his face, the thought occurred to him that he might be standing in his own ignominious grave, shared with this silly woman. One slip would be tantamount to a death sentence. The flood waters reached his shoulders. The woman was ten meters upstream, floating motionless, face down. A sense of elation energized him; there would be no struggle. He positioned himself within arm's length of her trajectory and waited with his arms outstretched like a cross.

The voluminous skirt of the woman's white *hanbok* spread out over the water. The skirt would make for an ideal grip, better than a slippery limb or unwieldy torso. When she came within reach, he seized the fabric with one outstretched hand and pulled the woman toward himself hand over hand. He towed her behind him toward the bank with a fistful of skirt in one hand, using the other hand for a rudder in the swift river. When the water was waist deep, he turned her over, lifted her in his arms, and charged up the bank, accelerating with adrenaline-fueled ease out of the river's death grip.

He laid her limp body on the ground and observed that the rain and muddy flood waters had failed to cleanse a mask of heavily caked makeup from her face. She would have been a beauty were it not for the curious incongruity of a country woman in thick makeup. From his army training, the soldier knew how to fill an unconscious person's lungs with air by mouth. Something, perhaps the disconcerting makeup, compelled him to elect a different strategy. He lifted her by both ankles and turned her upside down in the air. A gush of muddy water poured from her mouth and nose like a kicked bucket and splashed onto his boots. He laid her back on the ground. She began to cough and breathe on her own. Several farmers and the old woman gathered about them.

"She is breathing," the soldier said.

"She is breathing! She is saved!" shouted the old lady.

The young woman opened her eyes and beheld the commotion. She saw the soldier hovering over her with solicitous concern. She recoiled. Flat on the ground, garments in muddy disarray, she began to weep. The old woman sat her up, straightened her skirt, and scolded, "Stop crying. You are alive. This brave man saved your life."

Raising her wretched painted face to the soldier, she cried out, "You should have let me die!"

The soldier stepped back, dumbstruck. Immediately, the old woman and the farmers, who seemed to be her brothers-in-law, offered profuse apologies and thanks, and invited him to dinner in their home. The offer of food tempted him. But he only stayed long enough to collect his raincoat and his knapsack, and to ascertain that the drowning victim was the old woman's daughter-in-law. Unable to find dry kindling to start the kitchen fire, reproached by her mother-in-law, she had run into the river for spite. That was their version, anyway, shouted through the rain. The young woman, who had stanched her crying as instructed, slumped on her patch of mud, her face in her hands, and said nothing.

The soldier knew there was more to this story. But he had to move on.

2

Kim Young Nam
Occupied Korea
1942-1943

A boy burst from a grass-roofed farmhouse and hastened across the hardpan courtyard. Spread-eagled across his back was a squalling baby swathed in a blanket tied about the boy's midriff. As the boy and baby crossed the yard, a puppy with protruding ribs and gyrating tail yelped and nipped the boy's ankles, only to tumble aside as the boy swept past. At the gate, the boy hesitated. The baby wailed. Kim Young Nam set his face in grim determination and marched toward a plot of land where the children were strictly forbidden.

Beyond the gate, an obstacle more difficult to dislodge than the puppy jumped into his path. It was the boy's younger sister, clutching the hand of their toddler brother. The girl would have been pretty except for her hair, tawny from malnutrition, shorn to stubble in the vain hopes it would grow out black.

"*Oppa!* Where are you going?" she asked.

"I must find *Umma.*"

"She is in the forbidden field. She told us to stay home, remember?"

"Quiet! You go back home," he said with the authority of an older sibling. But the girl lacked the requisite respect for a seven-year-old boy nearly her own age, and took liberties.

"Please, *Oppa*. Do not go. *Abuji* will beat you."

"Go back home! Baby is hungry. I have no choice. Go!"

Every waking hour, hunger mauled the boy's belly. His sleep was plagued by the stabs of starvation. That a baby should suffer such misery could not be borne. He watched his sister and toddler brother run toward the farmhouse, then forged ahead in long, swift strides between a stream and a grid work of rice paddies. The verdant paddies stretched to the faraway horizon, where mountains of rock jutted into the blue-grey fog, an archetype of Korean countryside that inspired a thousand painters. But the boy did not raise up his eyes to behold the majesty surrounding him. He put one foot in front of the other.

"Yes, *Abuji* may beat me. But I have no choice," he said aloud.

As if in agreement, the baby urinated. Hot fluid spread across Young Nam's back like a luxurious massage, a sensation he relished on chilly days. He knew that, like any instant gratification, pleasure would turn to regret, and his back would soon become sticky and clammy. Under his loose clothing, the boy was a rack of bones, as were most all Korean children born and bred under the Japanese occupation. The natives existed to supply food and raw material to the empire's far-flung war campaigns while themselves consuming just enough to survive another day. Though thin, Young Nam was broad of beam, tall for his people, a handsome boy.

The baby on his back was nicknamed "Owlet" because of his large head and eyes. The moniker was a talisman against the misfortune that might strike a son whose parents had the hubris to assign a family name before a baby boy had survived his first year.

Owlet must have been approaching that twelve-month benchmark, but, preoccupied with the daily grind of survival, nobody was quite sure. His tiny size belied his age. He was the youngest, and would forever be regarded by the Kim family as the baby.

The plaintive mewing propelled the boy onward to the outskirts of the family farm. As he neared the forbidden plot, the boy smelled a sickly sweet odor. He continued on till he stood at the edge of the field. His head grew light and his legs gelatinous. The hazy vision of his mother and father in the center of the field of shoulder-high poppies blurred before his eyes. He opened his mouth to call to them, but could utter no sounds.

Earlier that spring, an edict had come down from the Japanese. The remotest plot of rice paddy had been supplanted with poppy flowers, monopolizing an acre of arable land and exacting a laborious harvest and processing. The yield of an acre of poppies would be pressed into a sticky brown brick of opium small enough to fit in the palm. The precious drug would be turned over to the colonial power in support of military operations incomprehensible to the Korean peasant farmer.

The petals had dropped from the poppies, and it was harvest time. The boy's parents toiled together under the sun, scraping the seepage from the scored capsules into bowls. Young Nam focused on the glint of metal bowls into which his parents were collecting the opium. It had been so long since he had seen anything metallic. His father must have buried these bowls in the yard when every other scrap of metal in their possession had been confiscated for the war effort. He envisioned his little rice bowl, recast, whizzing down the barrel of a gun, lodging itself into the heart of a man. Owlet twitched unnaturally against his back.

The boy gathered enough strength to call out to his mother. He heard from afar the strangeness of an unfamiliar voice, his, wafting over the field. He recognized, vaguely, that Owlet was suddenly still and that the earth was collapsing under him. Bright light flooded his vision.

Umma appeared before him. She seized him by the upper arm and dragged him away from the opium field. The boy collapsed on the ground while his mother extricated Owlet, laying the child on the blanket upon the ground. Owlet was sickeningly limp. She knelt over her child and slapped his cheeks.

Abuji approached, shouting. As if recognizing his father's voice, Owlet awakened and issued a weak cry. Mother put the child to her breast. She rocked, her head bowed over her child, humming a Western hymn the missionaries had brought to Korea.

The boy's heart constricted, and a lump rose painfully in his throat. He scrambled to his feet and ran. He heard his father call his name, but he ran on, not to flee a beating – he did not fear the switch – but to hide the shame of the tears filling his eyes.

Young Nam loved his baby brother as a father would love his son. No, better. Every atom of the Korean man's being yearns for a son, passionately, obsessively, beyond all reckoning. Yet when the son finally comes, a father must pay him less notice than he would a buzzing fly or be regarded as an insufferable braggart. A father must give his good son a grunt, his bad son a whipping. A father must brace the shoulders of his son to carry the weight of the future: the family, the property, the next entry in the genealogy rolls.

The boy, Young Nam, however, was free to love his baby brother with pure emotion, unfettered by expectations. That night, as the boy lay in the communal room, his mother breathing fitfully to the right, his brother snoring to the left, and Owlet draped over his stomach, nestling his hot oily head under his chin, Young Nam enfolded his baby brother in both arms and felt the counterpoint of their two beating hearts.

Shortly after the incident in the poppy field, Owlet was weaned, freeing his mother to work harder and longer, without interruption. The child quickly developed the telltale proportions of malnourishment: an oversized head and a swollen belly. The boy taught him to walk, and Owlet toddled about in a shapeless hemp shirt reaching to his jutting hip bones. His tiny buttocks peeked out the backside, and a tiny pepper dangled in front. The puppy was growing too and learned to follow the toddler about, gobbling up any stool that might drop and licking the floor spanking clean.

Owlet's first words, chirped with the insistence of a hungry hatchling, were to call his big brother, "*Hyung! Hyung!*" If the boy left his line of sight, Owlet flung himself to the floor, wailing, kicking, and pulling his hair. A grin of triumph lit his tear-stained face when his big brother materialized.

Over the course of just a few months, Owlet's speech exploded. To the boy's amazement, he asked a stream of questions for which the boy had no ready answers. Do fish have eyelids? Why does only my bottom jaw move? Why is the ceiling upside down? Why do shadows have no eyes? What is being you like? Where is God?

Owlet latched onto *Hangul*, the Korean alphabet. A master-piece of scientific simplicity, *Hangul* was invented by a scholar king of ancient times and disseminated to the masses, igniting a revolution in literacy. Crouched behind a stand of trees, checking over his shoulder, Young Nam slashed the simple marks in the dirt with a stick, pronounced their phonetic sounds, and quickly erased the symbols with his bare foot. Owlet saw *Hangul* every-where, in the knot of a tree, in the crook of a limb, and called out the sounds. "Quietly, quietly," Young Nam would admonish, lest an informer chance by. Under the Japanese occupation, the use of *Hangul* was a crime.

The regime also mandated practice of the Shinto religion to the exclusion of all other faiths. This the stubborn matriarch of the Kim family resisted. She was a deaconess of the Holiness Church in the village. Their services were held in secret, moving from house to house each week. Periodic raids and imprisonments of church leaders were routine. *Abuji* had sapped the family's resources bribing the authorities to leave his wife in peace after their youngest son's birth. But money and rice had run out. *Abuji* commanded his wife to quit the church. She declined to obey her husband. One Sabbath day, the pastor and elders of the Holiness Church were rousted out of worship and marched to the village jail. *Umma* was among them.

Each day following his wife's arrest, *Abuji* yoked the oxen and drove his cart into the village to petition for the deaconess' freedom. Young Nam's three older brothers shouldered their tools and went to work in the fields. At the end of the day, Young Nam, his sister, and two little brothers crouched along the dusty path for hours, awaiting the return of their father's cart which might transport their mother home from prison, or might return motherless, as it had every day for endless days.

At last one day, the cart rattled into view carrying two passengers. An ecstatic shout arose from the ragtag greeting party. But as the cart drew near, the children saw that their mother was slumped on the seat next to their father, her head on his shoulder. Her inert posture and the shocking sight of their parents in public physical contact silenced the children. The wagon lurched to a halt.

Umma raised her head and looked about in a daze. The upturned faces of her brood came into focus. The children's faces were grimy, their hair matted, and their clothing wrecked. The sorry sight lit her maternal fire. She sprang from the cart and chided them for their filth and sloth. She bustled them to the stream for a vigorous scrubbing, which left them shiny and raw. Tomorrow was Sunday, and they would be off to church in the village, where the congregation would celebrate the deaconess' release with tears and song and prayer till the sun set.

If a child had asked his mother what happened to her in prison, she would have meted out a swift smack. Nobody asked questions. Young Nam disciplined his mind never to stray to such frightening territory. Had he noticed the seepage of bright red on the deaconess' white jacket as she rejoiced in the front of the congregation, he would have turned his eyes away. *Umma* would be furious if she caught him staring.

On laundry day, Young Nam crouched by the stream, wringing the laundry his mother passed from her scrub rock. Out of his peripheral vision, the boy watched his mother mutter under her breath over the ruin of her best Sunday clothing. Sweat streamed down her flushed face as she beat the stain on her white jacket, a curious pattern of rust-colored streaks. While waiting for the next load to wring, Young Nam suspended little Owlet under the arms, dipping his toes into the water.

"What is frozen water called?" he asked.

"Ice!" said Owlet.

"And what is hot water called?"

"Ow!"

Young Nam recited a Psalm to the toddler, imagining that he would enjoy its cadence, even if the meaning were beyond his capabilities. To his astonishment, the child repeated the passage back to him, verbatim, with impeccable diction. *Umma*, absorbed by her furious exertion, did not hear it.

"*Umma!* You must listen to Owlet!"

She looked up from the laundry and blinked. She leaned back on her haunches, and the dripping garment fell from her hands onto the stone. The toddler recited his Psalm in all its somber beauty for his mother. As she listened, her mouth went slack. When Owlet was finished, his mother stared for minutes, her mouth still agape. Suddenly, she snapped her mouth shut, sighed noisily, and cried, "Not a scholar in the family!" She raised her head toward the heavens and lifted her voice.

"So homely. Useless! A scholar! I am a poor woman and will remain poor the rest of my life!"

Then she abruptly turned back to her laundry. But this time, she was humming.

Young Nam suffered a pang of jealousy. But it was quickly followed by a welling of pride. He was the brother of an extraordinary child. Owlet's memory was photographic, a gift highly prized for mastery of tens of thousands of Chinese characters and for recitation of poetry and literature. The family's scholarly *yangban* ancestry, dormant but never forgotten, had expressed itself in this child after generations of desuetude. The boy promised himself to teach his baby brother every shred of knowledge he managed to scrape together. If one family member, just one, could pass the government exams, they need never go hungry again.

In the warmer months, foraging provided relief from the hunger. The children fished and caught frogs, handing over any substantial catch to their mother, and gobbling the remaining tidbits themselves. Young Nam observed sparrows building a nest in the grass roof of their home. Biding his time till the eggs were laid, he climbed to the rooftop and collected the coin-sized eggs. Painstakingly, he poked two holes in each shell, blew the contents into the hollow of two wild scallions, and roasted them over an open fire. He split one between his younger brothers and the other between himself and his sister. He forced himself to eat slowly, to savor his green straw stuffed with golden manna. Owlet, with his immature digestion, promptly developed a case of flatulence.

"Perhaps it was the eggs," said Young Nam.

"Eggs do not fart!" said Owlet, punctuating his joke with another toot.

After this success, the boy made a habit of searching for bird's nests. Should indignant parent birds attack the boy while he was raiding their clutch, he would catch them bare-handed and stash them in a ready game bag, his roomy pantaloons, tied at the bottom with cord. The birds careened crazily in their hempen prison, pecking and shredding his legs. Undeterred, Young Nam would finish collecting the eggs while dancing a jig on the tree limb to shake off the peckers. A roasted sparrow would yield a morsel of meat the size of his thumb. Scrumptious.

Yet each month seemed worse than the last. On bad days, breakfast might be a small bowl of rice water with a few grains of rice floating in it. Lunch comprised three spoons of rice with three pieces of kimchi. If there was food for dinner, the men working the fields were fed first. More often than not, the children went without.

When winter came, the hunger grew fierce. The silent white beauty of the first winter's snowfall was lost on the boy. Sighing ruefully, Young Nam complained, "It is the first snow."

"No," said Owlet with a sly grin. "It snowed last winter too!"

How Owlet understood such things was a mystery, but one thing was certain. Owlet always put a grin back on the boy's face despite himself.

Like many exquisite things, Owlet was fragile. It was not long before the child was sick in bed with the first ailment of winter. What might have been nothing more than a common virus, ravaged its defenseless host. Young Nam observed his parents huddled over Owlet's inert frame, whispering to each other in desperate tones. He overheard his father say, *it worked on Young Nam.* With a start, he remembered the wretched episode to which his father was alluding.

Some years ago, Young Nam had been stricken deathly ill with malaria. Anemic and delirious, wracked with chills, he had convulsed on the floor under a mound of every blanket in the family stockpile. The radiant heated *ondol* floor, and coverings failed to still his quaking. At the peak of his suffering, *Halmoni*, his grandmother (now deceased), had exploded into the sick room. Old *Halmoni* ripped his blankets off with a wild shriek. The ancient lady tied a thick, coarse rope around his neck. She dragged him out of the room by the neck as he turned seven shades of purple, flipping like a dewatered fish. Ignoring this distress, and even perhaps relishing it, she hoisted the rope over her shoulder and charged with her captive out of the house, across the yard, and to the outhouse, heedless of the crashing of pots and scraping of garden tools against his writhing body. At the putrid threshold of the outhouse, she had flung her rope down and given him a swift kick in the ribs screaming: *Demons be gone! Leave the body of my grandson! Fly to the feces where you belong!*

The very next morning, the boy had fully recovered.

He was no doctor, but the boy knew Owlet was too weak to survive the outhouse curative. The howling of his own belly informed him that what Owlet needed was basic nutrition. He pleaded with his mother to forestall drastic measures. He rushed outdoors, overtaken by a primal urge. He would construct a trap. He would catch small game, perhaps a rabbit. He would cook a stew and feed his brother.

At the edge of a stand of white pines, the boy trudged through the snow looking for animal tracks. A penumbra of frozen breath puffed at regular intervals from his chapped lips. Clad in cotton padding under his hemp clothing, shod in straw shoes stuffed with cotton, he shivered as he hunted. Suddenly, he was distracted by a ruckus.

Pursuing the noise, he came upon Hiroshi Yamamoto, the only son of Japanese colonizers who operated a prosperous farm adjacent to their land. Young Nam's father, with his knack for the Japanese language, had occasionally served as a liaison between the Yamamotos and the Korean townspeople. Hiroshi was a small, though well-fed child, who peddled about on a shiny red tricycle and wore leather shoes. Every day, a teacher came to his home to tutor him.

Hiroshi was crying. A teenage Korean peasant had Hiroshi's arms pinned behind his back, exhorting a little boy of about five or six to pummel Hiroshi's stomach. A small crowd of ragamuffins had gathered to egg them on. Young Nam observed from behind the snowy pines, intending to avoid involvement. He could not help feeling amused at the sight of the tiny tyke enthusiastically bouncing his harmless fists off the belly of his overstuffed target. The peasant boy urged the bystanders to take a turn at his captive punching dummy. The ragged crew queued up, swinging practice punches in the air.

A larger boy came forward, drew back his fist, and punched the Japanese child with all his might. Hiroshi stopped crying and sucked in his breath. His captor released the child's arms. Hiroshi collapsed to his knees, threw up a little on the snow, and resumed crying. The teenager laughed, hoisted his captive back up, and invited someone else to take his turn. Another boy stepped forward, fists raised.

Suddenly, Kim Young Nam found himself stepping from behind his hideout and seizing Hiroshi's upper arm.

"I have come to take Hiroshi Yamamoto home," he said. "His parents sent me. You had better hurry home before they find out. Your families will be severely punished."

The ruffians dispersed like shooed flies. It was easier than expected. Young Nam was startled when Hiroshi hugged him and then surprised that the feeling of a Japanese child's arms around his waist did not repulse him. Hiroshi buried his face against the boy's worn, dirty cotton-stuffed jacket, and heaved in great dramatic sobs.

"Stop crying."

Hiroshi stifled his tears and slipped his plump mitten into the boy's raw bare hand.

"You must go home by yourself. I am very busy."

"Please? I am afraid of the bad boys."

"You make it worse if you cry. If you are strong, they will leave you alone."

Young Nam was loath to be discovered holding the Japanese child's hand or to step foot on the Japanese-owned farm. But he knew Hiroshi's fears were valid. He would walk the little Japanese boy back home and hurry back to his own people.

"Walk quickly."

At length, Hiroshi asked, "Is it true that your people are always hungry?"

"No!"

"My father says you do not use the modern farming methods and that is why your people are always hungry."

"It is not so!"

After walking some time in silence, Young Nam could not help adding, "It is because the levy on Korean farmers is too great."

"My father says I must be careful around starving people."

"Perhaps he is right. Perhaps I will gobble you up right now."

"When I am in charge, there will be no levy!"

Young Nam deposited Hiroshi at his doorstep. A Korean house servant with a frightened moon face bustled to the front porch and hurried the child into the house. Young Nam turned and trotted back toward the woods. He had not gone far when he heard a rapid clip-clop of wooden clogs on the porch, a sound that made his muscles seize. Hiroshi's mother called to him. He looked over his shoulder to see her hurrying toward him and gesturing frenetically. She scurried across the snow, wearing only her kimono. Perhaps she blamed him for what happened to her son. He considered fleeing, but the tiny woman was upon him before he could make the move. As a Japanese colonizer, Hiroshi's mother could choose to bring a world of hurt to him and his family with a snap of her fingers.

At this inopportune moment, a perverse notion intruded upon his composure. He had heard tell that Japanese women wore no undergarments beneath their tight kimonos and that they were capable of urinating in the standing position without disrobing. He kept his head bowed and stared at the woman's clogs.

In a beseeching tone that caught the Korean boy off guard, the Japanese woman entreated him to look after her child and keep him safe from bad boys. She pressed a sheet of dried squid upon him. He accepted the squid in the traditional polite manner, with two hands, and consented with mechanical respectfulness.

It was like manna from heaven, this dried squid. It would be salty and tough as leather. He would tear off shreds and soften them in his own mouth and tuck the pulverized wad into Owlet's cheek. Owlet would taste the rare treat and blink his eyes in surprise. He would suck the ocean nutrients into his depleted bloodstream. As the boy hurried home, planning the feeding, and mentally willing Owlet's revival, a stray thought gave him pause: the Japanese family must be terribly lonely.

What if he did make himself Hiroshi's protector? He was aware that he commanded enough respect amongst the village boys, by virtue of his size and intelligence, to do so. Rewards that would ease his family's suffering could fall his way. Perhaps he would be let into the Yamamoto house. Perhaps he could contrive to be present when the tutor came. He would remain quietly in the corner, absorbing.

But Hiroshi was not his kind. It would be tantamount to collaboration. Time and effort were finite resources which would need to be siphoned off from elsewhere. He shrugged off the idea and continued homeward. The child he loved most was quaking, hungry, and sick in bed at home. It would take all his faculties to safeguard such a precarious life. Owlet needed him.

3

Lee Hana
Occupied Korea
1943

A young girl hurried down a desolate dirt road. Though nauseous with hunger and exhausted from hours of walking, Lee Hana dared not stop. She pressed forward, head down, clutching a small satchel to her chest. The crimson wash on the horizon was fast fading, and her final hour's walk to her aunt's farm would be in darkness. But there she would be safe. People knew her aunt was childless.

There had been no school for over a year. Hana had been passing the long days at home helping her mother. Only that afternoon, she and her mother had been mending, the stack of freshly laundered clothes between them, yellow sunlight filtering through the paper window. The industry of her mother's nimble fingers and the sweet melancholy of her humming had lulled the girl into a peaceful doze.

Suddenly, her younger brother hurtled into the house and splayed onto the floor at their feet, clutching his heaving chest. His words spewed out in rapid fire bursts between gasps for air. He had been playing at his friend's house in the village. Without warning, police officers had marched in, brandishing papers, barking orders. His playmate's older sister had been apprehended. This neighbor girl, eighteen years old, had only just been betrothed to an elderly widower crippled by polio. The unfavorable match, made for her own protection, was too late to save her from the draft. When the girl's father had resisted, protesting that his daughter was soon to be married, the old man had been beaten with the butt of a rifle. Prostrate in a pool of blood, the father's last breath had been expended to warn Hana's younger brother to go home, to hide his sister.

No sooner had the little boy's message been delivered when his mother sprang from the floor, seized a cloth from the mending pile, ran to the kitchen, wrapped some burned rice crackers in the cloth, and pressed this meager survival package into her daughter's hands crying, "Fly! Fly to your aunt's house and hide. Run for your life. Do not stop. Do not look back. *Fly!*"

In the Lee family's village, the government had culled eligible young men from the village long ago, first for military service, then for manual labor. One day, an unexpected assembly had been called in the schoolyard. An official in a military uniform delivered a speech expounding upon the virtues of loyalty and subservience to the glorious empire in its inevitable march to victory. Then he read a list of names. Hana remembered the teenage girls who were chosen because, as everyone commented afterward, they were the prettiest in the school. They were ordered to bid their families farewell and report at dawn to the police station for duty in the Women's Voluntary Service Corp. It was explained that they would work in factories or as domestic servants, earning good wages in addition to room and board. If they failed to report, the girls and their families would be severely punished. This first batch of girls went obediently, terrified of the consequences of resisting, hopeful for financial relief for their families. There was even a tinge of pride in being the chosen ones.

Over time, a dark suspicion seeped throughout the village. It became known that recruitment to the Women's Voluntary Service Corp was an evil to be evaded at all costs. Hana was too young to know the reasons for this change in attitude. She believed it was because no wages, or girls for that matter, ever came back home. Families withdrew their teenage girls from school. Many of the young girls were rushed into marriage, often settling for any sickly, deformed, or elderly male specimen who had been left behind, unsuitable for the draft. Finally, the school had closed its doors.

They work you till you die, Hana thought. Therefore, I must run for my life. Lightheaded and exhausted, she stumbled to her knees. She scrambled to her feet and staggered forward while loosening her parcel. She had enough sense to realize that she needed to put some scraps in her belly or she would faint on the side of the road. She felt the sharp edges of the burned rice and her mouth watered.

There was an explosion. A vehicle backfired. An engine gunned. The girl dropped her parcel on the ground and froze. Headlights careened toward her, illuminating her white *hanbok* dress like a fluttering surrender flag. She lost critical moments fumbling to pick up her spilled rice crackers. By the time she had regained enough sense to abandon the parcel, turn, and run into the field, it was too late. A man in military uniform leaped from the passenger side of the truck, gained on her in a few swift bounds, caught her with ease, slung her over his shoulder, and strode back to the idling vehicle. He unlocked the back of the truck and flung her inside. The truck rumbled and backfired on down the road. Lee Hana, at twelve years of age, was thus drafted into the Women's Voluntary Service Corp.

Her eyes squeezed closed, she lay curled like a fetus till the blinding pain of her crash upon the metal truck bed subsided to a dull ache. Weeping sounds swirled round her. Was that her own disembodied cry? She heard a groan. Her own. So there were other girls in the truck with her, crying.

A hand touched her shoulder.

"Are you hurt?" a gentle voice asked.

"*Unni!*" Hana cried, recognizing the older girl.

She was the eighteen-year-old whose violent capture her own younger brother had witnessed earlier in the day. The girls, previously only acquaintances, hugged each other like long lost sisters and spilled their hot tears onto each other's necks. They sat close together holding hands. When her tears subsided, Hana discerned the forms of three other girls huddled together on the other side of the truck, their knees tucked up under their skirts, their arms linked together.

"*Unni*, where are they taking us?" Hana whispered to the older girl.

"We will all find out when we get there. Do not worry. If they wanted to kill us, we would be dead already," she answered.

"*Unni*, what will they do to us?" one of the other girls asked. All the young girls addressed her using the honorific for an elder sister, *Unni*, because she was the oldest.

"We will work in factories," *Unni* answered authoritatively, convincing even herself. "We will have to work very hard."

The girls were comforted by this. They were farm girls. They knew how to work hard.

They drove through the night, one dark-haired head resting on another's white-clad shoulder, like dominoes, in stoic silence absorbing the throbbing of their various injuries. After some hours, the truck pulled to the side of the road and stopped. The girls awoke from their restless half-sleep, hearts racing, wide eyes fixed upon the door. But their captors had only stopped to urinate, talking and laughing in a guttural manner, before switching places behind the wheel. Straining to overhear the men's conversation, the girls were able to ascertain that their captors were Korean, a recognition that provided no solace.

Sunrise leaked through the cracks of the truck door and awakened the girls. In the slit of light, Hana observed that the eye of one of the girls was swollen shut and that her face and the jacket of her dress were stained with blood. She must be a fighter, thought Hana with a tinge of shame remembering how she herself had gone as limp as captured prey when the soldier caught her.

Soon the girls were jarred by unfamiliar sounds: the eerie Doppler effect of a train whistle, the cacophony of a jam of honking cars, the barking of men and stray dogs. The truck lurched to a stop. The two soldiers flung open the rear doors, and the girls squinted and flinched in the sunlight. "Out! Out!" the men shouted at the cowering girls, jerking them roughly by their upper arms. They were lined up against the wall of a grey block building. One of the men guarded them at gunpoint while the other entered the building. Soon, a middle-aged couple emerged from the building behind the soldier. The frightened girls immediately recognized from their face, figure, and dress that the couple was Japanese. The Japanese man and woman sauntered down the lineup, leisurely surveying the haul. They stopped at the girl with the black eye and bloody bolero. The Japanese man expelled a grunt of irritation.

"What is this?" he asked.

"That one is trouble. You better watch her," replied one soldier.

"If you have to hit them, do not hit the face!"

"She is trouble. It was the only way," said the other soldier.

"Then perhaps I should delete her from your quota, as she is troublesome and moreover damaged."

"As you wish. But the supply is running low."

"Ha!" scoffed the Japanese man, his lips peeling back from his tangled teeth in a mirthless smile. "Your people keep breeding, do they not?"

Observing the soldiers bristle, the Japanese woman stepped forward and interjected, "Thank you for your excellent service.

We are all children of the same Emperor and must do our duty. These volunteers, all of them, look like good, strong workers who will bring much good fortune."

There followed a lecture in a hodgepodge of Korean and Japanese, shouted staccato military-style by the Japanese man as he strode up and down his lineup of recruits with his hands clasped behind his back. The girls were hereby inducted into the Women's Voluntary Service Corp. Should the volunteers refuse to obey orders, they would bring dishonor to themselves and their families. Both they and their families would be arrested and punished. Attempts to run away were illegal, futile, and punishable by death. The families of runaways would suffer dire consequences. They, like all children of the Emperor, must serve faithfully as an obedient child would serve her father. The inevitable victory of the Empire would bring recompense to all good volunteers and their families. They would have to work very hard.

The last bit was precisely what *Unni* had said. So it was true. A modicum of comfort crept into the girls' hearts. The Japanese woman, who had been inside the building during the initiation speech, emerged with paperwork she handed to the soldiers. The men accepted the papers, examined them, took a headcount of all five girls (during which the Japanese man rolled his eyes with an exasperated sigh), conferred over foreign writing, identified the number "5" with jabbing fingers, and, satisfied, went on their way.

Arms linked together, the girls followed the Japanese man, guarded in the rear by the Japanese woman, through the noisome clamor of a labyrinth that even the most provincial country girl must recognize as Seoul. They entered a restaurant. None of the girls had ever been served in a restaurant before. The bountiful meal spread on the table before their incredulous eyes could not fail to hearten them. "See how nice things will be for you if you continue to be good girls?" the Japanese woman simpered. The Japanese couple began to eat and urged the girls to fill up. At first, the girls nibbled timidly. But after a dainty sampling of the savories, they gobbled with abandon till every dish was cleaned.

During the meal, the Japanese man instructed the girls to address him as *"Papasan"* and the woman as *"Mamasan."* He assigned each girl a Japanese name. Lee Hana was renamed Suzuha. It was not her first renaming.

In school, the children had been required to speak only Japanese and assigned Japanese names. Hers had been Reiko Shiga. Some of her classmates, mostly the boys, were repulsed by their Japanese names, flinching every time it was called out by the teacher. Hana adopted a more pragmatic approach. She would submit and survive. She had been Reiko. Now she would be Suzuha.

The next stop was the public baths, another first-time experience, one considerably less gratifying than the restaurant. *Mamasan* escorted the girls into the women's section of the baths, while her husband – by now it was apparent they were a married couple in addition to business partners – waited outside. The girls undressed reluctantly, cowering in embarrassment, awkwardly covering their private parts with their thin arms and little hands, while *Mamasan* frankly surveyed their physiques, front, back, and flanks. "You girls are healthy," she pronounced with satisfaction and then summarily stripped down herself and marched them into the bath.

Following *Mamasan*'s instruction, the girls sat on low stools with buckets of soapy water and hurriedly scrubbed themselves clean. They rinsed off by pouring water over their heads. Beyond the scrubbing area, in the center of a dark, steamy room stood a massive concrete tub, circled about its perimeter by a concrete bench, overflowing with scalding water. The girls scurried to it and plunged themselves in, wincing from the heat, suffocating in the steam, but grateful for the burning water to cover their nakedness. With wide eyes peering over the water line, Hana looked about curiously.

The city women strolled nonchalantly with their breasts and pubic hair on full display, sat on stools casually exfoliating their bodies, unabashedly cleansed their private regions with one foot up on the bench, and chatted with each other just as if they were at the marketplace fully clothed. Hana had only that year developed breast buds the size of bird eggs, and had no body hair. She was shocked to observe the glandular ripeness and the black foliage erupting from the mature female flesh.

When the bath was over, the girls were issued new clothing, simple cotton kimono robes dyed indigo, which *Mamasan* helped them fasten. Their *hanbok* dresses and undergarments were wrapped into a satchel. The girls were relieved to be decent again, and they moved with stiff caution in their narrow robes. They helped each other braid their hair into the traditional maiden's hairstyle, single long plaits hanging halfway down their backs.

Fed, polished, clothed, and coiffed, the girls were taken to a nearby shop where *Mamasan* bought each of them a compact and small container of red lip stain. The compact cover was engraved with a pattern of cranes and opened to a mirror on one side and pancake makeup on the other. Then she positioned the girl with the black eye as a demonstration model before the tiny shop mirror and painted her face, taking pains to cover her bruises with an extra thick layer of makeup. Thereafter, each girl stood before the mirror to apply her makeup and red lips. The young girls smiled shyly and even giggled when it was their turn at the mirror. Hana was barely able to conceal her delight as she smoothed the thick pancake makeup onto her face, transforming her olive skin to a creamy mask. But when the last girl, *Unni*, who had been shrinking in the back, was beckoned to the mirror, tears were streaming down her cheeks and her tins rattled uncontrollably in her trembling hands. She dropped her gifts to the floor.

"Bad girl!" hissed *Mamasan*, pinching *Unni* on the upper arm.

"Please," *Unni* pleaded. "Please. We wanted to work in factories or as housemaids. We will work very hard. Please, I beg you."

Mamasan grasped *Unni*'s braid, shoved her head down toward the floor, and snapped, "Pick that up! That was expensive, you ungrateful girl!"

When the younger girls began to quake and then began to cry, threatening to erupt the peace, *Mamasan* executed a sharp about-face. "Of course you will work for very kind masters," she said in a saccharine voice. "You will cook and clean and do laundry. Your Japanese masters are very rich. They will expect their house servants to look pretty. Have things not been so nice for you girls so far? Crying is not pretty. Put on your makeup like a good girl."

With order restored, the curious entourage marched on. But *Unni*'s disquieting outburst in the makeup shop had cast a pall upon the girls. Hana noticed that passersby averted their gaze and steered wide to avoid the procession. *Unni* kept her head down and squeezed the younger girl's hand tightly. They turned into a side alley and stopped at an inn with a Japanese sign nailed over the lintel. "Your people are normally forbidden on these premises," *Papasan* announced. "But a special exception is being made for new volunteers."

As they aligned their shoes in the foyer, Hana looked to *Unni* for some sign. But her head was bowed so low that only her hair and reddened ears were visible. Spasms jerked her hunched shoulders. Beyond the foyer, there was an entrance hall where a boisterous party was in session. A group of Japanese military officers were gathered around a table drinking and eating and making merry, while a heavily adorned geisha filled their sake cups.

A rowdy cheer rose from the assembly when the Japanese couple led the girls into the room. The ranking officer staggered to his feet and wended his floridly drunken, bow-legged way over to them. The Japanese couple bowed at the waist. Motioning to the girls with grand flourish, *Papasan* announced, "It is guaranteed. Any one of these girls will assure victory and safe return from battle."

The captain inspected the lineup of new recruits, chucking a fist under each girl's chin to lift and evaluate her face. He made two passes in an agonizing leisurely fashion. Suddenly, he knelt before Hana, slung her like a sheep around the back of his neck, wheeled around to face his men and exult, "I choose this one! You men, follow the usual procedure."

The captain carried his limp quarry off to a private room. He laid Hana on a tatami mat in the center of the bare room. He knelt beside to her and stroked her face, speaking to her in an artificial high-pitched baby voice. "Pretty pet. Are your frightened? What is your name, my pretty little pet?"

She understood his question. But at that moment, she could not remember her name – any of them – and so remained mute. Presently, the sound of screams ricocheted all around the paper walls of the inn. Hana turned her head away from the captain and struggled to hold back her tears. He continued to pet her, speaking in Japanese which she understood only barely. "Do not be afraid. Some of my men are brutes. But I am not one of those animal types. You have nothing to fear. If I could, I would keep you in a little silver cage and carry it with me everywhere."

His hand wandered from her face to her neck while he rambled and slurred, "But I must do my duty. I must go back to war. You cannot imagine the things I have seen, the things I have done. Terrible things. I will suffer. I will inflict suffering. I will kill. I will be killed. Yes, one of these days, I will certainly die. Oh, my pretty pet, who will be caressing you then?"

Hana struggled to understand his soliloquy over the escalating screams in the adjacent rooms and the violent pounding of her heart. Oblivious to the din, the captain droned on, stroking her head with distracted affection, as one would stroke a lap dog.

His speech was interrupted by the crash against the sliding door, a man shouting, and a girl moaning horrifically. The captain cursed, rose, and slid the door open. The girl who had caused the disturbance fell into the room, doubled over, stark naked, clutching her abdomen. Quantities of blood poured onto the floor.

"What is this?" the captain shouted. A lieutenant, shirtless, fumbling to fasten his pants, explained that the girl had stabbed herself. The captain reached across the girl and slapped the lieutenant across the face. "Stupid bastard! How could you let this happen, you idiot?"

Then the two men studied the girl. An inhuman, low pitched wail, the braying of a mortally wounded animal, arose from the slender nude curled in her expanding crimson pool. "She is useless now," said the captain. He drew his pistol and shot the girl silent. As the captain kicked the body out of the way to shut the door, the dead girl's head fell to one side. Hana saw that it was *Unni*. A bayonet of fear gutted her heart.

The lieutenant asked, "Captain, I beg your pardon, but what do we do now?"

Shutting the door in his face, the captain growled, "Clean it up!"

The captain who turned on Hana was much altered. His face was as livid red as *Unni*'s blood and deformed with rage. With his arm raised across his chest, he stalked to the mat and struck the side of her head. "Why are your people so stupid?" he growled. He struck again and again. "Why do your stupid people not know what is good for you?"

Hana lay stiff and mute. The captain tore her kimono robe off, unbuckled his pants, shoved her legs apart, and rammed himself into her body. Bewildered and terrified, the girl believed she was experiencing imminent death, the throbbing pain from the blows to her head suddenly eclipsed by the excruciating ripping of flesh between her legs.

There followed a parade of officers through the night, each man sampling each of the four surviving girls.

When Hana had been a little girl, in more prosperous times, her father had raised rabbits. One spring morning, she had observed a pair of rabbits in a peculiar frenzy jumping over each other in their small cage. "Are they fighting?" she had asked her father. "They are getting married," her father had laughed. After a brief courtship, the male had mounted the female and finished his business. Soon there were baby rabbits. When the kits had grown, the parent rabbits furnished a delicious meal for the family and a fur muff for one happy little girl. One of the officers who visited that night flipped Hana onto her belly and mounted her in the manner in which the rabbits had mated. It was only in the course of this humiliating ordeal that she was able to recognize the nature of the atrocity being afflicted upon her. Then she was gripped with the wretched awareness that she had been awaiting her death in vain.

Her last visitor was the lieutenant who had been with *Unni* when she stabbed herself. Unlike the other officers who arrived in various states of undress, the lieutenant arrived fully dressed, tucked, and armed in his military uniform. He was a slight, baby-faced young man. The lieutenant lay himself on the mat beside her with a heavy sigh, folded his hands over his forehead, and stared at the ceiling morosely. During this interval of quiescence, the girl collected the tatters of her robe and undertook to her cover herself. The lieutenant took no notice and even appeared to be falling asleep. The first words Hana uttered that night were to awaken him before it was too late.

"Please, kill me," she begged in Korean.

He opened his eyes, blinked, and shook his head.

"Please, kill me," she repeated her plea in broken Japanese.

"No. I cannot," he answered.

"Please, have mercy," she begged again.

"I cannot help you. It is impossible. If I killed you, I would be severely punished, probably executed. One girl was bad enough. Although she did it to herself, Captain will punish me when he sobers up in the morning."

"I am nothing more than an animal. It will be nothing. You can say I killed myself," she sobbed.

"No. You are a soldier now. The truth is, you are more valuable than a real soldier," he intoned miserably. "Just do as they say. You must perform your duty. We all have to do our duty."

"What will happen to me?"

"What will happen to any of us? I should like to know the answer."

In the morning, the girls were collected by *Mamasan* and *Papasan* and, their new kimonos having been wrecked by the night's work, issued their old white *hanbok* dresses into which they were told to fasten their tins of makeup, their sole worldly possessions. Treading barefoot over the scarlet stain on the floor where *Unni* had fallen, Hana experienced a surge of admiration and envy. Like a mouse in the cat's claws, Hana's instinct had been to play dead. But *Unni*'s instinct had been to embrace death. If only she could be so brave!

Reunited, the four surviving girls, heads bowed, grasped each other's hands. The girl with the black eye had been badly beaten and stabbed in the thigh by a bayonet. A conference ensued between the Japanese couple and the captain concerning the loss and damage to their chattel. At length, the matter having been settled to the couple's satisfaction, the girls were each issued a rice cake, and marched to a hired wagon which transported them to the train station. The girls were loaded onto a cargo train carrying military supplies and munitions.

This time, none of the girls asked where they were going. It had ceased to matter.

4

Kim Young Nam
Occupied Korea
1943

K im Young Nam's craving for food was matched only by
his craving for education. He loved being a schoolboy.
To his everlasting chagrin, he was only able to attend
grammar school sporadically during the confluence of fortuitous
events which were becoming increasingly rare: when school was
in session, when he was well enough, and when his help was not
needed at home. The sight of other schoolboys in their uniforms
sent him running for cover to hide his rough clothing and bare feet.

Yet on those precious occasions when the boy was able to
attend school, the colonial schoolhouse grew more irksome with
each passing year. Korean teachers were replaced with Japanese
ones. He detested his Japanese name and the Japanese language.
He hated the lessons about farming and animal husbandry which
were taking up more and more of the curriculum. He remembered with longing more auspicious times when he had sampled
the glory of history, poetry, and Mandarin.

His teacher had a spleen. Beatings, knuckles ground into the
skull, whippings across the palms were the incidental nuisances

of every school day. At noon, the few children who had brought a lunch queued up front and opened their squares of cloth or wooden boxes for inspection. White rice was a luxury commodity, largely exported, and forbidden in the lunches of schoolchildren. Young Nam never had a lunch. As required of such children, he joined the majority of the class on his hands and knees with rag and candle to polish the wooden floor during lunch break. After the lunch inspection, his teacher would square her red lacquered bento box on her desk, align her chopsticks like two shiny red soldiers, raise bright quivering morsels to her mouth, and smack her lips while the lineup of backs and buttocks heaved up and down, burnishing the floor at her feet.

On one unforgettable day, a slight meek child, the only son of an impoverished widow, unexpectedly queued at the tail of the lunch inspection line. The teacher stalked down the lineup, tapping her child-beater stick on one open palm as she examined each humble lunch, till she reached the widow's son. He held his meal before her with two open palms together: a small rice ball. Her stick clattered to the floor. She bent to inspect more closely. She snatched the rice ball from the urchin's hands. She held it up to her eyes which rounded wide as saucers. Suddenly, she tore the rice ball apart. "White rice!" she shrieked. "Pure white rice! Where did you get this?" The quaking culprit produced no answer. The little rice ball was destroyed, bits scattered over the floor, the rest stuck to the teacher's fingers.

Livid, the teacher summoned to the front of the classroom three of the largest boys, each a head taller and strapping in comparison to the wretch. At that moment, though he had no idea what was in store, Young Nam was grateful to be the fourth tallest boy in the class. The teacher ordered the larger boys to strip the miscreant naked for his whipping. The three large boys hesitated, glancing nervously at each other. If they did not succeed, their teacher threatened, they would receive a like punishment executed by boys from the upper grades. Their abhorrence for exposure was motivation enough to propel the three large boys onto their quaking victim. The girls covered their eyes and hid their heads on their desks. Her eyes affixed to the scene, the teacher distractedly nibbled the sticky rice off her fingers, one by one, licking each clean.

The small child fought as if for his life. A mangle of flailing arms and legs crashed around the floor and slammed into the front row of desks. Blood splattered the girls in the front row, who screamed and pulled their knees up to their chests. When the teacher's chair crashed and splintered against the wall, she attempted to call off the operation. But the fight had escalated beyond control. The teacher howled and beat the maelstrom of body parts with her rod. Grim satisfaction filled Young Nam's heart, but he maintained an expression of stony blankness lest he attract attention.

Finally, under the rain of blows from the teacher's rod, the violent mass decelerated and the three large boys unfolded themselves, staggered to their feet, panting, gingerly touching their bloodied noses and inspecting their bloodstained hands. One of the large boys reached a hand down to help the small child to his feet. The widow's son sprang up, fully clothed. A stifled murmur of approval rose from the classroom. On that day, any modicum of respect the boy may have felt for his teacher soured irrevocably.

There were interminable outdoor exercises while the books gathered dust inside. The children were required to stand at attention in the schoolyard, the boys shirtless and ashamed, under the raging sun, to hear endless propaganda espousing the renunciation of selfish gain, the devotion of every thought and every action to the advancement of the empire. This was followed by calisthenics till the children resembled rows of boiled shrimp. After the first sunburn dried up and peeled off in sheets, a follow-up roasting was administered. The baked and browned children were lectured by teachers that this double skin shedding was a salubrious necessity for colonial children.

On a scorching day, a girl collapsed in the schoolyard. It was not an unusual occurrence, and the boy continued his exercises, as did the others, eyes straight ahead, without a break in discipline. Nobody dared to budge from formation and risk the ripping pain of rod on flesh. When the girl did not rise from the ground, one of the teachers descended from the dais, wielding a long black lacquered rod, the thick handle inlaid with intricate mother of pearl adornment, tapering down to the diameter of a cracking whip. She stalked between the rows of students to where the girl lay with her leg twisted unnaturally under her body and commanded, "Stand up, or receive your beating." The stillness was telling. The teacher took an involuntary step back and then bent over to have a closer look at the face of the fallen girl. She poked the child's side with her rod and then her shoe.

Then she proceeded back to the dais and whispered to a more senior teacher who whispered to the principal. Beneath their parasols, the teachers began to fan their faces. The morning exercises continued their normal course. After an orderly dismissal, as the students mustered to clean the schoolhouse, Kim Young Nam was summoned to the dais. The teacher announced that the girl who had collapsed during daily exercise was his sister, and he must bring his father immediately to collect her.

As Young Nam flew to his sister, he heard the teacher warn, "She is dead!" He knelt beside the dust-covered face from which no movement, no sound, and no breath came. The boy took his sister's body in his arms. They were only a year apart in age and nearly the same size. He struggled to his feet and took a step toward the schoolhouse. The teacher hollered, "You cannot bring that inside the school!" The boy turned his back to the teacher to hide the anger rising inside him. Staggering under the weight of the body, he made his way to the gate. As he attempted to cross the length of the schoolyard, weakened by the morning exercises in the heat, his knees buckled and his grip on the body slipped. He went down on one knee, secured his hold, and stood again. In a more conciliatory voice, the teacher called out, "You will never make it home. Leave that here. You must fetch your father."

Young Nam could easily carry Owlet all day long while simultaneously working his chores. But when Owlet clung on with his arms and legs, the load was considerably lightened. Dead weight was the most overwhelming burden a person could bear. The teacher was right. He would never make it. The boy laid his sister's body against the wall, arranged her limbs and straightened her uniform, and ran out the gate, neglecting to bow and clap at the Shinto shrine. It took an hour to sprint home full tilt.

The boy and his father sped to the school driving the team of oxen, *Abuji* whipping the beasts furiously all the way while the boy clung to the bucking cart seat. A black vulture circled over the schoolyard, its stripped head craning grotesquely toward the ground. Leaving his son to secure the oxen, the father rushed to his daughter. A cloud of flies dispersed from her body. He lifted the limp figure and walked away from the wall to the center of the schoolyard. He looked around. There was nobody. He carried her to the door of the schoolhouse. At a window, a face appeared and disappeared. *Abuji* waited. Nobody came. In the hot stillness, the flies ventured to resettle on the dead girl's exposed calves. Bolder flies buzzed about the father's face.

Abuji carried his daughter's body to the cart, her shorn head dangling over the crook of his elbow. The boy trailed behind him, his head bowed. His father carefully arranged the body into the cart, fanned the flies away with a rice sack, and covered her face with it. "Get in and watch over her," said his father. The boy sat, leaden and silent, beside his sister's body. The father, shoulders hunched, plodded beside the exhausted oxen. The vulture banked and circled, casting its hideous shadow over their creaking procession.

5

Lee Hana
Tianjin, China
1943

Lee Hana gingerly lowered herself onto the floor of the train boxcar. She propped herself on one hip to avoid pressure on her tumescent pelvic floor. Two armed soldiers boarded the car and took positions guarding the doorway. A blinding white light flooded her field of view, and shrill ringing pierced her eardrums. She steadied herself against the sooty wall. The soldiers took little notice of the girls. Hana let out the breath she had been holding seemingly forever.

Upon settling themselves, the girls joined hands again. Another group of young girls was already on the boxcar. Hana's attention was immediately drawn to a pair of identical twin sisters, round-faced and pretty as babies, clinging to each other and weeping in unison. Witnessing the doubling of their misfortune, Hana thought: how unbearable to be here with a loved one, how agonizing to witness her pain and humiliation, how wrenching to know she is witnessing yours, how magnified the worry and grief. She noticed the awkward position in which the sisters sat and leaned over to hold each other and the throttle marks on one sister's neck. She felt relieved that at least the taking of their innocence was over and done with.

For several days, the girls traveled in the boxcar. At station stops, the soldiers changed watch. On the second day, during the changing of guards, one girl suddenly bolted for the open doorway. With practiced ease, a soldier seized her by the braid and smashed her to the floor. Taking no more notice of his maneuver than of the squashing of an ant, the soldiers concluded their exchange of news and jokes before proceeding to their respective stations.

Closing the boxcar door, the soldier turned his attention to the girl who had attempted her escape. He grasped her braid and flung her away from the other girls who had crept nearby to give aid. With the mechanical proficiency of a wood chopper splitting logs, he beat the girl, delivering measured blows to her buttocks, thighs, and abdomen. She shrieked at first and then whimpered for mercy, and finally lay still as a corpse, absorbing the steady thud, thud, thud of the soldier's boots and fists. The beating seemed to last an eternity. The girls wept in absolute silence. When the soldier was finished, he stood up, breathing heavily, dark circles of sweat on the armpits and back of his shirt. He smeared the sweat from his face with his shirt sleeve, cracked his knuckles, and lit a cigarette. The girls were completely docile for the remainder of the long journey.

On the third day, the train reached occupied Tianjin, China. One of the girls could read the Chinese station marker, and the devastating news was whispered from one girl to the other. They had lost their families. They had lost their girlhood. Now they had lost their homeland. Hope was extinguished.

Mamasan and *Papasan* materialized to collect their property. The girls were taken to a staging area where there awaited hundreds upon hundreds of girls, in white dresses, black hair, and meek demeanor, like an enormous flock of sheep in a yellow dust field. All morning, a handful of flesh-peddlers, including

Mamasan, *Papasan*, and a Japanese army sergeant, sifted and sorted and negotiated over the flock. The twin sisters attracted the attention of the sergeant, who waded into the pen and separated them from the others. Then, he noticed Hana, who was standing nearby, and selected her too.

Papasan stepped forward and identified the rest of the girls in his group and presented them to the sergeant, loudly hawking their merits. The girl with the black eye and bayonet wound and the girl who had been beaten on the train and was still doubled over in pain were traded for an unblemished specimen of the sergeant's choice. A few more girls were chosen and haggled over. The remainder of the girls were divided into groups of about fifteen and loaded onto troop transport trucks under guard of armed soldiers.

Ten chosen girls were taken on foot to a block building with a corrugated roof. They entered a small, dusty room. The girls dared not speak, but their frantic eyes darted around the room. In the center stood a single wooden table blotched with dark stains, and against one wall a rusty cabinet containing bandages, jars of ointments, and a scattering of surgical instruments.

Rubbing his hands together, *Papasan* crowed, "Girls, we are in luck. This is an excellent assignment. You should be very grateful. You must continue to obey and work very hard…"

His speech was interrupted by the entrance of a young officer, an army medic in a blood-stained white jacket over his uniform.

"Line them up," he ordered.

Working down the row of girls, the medical officer swiftly surveyed each recruit, inspected her throat, and felt her neck glands. Reaching Hana, he turned to *Papasan* and inquired, "How old is this girl?"

"She does not know her age. We believe she is seventeen," *Papasan* said.

"This child is not a day over thirteen," the medic said.

"She is sixteen at the youngest."

45

"You lie," the medic snapped. "Have them disrobe completely. Then we will see."

The girls were silent except for the twins, who clung to each other and wept. They had each other to care and cry for.

"Do not cry," *Mamasan* hissed. "He is a medical doctor. He is only making sure you are healthy. Obey!"

One by one, each nude and bewildered girl mounted the stained wooden table and submitted to the first medical examination of their lives. The officer palpated their abdomens and brusquely forced apart their tightly clamped legs for a visual inspection. After all the exams were completed, Hana was separated from the rest of the girls who stood huddled together awkwardly shielding their nude bodies against each other.

"How old are you?" he asked. "Are you thirteen years old?" He held up ten fingers followed by three.

"As you can see, she is just as tall as the other girls," interjected *Mamasan*.

"Quiet!" the officer snapped at *Mamasan*, and turning back to Hana carefully repeated his question along with the hand motions.

"Yes. I am thirteen," Hana replied giving her Korean age in a barely audible, halting whisper using her country schoolhouse Japanese. She raised ten trembling fingers and then three. In Korea, the months of gestation in the womb were rounded up to a year such that a newborn baby would be one-year-old; thus she was twelve years from her birth.

The medic turned to *Papasan* and said, "What did I tell you? Did you ask her age when she was recruited? She is too young for service."

"She has already been used," *Papasan* replied, shrugging.

"Have you had your menses?" the medical officer asked Hana. She did not understand, so he rephrased his question. "Do you experience monthly bleeding?"

Mamasan translated. But the question was as unintelligible to the girl in Korean as it was in Japanese, a fact which provided the answer to the medic's question.

"She is too young for this work. She must wait until she is at minimum sixteen years old. She must be sent back to her home," declared the medic.

"She has already been used. Her family will not take her back."

"Then she will work as a housemaid until she is ready for service."

"Major Matsumoto's sergeant personally selected her. He is sure to have reported back to the major. You must obtain his permission."

"I decide these matters," said the young officer, but his voice was uncertain.

Papasan pounced upon it. "Major Matsumoto will be very angry. Very angry indeed. She is already broken in and prepared for service. The major is sure to ask for her tonight. You must obtain his permission."

"So be it," said the medical officer turning on his heels and stalking out of the room.

After a time, the medical officer returned. He snarled at *Mamasan* and *Papasan*, "They pass. Take them all. Instruct them on the hygiene procedures." He slammed the door behind him.

That evening, Hana sat on the edge of a narrow cot, her hands folded in her lap. She listened to the twins sobbing and comforting each other and pitied them. She and the twin sisters had been separated from the rest of the new recruits and stationed in a primitive Chinese house which had been converted into officer's quarters. The remaining new girls were dispatched to a separate comfort station to service the troops. A small back room of the officer's quarters had been partitioned into tiny cells using canvas cloth hung from ropes, each compartment just large enough for a cot. Straw matting was spread on the dirt floor beneath the army cot. In one corner was a jar filled with dark purple solution with a rubber tube hanging over the rim and a bowl containing a wad of cotton wool.

Major Matsumoto entered Hana's compartment first. He relieved himself quickly, much as if visiting the outhouse. But then he turned the girl out of the cot and inspected it, frantically passing his hands over her skirt and the bedding. Cursing, he stomped out and proceeded into the adjacent cell. Soon, one of the twin girls began to scream. Her sister, hearing her twin's distress, whimpered pitifully. Hana lay back on her cot with her skirt over her body and her arms at her sides and studied a moth which was hurling itself against the bare light bulb strung on an electrical cord across the ceiling. Between the screams, she heard the sizzle of the moth's body colliding against the lit bulb.

As the woeful outcry in the adjacent cell continued at some length, she remembered *Mamasan's* hygiene lecture. *Mamasan* had warned them that if they did not douche after every customer, they would catch a venereal disease from the men, go blind, rot from the inside out, and die a purulent death. Hana got off her cot. She squatted before the jar of purple solution and took up the end of the tubing. She struggled. Sweat poured off her brow and stung her eyes. Hana jabbed blindly, but the region was so raw that the lightest touch felt like a live ember on a suppurating wound. Hearing the major finish with the second twin girl and stalk out in a fury of cursing, she hastily swabbed herself with cotton soaked in the solution and scurried back to the cot. After the major had used all three new girls, his men took their turn. Five officers exacted comfort from Hana's body that night.

In the morning, *Mamasan* collected Hana and the twin sisters. On their way out of the officers' quarters, they overheard *Papasan* in a scrap with Major Matsumoto.

"You dirty thief. There was not a virgin among them!"

"I apologize, Major. I am deeply regretful. Next time, we will take care to reserve one for you."

"There may not be a next time. I may just chop off your deceitful head right now."

"I promise to bring you what you need. Upon my life, I promise it. But these girls are almost virgins. They were only used once before. Surely they will still bring some fortune."

"You idiot! There is no such thing as an almost virgin! None of these filthy slatterns will bring me any luck whatsoever!"

The girls put their heads down and hurried after *Mamasan*.

The comfort station was a rude wooden building, long and narrow, with a freshly painted banner nailed to the lintel proclaiming the arrival of new volunteers. The building was subdivided into narrow compartments like a horse stable. Each stall had a number and below that the girl's Japanese name on a shingle tacked to the door. The new girls who had arrived with Hana emerged from their cells, shell-shocked phantoms of their former selves. There had been a run on the fresh flesh, and the new girls had serviced twenty to thirty men each. Some of them bore the marks of the fists of soldiers infuriated by their encounters with what amounted to a lifeless carcass in a stall putrid with the sweat and excretions of the dozens of men who had preceded them.

The females filed into a nearby mess hall like nags to the slaughterhouse. Hana and the twins somberly ate their breakfast of rice and cabbage. An older woman, perhaps twenty, limped over and sat beside them. She leaned toward the three new officer's girls, her wild black eyes gripping the girls' attention with their insanity. In a rapid fire whisper, checking over her shoulder, bits of rice flying from between missing teeth, she unloaded her story during the ten-minute meal. She too had begun her service in the officers' quarters. The first time, she had resisted the customer with all her might, and he had beaten her and crippled her. While working for the officers, she had become pregnant, and the doctor had killed the baby while it was in her stomach. She had delivered her dead baby. She had begged the doctor to tell her the baby's sex: a boy. *A boy!* Killed. She had returned to work the following day. In less than a year, a new batch of recruits had come, and all the officers' girls had been transferred to the comfort station. One day, a girl ran away. She was captured in terrible condition, dehydrated and sick, and was beaten nearly to death. Another time, all the girls had been summoned to witness a woman's execution for spreading venereal disease. The woman abruptly ceased her rant when *Mamasan* approached and waved her off.

After breakfast, the girls washed the soldiers' laundry using buckets and washboards and hung the uniforms to dry. Then they were marched to their stations. It was just past noon, and a long queue of enlisted men already snaked around the comfort station. But Hana and the twins were directed to their compartments at the officers' quarters to prepare themselves so that they would be fresh and pretty for the officers. The three girls sat together on Hana's cot.

"We have decided to commit suicide today," a twin sister said calmly. "We did not want to leave you here all alone. So we decided to invite you to join us."

Hana was shocked. Remembering *Unni*, she stammered, "But...but we do not have a knife."

"See the curtains? There are two ropes available, and one of us can use the electrical cord," explained the other twin sister, having planned out this detail of the operation in advance.

"But...but I do not know how," gasped Hana.

"We will show you," replied one of the twins, taking down the canvas and rope partition. She extracted the rope and with nimble fingers tied it into a noose which she put around her neck, flipping her heavy braid over it. "Make sure your hair is out of it. You stand on your cot with the rope around your neck. You throw the other end over the rafter like so. You take out the slack like so. You tie it to the post like so. You kick your cot away from under your feet and let your body weight tighten the noose. Then you stop breathing and close your eyes. It will be so easy. It will be very quick."

"When would we do it?" asked Hana, unable to control the querulous tremor in her voice.

"We have to do it now. Before the officers come," a twin said.

"But I did not say goodbye to my mother," cried Hana, tears burning her eyes.

"None of us will ever see our mothers again," a twin said. "This is the only way. This is what our mothers would expect of us."

"Of course," answered Hana. "You are right. Thank you."

"And we must hurry!"

The sisters let Hana have the demonstration rope which was already tied into a noose. They took down the second rope and the electrical cord. After a polite skirmish in which each twin wrangled for use of the electrical cord in order to spare her sister the discomfort of it, the older twin prevailed. The twins hastily hugged Hana and then each other. They stood on top of their cots and went to work with no further ado. They were flush with excitement.

With the curtains gone, the girls were in plain view of each other. The three girls put the nooses around their necks and tied the free end taut. Hana, hands shaking violently, finished last. Observing that her compatriot was finally ready, the twin in the middle decisively kicked her cot, which fell over into her sister's cell. Her eyes were squeezed shut. Her body swung and twirled wildly, but the girl kept her hands and legs still until she finally settled into a billowing white pendulum.

Meanwhile, the older twin struggled mightily to dispose of her own cot, but her sister's was blocking the way, and there was no floor space left on any side. She flailed her arms and kicked her legs as if in a furious temper tantrum. After numerous agonizingly futile attempts, the girl finally lifted her feet behind her with simple grace and held her ankles, kneeling in midair, suspended by the electrical cord around her neck.

Hana was paralyzed. She could not move. She could not think. She watched and waited in horror for what seemed an eternity as the rafters creaked and life ratcheted away from the twins in terrible chokes and gasps. When it was over, scarcely aware of her actions, she removed her noose and stumbled from her cell, running, falling, scrambling on her hands and knees, crying for help. At the threshold of the front door, she was stopped by a man's arm. She recognized a young Japanese officer who had made use of her the preceding night. Gripping both of her upper arms, he rasped, "Never try to run away!" She gestured, frantic and wild-eyed, toward the suicide scene, silent screams dying in her throat.

The officer, holding her by the upper arm, rushed to the back room where the sisters were suspended. A groan escaped him. He cut the twins down and laid them side-by-side on the floor. Kneeling, he put his ear to their silent hearts. He stood up shaking his head. Surveying the suicide scene, the overturned cot, the canvas curtains which had been taken down and neatly folded in the corner, the single light bulb unscrewed and carefully placed beside the permanganate jar, the officer noticed the unused rope dangling free. "What's this?" he asked, grabbing the noose. Without waiting for an answer, the officer hastily untied it. He threw the coil of rope in the corner and took Hana by the arm to a storage room.

Pointing his finger between her eyes, he said, "Wait here until this settles. Remember. Those twins locked you in here. You had no idea. Or else you will be punished in the most brutal manner imaginable. Understand?"

Then he slammed the door shut and locked it.

In the aftermath of this incident, security was tightened. Armed soldiers stood guard at the comfort station. *Mamasan* or *Papasan* patrolled the officers' area. New partitions were hastily constructed of plywood. All ropes, cords, and sharp objects were removed. The ties on the girls' *hanbok* jackets were cut short. Even the glass jars of disinfecting solution were replaced with wooden bowls. Two comparatively fresher females were promoted from the comfort station to the officers' quarters.

Though suicide was vigilantly obstructed, attrition of the corps continued, from disease and injury. Collateral losses resulted from the routine deployment on every supply run and combat operation of small groups of women for ad hoc field recreation.

After some months, a new shipment of girls arrived to replenish the depleted ranks, and Hana was demoted to the comfort station. There, in cramped and sour stall number seven, she serviced soldiers for fifteen hours a day. During busy times, men came one every twenty minutes, leaving no time to eat or attend to hygiene. Any consciousness of the atrocity of her existence was stifled by primal sensations of continual hunger and raw ache.

No vestige of human feeling kindled her heart. Hope was a luxury she had long forgotten. She did not hope for relief. She did not hope for the black peace of death. She did not hope for anything. She was an amoeba twitching in a foul petri dish. Nothing more.

Then one day, a certain Private Koizumi came and changed everything.

6

Kim Young Nam
Occupied Korea
1944

It was dawn. The Kim family mustered in their courtyard, mother and father at attention in the front ranks, six sons in the rear. They stood before the village elder, who was dressed in the *yangban* scholar's white robes and a black silk hat. Behind the elder loomed two policemen, boots planted shoulder width apart, arms akimbo. The boy, Kim Young Nam, recognized one of the policemen. He was the son of the village butcher, an untouchable, once splattered with entrails, scraping in his lowliness. Now, in his Japanese uniform, he was invincible. As the confrontation progressed, the two youngest sons huddled closer to Young Nam. He took one under each arm. The village elder addressed their parents.

The elder informed the deaconess that she was fortunate. Number three son would be exempted from the draft because he was admitted to normal school. Number four, five, and six sons were too young for the draft. Thus, the Kim family would still have four sons at home. Many families in the village had no sons left. Furthermore, she was fortunate that her sons had not been drafted into the military. Nearly every other family in the village had sent a son to war. They were fortunate there were good factory jobs for the eligible sons. They would earn decent wages and learn a useful skill. They would be fed. They would be housed. They ought to consider themselves lucky.

"When?" asked the father. He had witnessed enough to know no recourse existed.

"Now," replied the elder.

With a wail of naked anguish, the deaconess threw herself at the feet of the elder.

"Not now!" she cried. "Do not take my sons now. I must feed them. We have been rationing. They have not eaten well in days. I am begging you. We will bring them tomorrow. You have my word. You have a son. You know my feelings."

"I am sorry, Deaconess," said the old man wearily. "I have been given no other choice. It must be now."

"Please. I beg you. You know. You have a son," she pleaded.

"Yes. I have a son. But only one," he said. "I have sold my soul to the devil for the sake of my only son. You have six sons. There is no recourse. I am deeply sorry."

"I beg you, can my sons stay together?"

"Yes," answered the elder.

"Do you promise?" she wept.

"I promise," said the old man.

The policemen lunged toward the young recruits. But the elder halted his henchmen with a raised palm. He turned to the heap of woman at his feet.

"We will wait at the gate. Send your sons alone. They are men now. Send them out like men or these two will take them by force."

As the reapers turned away, the deaconess raised herself and rushed at their retreating backs with another cry, but was restrained by her husband. Under his touch, her bones liquefied and she melted out of his grasp onto the ground. The children gathered around their mother. The eldest son raised her to her knees.

"Mother! There is no time. We must pray in our last moment together," urged her eldest son.

He was not especially devout, his Christian inculcation having come later in life, replacing a childhood diet of Confucianism, Buddhism, shamanism, and enforced Shinto, all blended with a strong dose of superstition; he was only anxious to end his mother's weeping.

"No. I must get you some rice to eat on the way. You will be hungry," she sobbed, making no move toward the kitchen, but gripping her son's shoulders and raising her streaked face to him.

"No. There is no time. We must go now. We do not want to be dragged off like animals. Come, let us pray. Quickly, Mother. Gather yourself. Let us pray!" he urged, deploying the only appeal likely to steady the deaconess.

Mother and sons knelt in the dirt, hands clasped. *Abuji* stood apart, his head hanging, not in prayer, but in defeat. Mother and sons began in unison, "The Lord is my shepherd; I shall not want. He maketh me to lie down in green pastures: he leadeth me beside the still waters…"

But the recitation dissolved into sobs. They could not go on. Powerless, they wept as their last minutes together sped by, the police at the gate. Their Psalm would be unfinished, like a life interrupted. Then from the ruins rose a voice. It was Owlet.

"He restoreth my soul: He leadeth me in the paths of righteousness for his name's sake. Yea, though I walk through the valley of the shadow of death, I will fear no evil: for thou art with me; thy rod and thy staff they comfort me."

Then, the child turned his head toward the gate and raised his tenor to its highest volume, saying, "Thou preparest a table before me in the presence of mine enemies: thou anointest my head with oil; my cup runneth over. Surely goodness and mercy shall follow me all the days of my life: and I will dwell in the house of the Lord forever."

The deaconess laid her ruddy hands on the bowed heads of her two teenage sons.

"Stay together. No matter what happens, stay together. Watch out for each other. Together you will be strong. Stay together."

On the dock at Pusan harbor, the sons were separated. Any flicker of hope was asphyxiated in the airless, fecal cargo holds of their ships. The nineteen-year-old was shipped to a metal working labor camp in Japan, the seventeen-year-old to a coal mine. In the camps, at the point of a gun, they would toil under conditions unfit for vermin, from sunup to sundown, day after day, without respite. Early on, one brother ventured to ask an older veteran of the work camp if wages were being sent directly home. "You are a slave now," said the specter. "Slaves are not paid."

In the camps, the work would not stop for injury or disease. Sanitation consisted of a communal pit dug in the ground. Those who could no longer work were disposed of. Alongside the male workers were women who were forced to work like the men, stripped naked to the waist. In winter they were hungry and cold. In summer they were hungry and hot. The air itself was parsimoniously doled, and the brothers gasped for each desperate breath, one in the flaming furnaces of a foundry, the other in the black tunnels of a coal mine. All around them, their fellow laborers died like flies, and, like flies, they were not counted.

With the farm shorthanded, sacrifices had to be made. There was money enough for only one tuition, invested in the eldest remaining son, who was already in normal school. Young Nam was obliged to quit school to work the farm. On his last day, he collected his polishing wax and floor rag with deliberate inertia, letting all the students pass him by while he lingered. Walking by the principal's office, he spied a small group of young girls in their school uniforms, huddled together with frightened faces, clutching each other's hands. Tied around their foreheads were white scarves with a red sun disc centered between the eyes. A Japanese official lectured them. The boy slowed his pace enough to gather that the school girls were being sent away to work in factories. The recruiter exhorted the girls to submit themselves and work selflessly for their emperor god. The boy's thoughts flew to his younger sister, to her sudden schoolyard death. A wave of relief, bordering on elation, washed over the boy.

Farm work was back breaking and mind numbing. Morning began the relentless cycle of stoop labor in the paddies, the fruits of which, after the government levy, could scarce quell the yowling of his hollow belly. At noon, the boy swallowed his rice water gruel in three gulps before returning to the fields. As he jogged for hours on the manually operated wooden water wheel to irrigate the fields, his stomach acids attacked his lunch gruel with such ferocity that he doubled over in pain.

But by afternoon, the boy heartened, because the time was drawing near when his elder brother would return home from normal school, change his clothes, and join him in the fields. Bent over their crops, his older brother would teach him all he had learned that day. The older boy recognized that teaching was the best route to academic mastery, and the younger made an eager and gratifying pupil.

Winter, and its companion, want, came too soon. The harvest had been poor. Though there were fewer mouths to feed, the labor of a nine-year-old boy produced a meager yield compared to that of two young men. It was not long after the first snowfall before illness struck the family's weakest member.

The fever claimed Owlet during the night, and by morning he could not arise from his bedding. Father moved the child's bedding over the warmest part of the *ondol* floor and fueled the fire in the plenum chamber below the house with extra wood.

Mother boiled rice water and dribbled one drop at a time down Owlet's throat. But the water spilled over his cheek filling his ear. The fever rose and delirium scrambled the child's burning head. Then, convulsions shook his frame and his eyes rolled back in his head.

In the yard was buried a gold Chinese coin, thick and round, with a square hole in the center, the final remnant of their currency. The father unearthed it, tied it around his neck, and hastened to the village on his oxen-drawn cart.

Later that day, he returned transporting an old man with a long beard like spider webs and skin wizened as a dried apple. The old man carried a basket in his lap and straddled a large bundle at his feet. He disembarked, one brown ropey hand hugging the basket, the other holding the lid shut, and entered the house.

Owlet lay like a desiccated wraith, silent and still under his covers, his sunken eye sockets staring into infinity. The shaman barely glanced at the child before turning to the father to demand, "First the money." He snatched the Chinese coin, put it to his tongue, and stashed it into a purse tied around his waist. A curious dry rustle shook the witch doctor's basket.

Then the shaman inspected the inside of Owlet's mouth, pulling open his cheeks, lifting the upper and lower lips, twisting the tongue up and around. He instructed *Umma* to keep Owlet's mouth moist to prevent breaks in the skin. The anxiety of his patient's parents, their hovering, their stream of questions – "What are you looking for in his mouth?" and "Can he be cured?" and "What is inside your basket?" – irritated the shaman. He instructed them to break the ice over the stream with rocks and drench themselves in its frigid water. They were to repeat this procedure morning, noon, and night to cleanse the evil spirits inhabiting their bodies and contaminating their son. They were to steer clear of him and his magic pot until their evil spirits were completely discharged: three days to be exact.

While his parents shivered at the frozen stream, Young Nam was dispatched to fetch the old man's bundle and firewood. The boy looked on with bated breath as the shaman gingerly unwrapped his bundle and revealed something resembling an oversized mud dauber's nest in the shape of a cauldron. "My magic pot," he said. Squatting on his haunches in the courtyard, the shaman arranged the firewood, placed the cauldron over it, and added a handful of snow.

Then, in a flash, the shaman lifted the lid of his basket and seized from it a hissing viper. Its diamond shaped head immobilized in the gnarled grip, the snake's body writhed and its bared fangs dripped venom. The shaman looked the snake in the eyes and cracked a toothless grin. He coiled it tail end first into the cauldron and swiftly topped it with a heavy lid. Then he lit a twig at a time under the snake pot, chanting and rocking on his haunches. For hours the shaman squatted in this position, building the fire with excruciating exactitude, one stick at a time. As the viper snapped and whipped inside the gradually heating pot, the shaman nodded and chanted.

All the while, the boy observed from a respectful distance, leaving only to replenish the wood pile. Gathering his courage, the boy approached the crouching figure and squatted opposite him in silence, watching. The old man squinted at the boy.

"So you are a curious one," the shaman said. "But you do not squawk like a magpie. I had to get rid of your noisy parents. They gave me a headache. Ask me the question that is in your eyes."

The boy learned that the shaman's magic pot was an iron cauldron coiled with rope and coated with clay. In this insulated pot, heated gradually, maximal venom would be extracted from the viper. If no open sores developed in the sick child's mouth and throat – entry through the bloodstream would be deadly – Owlet could safely consume the potion and be cured.

The sick child shivered and seized all night. The following morning, the boy awoke before the sun came up, slid out from the covers, and tiptoed out to the yard. A gentle snow was falling on the shaman who squatted over his cauldron in precisely the same posture as the day before. A small fire burned and the snake was still angry inside the pot. The boy offered to stand watch over the pot. The shaman refused. The boy offered to bring the old man some food and water. The shaman refused. After a time, the boy offered a cup of rice wine. This the shaman accepted. The vigil went on for three days and three nights during which the old man did not budge from his post.

On the third morning, the boy hurried to the courtyard. The scent of meat wafted into the frosty air. "My friend has surrendered all of the venom his body could make," said the shaman, lifting the lid to show the boy. The snake had been cooked alive in its own venom for sauce. The meat had fallen off the railroad of bones coiled in the pot. The old man wrapped the snake parts in a cloth and wrung out the liquids into the pot. After standing the pot in the snow for an hour, he soaked up the floating layer of yellow fat with paper.

Creaking audibly, the old man uncoiled himself to a standing position, studied the boy intently, and said, "The spirits spoke to me from the mountains last night. They told me something about your future."

Kim Young Nam held his breath.

"Do you want to know it?"

"Yes!"

"Your destiny awaits you in a great foreign land."

Then before the boy could ask any questions, he motioned to the magic pot and said, "Hurry up. You carry it in. I am weak."

No frankincense, no myrrh was ever transported with more painstaking care than that cauldron of viper stew. Once again, the shaman examined the inside of the sick child's mouth, throat, and tongue. When he was done, he examined it a second time. He lifted the sick child in the crook of his arm and gave him a sip from a spoon while the family gathered in hushed expectation. "More?" whispered Owlet. A yelp of jubilation escaped his mother's lips. The shaman glared at her. She stifled her sobs behind her hands. Owlet took another spoonful, his eyes focusing curiously on the shaman, then fell back to his mat. Over the course of the morning, he consumed the remainder of the viper elixir, and by the afternoon, he was healed.

Tears sheeting over her ruddy cheeks, the deaconess gathered her sons to kneel on the floor around their youngest brother and thank God for saving Owlet's life. More fervent prayers of gratitude were never sent heavenward than from the heart of the boy Young Nam. He loved his brother. But as his mother wept and prayed, and wept and prayed some more, the boy's private thoughts strayed to a different place. He replayed the shaman's tantalizing, inscrutable, and, in terrible times to come, sustaining words: *Your destiny awaits you in a great foreign land.*

7

Lee Hana
Occupied China
1944-1945

Suzuha: it is I," said Private Koizumi, rapping on the door of stall number seven of the comfort station. The soldier entered, stared at Hana, and then exhaled audibly. With a short joyless laugh, he placed his chit in her cupped hands.

"Welcome," said Lee Hana, and bowed mechanically, per required protocol. She wore an old army field jacket which the girls had been issued for the coming winter, blood stained and pocked with the bullet holes that had dispatched its previous owner, torn at the shoulder where the insignia had been ripped off, and nothing else. She stashed the receipt in its overstuffed receptacle and lay down on the straw mat that covered the dirt floor, her arms at her sides. She was not in the habit of heeding the customers. In fact, it was a violation of regulations to form social attachments.

"Suzuha," repeated the new customer.

"It is my honor to serve you," she robotically dispensed another stock phrase while staring at the ceiling. Some of the men got it over with quickly. Others expected extra attention.

Leaning over her face, the man whispered in fluent Korean, "Sit up. I have brought you something."

She jerked herself to a seated position, and shook her head in bewilderment. She focused her eyes and finally beheld what was unmistakable: a Korean man in a Japanese uniform. Scrambling to a kneeling position, she covered herself by tugging the jacket over her knees.

"*Annyong haseyo*," she whispered in formal Korean, bobbing her head in an abbreviated bow, then gazing at him in disbelief.

He squatted beside her, reached into an inner pocket of his coat, took out a cloth package, and placed it on her lap. "Open it," he said.

Hana unwrapped the small parcel and found a small piece of cold chicken. She sucked in her breath sharply. "Not for me, is it?" she gasped in disbelief.

"I saw you. I thought…you are a growing girl. You need some meat," said the private.

No morsel of tough boiled chicken was ever beheld with such awe. Was this a dream? The visitor pointed to the chicken saying, "You should eat it slowly. It may be hard for you to digest."

She swallowed it whole.

"What is your name?" he asked, reflexively checking over his shoulder at the closed door.

"Lee Hana," she mouthed in a barely audible whisper.

"I am Private First Class Koizumi," he declared loudly. Then he leaned close to her ear and whispered, "Pak Ki Jong."

"You are Korean."

"My troop arrived last week. I saw you with the women doing laundry. I thought I recognized you. But I was mistaken. How are they treating you?" he asked.

"Fine," she said. They both knew it was a lie.

"Is the meat good?"

"Yes. Oh, thank you. Thank you," she said. "Who are you?"

The private sat cross-legged at the end of her mat. He told her he was from Seoul. His father was a teacher, and his mother was a housewife. Times had grown difficult recently and his mother had begun to peddle their belongings on the street, a circumstance which depressed his father. The private had a younger sister who was about her age. His sister was very pretty…like her.

"Tell me more about her," she whispered.

His sister was smart. She was a hard worker. She could have been something. The private recalled a hot summer day years ago when his little sister had been about five years old. The little girl had set herself to work in the garden for hours. She had extracted miniscule seeds from the garden flowers without damaging a single living bloom. Brimming with pride, she skipped eagerly to him to show the seeds in her tightly clenched fist. Carefully, oh so carefully, she opened her tiny fist to display the miniature black pinpoints nestled in her palm. He could not resist. Taking a deep breath, he blew her seeds all over the ground. The child ran and cried to her mother who scolded him: one day you will regret all the mean things you did to your sister.

"My mother was right as usual," said the private.

"Another customer will come soon. May I offer you entertainment in the remaining time?" asked Hana.

"No. I only came to give you the chicken. I thought you were…you remind me of my sister," he said.

"This is an honor I do not deserve."

"Tell me about yourself," he said.

"I cannot remember anything. All I can think of is: today, I ate chicken," she said.

So he talked. His parents had run out of bribe money to prevent him and his sister from being drafted. They had become very poor. In his house there was a false bottom on the floor. Underneath was a crawl space, separate from the *ondol*, just large enough to conceal two people. To keep him hidden proved impossible. He would make too much noise until they had to let him out. He would run away and hide in the alleys. Finally, they were left with no choice but to surrender him to the authorities. His sister, on the other hand, could hide for days curled up in the darkness in deathly silence. She grew sallow and lame and lost her bloom from spending her youth in the crawl space hiding from recruiters. Her hair thinned and she had sores on her body that would not heal. She resembled the translucent white grubs curled on the damp black earth under a garden rock. His sister was an astonishingly disciplined individual. She would never be caught.

The next customer knocked on the door.

"Will you come tomorrow?" she pleaded.

"I cannot afford to. I must send my pay home to my family. My father cannot work nowadays. But I will come once a week for as long as my troop is stationed here," he answered gently.

A sharper knock rattled the door.

"Please come and talk to me again! I am not hungry! You do not have to bring food!"

"It is not the food that is dear. We must pay your proprietors for the chits. And I must bribe them extra to be allowed to wait for a turn with you because it is forbidden to request a specific girl."

"What? What? What do you mean?"

The financial aspect of her situation was a cipher to her. She never saw any money.

"I will come back next week," he reassured her.

Then he left. She never felt so alone. She had long been estranged from emotion. And now tears sprang from nowhere and streamed down her face as she prepared herself for the impatient customer. She fought to keep the chicken down as the next customer bore down with all his weight on her thin body.

Once a week, Private Koizumi rapped his secret code on her door, signaling Hana to don her fatigues before letting him in.

Normally, the girls remained bare from the waist down during work hours. In the frigid temperatures, she relished the temporary covering of her legs nearly as much as the morsel of meat or strip of dried fish he always brought. He fed her first. Then he sat on her mat and whispered to her in the precise syllables of her native tongue.

During one visit, before she could stop herself, she pleaded, "Can you save me? You are a member of the Imperial Japanese Army. Is there any way you can save me?"

The private was perfectly aware that the girl knew the answer to her question before she asked it. But he replied carefully anyway. His billet was to guard Korean and Chinese prisoners as they were hauled to labor camps or prisoner of war camps. It was a terrible job, but the only sort of work the Japanese trusted Korean soldiers to do. They would never place a Korean in an important combat role. Of course, the prisoners loathed him, especially the Korean Communists from the northern end of the peninsula who were fighting alongside the Chinese. The prisoners were diseased, starving, barefoot, and dressed in rags. They died left and right, and their corpses were left by the roadside for the animals to pick clean. Some of the Korean soldiers were overzealous in their desire to prove their loyalty and mistreated the prisoners in unspeakable ways. Others, while hiding behind the imperial insignia, resisted passively, perhaps by looking the other way when a prisoner escaped. These men were inevitably found out, tortured and executed. As for himself? He was marking time, staying out of trouble. He followed orders. What choice did he have? He did not want to die. He was an only son, and his family needed him.

"Will you stay here, *Oppa*?" Hana asked, addressing him as the big brother he had become to her.

"I know nothing. We came here from Manchuria. We were to continue south to Hankow. For some reason, we have been waylaid here. I do not know how long we will stay. I do not know why. They do not tell Korean soldiers anything until the morning of the maneuver. If I do not come to see you, it means we have moved out."

"But I could not bear it. I would die," she cried.

"When the war is over, I will find you. If you are still enslaved, I will find a way to purchase your freedom."

"I will die! I will die!"

"No. You must and you will survive! I will bring you home. I will introduce you to my sister. She is awfully clever. You will be her playmate."

"Your mother and father would never allow your sister to play with someone like me."

"Use your head, you silly girl! Of course, you must never, I repeat, *never* tell anyone about your work here. Say that you worked in a factory."

A rap on the door ended their time.

In the dead of winter, weeks passed without a visit from *Oppa*. Hana knew that his unit had marched on. With nothing to look forward to, the last remaining ember within her was extinguished. In their frustration with the lifeless form which provided no comfort, the soldiers beat her with increasing frequency. She saw their fists rain down on her like a faraway dream, and she felt no pain and no fear. She lost the ability to eat and listlessly passed her subsistence portion of rice to the other girls. Finally, when some customers demanded their money back, her proprietors brought her condition to the attention of the medical officer during their weekly inspection. Dismissing the rest of the girls, he turned on *Mamasan*.

"I told you she was too young. Had you listened to me, you would have prolonged your investment."

"We would be most grateful for your aid," said *Mamasan*.

"She has no infection. She has no specific ailment. My medicine is in short supply."

"The volunteers are in even shorter supply."

The medic filled a hypodermic needle. When the needle plunged into her arm, the patient did not flinch, but stared straight ahead in a glassy eyed stupor. The medical officer addressed Hana in a loud voice as if shouting through a wooden door.

"You must eat. You must force yourself to eat whether you feel any hunger or not. You must place the food inside your mouth, chew ten times, and swallow. It is part of your job requirement. Do you understand?"

The girl did not respond.

"Have you had your menses?" he shouted with his face in front of hers.

She shook her head. By now she knew from being with the other women what this meant.

"When you have your menses, you will receive two days off from work every month. Are you sure it has not come?"

"No," she replied blankly.

To *Mamasan* he said, "Give the girl two days off every month."

"And break the rules? But maybe the shot will cure her. The demand for her is still very high. I told you we are running low on volunteers..." said *Mamasan*.

"Quiet! Give her the rest of the week off," he interrupted. "Watch her closely. If she does not eat, bring her back to me. Thereafter, she will have two days off every month. No arguments. I do not want to hear the sound of your wicked voice again!"

"Yes, yes, thank you," *Mamasan* answered.

Turning back to Hana, he said, "It is your responsibility to force yourself to eat. Understand?"

"Yes," she answered mechanically.

"Remember to douche after every customer. Assume every soldier is infected. Require each customer to wear a condom."

"Yes."

"There is a great deal of swelling. Apply cold wet rags when you are not working. Get dressed and return to your place. You will have a week of rest."

"Yes."

After dismissing the girl, with a grim sigh of exhaustion, he said to *Mamasan*, "You would do well to listen to me next time. I told you she was too young. She will not last the winter."

Doubtless the medic's prediction would have come true had not another Korean conscript in the Japanese army passed through the encampment bearing a letter from *Oppa*. The Korean text of the letter was scrawled messily, as if in great haste. At the center of the paper was a stylized hand-drawn sketch of a young girl's winsome face with a heart-shaped mouth and oversized eyes sparkling with diamonds. Over her head, in the upper corner of the paper, was a constellation of stars, the big dipper and the little dipper, the North Star carefully labeled. The letter read:

Little Sister,

We march south. It is cold. Feet frozen. Lost toe but still alive. Remember. You will survive. This picture reminds me of you and my sister. Pretty. I cannot decide whether to keep it because I like it or to send it to you. I will send it and hope it finds your innocent hands.

Private Koizumi

In one of her countless readings of this precious letter, she discovered writing at the razor's edge of the paper so miniature she initially mistook it for a dirt smudge. Private Koizumi had written his true name, Pak Ki Jong, and beside it hers, Lee Hana. She survived the winter after all. She could not let herself die. Another letter might come.

Spring came. The snow melted into the muddy earth. Patches of weeds sprouted here and there. Beside the comfort station, a lone tree, twisted and moribund, eked out tiny green buds on its last living branch.

Something unsettling was afoot. The long winter of degenerate ennui was supplanted by an alarming sense of agitation. There was a rush on the comfort station, and the girls were used to the breaking point.

One morning, before the sunrise, Hana and a handful of other girls were ordered to pack all their worldly belongings, such as they were, and muster outside the mess hall for an important assignment. The girls wore their oversized hand-me-down army uniforms and arm bands imprinted "Women's Voluntary Service Corp." Hana stashed her letter from *Oppa* in one breast pocket and her compact of pancake makeup in the other, tied the frayed remains of her *hanbok* in a package about her waist, and donned only one straw slipper, its mate having been stolen for a talisman by a superstitious soldier. *Mamasan* and *Papasan* performed a quick Shinto ritual for the safe return of their meal tickets, whereupon they were hustled onto a supply truck behind a caravan of military vehicles. They rode all day and stopped at the outskirts of a sprawling garrison south of the Yellow River.

The girls idled under the guard of a soldier for several days, sleeping and eating on the truck, and waiting with dull apprehension. An immense mobilization, portending a division scale campaign, arose all around them like a fearsome dust storm. One morning, the girls were ordered to disembark from the truck. A dozen or so comfort girls attached to the garrison, most Korean and a few Chinese, visibly exhausted from the rush of customers they must have entertained, shuffled single file toward them, guarded front and rear by an armed soldier. The worn out nags joined Hana's group. Nobody spoke. They formed up behind a deployment of soldiers, horses, military vehicles, and supply convoy so vast as to be incomprehensible to the ignorant girls trailing at its rearmost ranks. The march commenced, engulfing the girls in a suffocating cloud of yellow dust and truck exhaust fumes. After an hour, the belching peristalsis of the division's advance reached the file of girls who plunged themselves into the sooty off-gas.

On the second day of the march, Hana recognized that the sun was rising on her left and setting on her right. They were heading in a generally southerly direction. Did *Oppa* not tell her that his unit was headed south? She switched her shoe to the other foot and stepped a little livelier.

"We are heading south," Hana said to the beast of burden plodding alongside her.

"South?" the girl croaked.

"Yes. See the sun? We are heading south. My *Oppa* is south."

"To Korea?" asked the girl, her eyes widening.

This incredible possibility had not even occurred to Hana. She had only been dreaming that *Oppa* might find her. Her farm girl's comprehension of geography was flimsy at best. Korea? Could it be possible? She felt her heart would burst.

On the third day of the march, her single ragged shoe, packed with dirt and horse manure, was lost. She walked on barefoot as did most of the girls. All she could see in every direction was dust. Nothing on the horizon hinted of the rugged mountainous terrain of her homeland. Hope went the way of her shoe.

On the fifth day of the march, a rogue soldier dragged one of the girls off the road, craving some quick recreation. There was a thunderous explosion. Body parts flew through the air spurting arcs of blood like crimson fireworks. To skirt this minefield, the division marched hours into the night in search of safer ground, leaving the dismembered body parts behind.

On the tenth day of the march, carcasses of horses and men began to appear on the side of the road where they had been dumped. The stench of decomposition announced a casualty before the girls trudged by the dead. A wake of vultures joined their military parade, wheeling overhead, descending en masse for mealtime.

On the untold day of the march, the girls' lips and feet were cracked and bleeding. Flies crawled over their faces, into their mouths, nostrils, and ears. Their skin was chaffed raw by the rough wool uniforms worn with no undergarments. Dust coated them from head to toe and filth ground into every crevice of their bodies. They were infested with lice, the crowns of their heads dotted white with nits.

Always there was hunger.

They arrived at a yellow-brown and dusty place. A sergeant took charge of the girls. He gave the standard speech, though it lacked the conviction of earlier renditions. "The war is nearly won. You are at the frontlines of the Imperial Japanese Army's greatest campaign. The men you serve today may die for you tomorrow. You must work harder than you believe possible."

The sergeant inspected the row of girls. He selected Hana from the group, took her to a tent, instructed her to wash up with a bucket of dirty water and a stained rag, and wait inside. Inside the tent was a thin, stained army futon, curling at the edges. She barely had time to wash her face and hands when an officer charged inside requiring service. Though she was on the verge of collapse from fatigue, hunger, pain, and malaise, she began the torturous duty which did not let up till the sun rose the next day.

Days bled into nights. Weeks then months came and went. The girls were herded, divvied up, and utilized like horses or equipment. Periodically, Hana would be appropriated for comfort duty on the front lines along with two or three others. They would be issued revolvers loaded with a single bullet to turn on themselves in the event of enemy capture. Thus equipped, they would be loaded onto supply trucks along with the food or ammunition, unloaded onto the dirt floor of a suffocating pillbox, and required to service combat troops who came in gangs and relieved themselves without a modicum of privacy. The girls suffered the same wounds, by gunshot, grenades, and mines, as the soldiers. When wounded soldiers overwhelmed the medical crew, the women would be put to work cleaning bodily wastes from the living and removing the gore exuded by the dead. Then, without any notice, there would be another long hard march, farther south, farther from home, with bombs raining from the sky, mines exploding from the earth, and bloated bodies littering the landscape.

There came a still and stifling day somehow different from the other days. The girls were given no orders. The soldiers crowded about the communications bunker. The men shouted, ran, shifted, and regrouped chaotically. Ignored, the girls gathered together in their tent, linked arms and held hands, and awaited instructions.

At length, the sergeant in charge of the girls rousted them from the tent. He marched them into a hole in the ground circled by sandbags. He ordered them to hunker down for an impending air strike and left them quaking there. Hana cowered against the dirt wall of a dugout. Ten other girls were packed in tight with her. They knew, as animals would, that they were in mortal danger. They hugged each other in the tight confines of the earthen bunker.

After about an hour, the same sergeant, accompanied by two soldiers armed with machine guns, returned to the dugout. Hana recognized one of the soldiers: a private who had become a repeat customer of hers, who had professed his undying love for her, who had wept like a baby on her neck while availing himself of her services.

The soldiers opened fire into the dugout.

Hana reflexively hit the ground, covering the back of her head with her hands. Searing pain ripped her upper arm. Bodies fell on top of her one after the other till she could scarcely breathe. The girls' screaming stopped quickly. But the machine gun fire continued at excruciating length. Finally, the sergeant barked an order and the men ceased fire and stalked off to their next chore.

Under the pile of bleeding bodies, rank with spontaneous defecation, Hana lay in dead stillness. She thought of Private Koizumi's younger sister hiding in the plenum chamber of her house. She did not flinch a muscle though the fluids of the dead flowed with agonizing stickiness over her face and neck. She played dead for hours until the black silence of night descended. When she could bear the weight and stench no longer, Hana struggled out of the death trap, dragging herself by one arm, the other having been hit by a bullet.

The moonlight illuminated a grotesque scene. Rigor mortis captured the girls in their final death throes, some scaling the walls of the dugout, some splayed on top of others, some hugging each other. Several girls, attempting a desperate escape, had been gunned down and left where they fell, draped over the sandbags. The garrison, along with its vehicles, horses, tents, and equipment, had vanished.

The girl's head reeled. She fell back and stared blankly at the dugout. What was the meaning of it? She reached for the letter from *Oppa*. It was soaked in bloody fluid and congealed in her hands. She turned her blood-encrusted face to the night sky. The seven stars of the northern dipper twinkled to her like beckoning eyes. Instinctively, with little more consciousness than a stray beast, she followed the constellation.

The summer of 1945 was at its end. Lee Hana had survived the war.

8

Kim Young Nam
South Korea
1945 to 1946

Astonishing news of Japan's unconditional surrender fanned across the peninsula. The country folk were stupefied, and Kim Young Nam was no exception. Born and bred under the occupation, the boy needed proof in order to believe that the only world he had ever known was ended. There was one sure way. He hastened to the Yamamoto farm to find out.

It was true.

In the yard, Yamamoto and the servant girl were securing a stack of crates to a wagon already hitched to oxen. Hiroshi, hovering at the doorway, spotted the boy. With a yelp, he ran from the house and hugged Young Nam.

"I will never see you again!" he mumbled into the boy's rib cage.

Hiroshi's father peeled his son off the Korean boy and deposited him onto the seat of the cart. Then he turned and put a hand on Young Nam's shoulder. The boy flinched involuntarily. The Japanese man quickly withdrew his hand.

"Is it true, sir?" asked the boy.

"Tell your father to take our house and our farm and everything we have left behind. You were the only people who ever helped us. I leave everything to your family. The papers with my seal are inside," he said.

Yamamoto helped his silent wife onto the seat of the cart. She put her hands on her lap and stared straight ahead. The Japanese settler filled his lungs with his last breath of frontier air and took a lingering last look about him: the house, neat as a gift box, the rock garden where his wife had begun to try her hand at cultivating bonsai, the koi pond, glittering in the sunlight, the fat chickens idly pecking in the yard, the luxuriant patchwork of rice paddies. He exhaled forcefully and took up the reins.

"You are free. Return to your people," he commanded the servant girl.

With those parting words, the Yamamoto family retreated from their homestead.

The boy sat on the porch, rubbed his face, and shook his head like a wet dog. The servant girl began to cry. Hiroshi's tricycle stood in the yard, gleaming red, the object of widespread envy, abandoned.

"Do you have family?" he asked the servant girl.

She continued to cry.

The outer door was ajar. Leaving his straw slippers at the doorway, he entered the house on tiptoe. To the right was the main room behind closed double sliding doors. He hesitated, peered through the paper door looking for shadows, and replayed Yamamoto's instructions in his head before daring to slide the door open. The room was bare, except for tatami mats covering the floor. In the center of the mats was a document stamped with the Yamamoto seal. He saw his father's name on the document and tucked it into his jacket. Perhaps it was the title to the property.

He looked around some more. In the kitchen, rich stores of rice, dry foodstuffs, pots of sauces and pastes, and rice wine had been left behind. The boy did not dare touch anything yet, but he knew the food would be much appreciated by his hungry family.

In the foyer between the kitchen and the main room was a lacquered bureau, inlaid with nacreous chrysanthemums, filled with Hiroshi's books. He crept to it with bated breath and caressed the spines. The skin shreds on his thick fingertips caught on the silk bindings. Some were in Japanese, some in Chinese, and some in exotic characters he did not recognize. His face burned as he reached for the foreign book with a trembling hand. A crash arrested his investigation and he scurried from the house, his heart pounding. It was only a fallen crate which, exceeding the capacity of Yamamoto's cart, had been hastily propped on the edge of the porch, and now littered its contents of western clothing and shoes on the ground. The servant girl was gone. The boy felt for the paper in his jacket, slid his shoes back on, considered whether to grab a fat chicken but, spooked, decided against it, and hastened home.

He smiled as he ran, thinking of Owlet dressed in the western pants and lace up shoes, riding merrily on the red tricycle. How proudly his little brother would peddle about shouting, "Look at me! Look at me!" while they all gathered and laughed at the spectacle. And the books! He could scarcely wait to sit beside *Hyung* before that chrysanthemum bureau and examine those books one by one.

At home, several men encircled his father in the courtyard speaking in excited tones. The boy waited in the background, but the men were engaged in a tongue wagging that could last for hours. So he crept before his father in the center of the circle of men and silently held the paper up with two hands.

"What is this?" asked his father. He was not angry about the presumption. Today was a day that anything could happen.

"It is from Hiroshi Yamamoto's father. He told me he is giving you his farm and everything in it!"

"Read it to me," said the boy's father.

The gathering listened intently while the boy read the document, a transfer of deed for the Yamamoto property to his father. When he was finished, he handed the paper to his father. *Abuji* studied the document gravely before handing it to the older man beside him, who stared at the paper and handed it to the next man. The paper went around the circle, to be handled with the utmost delicacy by the tough brown hands and scrutinized with the utmost intensity by the semi-literate eyes, till it wound up back in the hands of the boy's father.

"You should take ownership of the property immediately," said one wise man. "There will be widespread chaos soon. You need to squat there to assure your rights. You should move into the house today and leave your sons here with their mother for the time being."

"When your number one and two sons come home, you will need more land. Soon, they will take wives and you will be a grandfather," advised another.

"You have done much for the village to keep the peace. Your wife and your family have suffered much. No one will oppose it," concluded the third.

The boy's father listened thoughtfully to each of the arguments. Then, wordless, he went into the house, trailed closely by his son. He took the paper to the kitchen where his wife was at work. Startled by the peculiar expression on her husband's face, she asked, "What, *Yuboh?*"

The boy's father opened the paper and examined it again. Then slowly, deliberately, he crumpled it and, with a nonchalant underhand, tossed it into the kitchen fire. The boy gasped.

"What was that?" asked *Umma* as she watched the paper catch aflame.

"I do not want a Japanese farm," announced the boy's father to his bewildered wife.

"Father!" cried the boy. "What of the books? There were many books in the house. Hiroshi's father said he was giving you everything. What will become of the books?"

His father gazed quizzically at his son, then threw his head back and laughed. "Foolish boy. Can you eat a book? Can you wear a book? Well, tomorrow go retrieve your precious books."

Before sunrise, the boy slipped from the house and hastened to the Yamamoto homestead. The night before, he had put out a rice sack at the threshold to carry the books home on his back, and he congratulated himself on his forethought. No matter how fatigued he was at the end of the day, he would study the books every night; he would memorize every word. *Hyung* would help him. When he had mastered their contents, he would teach his little brothers.

Panting with exertion and excitement, the boy arrived at the Yamamoto farm. Even in the shadow of dusk, he instantly recognized it had been ransacked. The tricycle was gone. The chickens were gone. Even the koi in the pond were gone. The crate containing the clothing and shoes, and every molecule of food and wine in the kitchen were gone. The chrysanthemum bureau with its treasure trove of books was, like a euphoric dream that vaporizes at sunrise, gone. The boy slumped onto the porch and buried his face in the rice sack. He was furious with himself when tears came. He dried them roughly with the burlap and reminded himself that, with so much suffering all around him, with his brothers gone, possibly never to return, he must not mourn for material things, not even books. By the time the sun broke the horizon, he was stooped at the waist, ankle deep in the rice paddies, and famished for having missed his breakfast for a futile quest.

One day, the oldest son of the Kim family appeared on the doorstep. He bowed to his parents and tersely dismissed any inquiries. And in much the same manner, the second son materialized some days later. The sons were like distressed leather stretched over skeletons. But their wills were unbroken. Those who could be broken had died in the labor camps.

Shortly after the sons' homecoming, their father took a day trip into the village and returned in the evening with a mysterious sack. He took his parcel to an area behind the house where firewood and farm equipment were stored. He warned his two youngest sons to stay away from there. Naturally, Owlet and little fifth brother were irresistibly drawn to the forbidden zone. They heard the barking. Tied to a stake was a young dog, perhaps a year old, a yellow short hair, just like their deceased pet who had died of starvation long ago. The dog jumped up and put his paws on their shoulders and licked their faces. Beside themselves with glee, the boys cavorted with their new pet, offered it a bowl of water from the stream, and fed it some grass, the only edibles they could lay their hands on. Which of the mammals were filled with greater joy, the dog or the little boys, was impossible to say.

"Let us name him Happy," said little fifth brother.

"Goliath!" said Owlet. In a mock giant voice, he quoted from the Bible story, "Am I a dog?"

They agreed to name their dog Happy Goliath.

Their father came upon them and scolded, "Did you not hear me tell you not to come back here?" He picked up a switch and whipped them both. The little boys ran away crying, and the dog rolled onto his back with his tail between his legs.

Traditionally, dog meat was consumed only once a year, after harvest time, and only by the men folk. Dog was the only meat that could be digested by a starving stomach, infusing wasted muscles with vital protein. It had been a great challenge to find a reasonably well fed dog off-season.

The family bowed their heads over the homecoming meal. The two freed sons partook of the meat while the rest of the family satisfied themselves with rice and kimchi. Dirty tear streaks crusting the cheeks of their faces, and pins and needles smarting the cheeks of their buttocks, the two youngest sons somberly witnessed the consumption of Happy Goliath, an episodic dry sob escaping one tiny chest then the other.

Thus nourished, the older brothers were soon able to return to their farm work.

With the return of the two able bodied young men to the Kim family farm, and the lifting of the crippling levies on Korean farmers, the farm prospered. It was high time for a wedding. Many young Korean males were married as baby-faced schoolboys, at the brink of puberty, to older women fit to rear both their offspring and their young husbands. At twenty-one years of age, the heir of the Kim family farm would be an older groom. There was no time to waste.

A renowned matchmaker was commissioned to find a suitable bride. The hired expert proposed a young woman from a reputable family in the village. He touted her lucky face, a high brow signifying intelligence, and a prominent chin signifying the propensity for producing sons. After the preliminary negotiations through intermediaries, the groom's father journeyed to the bride's home to see for himself.

Two fathers conferenced behind closed doors. The proposed bride-to-be was bidden to carry in a tray of barley tea and rice cakes for the men. The visit went on. Called upon to carry in tray after tray, with increasingly generous offerings, the young lady bristled at the squawk of her mother's summons. Only when her mother's best rice wine was served up, did a worrisome yet exciting inkling dawn upon her. She tidied her hair and put on an ingratiating manner, though she need not have troubled herself. With each cup of rice wine quaffed, her future bloomed as rosy as the rising flush on the cheeks of her future father-in-law. She was not quite as beautiful or as gracious as advertised, but then again they never were. Matchmakers were salesmen, as everyone knew. One look at her auspicious strong chin, portent of future sons, and her fate was sealed.

In a blaze of excitement, *Umma* prepared the wedding chest, stationed in its massive grandness in the center of the main room. At night, the boys arranged their bedding against the perimeter giving the chest wide berth; it was not to be sullied by dirty fingers. Peddlers bearing fabric, wood carvings, metal wares, and household goods swarmed the house, invariably finding a receptive audience with the deaconess. Two silver wedding rings, thick and heavy with the import of future generations, were forged for the bride and groom.

A fourth wing was added to the house which now completely encircled the courtyard in a protective perimeter of familial solidarity. The new honeymoon suite was the beneficiary of obsessive cleaning. Its floor was shellacked with paper and rice glue to gleaming perfection, only to be layered over with more paper and more glue for more perfection. The room was equipped with a great armoire of dark varnished wood, its square doors secured with a heavy brass lock in the shape of a fish. The armoire was stocked with new bedding which was removed, aired and admired, inspected for flaws, and then repacked again and again.

Beneath the hubbub, a fastidious attention to detail underscored the preparations, the unspoken aim to nullify any bad fortune foretold by an earlier, troubling turn of events. Since birth, the groom had been promised to a different bride. On the one hundred and first day of his firstborn son's life, though bleary from the baby's hundred-day celebration where the rice wine had flowed like a river, the dogged new father undertook a two day journey on business of utmost urgency: to seal the future of the Kim lineage.

Word of a comely child in a neighboring village, an astrologically perfect match, drove him onward. How disappointed he was to meet his would-be future in-laws! The man appeared chuckleheaded with his flared nostrils and protruding ears. The brown-faced wife squinted at him through stingy eye slits. The elder Kim began to plead illness and turn around for home when the daughter toddled out to see who had come. As rumored, her beauty was striking. The little girl had inherited from both blood lines the finest gifts of bygone generations. The very same features which were overshadowed by unfortunate glitches on her parents' faces were organized perfectly on hers, tweaked a millimeter here and there by the blessed miracle of random mutation, to produce a visage of symmetry and delicacy, untouched by the ravages of weather and hard work. She was a butterfly in springtime. She fluttered about the courtyard collecting petals from the peonies and glancing shyly at the guest who so intently admired her with his bloodshot eyes. That happy day, amidst a field of flowers, she was pledged as the future wife of the firstborn son of a landowner. The two fathers would procure a matchmaker's stamp when the time came to make the agreement official.

Every year, for fifteen years, gifts had been exchanged to renew the promise. Then the gifts had suddenly stopped. The bride-to-be had been conscripted by the Japanese. She died overseas under unexplained circumstances: the brief life of a rare specimen, punctured by an unrepentant lepidopterist's needle. Regarding this, the Kim family kept silent. Why plant a seed of doubt as to the eligibility and luck of a fine young man, a firstborn son?

On the morning of the wedding, the bridegroom rode on horseback, with attendants on foot flanking him, one guiding the horse's decorated reigns, the other holding a parasol on a long pole over the groom's head. Second elder brother rode another bedecked horse behind the groom. Then came two more horses abreast, on one side third elder brother, his arm wrapped around little fifth brother, and on the other side Young Nam securing Owlet. Behind the parade of sons, came their mother and father riding their cart hitched to the pair of oxen garlanded with fresh cut flowers. A large entourage of the groom's family and friends followed on foot.

"I am a very poor man with too many sons! See how many horses I had to rent," exclaimed *Abuji* in a loud voice of mock exasperation. Those within earshot of the cart laughed heartily, and the vanity was repeated through the crowd eliciting a rolling wave of laughter.

The wedding party reached the bride's gates. No sooner did the bridegroom dismount than he was whisked off to change into his ceremonial garments, sewn by his fiancée's own hands. He disappeared a plain white clad farmer and reappeared a resplendent peacock, blazing, glorious, to be passed around so the intricate handiwork of his bride could be admired by his people. A wild goose, tightly bound in red silk, was extracted from the cart by an attendant and handed to the groom. He proceeded with his live offering, a symbol of societal order and lifelong fidelity, to a low table outside the main door of the house, placed the goose upon the table, and stepped back. The goose, having struggled wildly in its bindings throughout the long journey, was now a limp bundle of fatigue and resignation. The bride's mother appeared, picked up the goose, and carried it into the house. The guests jostled for position in the courtyard.

Finally, the bride appeared in the doorway, a vision of cascading silk. A delicate headpiece, aglitter with trinkets, crowned her head. Her ebony hair was slicked back into a chignon at the nape of her neck and secured with a long silver hairpin draped with silk ribbons. A golden coat embroidered with flowers overlaid her bolero jacket with variegated half-moon sleeves and a half bow at the breast. Her full crimson skirt shimmered with Chinese characters in gold at the hem. The bride's hands were clasped, hidden inside her sleeves. As she stepped onto the porch, two sisters emerged to support her at each elbow. The bride stared steadfastly at the ground.

Owlet, riding piggyback for a better view, tightened his arms around Young Nam's neck and whispered in his ear, "*Hyung*, she is so beautiful! Do you think she is beautiful?"

"Yes!" replied the boy with all his heart, although he had yet to see his future sister-in-law's face. He glanced at his eldest brother. The groom's face remained an expressionless mask – quite right – but his eyes burned with intensity, fixed on the bride's headdress. It was all they could see with her head downcast.

There was a hush of exquisite anticipation. The rustle of the bridal silks was audible as the bride and her attendants proceeded slowly to the center of the courtyard. The bride and groom stood opposite each other across a basin of water atop a table. The attendants washed the hands of the bride and groom and spread mats before them.

The bride tilted her head slightly to one side, then, with deliberate languor, sank to her knees onto the mat, her skirt a dramatic mass of parachuting silk. She bowed her head down till it touched the ground. Her sisters went down with her, supporting her at each elbow, but did not bow their heads quite as low as required of the bride. The bride gracefully arose, with the assistance of her sisters. A murmur of appreciation passed through the wedding assemblage. Then, a second time, she descended gracefully to the mat in obeisance. When she stood again, it was the groom's turn. Hands free, he bowed to the ground, only once, more brusquely than she, touching his forehead to the mat and raising himself upright on his own power while his attendants remained upright on either side. The bowing ceremony was repeated, the bride bowing twice, the groom reciprocating once. During the entire proceedings, it was evident that the bride had not stolen a single glance at the groom and that the groom had to satisfy himself with a detailed observation of the gewgaws on the bridal headdress.

At the wedding table, a gourd of wine was passed to the groom, who took a drink. The gourd was passed to the bride's attendant. All eyes watched. The bride would raise her head to take the wine, offering the first view of her face. The trinkets on her hat trembled as she slowly, tantalizingly lifted her chin.

She looked dreadful. Her blood-shot eyes were swollen nearly shut. The scarlet circles painted on each cheek streaked down her splotched face. Mucus coursed from her nose, which she was helpless to redress with her hands clasped inside her sleeves. One sister hastily mopped up the wreck, then proceeded to weep noisily herself. Presently, the other sister joined in with wanton abandon. The bride quickly touched her lips to the gourd and bowed her head back down, her shoulders quaking.

Now they were married.

The new husband and wife performed the obeisance ceremonies for both sets of parents, and in the ritual of these elaborate ceremonies, the bride finally calmed herself. At last, they were seated on mats at the wedding table, piled with a munificent bounty. A live chicken and rooster, bound together in a blue and red silk cloth, were placed under the wedding table. The groom ate heartily; it had been a long day for him. The bride ate nothing. Her attendants touched every variety of dainty rice cake to her lips, but she only pretended to nibble.

Suddenly, under the wedding table, the chicken broke free of its silk binding and flapped up a feathery fracas. One of the attendants lunged to capture it, but it slapped its wings violently in the girl's face. The girl screamed and the chicken escaped. With the silk now loosened, the rooster unbound itself and made its own raucous escape. The guests, lubricated by wine, laughed uproariously at the fowl escapade.

The bride commenced anew her weeping and her sisters followed suit. It was certainly expected that a bride should be quite solemn and even cry on her wedding day. Weeping was preferable to the bad luck attending a smiling bride. But the wracking wet noisy sobs from the trio of young women might have threatened to dampen the festivities were it not for the good cheer of the freely flowing rice wine. Through hours of revelry, poetry recitations by the more educated elders, unruly waves of bean paste smeared children, interminable greetings and congratulations and bowings to the new in-laws, the bride and groom sat at their banquet table, a couple of adornments, waiting.

Evening came at last. The family and relatives gathered around the house as the core bridal party mustered into formation to march to the bridal chamber, newlyweds side-by-side in front, their respective attendants directly behind. They proceeded into the bridal chamber, and the attendants slid the doors shut behind them. After a short interval, the attendants emerged carrying the headpieces and silken outer garments they had assisted in removing. The rest would be up to the groom.

A posse of unruly boys, relatives of the bride's family, raced to the outside wall of the bridal chamber. They licked their fingers and poked holes in the rice paper of the windows. The brothers of the groom, though not lacking in curiosity, did not participate in the mischief. They had been promised a whipping for misbehavior and did not relish the sting of eldest brother's switch. The brothers stood to the side, feigning nonchalance, while riveted to the commentary of one of the rapscallions squinting through his peephole.

"Shhhh! Quiet! He is removing her jacket. He is folding it neatly and laying it aside. He is removing her skirt. He folds so neatly. How considerate our new uncle is! She is wearing only her top and petticoat. Oh, now he is removing his own jacket. He folded it and laid it on top of hers. Our new uncle is a tidy gentleman. He is removing his pants. He folded them too. He is wearing only his long underwear. Move over, rice pot. This is my peephole. Make your own. He pulled out her hairpin. Her hair has come tumbling down. He is lifting her like a baby. She is covering her face. You! Get your elbow out of my ribs. He is hiding her under the covers. Now he is crawling under the covers. I cannot see anything. What are they doing? It is too dark. I cannot see anything. Come on, let us hurry and eat up the last rice cakes before we have to go."

Following tradition, after three days at his bride's home, eldest brother brought his new bride home. For the homecoming party, the courtyard was choked with some hundred friends, relatives, and hangers-on. On the porches of the four wings encircling the yard were feast tables piled high with pyramids of victuals.

Eldest brother alighted from his horse and made his way in, bowing at the waist to guests along the way. Four bearers carried the bride's palanquin into the courtyard. After a length of time, the curtains on the palanquin parted slightly, and only one arm emerged to hand out a round celadon vessel. An attendant took it and scurried past the guests to the gates, splashing its contents of vomit along the way. The ride had been stifling and bumpy from daybreak to noon. Along the way, one of the original litter bearers had taken ill and stopped at a farmhouse to rest. The replacement bearer was shorter than the rest, and the palanquin had listed to one side for the remainder of the long, turbulent journey. A pale, limp bride was escorted to her table where she presided listlessly with her new husband over the second celebration.

The following day, it became clear that the bride was suffering from more than exhaustion. She took to her sick bed with a high fever. Next the groom fell ill. Soon typhoid fever raged through the household.

Abuji succumbed. He passed the night groaning and thrashing, and, for the first time in the boy's memory, could not rise from his bedding in the morning. The fever then spread to second and third elder brothers. *Umma* shuttled hot rice water in to the sick rooms and full chamber pots out, back and forth, without respite. She instructed Young Nam to keep his two younger brothers out of the sick room and sleep with them in the entryway. But the typhoid struck the youngest two boys anyway.

A familiar panic gripped the boy as he witnessed the ferocity with which the fever consumed its meager prey. Owlet's slight frame seemed to have shrunk overnight, still and limp, except for the periodic chills rattling his bones. Mother struggled to build a fire for the *ondol*, but the wood was not yet seasoned and refused to catch fire. She staggered in from her failed efforts to find the boy lying on his side hugging Owlet to warm him. She gasped.

"Young Nam!" she chided. "Let him go. Go empty the chamber pots. Not in the outhouse. Take them farther out. To the poppy field."

The boy collected the diarrhea-filled chamber pots from the sick room and emptied them into two buckets outside. He shouldered a long pole, knelt to hook a bucket on each end, and trudged with his burden to the farthest plot. The old poppy field was ploughed over, waiting to be converted into rice paddy. He emptied the buckets into irrigation channel flooding the field, and rinsed them in the water, relieved to be rid of the noxious stench of disease. The boy wended a circuitous path back home. Perhaps if he made a slow-cooked stew from a live snake he could cure his baby brother. When he reached the path to his house, he hesitated, then turned away and jogged toward the stream. He would easily capture a frog there. Frog was delicious, the closest thing to snake he could think of.

His head cleaved a cloud of gnats as he reached the stream. Silently, he set his buckets and pole down in the grass. Dragonflies hummed above a trio of turtles sunning themselves on a rock in the center of the shimmering stream. *They know nothing of misery*, thought the boy...*yet*. He crept toward the bank. The rocks and branches along the water's edge were loaded with fat, lazy frogs just waiting to be captured. It would be easy pickings. But the boy stumbled and fell. All the wild things fled.

Sitting back on his haunches, the boy felt the side of his head. It was slimy. He looked at his fingers. Blood. He forgot why he was here. The sun hurt his eyes. So bright. Blindingly bright. Collapsing onto his rear, he folded his arms over his knees and rested his forehead on them, closing his eyes. The dragonflies returned first and whirred overhead. A fly buzzed by to sample his blood. Why had he come here? Oh, yes. He needed to catch a frog.

He rose and made his way upstream where the animal population was oblivious to the great splash he had made. A bloated specimen, dormant at the edge of the stream, would be his easiest target. But the boy's pounce was leaden and the overweight frog made a leisurely escape. Did that spiteful amphibian actually glance over its shoulder to taunt him? The boy sat back on the bank again and closed his throbbing eyes. The din of insects ricocheted in his skull. A chill spread from his spine to his fingertips. He could not be sick. *Get up*, he commanded himself. He forced himself up and walked with conviction to the buckets. Yes, he felt fine. He resolved to lower his sights to a sunning turtle. It would be impossible to fail.

He took a bucket and proceeded farther upstream till he identified a sizable turtle sunning itself on a rock. Turtles and snakes: were they not cousins? The meat of the older turtle would be tough, but it was a certain catch. With his overturned bucket in his outstretched arms, the boy silently waded into the stream and trapped the animal. The dull thud of wood on shell was unmistakable. He had it. Reeling from his triumph, he steadied himself. He would take his catch home and scrub off the slime and the mites. He would boil it slowly, slowly over an open fire. He would dribble the broth a droplet at a time into the inside of Owlet's cheek. Painstakingly, he lifted the bucket and slid his hand underneath. *Let it bite me*, he thought, *I certainly do not care now*. He felt nothing. The oversized reptile must have been wedged up inside the bucket. He flipped the bucket over to trap the turtle on its back, and peered inside. It was empty. Impossible.

By now, *Umma* would be in desperate need of his help. He circled the rock, searching for the turtle which had vanished. When he stopped short, the stream continued to revolve. The boy set his bucket down, sat on it, and put his head in his hands to still the vertigo. In the darkness, he felt the nauseating acceleration of a world spinning wildly out of control. He fell to his knees in the water and hugged the bucket lest he drown. Then there was blackness.

The violence of water rushing down his windpipe jolted the boy from the river rocks. With a roar, he scrambled on all fours up the bank, doubled back to retrieve his bucket, retook the high ground, vomited, reassembled his pole and buckets, and turned homeward. As he walked, a quantity of stream water gushed from his mouth and nose onto his feet, but he marched on without pause. He congratulated himself. *Look at me. I am strong. I am perfectly fine.*

That night under his bedding, the boy was shaken to the marrow with a dead chill. If only he could find the warm spot on the floor, he would not rattle like dry bones. *Move*, he told himself, but he could not. He must get up and give Owlet a drink. Owlet would dehydrate.

Then he was running through the rice paddies clutching a pot of stew. The pot burned hot against his chest and the steam rising from the broth suffocated his face. The labyrinth of rice paddies and irrigation ditches was interminable. He was lost. He doubled back to retrace his steps. The paddies gave way to the poppy field. He smelled the fumes of opium. A curse escaped his lips. He turned and ran in the opposite direction. Now the pot of stew was stone cold, and he shivered uncontrollably.

He veered in a perpendicular direction and ran along a dirt road. He tripped and fell, spilling a great portion of the stew. He dug his fingers into the sodden earth where the precious brew had soaked in and inexplicably put the clod of mud into his mouth. It was a regrettable impulse. He spewed the foul dirt and clawed it from his mouth. He continued his desperate, yet aimless, trek.

He found he had arrived at the village school. Why was he here? He was drawn inside the gates. The schoolyard was vacant except for a slim form lying in the center of the scorched hardpan. He crept to the form. It was the corpse of a young girl. It was his sister, covered with a writhing blanket of maggots and flies. The pot fell to the ground, spilling the remainder of its contents. Frantically, the boy waved the flies off. In a great black undulating cloud, the flies lifted from the girl's decomposing form and descended upon him. A cry, his own, awoke him.

His face was in a puddle of vomit. It took a moment to realize that the turtle stew did not exist. A square of diffuse light from the morning sun shone through the paper window. The boy hoisted himself onto his hands and knees, and crawled into the patch of sun, paused there to collect his strength, then continued to the threshold of the sick room. He stopped at his mother's feet planted in his path.

"And now you are sick," she pronounced grimly. "Go back to bed. Your brother and his wife are better now, and they will help me."

The weary mother put the last of her ailing sons to bed. If his brother and sister-in-law had recovered, all would be well. The boy finally granted himself permission to rest. He surrendered himself to a sound sleep.

No thrill could match the euphoria of his flying dreams. Standing in the courtyard, the boy recognized the familiar signs, the telling lightness: he would fly again. It began with weightless, effortless bounds, buoyantly graceful, lighter than air. Each leap higher than before, he lifted off the ground and touched back down on the tip of a toe. In his final leap, he willed himself up and up, over the house, over the fields, over the village. He stretched his arms upward. A zephyr caressed his cheeks and lofted his hair.

Now he was flying higher, now faster than ever before. Like bleached white sails in the cerulean atmosphere, his jacket sleeves and baggy pants billowed and snapped. Below, the rice paddies were shrinking squares and the roof tops vanishing dots.

He willed himself to descend, but he had lost control of his trajectory. In a blink and he was gliding over the ocean, still and green and everywhere. He flew a wide circle, searching the horizon for a shoreline. The water stretched deep and wide in every direction. He flew a wider circle. The ocean was infinite. *See where this takes me*, he told himself, and he flew on and on.

Then he heard a sound. He found himself inside an unfamiliar building. He went to the window, where a tiny finger stabbed at the glass as if in a futile effort to poke a hole through it. The finger belonged to a small boy. The whites of his wide eyes glowed in the night. He pressed both hands against the window, and the small boy mirrored his gesture with his own little hands. The boy fumbled with the unfamiliar mechanism of the glass paned window. Suddenly, the delicate figure pitched backward into the swallowing blackness, his arms outstretched, his fingers grasping, with a frightened cry, "Do not leave me!"

The boy awoke. He was lying on the floor, covered with a pile of cotton blankets. The closest layer was drenched and clung to his skin. Sunlight permeated the paper walls. The house was silent, and the room appeared empty except for his bedding. Raising himself to his elbows, he called weakly for Owlet. His mother was sitting directly behind him, dozing against the wall, her sewing having fallen to her lap in the exhaustion of her vigil. Hurriedly, she set her sewing aside, picked up a bowl, and hastened to her son.

"*Umma*, what happened?" he asked, sitting up.

"Drink this," she said, holding the bowl of rice water to his lips. He drained the bowl. She sat heavily, took the empty bowl in her lap, and studied him, taking stock of his condition. The boy straightened up. He saw in her stricken face, swollen and red, that something terrible had transpired while he slept. With a pounding heart, he waited for her to speak.

"Tell me, *Umma*."

She did not speak.

He said with all the mature strength he could muster, "I am well enough. Something bad has happened. Tell me, Mother."

"Your younger brother is dead," she said.

From his bloodless face, she knew that he had misunderstood, and quickly clarified, "No, not Owlet. It was the fifth, Young Jae."

So Owlet had survived. But little fifth brother was dead. A welter of guilty relief tangled his sorrow into a disorganized wreckage. The boy struggled to compose himself.

But then his mother cried out in anguish, "And your father is also dead."

9

Lee Hana
South Korea
1945

Trekking on foot, foraging on roots and bark, sleeping in the open, surviving moment by moment like a wild animal, Lee Hana made her way home. She went unnoticed, just another starving refugee, until allied soldiers collected her from a ditch where she had collapsed. They saturated her with DDT, performed field surgery on her bullet wound, fed, clothed, and shod her, and, along with hundreds of Korean refugees, transported her to Seoul. From there, she made her way home on farmer's carts and by foot. In her pocket, she safeguarded her only recompense for her years of slavery: a compact of pancake makeup.

Hana left home at twelve years of age and returned at fourteen. She had not grown during her two years in captivity, and her figure was thin and undeveloped. Her hardy olive complexion was none the worse for the harsh elements, and the soldier's blows had spared her face. But her haunted eyes, alternately dull and lifeless, then darting with primitive fear, had rendered her almost unrecognizable.

She slunk into her home like a thief on silent feet. She came upon her mother squatting on her haunches before a buried earthen jar, scooping out pickled cabbage into a bowl. Hana opened her mouth, but no sound emerged. Stock-still, she waited to be noticed. After an agonizing interval, her mother stopped digging and glanced over her shoulder. The woman leaped to her feet, scattering the kimchi to the ground. She stared with wild eyes, unable to recognize her daughter for several excruciating minutes. Hana soundlessly mouthed: *Umma*. Suddenly, with a cry of disbelief, her mother rushed to the cowering girl and enfolded her in her arms. Hana buried her face in her mother's shoulder, smelled the familiar scent of wood smoke and garlic, felt her mother's arms tighten around her, tasted the tears that streamed from her mother's eyes onto her own face, and believed her life might be right again if only she could stay this way forever.

Hana's parents asked no questions. But over her homecoming dinner, her younger brother hectored his long lost sister for an explanation. Hana had not forgotten Private Koizumi's admonition to keep silent about her service as a comfort woman. She pretended not to hear her brother until he finally shouted, "*Noonah!* Can't you hear me? Where have you been? What have you been doing?"

Her mother laid her chopsticks down on the table and searched Hana's face with frantic eyes. Her father stopped eating and stared at his bowl, his chopsticks suspended in midair. They wanted an answer too. The girl had never lied to her family before, but knew well that now was the time if any.

Hana swallowed hard and murmured that she had worked in a factory in China. But she had never stepped foot in a factory of any kind, and when pressed for specifics by her inquisitive brother, she grew confused and agitated. She stuttered that she had worked as a laundress in a laundry factory. Her eyes flitted from one troubled face to another. Her mother and father exchanged a tense glance. Suddenly, her mother smacked her little brother across the mouth and said, "Enough!"

Hana threw herself into home life with a lunatic fervor. Farming, cooking, cleaning, and laundry distracted her from the torture of memory. But sounds as banal as the barking of a dog could incapacitate her with a paroxysm of panic. A pot falling with a clatter could precipitate violent tremors. Hana was attracting notice when all she wanted was to be invisible. She attempted to exercise control by emptying her mind and setting her body to work. She worked from sunup to sundown till her muscles ached. She would be the best daughter in the village. She would make everyone's life easier. It was her purpose. It was the reason she survived.

But during the night, when the family settled themselves to sleep in the common room, the trouble came. In her sleep, she thrashed and screamed. One night, her mother found Hana on her hands and knees frantically pawing at the floor. She grasped her daughter by the shoulder and called her name.

"Hana! Hana! What are you digging for?" her mother asked.

"Hide! Hide!" she screamed, awakening herself from the night terror.

Her mother took her into the kitchen and forced her to reveal what had happened to her during the war. The secret had been a demon roiling inside her, and its release, like violent retching, was both terrible and exhilarating. In wrenching, hysterical sobs, Hana told her mother everything: the kidnapping, the rape at the inn in Seoul, the comfort station in China, the long hard march, and, finally, the pill box where the girls were shot. At the end of the confession, wrecked, drained, stained with the tears of her exorcism, she stretched out her arms like a baby to embrace her mother.

A slap stung her cheek. The pain, slight though it was, felt unbearable, worse than a man's fist, worse than a bullet, worse than a rape. Like a mortally wounded beast, her mother brayed, "Why did you not kill yourself?"

Hana raised her swollen eyes to witness her mother's unrecognizable expression, drawn and quartered with furious anguish. The woman raised her hand over her shoulder and paused in this position for a moment as if to gather all the strength of her horror and rage and pain. Then she slammed a backhand down on her daughter's face. The girl hurtled to the floor. She closed her eyes and lay still as a grave, as she had done so many times before. She heard her mother scream again and again.

"You should have killed yourself!"

10

Kim Young Nam
South Korea
1947 to 1948

Ll agreed: the new wife had brought bad luck to the Kim
family. It could have been predicted. Her cheekbones
were prominent, widow-making cheekbones, very omi-
nous. She had cried excessively on her wedding day, attracting
evil spirits. Compounding matters, unlucky foreheads cursed her
sisters. The omens had howled out to any who would pay heed.

When the typhoid passed, and the dead were buried, the
deaconess hauled her new daughter-in-law to church, now held
regularly and openly in the village rectory. The pastor summoned
the unlucky woman to stand before the congregation. She must
show remorse. She must confess and accept her Savior. Her heart
was black with sin. Merciful God would forgive her. He would
wash her heart white as snow.

The hands of the congregants shook like a ruddy storm over
her head, tears rained down, and shouts thundered all around.
The good people did their very best. But nothing on earth is as
stubborn as a Korean woman. The new wife stared at the door,
those unlucky cheeks as dry as a bone, unmoved and unmoving,

for three solid hours. When the ordeal drew to a close, she stood alone outside, her back turned to the huddle of mourning brothers-in-law, her parched gaze trained toward the village, *her* village, *her* people. Inside the church, an interminable conference took place among the deaconess, her eldest son, and the pastor.

It was not against their religion, the pastor decided, merely an insurance policy. He sanctioned the commissioning of a shaman to ensure that any lingering evil was expunged from the household.

This shaman required a feast. The deaconess charged her daughter-in-law with the preparation of the pig's head. It had been a hefty beast, and its decapitated head was unwieldy and caked with dried blood. The new wife hauled bucket upon bucket of water from the stream and, squatting on her haunches before the head, washed and scrubbed and plucked. During this laborious chore, her mother-in-law would suddenly fly out from the kitchen to holler, "clean out the mouth and the ears" or "comb the eyelashes." When the head was deemed adequately cleansed, the young wife sought her husband to carry the offering to the cauldron of boiling water in the kitchen.

The deaconess shouted, "No! Let my daughter-in-law bring it to me. She is dirty already." In her delicate attempts to avoid embracing the pig's snout to her breast, she could not gain proper purchase on the slippery head. The pig's ears proved insubstantial as lifting lugs, and they slipped right through new wife's hands. After a brief wrestle, she gave up, turned her back to the kitchen, and stood staring impassively out into space. The deaconess marched in a terrific huff from her observation post, lifted the pig head in one deft motion, and marched to the kitchen, but not before stopping to fling her worst insult over her shoulder, "Useless!"

Dark and deformed, the shaman, a hereditary *mudong*, descended upon the afflicted household. She was stooped in half, and a jagged hump projected from her back. Straightaway, the old hag hobbled to Owlet, pulled him by the arm from his hiding place behind his *Hyung*, pinched his cheek, and flashed him a rotted smile. Owlet squealed, wriggled his arm free, and stuffed himself between his brother's legs. The *mudong* humped her way over to the new wife, stretched out a gnarled hand, and twisted the young lady's nipple. She proceeded to the feast table where the pig's head had been arranged on a polished brass platter, with a garnish of fruit around its neck and rolls of won stuffed into its orifices. She snatched the money from the ears and mouth and stuffed them into her garments. The deaconess shut herself and her daughter-in-law up with the witch to avail herself of the rites now due.

Eldest brother retreated into his chambers. But his younger brothers milled in the courtyard, eavesdropping, sniffing the burning of papers. They were anxious for it to be over so they could eat the leftovers. Owlet asked Kim Young Nam what was in the shaman's hump. The boy replied dryly, "the evil spirits." Owlet's eyes grew round. The brothers stifled a snicker.

At long last, the women emerged. The *mudong*, in a glassy-eyed trance, chanted gibberish while waving in her clenched fist a straw doll, wrapped in a scrap of eldest brother's wedding clothes. Eldest brother was rousted from his room. He was made to lie on the ground in the middle of the courtyard with the doll on his chest while his wife supplicated herself at his feet, full bow, her face to the ground on the backs of her hands. The shaman chanted and circled the couple, squatting with her elbows on her knees in a posture of defecation. Then, drawing a knife from her belt, she waved it back and forth across eldest brother's neck in a slicing motion. She snatched the straw doll from eldest brother's chest, chopped its head off, and instructed second and third brothers to bury the pieces near their father's grave.

The *mudong* filled her mouth with water and spewed it full blast on the young wife's face, then pelted her with fistfuls of rice. She fetched a large metal pot from the kitchen, put it over the new wife's head, danced around her, banged on the pot with the knife handle, and shouted profanities.

The sight of his eldest brother playing dead on the dirt like an idiot, his new sister-in-law with a pot over her pretty head, this troll whom they would ordinarily shun riding roughshod over his elders, and, worst of all, his revered mother, a deaconess of the Holiness Church, succumbing to the tomfoolery she had long ago rejected for the teachings of Christ, was too much for Young Nam to bear. Besides, the food was getting cold.

Finally, the old hag shambled off, a substantial portion of the family's humble fortune in her pocket, a bolt of Mother's hand-woven hemp strapped beneath her hump and an enormous metal bin brimming with foodstuffs, including the pig's head, balanced on her head. As soon as the *mudong* was out of sight, the new wife rushed out, across the courtyard and through the gates.

"Follow her. Make sure she comes back home," said the deaconess.

Young Nam obeyed. Carrying Owlet on his back, he trailed his sister-in-law from a safe distance out of the courtyard, across the fields, all the way to the edge of the farm. As she approached the last rice paddy, she slowed, and stopped. She had nowhere to go. She stood hugging herself and swaying, grains of rice still stuck to her face and hair. Owlet hopped down and, before Young Nam could stop him, approached his sister-in-law.

"Auntie?" The new wife turned to find Owlet offering a wilted sprig of azalea blossoms. "I think you are so very beautiful," he declared. She took her hand out of her sleeve, accepted the flowers, touched them to her lips, and closed her eyes. Then Owlet smiled shyly and recited a poem he had remembered from her wedding day. It had been written by a Buddhist monk and recited by one of her educated *yangban* relatives to the bride and groom as a wedding gift.

> In heaven shines no moon.
> On earth there blows no wind.
> The field is soaked in blood.
> The river flows with tears.
> The living song of my love,
> up to the firmament high,
> born from my humble lips,
> reaches the moonless sky.
> A vision of a princess bride,
> steps out of the shadow of death,
> one hand holds a sword,
> the other a golden seal.
> On earth there may be death.
> Humanity may shed tears.
> Princess of the sword and seal,
> on this day we revere.

A single tear welled up and spilled over the precipice of the young woman's cheek. She stretched forth her hand and caressed the little boy's face. "You will be a scholar," she whispered, paying the small child the highest compliment. The little boy gazed at his sister-in-law with the most pure adoration of an infatuated boy.

Shot out of nowhere, the deaconess fell upon them and smacked Owlet on the side of his head. "Get home! You naughty boy!" she screamed. Owlet scuttled to his older brother, clutching his ear and whining. The pair hurried home while their mother shouted at their sister-in-law, "Who do you think you are? Are you crazy? Stay away from my sons! Do not bring them your bad luck. Why are you so lazy? Lazy, good-for-nothing. There is cleaning to be done. Do you expect me to clean all your mess up myself? You are a no-good daughter-in-law…"

Wearied by the strife between his mother and wife, plagued with guilt by association for deaths of his father and brother, eldest brother announced his intent to relinquish his birthright and move with his wife to Seoul. The deaconess did not object. Perhaps it was for the best. Perhaps the evil spirits would depart along with her daughter-in-law and spare her remaining sons.

Young Nam was both horrified and thrilled. To lose the man of the house, so soon after his father's death, could cast the family into peril. But the concept that it was possible to escape the shackles of subsistence farming, to move to the big city, set the boy's mind on fire. When the family gathered at the front gate to see the newlyweds off, the boy overcame his natural reticence to speak his mind.

"*Hyung*! I wish I could go with you."

Eldest brother put his hand on his brother's shoulder.

"Work hard. Study hard. Obey your older brothers. Take good care of Owlet. When I am established, I will send for you. I will send you to school."

And with that promise, from the family farm passed for centuries from firstborn son to firstborn son, a man and his wife, each carrying a modest parcel of belongings tied in a square of cloth, departed for good without a backward glance. The young couple joined a post-war diaspora, a teeming convergence of humanity, suddenly free not only from the manacles of the occupation but also from those of caste and family, free to pursue prosperity and education.

Eldest brother remembered his promise to his younger brother. He lived and worked toward it every waking moment, with the infinite endurance of a subsistence farmer and labor camp survivor. He toiled in a variety of occupations for many grueling months, performing whatever work he could get, always sending something home to his mother. Eventually, he was able to make a respectable living in the taxi business, enough to buy a two-room house with a small yard. In a little over a year, he was able to send for Young Nam.

When the day finally came to leave the farm for the first time in his life, Young Nam felt excitement and dread in equal measure. The shrinking family gathered to take leave of another member.

"Go quickly," said the deaconess brusquely. "Go!"

The boy knelt on one knee before Owlet and put his hands on the child's shoulders. He intended to say something cheerful, but he blurted, "I hate to leave you."

To his surprise, Owlet responded calmly, "*Hyung*, mother said you must go quickly."

"Make sure you eat. Eat as much as your belly will hold."

"I will."

"When I come back, I will teach you everything I have learned. But only if you promise to eat as much as possible."

"Do not worry about me, *Hyung*. When you come back, I will be taller than you."

"Go quickly. Go!" interjected their mother, her voice shaking with welling tears.

The family followed the boy out of the gate and walked him to the edge of the property line. Young Nam bowed to his elders, patted Owlet's head, and turned away. He walked as far as he could bear before craning back around for a last look. His mother was wiping her eyes on her sleeve. His two older brothers were waving him on. Owlet, perched on second elder brother's shoulders, squealed, "Go, *Hyung*. Go!"

* * *

Imploding with anticipation, giddy with ambition, the boy arrived, after two days of travel on foot, by bus, and by train, at Seoul Station. Eldest brother cleaved his way through the crowds and reached his younger brother. He flung a welcoming arm over his younger brother's broad shoulders. "You grew!" he exclaimed. He took the boy's small parcel. The pair strode forth, stepping more jauntily together than each had alone.

The city whacked the boy over the snout like a sack full of excrement. Certainly, the farm smelled of animals, manure, and human fertilizer. But in the teeming city, no pine forests, no fresh breezes diluted the atmosphere. There was no respite from the stranglehold, the acrid reek of a densely packed population lacking sanitation. The miasma hung trapped in an endless labyrinth of stone, cement, and mud walls with razor-sharp bottle shards grouted along the tops, dark parabolas of urine staining the sides, and mounds of fly-covered feces piled along the base. The dusty streets were crammed with trolleys, cars, buses, trucks, taxis, rickshaws, bicycles, beasts of burden, and humanity in a hustle.

Eldest brother asked, "Are you hungry?"

It was a rhetorical question. They stopped at a street stand and eldest brother bought the boy a cup of hot silkworm broth. The boy inhaled, displacing the city stench with the pungent steam rising from the boiling pot. Eldest brother watched his young charge suck down the brown syrup in one gulp, laughed, and shelled out more pocket change for a paper cone filled with boiled larvae.

They continued only a short distance before stopping at the next stand where a vendor squatted on the ground before a low coal fired stove. "Don't tell," eldest brother said as he reached into his trouser pocket for more change to buy the boy a *boki*. The street vendor stirred a tablespoon of sugar into a ladle over the small fire till it melted sticky brown, then added a wet chopstick tip of white powder, puffing the liquid sugar and lightening the confection to a caramel color. He poured the ladle's contents onto a flat metal griddle, flattened it with an iron, and imprinted upon the candy the shape of a star. He handed the candy disk to Young Nam. "If you separate the star perfectly, you get a second one for free," explained eldest brother. But the boy had already crammed the rare treat whole into his watering mouth.

Swarming every patch of real estate, peddlers hawked every known species of the animal, plant, or fungal kingdom, from every phase of life cycle, eggs to embryos to adult, from live creatures squirming in tubs to hacked and pickled remains in rows upon stacks of jars. An old lady shuttled from door to door, balancing on her head a metal bin three times the diameter of her shoulders piled high with a tottering pinnacle of eggs. A *yangban* sauntered languidly, a penurious peacock in full regalia of embroidered silk overcoat, black horsehair hat, and filigreed ivory fan. A muddy, legless beggar child scooted on a makeshift wheeled pallet to escape the boot of a policeman. A fraternity of uniformed high school students, arms linked together, sang anthems in boisterous camaraderie. A feces-crusted untouchable balanced a long pole across his shoulders with two overflowing honey buckets, sloshing human waste indiscriminately as he trudged through the crowd. A businessman in a smart western suit and fedora carrying a handsome molded plastic briefcase strode purposefully to his place of commerce. The wildly disparate forms of humanity mixed on the city streets like the scrambled contents of an overturned treasure chest and garbage dumpster.

Suddenly, a swarm of screaming schoolgirls streaked past, shoving their way past their elders. Eldest brother gripped the boy's upper arm and pulled him out of the way. Pursuing the hysterical girls followed a leper, clothed in tatters, topped with a skull-like head, its nose and lips rotted off. The leper's outstretched arms ended in palms with vestigial stumps.

After the ragged apparition had passed, eldest brother released his hold of the boy and said, "It is believed that the flesh of a child will cure leprosy."

"Truly?" the boy asked incredulously.

"Maybe he's just having fun in his last hours," laughed eldest brother.

The most astounding spectacle, one that far surpassed the boy's wildest expectations, was that of the American soldiers. Indeed, the fabled tall, blond, blue-eyed American roamed the alleys of Seoul. But the riot of shape, color, and size, the mind-boggling disparities from one to another bowled Young Nam over. On the whole, to a boy expecting a heavenly host of angels, the Americans struck him as monstrously ugly. Some were as short as a Korean, some as tall as a tree. American hair came in yellow, black, every hue of brown known on earth, and even in flaming orange. The light-eyed Americans could evidently see just as well as the dark-eyed ones. Erupting from the centers of their faces were eagle beaks and sausages equipped with great cavernous nostrils. Only the black soldiers – another startling cultivar – exhibited the low-profile, wide Korean noses familiar to the boy. The American soldiers wore their shirts open, their dog tags buried in thickets of chest fur. They carried candy in their pockets and tossed them at the crowds of urchins who followed them everywhere.

The Kim brothers passed an American military garrison, a cluster of wooden buildings and a steely formation of Quonset huts. A few meters from base, outside the barbed wire, towered a mountain of refuse: tires, scrap metal, razors, cans, broken bottles, cigarette butts, wrappers, soiled paper, and food waste. The garbage dump was crawling with activity. Mothers and fathers sifted through the maggots, roaches, and rats, filling their rusty buckets with ribs and chicken bones. Children crawled on top of the heap, foraging half-eaten chocolate and hard candy, stuffing waste food directly into their mouths and other reclaimed refuse into their pant legs. Wild dogs circled the periphery, diving into openings in the crowd to snatch a bone. An undulating tarp of flies blackened the lot.

"You would never believe what the Americans throw away," said eldest brother. "There are piles of bones with hunks of good meat left on them. Beef, pork, chicken. These poor people collect the bones and wash and boil them to make a stew. This single dump contains enough meat to feed the entire city of Seoul. The Americans also discard entire loaves of bread because of one mold spot. Their bread is sweeter and softer than a rice cake. They must eat it as a dessert. They throw away partially eaten candies of every color and consistency imaginable. American candies are so sweet they burn your teeth..."

Eldest brother noticed a queer look on the boy's face. He ceased his detailed recounting of the contents of the dump, and a stilted silence ensued.

"When people come here with no money and empty bellies, they must do anything to survive," he said.

"I would too," said the boy.

At eldest brother's home, when they sat down to dinner, to the boy's relief, there was no mystery stew, only the standard fare of rice and a spread of side dishes. The two brothers fell upon their meal. The lady of the house rearranged her food in various patterns in her rice bowl, listlessly eating one grain of rice now and again. The boy noticed then that she was rather pinched and thin.

"Do we have *jangjorim*?" said eldest brother to his wife.

"We ran out."

"My younger brother needs meat. He has traveled all day."

"This meal is too plentiful already," exclaimed the boy.

"Go get some," insisted eldest brother.

His sister-in-law rose abruptly and headed for the kitchen where a great clatter ensued. She returned bearing a small dish of hard boiled eggs, pickled black in vinegar and soy sauce.

"Thank you. Aunt, I am very grateful for your kind hospitality," said the boy, making a special effort to ingratiate himself to his hostess. He received no acknowledgement.

When the eggs were consumed, she addressed her husband, looking past the boy who was seated next to her, "Ask him how his little brother is doing."

"How is the family?" asked eldest brother, though the two had already covered this turf on their walk from the station to home.

"Mother is well…" began the boy.

"I asked only about Owlet. The *smart* one," she snapped at her husband.

"Then, how is Owlet?" sighed eldest brother.

"Owlet is very well," said the boy, suddenly missing his little brother; happy, funny Owlet, his warm weight on the back, his moist breath on the neck.

His sister-in-law knelt and began to collect the bowls, saying, "Ask him if he has had enough to eat."

"Yes, Aunt. It was too delicious. Thank you."

There came no reply. No eye contact.

The stone wall would block the boy out for the duration of his short stay. For a necessary communiqué, she would wait till her husband came home to serve as her medium. The moment the weary man stepped foot onto the threshold, before he had a chance to remove his shoes, she would discharge, "Tell your brother not to leave his books around," or "Have your brother load in the coal before he goes out."

The boy wasted no time. He identified the area middle school, secured permission to sit for exams, and, despite his threadbare country education, distinguished himself. The curriculum in Seoul was echelons above that of his country school. He aimed to be the top student in every subject.

Most exciting of all was the prospect of English class. The teacher was Korean, a disappointment the boy swallowed manfully. The class repeated in sing-song unison such essential phrases as, "I amma boh-yee" and "I amma gull." The boy practiced his precious handful of phrases over and over and yearned for more. He learned the twenty-six letters of the English alphabet which he recognized with a pleasurable shock from the foreign books he had seen in Hiroshi Yamamoto's house. There were several characters – capital "O" and "E" and lower case "l" – which were the same as *Hangul*; what could it mean? Observing the writing on American military signs, he ascertained for himself that the letters were not grouped into a little block of syllables arranged in columns like *Hangul,* but rather aligned individually in a horizontal line. But he did not learn much else. Within the first month of class, his teacher's shallows had been plumbed. But the exposure was enough make him recognize that the mastery of the English tongue could be a lifetime endeavor.

One afternoon, a man named Sun, proprietor of a watch crystal manufacturing operation, came to the house for a visit. The boy sat cross-legged on the floor in the corner of the living room studying while eldest brother hosted Sun.

Straightaway, unsolicited, eldest brother announced loudly, "My brother scored the highest grade of all the applicants in his entrance exams."

"Oh! Is that so?" said Sun, studying the boy and rubbing his chin.

"At the end of this term, they say he will skip ahead a year."

"Is that so?" said Sun.

"His teacher actually came to visit me here. Can you believe it?" said eldest brother, laughing and slapping the table.

"Is that so?"

"And how are your sons? Has your oldest managed to pass his exams yet?" asked eldest brother kindly.

"I have to say, what I mean to say is, it must be said that, ah! Not exactly. Not yet."

The boy's sister-in-law set down a tray of hot tea and rice cakes and whisked herself back to the kitchen.

"He will pass next time. Sometimes it takes several tries. I hear many boys try over and over many times till they pass. The ones who pay their way in get expelled the minute the money runs out. As for my little brother, he had traveled from morning to night to get here, sprang out of bed the very next morning at sunrise, vanished from my house, sat for the exams, and somehow or other managed to make the highest score. And the boy has barely had any schooling in the country. Have you ever heard of such a thing?"

There was a violent metallic crash in the kitchen. The conversation stopped for a moment while eldest brother measured the silence.

"Have you ever heard of such a thing?" eldest brother continued in a more furtive voice. "A poor country bumpkin *chonnom* beating out all those rich city boys?"

"Say," said Sun, rubbing his chin. "Say. Might I hire him to tutor my sons? The oldest could use some tutoring to pass his entrance exams. He is a smart boy. He just needs a little boost. He works too hard at the factory. He would rather spend his time helping me than devote himself to his studies. He is really a selfless, good son. My younger son also needs help with his grammar school work, easy stuff, but he works too hard for me, you know. I will pay handsomely."

The boy kept his face in his book, but his ears burned. Some money in his pocket would be reassuring. And he knew he must save for high school tuition. He would send some home to mother. He would give some to his sister-in-law. He wanted to do it.

"No," replied eldest brother without hesitation. "I am afraid that would be impossible. My brother must focus every moment on his studies. He will pass the government exams."

That evening, the boy lay in his bed with a book of poetry his teacher had loaned him. He moved the book closer and closer to his eyes as the light dimmed till it was a centimeter from his nose. Finally, in the pitch darkness, he laid the book over his face. As his heavy lids closed, the boy heard a disturbance, the din of marital discord. He ducked his head under the covers and blocked his ears in a vain attempt to muffle his sister-in-law's voice.

"You treat him like your son. What about *our* son? When will we finally have our own son?"

In a barely perceptible low-pitched murmur, eldest brother spoke to her. "Be patient. It takes time."

"I will never conceive a son because in your heart you already have your own son. You lack the desire now. Your brother is everything to you. Always bragging about your brother. All he ever does is read. He is the laziest boy I have ever met in my life. He reads and he eats. Reads and eats. Reads and eats! *Reads and eats!* I am sick to death of him. I cannot stand the sight of him."

There was another conciliatory response from eldest brother. But she ranted on.

"How will our son go to school when you send all your money to your mother, and whatever is left, you spend on your brother? Our son, if we ever had a son, which we never will, could be a smart boy. But there will be no money leftover to send him to school. Our own son will be a butcher to support your precious scholar brother!"

The strife continued deep into the night. Before sunrise, his eldest brother arose, eyes bloodshot, purple bags underneath. His sister-in-law was curled up in a heap under her covers facing the wall. Eldest brother put his hand on the boy's shoulder and whispered, "Study hard today," and slunk out of the house without his breakfast, his posture flaccid.

Young Nam folded his bedding, gathered his few belongings, scribbled a quick letter, rolled it, stuffed it into his eldest brother's house slippers, and hurried off to school. After school, he paid a visit to the Sun family at their watch crystal factory. Their mean section of the city wound with narrow streets flanked by industrial row houses and yards in which crates and pallets tottered high with raw materials for every homegrown entrepreneurial enterprise ancillary to the country's emerging manufacturing industry. Not a sapling or flower impinged upon the dirty shades of black and grey kicked up by the soot of round-the-clock production. The boy's eyes stung from filthy vapor. He knocked on the door.

A woman put her face at the door crack, her eyes narrowed to suspicious slits. The boy introduced himself. A twitch of recognition animated her coarse features. She opened the door and motioned the boy inside. She lit into him with the swift rapaciousness of her kind.

"I will give you room and board, two meals a day, and one thousand won a month. For this you must work in my factory. In your free time, you will tutor my boys. It is a very generous offer. You will find none like it in the city. I only offer you such a handsome package because my husband spoke so highly of you. Answer quickly. Yes or no. Before I change my mind."

What with runaway inflation, it would take years to save enough for high school tuition at such a meager salary. Furthermore, factory work was not what he had in mind, and the prospect of living with the Sun family was repugnant. He had envisioned himself renting a small room in some kindly widow's tidy home. He coughed.

As if reading his mind, the woman added, "My neighbor is renting a room to a Seoul National University student for one hundred won a day. There is a terrible housing shortage. You will not find a better offer. Yes or no. Quick."

He looked around. The slice of light from the open door illuminated a dense concentration of airborne particulates. Bare light bulbs strung from the ceiling on an electrical cord glowed dimly in a penumbra of dust. The stench of machine oil and burnt rubber drive belts seared his nostrils. Sawdust and newspaper littered the floor.

Then he noticed the sons. Behind a work table, the older son, in a greasy undershirt, glowered at the boy. The younger son, his frantic eyes oscillating from his mother to the visitor, seemed to be transmitting a warning. Young Nam involuntarily stepped back toward the door.

"There is another boy, a high school student, very smart, coming to seek this position. He has already agreed to my terms. I only make you this offer because my husband wants you. So you had better decide quickly. Yes or no. Quick, quick."

Just as the boy resolved to slink back to his angry sister-in-law with his tail between his legs, Mr. Sun burst from the adjacent living quarters. With a warm smile and flattering words, Mr. Sun ushered the boy into the living quarters and offered him a cup of tea. He shooed his wife away, and offered a better deal: three thousand won per month plus room and board in exchange for the boy's factory labor after school and tutoring services in his free time. Like his wife, Mr. Sun pressed the boy to decide on the spot and start right then and there. The boy said yes.

Thus began Kim Young Nam's independence, the life of a child laborer at twelve years old.

Factory work was a muscle-knotting grind. At sunrise, the boy rose to polish and pack a crate of crystals before sprinting to school. More often than not, he arrived after the first bell to receive the teacher's rod across his open palms. The punishment he took in stride. It was the grease in the creases of his palms and the black crescents under his broken nails that made him flinch.

After school, he worked in the factory until suppertime, then tutored the sons. But knowledge passed through them undigested, like grass through a dog's tract. The older son, to relieve the shame of his position, mimicked his younger tutor, a shrill incessant torment. He crunched his tutor's toes under his heel and stabbed his thigh with a pencil under the table. The younger son cried, "I do understand, I do not understand," a pathetic refrain that infuriated Young Nam even more than the older son's abuse.

Finally, at the end of his long day, as the sun set, the boy turned to his own studies. Having declined to sleep with the Sun family, he lay on his straw mat spread upon the sooty factory floor, and read till he fell asleep with the book covering his face.

In Young Nam's classroom, the boy who had played the perennial runner up to him gained ground, vying for the top grades and at times winning. The boy withdrew from his friendships. He no longer kicked the pebble-filled sack his gang used in lieu of a soccer ball in the schoolyard. He needed those precious minutes to study. He no longer walked home singing arm to shoulder with a friend on each flank. He was different now. They were still children; he was a laborer. They were carefree; he was careworn.

One day, his teacher summoned the boy to her desk.

"Kim Young Nam, I am aware of the change in your circumstances," she said under her breath. "But I cannot treat you differently from the other students. You are a smart boy. Always do your best."

The unexpected kindness swelled his throat and filled his eyes.

At the end of his first month, Young Nam approached Mr. Sun for his pay.

"How are my sons doing in their studies?" asked Mr. Sun.

"Improving," the boy lied.

"Work them as hard as you can," Mr. Sun urged as he opened the cash box with the key from the chain around his neck. And as he counted out the wages, the boy tallied in his head: one thousand won for his mother, one thousand won for next term's middle school tuition, one thousand won put away for high school tuition. The heft of the money in his pocket did feel good. Perhaps the scratchy eyes, prickly throat, aching shoulders, and weary brain were worth it.

On his way to the outhouse, the boy was intercepted by the Sun boys. The older boy did the talking while the younger boy stood by, violently twisting the button on his uniform.

"You were paid. We do the same work, but we were not paid."

"Talk to your father about it," replied the boy.

"Share the money with us."

"Talk to your father if you want your own pay. Please step aside. I have to go."

"I did talk to my father. He said to talk to you," he said, shoving the boy on the chest.

"He did not."

"Yes he did. If you do not believe me, ask him yourself. We do the same work but only you get paid," he said, stabbing the boy's chest with each phrase.

"If you will recall, I tutor you in addition to the factory work."

"You tutor. I eat the shit you feed me. Like I said, we work the same."

"Leave me alone. When I am done, we will go and talk to your father together."

"I will go to your teacher and tell her you stole from us. You will be expelled."

"Try it."

"I will break your fingers so you cannot hold a pencil. I will do it to you in your sleep. You will fail all your exams…"

In the end, the boy turned over two thousand won to the sweatshop sons, leaving him with one thousand won, just enough to stay in school another month.

Shortly after this encounter, a better one came. Young Nam met eldest brother waiting for him outside the school gates. In his sharp black suit and chauffeur's cap, eldest brother cut a handsome figure.

"Little brother! I have come to see you."

"*Hyung!*"

"I read your note. On the same day, Mr. Sun came to me to ask for permission to hire you. I said only if it is what my brother truly wants. He said he thinks of you as a third son. He begged me to give you a month to settle in, so I agreed. It has been a month. Are they treating you well?"

"Tolerably well."

"So you are a man. I am proud of my little brother."

"Has my aunt been well?"

"Your aunt has been terribly sick. She cannot get out of bed except to use the chamber pot. To tell the truth, her condition is what kept me from coming sooner, never mind any promises to your employer."

"Oh, no!"

"In fact, it is happy news. She is pregnant. But she is having such a terrible reaction. So I have been very busy. I have to work, take care of your aunt, cook, clean, and manage everything alone. I want to come see you every week but…"

"No, no. I would not expect that. I am happy to see you today. But I am also very busy."

"And your studies? Are you still the number one boy?"

"Sometimes," hesitated the boy.

"*Aigo*! Always modest. I spoke with your teacher, and she has already told me that you are the top boy. Here, this is for you," said eldest brother, handing him a roll of bills.

"No. I make my own money now. You will need it for the baby!"

"Use it for books," said eldest brother, grabbing the boy's hand and pressing it into his palm.

"No. I do not need it," said the boy. A friendly tussle ensued, till eldest brother shoved the bills deep into the boy's trouser pockets.

"Promise me you will come to me if you need anything. You can come back anytime, no matter what. Know that."

"I know."

"Study hard," eldest brother said as they parted ways.

Every month, the oldest Sun boy sat for his upper school exams. Every month, he failed. Every month, the factory proprietress tongue-lashed Young Nam for bad tutoring and her own son for stupidity. She threatened to fire Young Nam and throw him out in the street. She threatened to disown her son and throw him out in the street. Worst of all, she threatened to disown her son and adopt Young Nam to take his place. The drumbeat of accusations and insults and threats would pound on for a week out of every dreary month.

Several rounds of failed high school exams later, the Suns lowered their sights to vocational school for their heir apparent. Mr. Sun excused his son and tutor from factory work for a week before the entrance exams. They crammed desperately into the night, and Young Nam was forced to neglect his own studies. The exam results were posted on the weekend. While the Suns were eating lunch with their mother, a meal not included in his pay, Young Nam sprinted to the vocational school to check the results. On the roster tacked to the front door, the Sun name was emblazoned under the *failed* column. Despite himself, a laugh escaped his lips.

"What a dunderhead," the boy blurted out loud.

Later, at dinner, the boy was applying himself to his rice bowl when he felt something hit his forehead. The object fell into his rice bowl...a piece of kimchi. How curious. But without a break, he scooped up the fallen cabbage with a mound of rice into his mouth. Then he felt another piece smack his nose. This time, the kimchi landed on the table. The two Sun boys snickered. The boy glared at them. But while his eyes were on them, another bit of food hit his chest. So it was not the sons. It was their mother who was steadily pelting him with food.

"What are you doing, *Yuhboh?*" asked Mr. Sun.

"He did not teach my sons. He robs us of food and money and gives back nothing in return."

"Stop doing that," said Mr. Sun.

"Did you know that your son failed again? That thief could not even get him into vocational school. He wants him to fail. He taught him everything upside down and backwards to make sure he would fail."

"Stop. Do not blame the boy," said Mr. Sun.

Eyes slit and lip curled, she snarled at her husband, "Who should I blame? Your son? Is your son an imbecile then? An idiot who cannot even get into vocational school?"

"I told you to stop!" shouted Mr. Sun, rising from the table.

She pounded her fists on the table and screamed, "I am going insane. You brought another mouth to feed into my house. He is stealing from us. He is laughing at all of us..."

She raked bloody scratches down her face and pulled fistfuls of hair out of her head as she ranted. Her sons cowered.

To the collected horror of the three children, Mr. Sun stood to announce, "I am leaving!" and stormed out the door. The boy took a blinding blow to the head with a metal rice bowl. He collected himself as his vision cleared. He had had enough. He said, "I am leaving too." Then, he gathered his books and change of clothes, dodging the flying dishes. The berserk woman turned upon her sons.

"You are not my sons! You are not my sons!" she shrieked as she beat their faces and heads with a bowl in each hand. Invectives pertaining to their idiocy and bastard origins spewed from her like a septic explosion. The sons cried like babies, professed their love for their mother, begged for mercy. Young Nam slammed the door on them.

His head was throbbing. Gingerly, he felt the egg on his forehead. He stopped on a curb and tied up his books into a knapsack fashioned with his spare shirt and pants. With this parcel slung over his shoulder, he meandered in the general direction of his brother's home. But on the way, he came across a room for the night for one hundred won. It was little more than a closet, but no worse than the factory floor. He lay himself on the bare floor using a book for a pillow. At least it was clean. His head ached, and he tested the lump on his head with his fingertips. In games of soccer at school, even if there was a real ball instead of rocks, the boy steadfastly refused to head the ball (idiotic maneuver he always thought) to avoid possible damage to his brain. He never employed the head butt when jousting with his friends. Why did that fishwife have to hit his head of all places, the repository of his most treasured organ? Shivering, he curled up and thrust his hands into his pockets. He had only two hundred won left. He wrapped his fist around it. In the morning, he would decide what to do next.

As darkness fell, he thought about his own mother, how in the bleakest of times she went begging from morning to night at the neighboring farms for rice to feed her children, how coming home limping and empty-handed she would crumble to her knees and wail pitifully, how the little ones crept to her and told her not to cry because they were not hungry, how she crushed them to her bosom and soaked their heads with her hot tears. How desperately he missed her now. He recognized this painful longing for what it was: a blessing. Any trial he had to endure, no matter how grueling, painful, lonely, or humiliating, was preferable to abuse by a parent.

In the morning he went to school on an empty stomach. At the end of the day, as the schoolchildren shoved past him to hustle home, the boy moved as slowly as he could across the schoolyard, not sure where to go or what to do. Only at his lowest moments, did he resort to prayer. And this was such a moment. *Lord, show me the way*, he prayed silently.

Miraculously, at the gate was waiting his second elder brother, come from the farm.

"Am I a ghost? Do not look so shocked, little brother!"

"My prayer was answered!"

"Eldest brother sent me to find you. I went to the watch factory, and they told me you ran away. What happened? What is that on your head? Who did that to you?"

"An accident. What brings you to Seoul?" asked the boy.

"I came to visit my brothers. Mother sent me to check up on you and to bring home a report of eldest brother's new baby son."

"A son!" exclaimed the boy.

Young Nam accompanied his brother to their eldest brother's home, not without trepidation. He hoped that the parcel of worldly belongings he carried would not be misinterpreted. The front door was still festooned with a rope woven with charcoal and peppers, heralding the birth of a boy, and warning outsiders that a twenty-one-day quarantine period was in effect to protect the newborn baby. Only nuclear family would be welcome into the home. A lump rose in the boy's throat.

But the new mother came to the door behind eldest brother to greet her brothers-in-law and usher them in. Her old sour glare was replaced by sparkling eyes. She addressed Young Nam directly with gracious words of welcome, and the boy was taken aback to see her smile for the first time in their acquaintance. She seemed taller. She wore a new celadon *hanbok,* and her hair was in a sleek chignon adorned with jade hairpins. In the cradle of her arms she displayed her sleeping infant son. He would be called Tree until his first birthday celebration when a proper name would be given.

Eldest brother now had a housemaid from the country. The maid shuttled back and forth, whisking away empty dishes and returning them mounded high with fragrant offerings of savory meat and succulent vegetables. The new mother consumed voraciously and, both cheeks stuffed with food, chattered about her son's upcoming celebrations. The one-hundred-day party would be in Seoul. It would be very crowded in their small house, but they would manage. Nobody would mind the crowding once they tasted her maid's cooking.

On Tree's first birthday, they would travel back home for the birthday party so both sides of the family could join the celebration of the first grandson. A party even more munificent than their wedding would be arranged. The ceremonial tables would be loaded with pyramids of glossy fruit and silver trays of rice cakes of every shape, hue, and texture. Baby Tree would be adorned like a tiny prince in sumptuous regalia of embroidered silk. For the denouement, following tradition, a string, chopsticks, money, and calligraphy brush (or nowadays a pen) would be set out on a table before their son. Which of these objects the birthday boy picked up first would foretell his future. If he picked up the string, he would enjoy a long life; if the chopsticks, he would always be well fed; if the money, he would be rich; if the pen, he would be a scholar.

"I hope my son picks up the money!" the new mother laughed giddily.

She was dissembling to avoid jinxing herself. They all knew that she, like every status-conscious Korean mother, yearned for her firstborn to pick up the pen.

"You must have picked the pen, did you?" she asked Young Nam kindly.

"I do not know," replied the boy.

"What? You remember everything. How could you forget such an important thing!" she playfully chided and turned to her husband. "What did he pick up? I predict it was the pen!"

"It was hard times," replied eldest brother quietly. "My little brother did not have a party."

"Young Nam does not need a party to prove he will be a fine scholar!" she said.

Then, the conversation took a turn for the worse. Second brother announced that Mother needed Young Nam to return home to the farm. Third brother had landed a teaching position in a neighboring village and had moved away from home. With only two able-bodied adults, and one of them an aging woman, the farm was in extremis. The village school had grown, and new teachers had been hired. He could attend the village school and help on the farm.

"But I have final exams coming up!"

"We will come to visit you at Harvest Moon Festival," offered his sister-in-law.

"Mother needs you," insisted second elder brother.

Young Nam remembered he had asked the Lord to show him the way. Could this be the terrible answer?

The reluctant expression on the boy's face made second elder brother add, "And Owlet misses you terribly. He needs you."

"Then I must come home."

On the train ride home, the boy forced himself to overcome his deep regret and look forward to seeing his mother and brothers. He wondered how much Owlet had grown. Would his baby brother hide shyly or would he leap into his outstretched arms? It had been a long time since his piggyback had been commissioned. As the stained slabs of concrete, foul yellow smog and chaotic hustle of Seoul receded farther and farther behind him, as the verdant panorama of the countryside spread before his eyes and the fresh air filled his lungs, he sank deeper and deeper into despair.

Second elder brother filled the silence with encouraging talk. In the old days, their father had hired two laborers to work the farm in exchange for room and board, two changes of clothing, and three sacks of rice after harvest time. They would hire laborers again. Some of the neighboring farmers were pooling resources with their family to purchase a mechanical harvesting machine that would increase their efficiency. It was agreed that their mother, being a widow, would get her turn at it first come harvest time. The money the two brothers were sending home was being saved for this purpose. With these improvements, the boy would have more time to devote to his studies. Eldest brother had given up his inheritance, so the farm would pass to himself. What with third brother going into the teaching profession, he and the boy would be equal partners.

The more second elder brother prattled, the darker grew the storm that clouded the boy's mind. He excused himself to stretch his cramped legs – a fellow cattle car passenger seized his seat before he could change his mind – and made his way through the crowd and cargo to the open doorway. His eyes squinted against the rush of air. He braced himself within the doorframe. He would be missing his final exams. Well in advance, he had prepared to attain perfect scores, fiendishly studying through the night sitting cross-legged on the floor of that gritty factory, memorizing where familiarization would have sufficed, erasing and rewriting recitations until the precious paper wore clean through. If he ever made it back to Seoul, he would be made to repeat the entire year of schooling. What difference would one week make to the farm?

He felt the rumble of the tracks and looked down at the ground blurring past. From the doorway where he stood, he was so close to the ground. The trick would be to stay loose and roll, to yield to gravity. He checked his trouser pocket for his money. No. Owlet would be expecting him, counting the days and hours no doubt.

Then, to his surprise, he leaped.

Tumbling down the jagged precipice, ripped by rocks, stuck by sticks, Kim Young Nam tucked his arms tight and covered his face and rolled for what seemed like an eternity, punctuated by tearing of clothes and cracking of joints. Finally, a ditch halted him. Sorely battered, he staggered to his feet and watched the train disappear over the horizon. He examined himself and found he was, for all intents and purposes, intact. He felt in his pocket for his money, enough to get by two more days. He wondered, *Am I possessed by the devil?* He laughed out loud.

He turned north, toward Seoul, toward school, and limped forward. He grew hungry and thirsty. After an hour of walking, he took off his shoes, stuffed in his socks, and carried them under his arm. They had been too small for quite some time, and his feet were throbbing raw meat slabs. Barefoot, he made quicker progress. He walked on until dusk, swallowing saliva to mollify the rumbling in his belly, until the supply ran out.

It would be necessary to stop for the night. A grass-roofed farm hut beckoned in the distance. He would go there. First, he would ask for a drink of water. Then, if the woman seemed amenable, he would ask for some food and a dry corner to sleep in. It was not an unusual thing to do, and a decent young student would be more than welcome in a humble country home.

At the doorstep, he brushed off and straightened his uniform in anticipation of some old-fashioned farm hospitality. He knocked on the door and shouted a confident, "Hello!"

A jolly-sounding woman's voice answered, "Wait! I am coming! Do not go away." He wondered if she was a good cook. It hardly mattered in his present parched and ravenous state. The slow, heavy tread of a well-fed woman lumbered to the door. So she must be a good cook then.

The door opened. The woman took one look and blasted his face with a hysterical scream. She slammed the door, nearly bashing his nose. Shocked by this reception, the boy heard her hysterical cry, "Husband! Help!" The boy turned and ran.

Dispirited and exhausted, the boy trudged along the train tracks until in the dwindling light he found a grassy depression to rest in. As insects feasted on his face and neck, he fell asleep wondering whatever could have been the matter with that absurd farm woman.

He awoke to find second elder brother gently shaking his shoulder. For a sinking moment of confusion, he thought he was at home. "I found you," said his brother. A farmer on a horse-drawn cart waited above the embankment. The brothers scrambled up the hill.

"Make it quick. I am in a hurry," groused the farmer.

The boy drank from the farmer's jug and shoved a rice cake into his mouth. Second brother, arms akimbo, shook his head as he watched his younger brother refresh himself.

"You gave me a lot of trouble."

"I am sorry."

"If you want to go to school so badly, I will not stop you. But you may not go back to the factory. You must go back to eldest brother's home," he said.

"Hurry up. I have work to do," grumbled the farmer.

The older brother handed the younger a cloth saying, "You better clean your face. It is covered in blood. You look monstrous."

"So that is why that farm wife screamed and slammed the door in my face!" exclaimed the boy.

"You went to someone's house looking like *that*?" And the brothers began to laugh.

"I thought I looked handsome."

They laughed even harder. The farmer on his cart began to chuckle despite himself.

"And you…crazy boy…and you jumped off a moving train *to take an exam*?" the older brother gasped between guffaws.

"Did I really do that?" the boy sputtered.

"This is the smart one in the family. He jumped off a moving train because he wanted to take exams!" second brother said to the farmer. By now, the farmer was shaking with hilarity, gripping his sides.

When their laughter subsided, second brother said, "I must return to Mother quickly. It is only a few hours to Seoul. Can you walk?"

"Yes I can!" exclaimed the boy.

The farmer, still chuckling, gave the boy the rest of the rice cakes and the jug of water. The old man grunted, "You show those city boys how the country boys get the job done!"

The brothers parted ways. The older brother, in the farmer's cart rumbling south, craning around to face his brother, waved and shouted, "Go on! Go quickly!" The younger boy, headed north, but walking backwards to face his brother, waved and shouted, "I am! I am!" The moment his brother was completely out of sight, Kim Young Nam wheeled about and broke into a sprint.

11

Lee Hana
South Korea
1948

Lee Hana's wedding was quick and quiet. There were no guests. There was no feast. There was no joy. Only relief. The match had been costly to arrange. Rumors had spread. The girl's haunted face and cowering posture raised suspicions. People suspected she was an apple with a worm hole. Hana's father traveled farther and farther from the village to find a matchmaker who would take the difficult case on. After over a year of search, negotiations, and financial sacrifice, a match was made. With the bad apple removed, their son would be able to bring a decent wife into their home. Hana knew better than to argue or plead. She submitted to her marriage with her head down and her mouth shut.

At first glance, Hana's intended husband appeared a tall, handsome, well-built man. But any initial favorable impression quickly spoiled. The bridegroom drifted through the abbreviated marriage ritual like a sleepwalker. On their wedding night, the family cleared out of the common room to give the newlyweds a private moment to consummate their marriage. But Hana's new husband stood by the window and stared outside in a listless daze.

"What was your name again?" he asked in a dull voice.

"Lee Hana."

"It hardly matters."

He heaved a laborious sigh. After an endless time, a groan escaped him. He slid to the floor and put his forehead on his forearms.

"How long will this be?"

His speech was torpid, as if every word were an obstacle to be surmounted.

"I do not know."

"I wish they would leave me alone," he said.

"Me too."

The bridegroom looked at his bride and saw her for the first time that day. His eyebrows shot up in alarm over his widening eyes.

"Are you pretty?" he asked.

"No!"

"What is wrong with you? Why did they let you marry me?"

"I...I consider myself fortunate to be a married woman."

"You appear to be a beauty."

"Not me," she whispered and bowed her head down.

"But what is the use? The worms will eat that pretty face of yours in the end."

Hana had married the youngest of five sons. As such, she entered the populous household as its lowest ranking member. This suited her. She made herself small and silent. She answered to the constant orders of her numerous female superiors. Mindless obedience and ceaseless industry diverted her mind from wretched memories.

Her eldest sister-in-law spread her corpulence about the center of the room directly over the heat source, and from this comfortable throne, demanded constant feeding. Cheeks stuffed to bursting, flecks flying from her mouth, she complained that nothing from the kitchen was worth the effort of chewing. Hana's rice was overcooked and her dumplings bland and her portions stingy. This vast female was immune from reproach, having married the ranking male and produced the only grandson in the family.

The second sister-in-law, childless, cried daily. She came from a distant village on a one-way trip to a loveless marriage. Her husband ignored her. She loathed Hana before the new wife stepped foot in the house. What if her newest rival produced a child before she did? There would be yet another sister-in-law to torture her with sidelong glances and pitying comments.

The third sister-in-law had an infant girl on the right side, a toddler girl on the left, and was pregnant in the middle. She greeted Hana's arrival with a campaign to latch her daughters onto their newest aunt. It failed. The girls clung with ferocious neediness to their expanding and nauseous mother.

The fourth sister-in-law was the worker, her assiduousness matched only by her vociferousness. She complained about the other wives and their excessive eating, crying, and sleeping. She was the only one who did anything around the place. Nobody ever helped her. This had been her lot all her life. She had worked hard since the day she could pick up a broom. Having spent a year being bossed by the women above her, she welcomed the new underling with a vengeance. She still dominated the house and garden work, as such was her industrious nature. But Hana served as both audience and accessory to her diligence. She summoned Hana from the far end of the house to fetch her the ladle an arm's reach away. Hana stood by to hand her clean rags and gather the dirty ones when she scrubbed. And Hana absorbed the steady stream of grievances and self-congratulation.

And then there was Hana's mother-in-law, *Uhmonim,* all bone, sinew, nerves, and tongue. The old lady, though feeble in body, whipped her sons into submission with her tongue...except for the youngest, Hana's husband. He alone was immune from reproach.

Shortly after the newlyweds came home, Hana's husband ran away. *Uhmonim* ordered her sons to canvas the property and surrounding farms for him. She dispatched the eldest son on horseback to search the village. It was apparent from the well-rehearsed emergency response that his disappearance was not an isolated occurrence. But this time, someone was to blame.

"Where is your husband?" demanded the old lady.

"I do not know," Hana answered.

"Were you a good wife to my son?"

Hana hesitated.

"Answer!"

"Yes?"

"Stupid girl! On your wedding night, did you perform your wifely duty? If you did not, you will bring us very bad luck!"

"Yes, I did," she lied.

"Then where did your husband go? I expect you to be a good wife and take care of my son! You were to be abandoned like a dog. I took you in. Nobody wanted you. Do you understand?"

"Yes."

"Am I to feed and clothe you for nothing? Nobody would notice or care if I cast you out. I raised five sons. What have you accomplished with your life? You are to mind your husband and prevent him from running off like this! Do you understand?"

"I do."

It happened that the old lady had hired a shaman to treat her troubled son. After performing his obligatory rituals, the shaman came up with a practical suggestion: the old lady should find her son a wife to manage and care for him. But the youngest son's notorious reputation in the village had prevented a match. Undeterred, the old lady had sent her oldest son to journey to neighboring villages and scare up an unsuspecting female. Fortuitously, Hana's availability had been circulated among matchmakers. And so the match was made, the marriage executed.

Hana relished her husband's frequent, prolonged absences. She devoted herself to the hard work of the lowest ranking farm wife, tending the animals, working in the vegetable garden, laboring in the fields, cooking meals, cleaning, washing laundry, serving her superiors, pausing only to stand in the kitchen and choke some food down. The only disturbances to the simplicity of her servitude were the strident heckling of *Uhmonim* and the episodic reappearance of her husband.

After lengthy absences, he would return home disheveled, drunk, smeared with dirt, splattered with blood, sometimes on horseback tied up like a prisoner behind his eldest brother, sometimes on foot of his own accord. He would career about the yard and collapse in his own vomit. Inevitably, someone from the village would knock on the gate seeking recompense for the havoc he had wrought. Groveling with apologies, the old lady would produce an offering of a liter of rice and a basket of fresh laid eggs.

During one of her son's manic episodes, the old lady hauled Hana out of the house and pointed to him. He was picking up chickens and throwing them against the coop and, in the maelstrom of chicken shrieks and flying feathers, bellowing, "Something is wrong with me! Something is wrong with me!"

"Look at him!" hissed *Uhmonim.* "Are you being a good wife? Does the husband of a good wife behave this way?"

Hana observed in silence.

"Are you deaf as well as dumb? Do something! You are his wife!"

Hana approached her husband and patted his arm. With insane strength, he picked her up with one hand and flung her to the ground like a heap of white rags. He stalked to the splayed figure, gathered a fistful of her hair, and dragged her in a haphazard zigzag around the courtyard till he settled on a good spot upon which to throw her down and beat her. The old lady rushed to the chicken coop, gathered the limp chickens, ran into the house, and slammed the door behind her. Hana's husband pummeled his limp wife crying, "Something is wrong with me! Something is wrong with me!"

When it was over, Hana crawled on her hands and knees to the far end of the yard and huddled there till the knife blade of the pain subsided to an ache. She had a purse tied to the inside of her skirts where she had secreted away her sole personal possession, a corroded metal compact with a cracked mirror on one side and some dry, crazed makeup on the other. She opened it and winced at the image of her swollen face. She spat into the makeup to soften it and gingerly dabbed the paste over the cuts and bruises on her face. Then she limped to the kitchen to help her sister-in-law prepare the sacrificed chickens for dinner.

After serving the meal, she retreated as usual to the kitchen to eat her supper. But her mother-in-law came to the kitchen and said, "Come, Daughter. Your husband is home, and you must sit at the table like a proper wife."

Her husband's hair and clothing were still in disarray, but his demeanor was entirely altered. He hung his head over his bowl and did not take a bite. The meal lasted forever. At the end of supper, suddenly, a terrible animal noise escaped him. Hana's heart lurched. Her husband looked into her eyes; his own were welling with tears. He dropped his head again and cried like a baby. He continued to weep while the dishes were cleared and the table put away. He wept on while the floor was cleaned around him. He wept while the bedding was spread out. Then, abruptly, he keeled over onto his side, with his legs still crossed, and fell fast asleep.

The next day, he led Hana on a long walk to the edge of the mountainside. They entered a small grove of pines.

"I cannot do it with all those people in the house. This place will do. Take your clothes off and lie down. Mother told me what I must do."

Readily, in practiced, mechanical fashion, she disrobed and spread her skirt and jacket and petticoat on the ground. She removed her undergarments. She lay upon the clothing, nude, with her arms at her sides. Since the last time she performed this service, she had grown into a woman. The slope and the silk of her resilient body belied the ravages of her girlhood. Her husband untied his pants and let them drop to his ankles. He stared balefully at his penis, which shriveled like a brown grub in a black thicket.

After an extended wait, he asked, "When will it work?"

"Maybe never," she whispered. Among her countless customers, she had witnessed this condition now and again, always with great relief.

"Is there something wrong with you?"

"I think there must be," she replied.

"What do I tell Mother?"

"Tell her…tell her we did it."

"She will be angry when we do not make a son."

"Tell her it is my fault. Say I must be barren like my sister-in-law."

"Yes, good. Then she will only be angry with you."

"What if we pretend we are living as a married couple?" she suggested cautiously. "But we can secretly live as brother and sister."

"Yes. That is a good idea. We will do that."

Her husband yanked up his pants and retied the belt while Hana scrambled to her feet and threw her clothing on. As she followed her husband back to the house, she felt elated. She had spoken. He had listened. They had agreed. If this was marriage, it was good enough.

Hana's husband slept, moped aimlessly in a daze, and then slept some more. In the hardworking household and backbreaking farm, nobody groused about the youngest son's torpor. He was awakened for feeding time and otherwise left alone.

His wife, however, was not. Frustrations needed to be vented, and she was the soft target. After all, the shaman had promised he would be cured if he married. Precious funds had been expended toward this end. If she were a better wife, he would become a better husband. The old lady flagellated her daughter-in-law with this whip daily.

After a particularly grueling diatribe, the diligent fourth sister-in-law whispered to her, "No woman deserves a husband like that. The old lady is wrong. You are not at fault for anything. You are only a woman. What power do you have? None. You have bad luck. That is all. Bad luck."

So that was it? She simply had bad luck? It was not her fault. She had done no wrong. The kind words filled her heart.

12

Kim Young Nam
South Korea
1949-1950

American soldiers gathered at the base of a craggy bluff to watch. An old, white-haired Korean man, bearing on his back a towering load of army cargo strapped onto an A-frame, scaled the steep slope with the sure tread, steadfast diligence, and proportionate strength of a worker ant. The Americans hooted and hollered. At the top of the hill, the old man stacked the payload neat and square, and scrambled down, grinning agreeably, bowing at the waist to the semi-circle of clapping soldiers.

"If ole' *Halapuji* can do it, I'll be damned if I can't," said one of the Americans. The strapping six-footer commandeered the A-frame off the old man's stooped back. His platoon members obliged him to make good on his boast, mounting the A-frame to the linebacker's broad back and securing a stack of crates upon it. The whooping and whistling resumed as the American began his precarious ascent. His boots hunted for footholds which only crumbled into a shower of rocks under his great weight. He clutched at saplings which uprooted under his ham-fisted grip.

Suddenly, the American lost his footing. He slid face down the unforgiving precipice, until a ridge wedged him fast. The old Korean man scurried to his aid and took the load off his back. The American skidded to the bottom of the hill, complaining of a bad back from a high school football injury.

"You big pussy! Ole' Grandpa kicked your fag ass," howled one of his compatriots, thereby volunteering himself as the platoon's next Sisyphus. The spectacle continued until all the men had a go at the climb. Finally, with chow time coming, it became expedient to allow old *Halapuji* finish the job without further ado. After the old man double-timed it down the hill the final time, one of the soldiers gave him a congratulatory slap on the back, which sent him rolling like a tumbleweed. The good soldiers picked him up, dusted him off, and stuffed his shirt with candy bars and packs of cigarettes.

From a distance, the boy, Kim Young Nam, observed the escapade. How in the world had this race of giants, unable to climb a hill, defeated the Japanese? Then he remembered something his older brother had once told him, a story he had listened to with skepticism at the time, but now understood to be, astonishingly, factual: the Americans had twice obliterated entire cities in Japan with a single bomb. They did not need to scramble up hills. As the American soldiers ambled past the boy, one of them tossed him a chocolate bar.

"Good catch," said the soldier.

"Good catch," repeated the boy. He had observed the tattered urchins who followed the American soldiers to collect the candy and coins they doled out with such casual generosity. But this "good catch" was his first. He could smell the sweetness right through the fancy packaging. He unwrapped the candy and took a bite. It was the richest, sweetest food he had ever tasted. Saliva erupted into his mouth as the chocolate melted on his tongue like a heavenly dream. He could hardly believe his good fortune.

Such munificence. Such inexplicable kindness. He devoured the rest of the chocolate bar in one gulp.

"Good catch," he repeated out loud. He already knew what "good" meant. "Catch" was new vocabulary. "Catch" must mean candy, he figured. Yes, it *was* good catch.

The boy was on a mission to find a summer job working for the Americans, a job that might afford the opportunity to learn English from native speakers. And if a regular supply of good catch was part of the bargain, so much the better.

Young Nam waylaid *Halapuji* and importuned him for advice. The old man looked with favor upon the boy's smart turnout in his school uniform and slicked hair. He led the boy into Yongsan Garrison, a complex of brick buildings, originally constructed for the Japanese Army, and now occupied by the US Army. The boy was introduced to a Korean agent in charge of hiring locals to serve the American military. The boy was hired as a gofer to the Korean mechanic who was the gofer to the American mechanic in charge of maintaining the military vehicles. While it was disappointing to report to a Korean, at least it was an entrée.

The boy's summer work was both easier and harder than his first job in Seoul at the watch crystal factory. There, he could not work fast enough, long enough, or hard enough to suit the boss lady. At Yongsan Garrison, much of his work day was spent idling in a state of suspended animation. The boy wore inactivity like a horse hair shirt. He sweltered in the sun at his post, infrared radiating from buildings the color of dried blood, waiting for an order from his supervisor. The air was saturated with humidity and a monsoon loomed over the mountains. Ennui pervaded the garrison during the muggy hours in the rank stench of the city. The Americans were marking time, waiting to return to their own land of flush toilets where the streets were paved with gold, not fringed with feces.

Come sunset, the soldiers caroused in a nightly bacchanalia that rocked the alleys of Itaewon. The dingy watering holes filled with American soldiers and the barkeepers' money boxes filled with American greenback. Painted women in flimsy western dresses hung on the arms of the soldiers and paraded brazenly. One evening, as the boy walked home, a soldier crossed his path, swinging a bottle of liquor in one hand, dragging his prostitute by the hair in the other. She screamed wicked obscenities and kicked violently as she flopped behind the soldier like a rag doll. She had lost one shoe, and her toenails sticking through the ripped nylons were painted crimson. The boy cringed, cast his flushed face to the ground, and quickened his pace.

A summer storm had been gathering like an immense grey mass over the mountains for days. The boy was on base when the monsoon suddenly metastasized. Black spilled across the sky, thunder detonated, and rain pounded the earth. The soldiers outside in the yard cursed and sprinted for cover. As the boy had nowhere to retreat to, he stood in the rain, rather enjoying the clean soaking, watching the dust liquefy into a mud slurry. He thought of the farmers out in their paddies, their parched, brown faces raised to the sky in gratitude.

Hours later, the storm tapered to a steady shower. The boy still stood at his post. Suddenly, a group of soldiers burst from their barracks, running toward the parked fleet of troop transport trucks in a distant dirt lot. The men shouted. They circled the trucks, bent at the waist, and called out names. Horror stricken, the boy realized what they were looking for.

Many of the soldiers habitually napped underneath the vehicles for shade from the scorching sun. On weekends, after bouts of heavy drinking, revelers were often to be found under the vehicles passed out in pools of vomit and motor oil. In the soaked earth of the monsoon rains, the wheels of the trucks had sunk so deep that the running boards barely skimmed the mud line. The boy raced to find his supervisor, who was napping in the mechanic's garage. The pair sprinted to the lot bearing jacks, blocks, and shovels.

The boy, his supervisor, and the soldiers worked frantically in the unforgiving rain. The sodden earth, like quicksand, gave no purchase to the blocks and jacks which sank under the weight of the trucks. Abandoning this method, the boy and the men took up shovels. But the more they dug, the deeper the trucks sank. The stockpile of shoveled silt thinned in the rain and slid back between their legs and under the trucks.

With a great roar, a soldier plunged himself head first, arms outstretched into the quagmire under the truck. In short order, spasms convulsed his exposed legs. Two men grasped a flailing leg each, heaved with all their might, and extracted the soldier. Vomiting sludge and bar swill, he collapsed off to the side, sucking violently for air. The remainder of the rescue party moved from one truck to another, digging with frantic abandon.

A soldier ran for help. He returned accompanied by an officer. The officer assessed the scene. He asked some questions of the enlisted men. The men and the boy gathered around the officer with hopeful expectancy. The officer looked at his watch. He shook his head. He addressed the assembly in measured tones. The boy required no English comprehension to understand the officer's pronouncement. They all knew the men under the trucks were long dead.

One of the soldiers wept like a child. Another cradled the weeping man's head on his chest and comforted him. The officer noticed the bedraggled Korean boy standing among his men, shin deep in mud, panting madly, with a shovel in his hands. The stricken expression on the boy's face must have affected the officer. He waded through the mud to put his hand on the boy's shoulder and said, "You did your best."

After this incident, the boy grew vexed by a disquieting sense of vulnerability. The preceding year, the Republic of Korea had been inaugurated under Syngman Rhee. Less than a year later, the American troops withdrew from their half of the peninsula, leaving only a skeletal advisory group behind. The boy lost his job. More importantly, the vacuum struck the boy like the death of his father, like a safety net spirited away. He shrugged off the unwelcome feeling and shouldered on.

One year later, civil war broke out.

Radio broadcasts admonished the citizens of Seoul to stay home and remain calm. Yet droves of frightened civilian refugees from North Korea fled chaotically through Seoul bringing word of the communist attack at the border. Advancing in the opposite direction, toward the 38th parallel, marched columns of South Korean soldiers, some on trucks and jeeps, some riding ox-drawn carts, some peddling bicycles, and some on foot. The troops were met with the fervent cheers of patriotic onlookers. The citizenry, from wizened grannies behind their fish stalls to *yangban* in their silk robes and black hats to barefoot street children, whipped themselves into a patriotic froth: reunification of their divided nation must be imminent.

The sky over Seoul was slashed by Russian-made Yak fighter jets, strafing the city on their way to destroy Kimpo Airport. The ignorant populace redoubled their frenzied victory cries. They could not distinguish friend from foe. They did not know that at the parallel, the South Korean army, equipped with hand grenades and makeshift explosives tied to poles, had been ground into the earth like so many cockroaches under treads of the advancing Russian-built armored T-34 tanks.

Within days, cannon fire could be heard in the city. Radio broadcasts fried into blind static. Rumors of the Rhee government's helter skelter flight from Seoul disseminated mass panic. Yongsan Garrison became a ghost town overnight. On his lone reconnaissance forays, the boy had witnessed American officers of the Korean Military Advisory Group motoring south in jeeps stuffed with their Korean aids. He reported his findings to eldest brother. His wife and baby tucked in for the night, eldest brother convened a sober conference with the boy on the front step.

"What do you think? You say the Americans have fled. That is very bad. I wonder if you should go home and help protect Mother and the farm," he said.

Despite the desperation of the situation, the boy was proud that eldest brother was addressing him man to man. He straightened his back. He declared, "We should all go together."

"Your aunt cannot travel. The baby will be coming any day."

"We can wait until the baby comes. Then we can go together. I saw that the trains and the roads are all impassable. We may need to walk. I can carry my nephew on my back, you can carry food, water, and necessities, and Aunt can carry the newborn," said the boy.

Eldest brother knit his brow, thought for a long minute, and concluded, "Your idea has merit. But under the circumstances, I can protect my wife and son and baby best here. I have the livery cars which may prove to be useful. Owlet will need you. He is a fragile child and will be frightened to death. You will be able to move more quickly and more safely alone."

"Owlet," remembered the boy. "He *will* need me."

"It is the best way."

Eldest brother read the hesitation on his brother's face and added, "Anyway, the schools here will be closed until the country is reunified."

"When should I leave?"

"Tonight. After reunification, you will come right back to school."

Around midnight, the boy plunged headlong into the tumultuous exodus, with a small parcel of provisions hurriedly packed by his weeping aunt. He was thankful to be shod in the sturdy US Army boots he had scavenged from the garrison's dump. They were too big, but he had stuffed the toes with rags, rendering them perfectly serviceable.

Every major thoroughfare out of Seoul was choked with vehicles, draft animals, military personnel, and civilian refugees. Where possible, the boy scrambled through side alleys to skirt the traffic jam, forging his way toward the Han River Bridge.

After two hours of jostling through the crush of desperate refugees, the boy finally stood at the top of the bank of the River Han and surveyed the scene below. The Han was flowing full but calm. The black steel arches of the Hangang Bridge spanned several hundred meters across the dark waters. On the bridge, a bumper-to-bumper lineup of military vehicles was at a dead standstill. A teeming rabble of humanity, carrying their worldly belongings on their heads and babies on their backs, clogged the remaining lanes. At the entrance to the bridge, military police beat back the burgeoning crowds with clubs.

Gun shots rang overhead. The mob surged toward the bridge like a ragged white wave. The boy reckoned that it would take all night to get across the bridge. By then, the enemy would be upon them. Perhaps he would swim across. But he had never swum such a distance before. Perhaps there was a narrower crossing downstream. But the current would be stronger. The boy trekked down the river bank away from the bridge evaluating his alternatives. Then the decision was made for him.

An immense explosion threw him to the ground. He crashed face down on the bank and covered the back of his head with his hands. The fury of a blood red inferno enflamed the earth and sky. The earth shook once, twice. Then there were shrieks. The inhuman cries of the wounded and dying, widowed and orphaned, pierced the night.

Before he could think, the boy was back on his feet and running for his life, shedding his parcel on the way. A wall of flame and billows of smoke rose from the bridge. He outran the ash cloud, past the gaggle of frantic peasants on shore jostling to board the pathetically inadequate ferry boats. He scrambled as far downstream as his nerves allowed before hurtling himself into the water. He swam with every dram of his youthful ferocity.

In his peripheral vision, he witnessed white clad figures plummeting off the bridge into the black water, one after another. He struggled to keep his head above water. The opposite shore was barely visible, and he was choking with foul river water. Something was wrong. He feared he would surely drown. Then he recognized that his waterlogged army boots were pulling his body down like a ball and chain. He untied the boots and kicked them off. Better. If he kept his head and paced himself, he might make it. With steady, measured power, he stroked through the water.

Ahead, the boy discerned a small wooden rowboat so overloaded with Koreans in white peasant clothing that the hull barely skimmed above the waterline. They sat in eerie silence like a congregation of compliant ghosts, their frightened eyes fixed to the stern. As he overtook the boat, he saw an American soldier holding the back of the boat, kicking furiously to propel it through the water. He thought about joining the American. But the added downward vector of his weight could sink the boat. So he swam wordlessly alongside, grateful for the company.

At the southern bank, the boy dragged himself on his hands and knees out of the river and caught his breath. He looked at the burning bridge over the River Han. Headlights still shone on parts of the Hangang Bridge. But two spans of the bridge had collapsed, to be swallowed by the black water. *When whales fight, shrimps' backs are broken.* The meaning of the ancient aphorism stabbed his heart. He rose and continued his long journey home, barefoot and empty-handed.

He was a wretched sight at the conclusion of his trek. At the threshold of his mother's home, he called for her. She came running. She threw her hands to the sky and cried, "Glory to God! The Lord has answered my prayers!"

Heedless of the grime, the deaconess hustled the boy, sediment and all, into the house. In the main chamber, Owlet lay flat and still in his bedding.

"The planes fly over us. They make a terrible noise in the sky. Then Owlet trembles and trembles. He cannot still his trembling body. Then he falls ill. Thank God, you came home. He will regain his strength when he sees you."

The boy leaned over Owlet and smoothed his hair. His caress left a streak of mud on the pale expanse of the sick child's forehead. He whispered his brother's name. Owlet's eyes opened large, blinking in disbelief. Suddenly, the invalid stretched out his arms and embraced the boy's neck crying, "*Hyung, Hyung!*"

"I knew it!" exclaimed their mother. "The Lord heard my prayers. And the Lord answered my prayers!"

In short order, the boy assimilated back into farm life which, for now, was largely untouched by the war being waged up north. Owlet, now eight, a bit too old but none too heavy, hitched a piggy back ride on the boy's back once again. With his chin hooked over his brother's shoulder, he chattered happily into his ear. When he grew up, he would move to Seoul with his older brothers. He would attend school in the city. He would come back home. He would become the head schoolteacher. Everyone would address him with the honorific *Seon saeng nim*.

The boy acknowledged the banter with abbreviated chuckles. A constant weight of worry distracted his attention. Refugees from the north were streaming through their village on their way to Pusan, bearing news of a massive military retreat. He agonized over what might have become of eldest brother and his young family trapped in a city now overrun by the North Korean communists. If the communists advanced much farther, the farm and the family could be in jeopardy. Guiltily, he could not help but regret the days, weeks, and months of missed education.

Sunday, on their way home from church, the family had

witnessed an ad hoc outdoor worship service of some hundred refugee families. Their minister stood on a hillside, one hand balancing an open Bible, the other raised to heaven. A lens of the minister's spectacles was cracked. He wore a western suit, coated brown with dust from necktie to trouser cuffs. His big toes protruded from the ripped leather uppers of his shoes which were tied with twine. The minister held forth with imposing presence and booming voice, undiminished by his reduced circumstances. His congregation of refugees sat on the grass clutching all the worldly goods each could carry, some in traditional dress, some in western dress, some clutching Bibles, some weeping openly, all with eager eyes and ears riveted to their leader. At the minister's feet sat his steely wife and flock of children. When his raised hand came down, it lighted upon the head of his young daughter whom the boy noticed appeared to be about his own age. Her slender arms surrounded a pair of chubby baby brothers upon her lap. The boy caught a snippet of the sermon as they trudged back to the farm: "Let us trust in the Lord. The Lord will provide."

"The Christians are fleeing," Young Nam whispered to second elder brother.

"Everyone is fleeing."

"Must we flee?" asked Owlet.

"Do not be afraid," Young Nam answered quickly, regretting that Owlet had overheard him. "We will be safe. We will stay on the farm."

"What else can we do?" said elder brother.

"Let us trust in the Lord. The Lord will provide," said Owlet, repeating the phrase he too had overheard.

"What else can we do?"

By the end of that summer, North Korean communists occupied the village. The remains of the pummeled South Korean army, the American military, the United Nations peacekeeping forces, and thousands of refugees were driven to the Pusan perimeter, a precariously small patch of land at the southern tip of the peninsula. Shops closed. Churches closed. North Korean soldiers in their uniforms the color of dung and urine prowled the streets with their rifles drawn. It was rumored that the wealthiest caste of villagers, merchants, and landowners were being rounded up and executed.

Soon a pair of North Korean soldiers came to the boy's home. What remained of the Kim family assembled for inspection: Mother, second elder brother, Young Nam, Owlet.

"Are there no other males in the household?" one of the North Koreans asked suspiciously.

"My husband is dead. I am a poor widow," replied the deaconess.

"I am the only man of the house," declared second elder brother, stepping forward.

"What about him?" asked a North Korean soldier, pointing to Young Nam.

"He is my young brother. He is only twelve years of age."

"He looks older. He looks sixteen," said the North Korean.

"He is unusually tall for his age. But he is twelve. He is an idiot. Of course that type of boy grows very fast," said second elder brother.

The boy bore the demotion in age and intelligence with stoic forbearance, staring ahead with a dull expression: anything to avoid the draft. He heard the blood pulse in his ear.

"And this one is the baby. A very sickly child, as you can plainly see," said second elder brother motioning toward Owlet.

"Are there no other males in this household?" repeated the North Korean.

"None."

The soldiers conferred with each other in private. One addressed second elder brother, "The People's Army is in need of food."

Mother brought two bags of rice and handed them to one of

the North Koreans. The soldiers conferred again. Then one soldier relieved his comrade of one of the bags of rice and returned it back to the deaconess with a magnanimous flourish.

"Take this to feed your children. You are a poor widow."

That evening, with chores finished and Owlet put to bed, the boy stole out of the house and walked alone, beyond the farm, beyond the stream, to the woods at the foot of the mountains. He was restless and agitated. It had been months since he picked up book or pencil. After less than an hour's trek, he came upon an odd sight. At the edge of the woods, in the center of a grassy clearing, was a rectangular patch of disturbed earth, clearly man-made. He crept closer. A layer of freshly dug earth covered the pit. He walked around its perimeter and knelt to sift a handful of moist dirt through his fingers. He thought he saw the dirt shift. His stomach lurched.

Suddenly, a hand thrust forth from the earth. The boy fell to the ground with a smothered cry. Another hand erupted from the dirt. The hands clawed frantically, unearthing a human face. The buried man struggled to a seated position and then to his hands and knees and crawled away from the pit. He spat dirt and vomited and then shuddered with dry heaves. The boy crouched in full view, frozen in shock.

At length, the man staggered to his feet. He looked back at the death pit and fell to his knees, groaning and coughing. The man raised himself with agonizing effort to his feet again. He was a giant, with angular features, and an eagle beak for a nose. Spikes of straw-colored hair protruded from his head as the dirt fell away in clods to his massive bare feet. His astonishing cerulean eyes, pale orbs in their sunken sockets, searched wildly all around but did not see the boy directly before him. He looked at the pit again. The monstrous, earth-crusted behemoth growled: *"Fuckin' gooks!"*

The boy crab-skuttled backwards on his palms and soles.

"Motherfucker!" shouted the blue-eyed Lazarus, lunging toward the sound, reaching over his shoulder for his phantom M-1. "Goddammit!"

The boy sprang to his feet and raised his hands over his head. In his best schoolhouse sing-song he announced, "I amma boh-yee."

"Jesus fucking Christ!" replied the earth-crusted monster, bent at the waist with his hands in defensive position, like a wrestler angling for a takedown.

Perhaps, in extremis, the boy had chosen the wrong phrase. He stammered, "I amma gull?"

"Oh, for fucking Christ's sake," grunted the Lazarus, the adrenaline draining from his voice. The man steadied himself with his hands on his knees and looked the boy over.

Although it was plain where this blue-eyed giant must hail from, the boy, in addition to seeking confirmation, wished to offer his respectful acknowledgement, and carefully pronounced the Korean word for "American": *Me gook?*"

"I already figured out you're a fuckin' gook, kid," said the American. "What the hell's your name?"

The boy elaborated with the Korean words for "American person": *Me gook sa ram?*"

"I know. You gook. You gook," he said, punctuating his affirmation with finger stabs at the boys chest. "But what the hell is your name? I know you got a name. Is it Kim? Lee? Kang?"

"Kim," the boy answered quickly, understanding now. "Kim!"

"Shoulda' known. All you fuckin' gooks are named Kim. You Kim. Me Doug," he grunted, pointing at his own chest.

"Dug-ras-suh Ma-kah-tuh," the boy pronounced with reverence.

Doug's pale blue eyes shone brighter from his smeared face. "Well, you ain't as dumb as you look."

The American giant suddenly started.

"Come on, Kim. We gotta' start diggin'."

They extracted another survivor from the pit, a South Korean army officer. The two soldiers and the boy now dug with their bare hands. It did not take long, as only a cursory layer of dirt had been thrown over the shallow grave. Most of the men in the pit had been shot dead. They dragged the corpses to the grass and laid them out side-by-side. Some of the prisoners-of-war had been burned and bound with barbed wire about the wrists, ankles, and faces. The handiwork of a godless people, Young Nam thought.

At the conclusion of the grueling task, ten dead, mostly Korean, along with one barely conscious American army officer had been unearthed. The large American slung the officer's arm over his shoulder exhorting, "Come on, Sir. You can do it." And the three survivors of mass execution hobbled behind the boy to the Kim family farm.

The following morning, the South Korean officer, who had only been grazed by the firing squad, stuffed his belly with rice and, against the urging of the deaconess to stay and recuperate, set off to rejoin his regiment. Second elder brother hitched the ox-drawn cart and set off to gather trusted farmers to help bury the dead.

The two Americans were hidden in the side wing of the house that had last been occupied by eldest brother and his wife. As it happened, the enlisted American, Doug, had taken two bullets, one in the arm and the other in the thigh. The deaconess was unable to extract the bullets, so she plastered over his entry wounds with a poultice of ground tree bark and bandaged them with lengths of hemp cloth.

The boy brought two sets of his late father's jackets and pants for the Americans to wear so his mother could wash their fatigues which were caked with mud, blood, and excrement. The boy remembered his father as a large man. But Doug emerged in the Korean clothing looking as if he had crammed himself into a child's suit. The sleeves ended at mid-forearm and the pants at mid-calf. The voluminous pants, with extra fabric meant to be gathered and secured with a belt, adequately covered his lower half, but the jacket would not close over the vast acreage of blond pelt on his chest.

At sunrise, the boy would carry Owlet on his back on a tour around the farm and, if no intruders were in sight, knock on the Americans' door. Despite his injuries, Doug arose every morning and performed calisthenics on the front porch, cursing liberally in pain. He shaved his face with a knife peering into the lid of a metal rice bowl and cleaned his teeth with his index finger. After his morning ritual, he received two bowls of rice porridge from the boy, which he carried into the chambers to eat and to feed his superior officer.

This superior, a lieutenant, bore no discernible injuries, yet was considerably more debilitated than Doug. After several days of isolation, the lieutenant finally emerged into the light of day. He was still dressed in the Korean suit, and a mangy beard covered his face. Of compact build, he reached up awkwardly to hang his arm about Doug's neck for support. Doug sat the lieutenant on the front porch. "Goddammit, if you don't smell like goddamn shit," said Doug. The officer stared a thousand yards ahead while Doug chattered at him in an artificially cheerful voice. After only a few minutes, the lieutenant rose abruptly and retreated back to the room. Doug said, "Sir! You come back out here, Sir!" Then heaving a great sigh, he followed the lieutenant inside.

With church closed down, the deaconess had established a Sunday devotion time of prayer and hymns. After the singing, Owlet and Young Nam would each recite a chapter of the Bible they had committed to memory. During this time, exhausted elder brother would sleep in the seated position, snoring steadily. One Sunday during the family service, mid-verse into "Amazing Grace", the chorus was unexpectedly interrupted. The Kims were startled to find Doug standing in the doorway. Slowly, the pale giant reached into his shirt and extracted from the thicket of chest hair a silver chain bearing a cross pendant. He pointed to it. He said, "Jesus Christ." For the first time, the name was not associated with an expletive. To the family's collective astonishment, tears rained from the American's sky blue eyes.

Only months after their invasion, the North Koreans evacuated, taking all the stores of food and supplies they could transport with them. The country folk surmised that the tide of the war had changed. News of the US Marines' landing at Inchon and the break out from the Pusan Perimeter trickled down to the boy's village. Young Nam debriefed Doug in a combination of Korean and English, and made him understand that the communists had cleared out of town. An increasing number of military aircraft exploded the country skies. Doug explained to the boy by pointing to the planes and then to his chest and to his insignia that the aircraft were American.

In quiescent moments, Young Nam explained to Owlet that the American fighter jets were welcome in their country, that the pilots were good brave men like Doug who had come to protect them. He repeated the mantra like a hypnotist. He made Owlet repeat his words. But the effort was in vain. When the swept wing monsters ripped the clouds asunder, their deafening mechanical screams electrocuted the little boy's nervous system. The rattled waif took to his sick bed. The family tended to him from sunup to sunset in shifts, praying for a few days' respite from the fighter jets so Owlet would regain his strength.

One evening after dinner, Doug had settled his lieutenant on the porch. Across the courtyard, on the opposite porch, the boy had settled Owlet, just recovered from another illness. The boy and Doug made eye contact with each other. Doug cracked a wan smile. He crossed the dusty courtyard.

"We're leaving soon," Doug said.

"I am sad," answered the boy. His English had improved with Doug there.

"I am too," Doug said. "You take care of your ma and them."

"Yes."

"And you tell her from me, *komapsumnida*," Doug said, bowing with his hands pressed together, his version of oriental formality.

"We are have to say *komapsumnida*," replied the boy.

That evening, there was an urgent rap on the family's door. The lieutenant, for no apparent reason, had died in the night. Second elder brother agreed to bury the lieutenant alongside the slain American and Korean soldiers in the clearing near the woods. Doug would proceed toward Inchon to rendezvous with his fellow Americans. The deaconess packed a generous satchel of provisions for the American.

As the family escorted their guest to the edge of the property, the boy noticed that the furrows in Doug's brow had smoothed and there was a spring in his bullet-riddled gimp. Though he had been another mouth to feed, though his presence had endangered the family, though he was an oversized, yellow-headed eyesore, each of them was sorry to see him go. They stopped at the edge of the farm and bowed to the soldier. Then, before they knew what was happening, Doug bent his great frame downward and hugged his hostess. She stood at attention, wordless, hands at her side, rigid as a tree. She remained in this position until Doug was out of sight. Then, she staggered backwards and fell flat on her back.

"He hugged me!"

Owlet clapped his hand over his mouth and shook with muffled laughter. The boy knelt at his mother's side and reassured her that this hugging was an American act of friendship and gratitude, that it was a customary gesture for their race. But the poor deaconess lay splayed on the ground, aghast, staring at the sky, repeating, "He hugged me!"

When they returned home, mother and sons balefully

evaluated the larder they had cleaned out to supply Doug. During their sudden retreat, the North Korean army had confiscated all the rice, tools, and valuables they could carry. The locust plague of needy refugees, the communist occupation which sucked up able-bodied men along with food and goods, the pounding of relentless air raids that afflicted the summer, resulted in an autumn of meager harvest. The *Chusok* harvest festival, the most important celebration of the year in the farming villages, was altogether forgotten. It would be a long hard winter.

With the invincible self-confidence of youth, the boy knew he would suffer but survive the food shortage. But this confidence was infiltrated by a dull grey fear for Owlet. Years ago, in bitter winter, the old shaman's snake elixir had rescued Owlet from the grip of death. The boy thought he would capture a rattlesnake and keep it alive till it was needed. But no rattlesnakes were to be found. The fish in the stream were sparse. It occurred to the boy that since his return home, he had not sighted a single white heron fishing in the stream. Even the wild animals were poisoned by the war's scorched earth.

For a year there was no word from eldest brother. The boy collected what news he could in his forays into the village. Seoul was being dredged into and out of enemy hands like flotsam and jetsam in a tide of blood. North Korea was being bombed and burned to an ash heap. The worst news of all: communist China had entered the war.

The boom came first, a pressure wave that shocked the eardrums. Then, out of nowhere, a sortie of fighter jets shrieked through the atmosphere. Young Nam stood gawking slack-jawed at the machines, sleek and violent, carving the sky, and vanishing over the horizon just as quickly as they had appeared. Then he shook his head clear and remembered Owlet.

Young Nam canvassed the house, the yard, and the rice paddies calling for his little brother. His mother and older brother joined the search. Owlet was in none of his usual hiding places. After a frantic hour, he threw his head back in frustration and spied Owlet, high in a crabapple tree, arms and legs twisted around a branch, cheek pressed against the bark, eyes sealed tight, pale as a cocoon. His calls elicited no response, not a flicker of an eyelid. Young Nam climbed the tree to disentangle his brother. It took every bit of the boy's considerable strength to prize Owlet's thin arms and legs from the tree limb he gripped as if in rigor mortis. During this operation, his mother and brother stood below with their arms stretched upward shouting exhortations. Finally, the boy peeled the child from the tree and handed him down to his older brother who carried him into the house. They settled Owlet, stiff and cold, on his bedding. His hands were curled and marks bruised his forearms. Owlet suddenly opened his enormous sunken eyes.

"We are so small on this earth," he whispered.

The child closed his eyes and stopped breathing.

In good times, Owlet's fragile existence was a painstakingly cultivated labor of love. In wartime, his loss was inevitable. The family had spent much of their lives battling to keep their beloved child alive. In the flash of a fighter sortie, the battle was over. Kim Young Nam released a breath he felt he had been holding unbearably for years. Tears drenched the humble deathbed.

After the burial, the two sons escorted their mother into town. Their lives had been so fraught with turmoil and want that Owlet had never been given a proper name nor enrolled in the official genealogical register. It was the family's most prized legacy, bearing in the stamps of preceding generations the testament to their *yangban* ancestry, conveying the privilege of advantageous propagation, regardless of their current poverty. In wartime, money had no value, so they paid the genealogist with a half-liter of rice.

At the bottom of the roster of sons born to the deaconess and her deceased husband – from eldest to youngest, Kim Young Ho, Kim Young Soo, Kim Young Min, Kim Young Nam, and

Kim Young Jae – the genealogist, using red ink reserved for the dead, documented the child's earthly existence for posterity, Kim Young Il. The genealogist sighed and quoted an ancient proverb.

When a tiger dies, he leaves a pelt; when a man dies, he leaves his name.

Owlet was gone. Doug was gone. Harvest was over. The food stores were low. His continued presence would only serve to sap the resources. Waking was a chore. Breathing was laborious. Life on the farm, with no prospect of education, no foreseeable future, no little brother to care for, had become a stultifying stalemate, unbearable and pointless. The boy decided to forge out on his own.

Armed with the English he had learned from Doug, and the skills he had learned from his summer job at Yongsan Garrison, he would seek employment with the United States military. His mother and his older brother knew they could not stop him. He donned his school uniform, though it was too tight and short, and set out for Inchon, scene of the first decisive American victory.

13

Lee Hana
South Korea
1950

It was a new year and a new war, but the sound of gunfire was nothing new. Lee Hana was working in the garden when she heard it: the mechanical rat-a-tat of high capacity killing. She dropped her basket and scrambled into the house. The bare rooms, devoid of furniture, offered nowhere to hide. She scuttled around in a tight circle, like cornered prey, then veered to the kitchen, where she wedged herself between the stove and a tall clay urn. Observing this, her mother-in-law stalked after her.

"What is wrong with you?" the old lady chided.

Hana neither saw nor heard. Eyes squeezed shut, ears covered with bloodless hands, soaked in cold sweat, she jerked in spasms.

The old lady leaned closer, gripped Hana's forearms, and shouted louder, "What is wrong?"

"Guns! Listen! They are shooting!"

The old lady straightened up and tilted her ear toward the window. She too heard the distant popping sound. She put her hands on her hips and turned to her daughter-in-law.

"It is a woodpecker."

"Guns! Shooting!"

"Guns? What do you know of guns? Are you a man? Are you in the army? Foolish girl! Have you never heard a woodpecker before?"

They found the corpse at sunset. The second daughter-in-law of the household, still childless, scolded by *Uhmonim* for crying, had taken to disappearing on long, solitary walks to indulge in her daily weeping. When she did not return for supper, the four able-minded sons fanned out over the farm and surrounding fields searching for her. They found her body at the edge of the farthest rice paddy, face down, bullet holes in her back.

Hana knew what death looked like. She did not gasp in horror like the others. She watched with glazed numbness as her brother-in-law threw himself over the corpse, rent his clothing, and wailed. It seemed he cared for his wife in death as he never had in life. The family buried their slain member quietly. There was no ceremony. There was no funeral procession. No effort was made to discover what had happened. It was wartime: people got shot.

North Korean Communists overran the village, but withdrew as quickly as they had come, confiscating all the food and supplies they could carry. As the invaders drove south, the peasants hunkered down on their farms. Their war news was delivered by the roar of jet planes overhead, which sent them scurrying into their thatched roof houses. The summer passed in the shadow of vague but omnipresent dread.

Autumn came. The men were in the paddies harvesting rice when soldiers stomped into the farmhouse without removing their boots. They shouted for the inhabitants to muster before them. The old lady hobbled out of the kitchen, flapping her arms.

"Bad men! Look at the mud you have brought into a poor old woman's house! What would your mother say?"

The younger soldiers, Korean boys after all, bowed in a succession of quick, obsequious head bobs, while shuffling backwards toward the door. But the officer among them stamped forward and spoke.

"I am Lieutenant Paik Kyung. Republic of Korea Army 1st Division. We are authorized to draft any able-bodied, unmarried male in this household. We need laborers. Every member of this household must present himself for inspection, along with his wife and children."

"All my sons are married!" cried *Uhmonim.*

"They must show themselves and be counted."

The four working sons were rousted from the rice paddies and assembled in the yard, still clutching their scythes, barefoot, pants rolled to their calves. Four daughters-in-law and their children assembled behind them. The wives trembled. The children bawled.

Satisfied that all the able-bodied men were married, the ROK soldiers turned to depart. And then the fifth son wandered into the gate.

"Is this your son?" asked the lieutenant.

"Yes, but you cannot take him. He is married."

"Where is his wife?" asked the lieutenant.

The old lady pulled Hana forward by the elbow and said, "This is his wife. Daughter, speak up! Tell them he is your husband!"

Hana, shaking violently, managed to mouth, "He is my husband."

"Then one man is not married."

"I did not lie to you. All my sons are married. But one wife is...is not here."

Uhmonim's second son, unable to produce a wife or children, was issued an M-1 rifle on the spot, and marched off the farm, still barefoot.

"He might come back alive," said the old lady to her youngest son. "But you would not have stood a chance. It is a good thing I was wise enough to get you a wife."

A man was spared from a bloody civil war because of Hana. Certainly, that man caused his family nothing but sorrow and troubles. He was a beloved son nonetheless.

Sure enough, the sorrow and troubles arose in due course. The youngest son wandered off the farm. As the sons saddled up to hunt down their errant youngest brother, one said to the other, "It should have been Hana who got shot."

"Why? Poor girl suffers enough."

"Because the army would have taken *him*. Think how convenient that would have been for us."

But the old lady loved her crazy son, perhaps more blindly, more fiercely than she loved her capable sons. That was enough to make Lee Hana feel her worth.

14

Kim Young Nam
South Korea
1950 to 1953

Somewhere outside Inchon, Kim Young Nam encountered the signal company of the United States Army 24th Infantry Division, engaged in a mobile operation. Having hemorrhaged troops and support personnel up and down the peninsula, the US Army was desperate for manpower. The boy presented a civilized appearance in his school suit, and intelligence lit his handsome square visage. Even more compelling was the modicum of English he could speak. He was hired and set to work immediately. His billet was to change flat tires along with whatever grunt work was called for. It was the summer of 1951. Kim Young Nam was sixteen.

A farm boy is no stranger to hard work, a child laborer no stranger to deprivation. But an employee of the US Army in wartime will work harder, endure more, and sleep less than he imagined physically possible. His compensation included a head-to-toe baptism with DDT, two to three meals a day, a spot to sleep in (be it tent, truck, bunker, or trench), and one thousand won per month (the equivalent of twenty-five American cents).

The infantry advanced laboriously on foot, while the drivers, officers, and injured humped along in the half-crippled, jerry-rigged, rust and bullet hole riddled fleet. The regiment was constantly on the move. Movement meant flat tires. Flat tires meant the boy, wielding tire, jack, and iron, hustled on the double. Before he tightened the last lug and choked on the cloud of exhaust spewing from the tail pipe of the repaired vehicle as it sped off to rejoin its convoy, the next truck or jeep would require attention. In this grueling manner, the boy accompanied his regiment to the front lines near the 38th parallel, where the main line of resistance had been drawn in blood.

There was no time to contemplate the spectacle of entire villages reduced to rubble, of decomposing corpses of soldiers in their foxholes, of white-clad civilians gunned down in ditches, of orphaned children wailing over the bodies of their slain parents, of land and flesh scorched by napalm. To stop and shed a tear was a luxury he could not afford. Here was a jeep with a flat. There was a truck stuck in mud. Here was a tent to pitch. There was a latrine to dig. Always his sergeant sounded off like machine gun fire: *Get the lead out! Get them knees up! Look alive!*

During the march north, a radio man strayed off the road and triggered a landmine. Chunks of seared flesh showered the vicinity like bloody hail. Instantly, a small cadre of men surrounded the injured soldier. One soldier removed the wounded man's weapons and equipment shouting, "The radio! Secure the radio!" Another stashed the radio with his own gear. One installed a field tourniquet around the gushing thigh. Another radioed the medical battalion. One held the shocked silent victim's hand saying, "Hang in there, man. You're good, you're good."

Two corpsmen carrying a litter leaped from the moving ambulance. They started a blood transfusion and whisked the patient off with practiced efficiency. Then the soldiers checked and double-checked that the fallen soldier's radio had been properly secured. The entire episode was over before the boy could release the breath he was holding.

The other ground pounders in the area, having ascertained that the situation was under control, had trudged on with battle-hardened pragmatism. The soldiers involved in the rescue fell back into their ranks without a hint of drama, as if they had only stopped to tighten their boot lace. As he trudged along, the tourniquet man picked morsels of flesh off his field jacket and flung them aside noting, "Got some barbecue on me."

Despite its intimate and constant presence in his newfound circumstances, death was not a variable that the boy figured into the formula of his own life. He simply never contemplated the possibility or the probability of himself becoming another statistic. To learn English and to earn money were the dual goals to which he applied himself with youthful vigor and faith in his own survival.

While his hands worked, his mind laid plans for his future. By the time UN forces reached the Yalu River bordering Manchuria, the war would be won, the country reunited. At the current rate of progress, it would take six months to a year at most, he estimated. By then he would have enough money to go back to school. He would resign his position and return to Seoul to find his eldest brother. On the way, he might visit Pyongyang. He had heard tell that Pyongyang boasted the most beautiful scenery in Korea… and not just the mountains. What was the saying? The strong men are in Seoul, but the pretty women are in Pyongyang. That was it. But what if he should arrive to find the city ravaged? Doubtless it would be. On second thought, perhaps it would be best to return to Seoul without delay and resume his academic career.

The 24th was moved into reserve south of the frontlines. They encamped in a narrow valley formed within a perimeter of ridges in a complex of bunkers left behind by the combatants who had preceded them. The men immediately established round-the-clock patrols, reinforced the bunkers, and dug trenches. Triple rows of barbed wire were strung out and festooned with empty c-ration cans filled with rocks as an early warning system. Red panels were propped up on the hillside to ward off friendly fire. The command post and mess tents were pitched and reinforced with two-by-four frames. The weapons and equipment were repaired and maintained. Most importantly, the mobile kitchen, fitted in a two-and-a-half-ton truck, was fired up for hot grub. They settled into a routine, not a comfortable routine, but a routine, and looked forward to the forthcoming hot meals.

On a sultry afternoon, the sickly sweet odor of ozone suffused a stiffening breeze. Young Nam sensed it and knew what was coming. A white hot gash tore the sky, and thunder rattled the earth. The rains came. Instinctively, the boy turned a grateful face to the sky to feel the first drops from the storm that would flood the farmers' thirsty rice paddies. He was quickly reminded of where his new loyalties belonged. As the storm consolidated over them, dumping its driving downpour, the exasperated soldiers cursed as they unfurled and donned their ponchos.

"Is this a monsoon?" the sergeant shouted through the watery din to Young Nam, whose rudimentary English comprehension had already come to his attention.

"Yes! Time monsoon come," the boy answered.

"Goddammit!"

The sergeant stalked about shouting orders, and he and his men busted their guts to secure their materiel. The tents were broken down and stowed. Oxen-drawn carts were harnessed to tow ammunition, food, and equipment up the rugged hills into positions of elevated redoubt. Korean bearers carried A-frames on their backs and crates on their heads. After more than a year of relentless combat up and down the rugged terrain, the American soldiers easily scaled the ridges on their fortified mountain legs bearing their radios, batteries, and portable generators. Soon, the bunkers washed away, dragging along tangles of barbed wire. The dirt road they had traveled over to reach the encampment flooded into a mudslide of boot-topping sludge. Trucks and heavy equipment mired in sucking slop.

At night the men slept in and on top of trucks and tanks covering themselves with ponchos and tarps. The less fortunate who slept in shallow trenches dug into the hillside were soon jolted awake by rising water filling their nostrils. There was no escape from it; everyone was soaked.

One of the radio operators ascertained that an offensive was taking place in the deluge in the territory their division had last occupied prior to being pulled into reserve. "Them poor bastards," the men grunted. They knew from prior experience that the combatants would be carrying ten extra pounds of water weight with every grueling step, that foxholes and trenches would be bogged with muddy water, that radios would short circuit and guns would crap out. Before all communications drowned out, though, they understood that the line was holding and even advancing north toward Pyongyang, inch by sodden inch. This would afford their division time to dewater and regroup when the monsoon passed.

When the monsoon was over, soldiers on patrol discovered a farmhouse nestled in the valley on the far side of the hill behind which they had retrenched. They took the platoon's sergeant to see it. The sergeant brought the boy along in case an interpreter was needed.

A bamboo fence in good repair surrounded the house. Stepping stones led from the gate to the front door and circled the perimeter of the house. On the wooden porch, clay urns were aligned outside the door. The doors and windows, constructed of paper over wooden grid, were shut tight. The roof was thatched with yellow grass. The house was still.

One of the men asked the sergeant, "We're down far enough from the chinks, right? Why don't we light it on fire so as we can dry our shit up?"

"Yeah right, Einstein," the sergeant replied drily.

"I'm serious as hell. We're going be sent back up for the next one, ain't we? Only one reason we're in reserve now, ain't it? All our shit is waterlogged. My gun don't shoot no more. We're dead. And if we're dead, whatever gooks live here is good as dead. Look at it. It's a matchbox. It'll burn real good."

Upon reflection, the sergeant said, "Check it first. We don't want any crispers."

Two rookie privates, along with Young Nam, were sent to evacuate the house. The boy stood outside and shouted a greeting. He circled the house and shouted into each window. There was no answer. He returned to the front of the house and reported his findings.

Then one of the privates kicked the door and his boot went through the paper. The sergeant shouted, "Slide it, bonehead!" The privates charged inside, rifles drawn, yelling, "Come out with your hands on your head, and you won't get hurt." The sergeant rolled his eyes. After a few minutes, the flushed, panting recruits emerged and reported the house empty.

"Do it," ordered the sergeant.

Presently, the farm house was up in flame. The fence was pulled up and added to the bonfire. The men surrounded the conflagration, spread out their olive drab ponchos, and laid out their disassembled radio equipment on top to dry. When a reassembled radio crackled back to life, there was shout of exultation. They dried and cleaned their rifles and light machine guns. When their work was done, and the fire still crackled and popped, one of the men broke into "Kumbaya." He was quickly drowned out by "napalm sticks to kids" and a medley of lewd jodies.

The boy observed the burning from a distance. His mind's eye visualized his family home: his father painstakingly thatching the roof with dried grass, his mother laboriously gluing layer upon layer of paper to the floor with rice paste and polishing it to a glossy golden sheen. Generations of backbreaking labor could be devoted to building and maintaining a home. Yet it only took a whim to raze it to the ground. Any regret the boy may have suffered on behalf of the now homeless farmers passed quickly. He had only to recall the teenage boys rousted from just such farmhouses by the KATUSAs, Korean Augmentation to the United States Army, who summarily thrust upon them the rifle and bandoleer salvaged from the last batch of freshly killed Korean youth, and issued on the job training as they marched. These peasants were lucky they were not home.

When only ashes remained of the humble farmhouse, a fine drizzle began to fall. "Good timing," commented the sergeant as he stalked over the smoldering heap and kicked the ashes. He stopped and peered curiously into the cinders. He retrieved a tiny white object, which he examined closely between his thumb and forefinger. "What the hell?" Then he found another and another. As he continued to collect the little white shards, he grew increasingly agitated.

"What is it, Sarge?" asked one of the men.

The sergeant did not answer but summoned the new privates who had cleared the house. He shouted in their faces, "You dumb shits! Did I or did I not tell you to clear out the house?"

"Yes, Sarge," they answered.

"And what happens if you idiots fail to follow orders?"

"But, Sarge, we did what you said," they stammered.

"Answer the question! What happens if you fail to follow orders?"

"Someone could die?"

"No! Not *someone*. You! Me! All of us! One lazy bastard makes a mistake and we all fucking die. Training is over. This is reality. Look what you couple o' retards left in there!"

He opened his hand to display a small pile of what appeared to be tiny white pebbles. The recruits studied them and then looked at each other blankly.

"They're baby teeth, brittle dicks! You fucking roasted a baby!"

The privates recoiled. They were not yet inured to war and still possessed the capacity to experience horror. For the veteran sergeant, though, incompetence was the only horror of concern on this occasion.

"If we have to pay off a gook for this, it's coming out of your pocket," the sergeant threatened, continuing a profane tirade that peeled the young men's faces back like a shock wave.

The boy hurried forward and stood behind the privates waving his hands and shaking his head saying, "Sarge! No baby. No baby."

"What is it?" snapped the sergeant.

The boy explained with the aid of exaggerated pantomime, "Baby tooth. Baby grow. Little boy. Little girl. Baby tooth fall out. We happy. Mean baby grow big. Throw baby tooth on roof. Make good luck. Again baby tooth fall out. Again throw on roof. Good luck. Make good luck throw baby tooth on roof."

"Didn't work for them," snorted one of the privates, jerking his head toward the black cinder heap.

The other private laughed and said, "You crazy gooks need the tooth fairy."

The sergeant turned to the men and, because his fury had a hang time and because he was irked by his nonsensical mistake, shouted, "You got lucky this time! But remember everything I said! It still goes!"

The sergeant tossed the teeth over his shoulder into the ashes and stalked off. The boy approached and squatted on his haunches peering at the tiny ivories. How merrily Owlet had clapped and danced a silly jig when his baby teeth landed on the roof, a moment, as it turned out, which would prove to be one of the highlights of his brief life. He envisioned the family collection of baby teeth still embedded in his mother's grass roof, tokens of an innocent age, white and shiny. Adult teeth were yellow and ugly and throbbed with pain, like unwelcome harbingers of the adulthood to come. The boy gritted his bad teeth and returned to his work. All hands were needed for flood recovery.

Around this time, a certain Corporal Jack Howard was integrated into the unit following the dissolution of the army's all-black battalions. He was transported to his new unit atop a jumble of crates in an open three-quarter ton trailer hitched to a supply truck. Several lower ranking white soldiers rode the crates with him, one reporting straight from basic training, two discharged from a field hospital. In the cab of the truck rode several more senior veterans, white, of Corporal Howard's rank. The men dismounted and regrouped. The white men clustered together, reflexively segregating themselves from the quiet tall black man.

The corporal took stock of his surroundings. A reputation for poor combat performance by the all-black units had preceded him and cast a pall over his arrival. Young Nam had been instructed to meet a black-skinned soldier and to escort him to the sergeant. He knew this responsibility was not an honor bestowed upon himself, rather a degradation for the black American soldier, to be greeted and led by a native boy. With ramrod spine and forward gaze, the corporal steeled himself against the undermined foundation upon which he trod. He strode the gauntlet of hostile eyes and followed the Korean boy into command post.

The sergeant examined the corporal head to toe. He lit a cigarette and squinted at the black man through the puffs of smoke. "You the only one we got. You aware of that?" he asked.

"I am now, First Sergeant," Corporal Howard replied with rigid formality.

"How will that be for you? All alone?"

"I'm a soldier in the United States Army. I better not be all alone."

"Yeah, you're right, you're right. Well said. Fair enough, fair enough."

The sergeant spat and cocked his head to one side. He asked, "Say, Howard, have you heard the saying 'negroes won't fight'? Have you heard that one?"

"No," Howard replied quickly, although, of course, he must have. Everyone was saying it.

"Well? Is it true what they say?"

"I can only speak for myself. I fight."

"Uh huh. That's good. That's good," nodded the sergeant. He glanced at Kim Young Nam who stood at attention near the tent opening with the same impassive stoicism of the black man before him.

"Ahem. Say, have you heard the saying, 'Koreans are the niggers of the orient'? You heard that one?" the sergeant prodded.

"I have," Howard answered with unflappable blandness.

"So what the hell does it mean?"

"I'm a soldier. Not a sociologist," he replied.

"Fair enough. Fair enough. You're a soldier. Uh huh. So what can you do, soldier?"

Here, Corporal Howard grew animated despite himself. He said, "I am a communications specialist. I'm good. I know Morse Code, encryption, decoding, field telephones, FM gear, SCR..."

"We need a wireman," the sergeant interrupted.

Corporal Howard blinked. He cleared his throat and spoke carefully, "With all due respect, First Sergeant, I started out a wireman as a private."

"Good! Then you have experience. 'Cause we need a wireman. See?"

"I see."

"What. You got a problem with that?"

After a pause and a heavy breath, the corporal answered steadily, "I'll do what is needed."

Corporal Howard turned away to exit the tent. The sergeant called, "Hey, Howard!"

"Sergeant?" he said, his back still to the sergeant.

"Just do it for a little while. Show the guys you're okay. Trust me. You'll make out better this way in the end. Get it?"

"Got it," the corporal answered and continued toward the exit. He paused at the tent opening, turned, and paced back to the sergeant. He extended a broad hand.

"Thank you, Sarge," Howard said.

The sergeant stubbed out his smoke and stood to shake Howard's hand. "Welcome."

Corporal Howard went to work. The task most loathed by the signal company fell to him: testing the lines of communication to battalion headquarters on the hour. If a fault was found, Howard, assisted by two privates, a Korean bearer carrying a spool of wire on his back, and, if available, the boy, who was now regarded as the enlisted rank's company interpreter, traced miles of wire till the break was found and repaired. The protocol called for a wire crew from both ends of the line to search and repair till they met somewhere in the middle.

On the first of Howard's forays, his wire crew met their counterparts from headquarters well over a mile beyond the midpoint. The second outing, they covered two extra miles. On the third, they had humped it many miles past the middle, detecting no trace of the detail from headquarters. A steep ridge loomed before the weary men, one of whom suggested they turn around and return to camp. The other crew must be just over the hill, and if they did not turn around, they would miss hot chow.

"We will finish this," pronounced the corporal and began the climb. The men cursed under their breaths, "Just because *you* have something to prove." But they followed him up the hill and traced the wire all the way to headquarters. There, at the bitter end of the line, Howard discovered there had been no wire fault at all, but an open circuit at the command post switchboard.

The trek back to camp in the threatening darkness was grim with disgruntled underlings and their grumbling bellies. Corporal

Howard lifted the wire spool from the old Korean and carried the burden on his own broad back, trudging up the rear in silence.

At the edge of the encampment, in a radio bunker constructed of a triple layer of stacked sand bags and a corrugated tin roof, radio operators were stationed round the clock to receive and send messages. Inside the communications bunker, a decoding machine and a lineup of radio transceivers were set up on wooden spools, wired together, and hooked up to a common portable generator. Outside, stood an auxiliary foot cranked generator. When a Korean laborer mounted its tripod and peddled like mad, a spectacle termed, "riding the donkey," the men gathered around and howled with laughter.

No one was laughing the day communications with forward patrols crackled off. As the radiomen cursed and gnashed their teeth, Corporal Howard sat in a small corner of one spool and set to work on a tin can.

One of the men asked another, "Does that boy know what he's doing?"

"Ask him. He's sitting right next to you."

"Hey, Howard. Know what you're doing?"

The corporal ignored the question and focused on his project. When he was finished, he secured his tin can in his field jacket pocket and loops of wire over his shoulder. Using a climbing harness fashioned from a canvas strap, he hoisted his great frame to the top of the tallest pine tree, letting out wire as he went. At the top, he set to work installing his homemade device.

One of the soldiers pointed to the treetop and shouted, "Hey, guys. Look! The jig is up!"

Corporal Howard studiously ignored the guffaws. He completed his installation and shimmied down the tree, securing wire to the trunk as he descended. He connected the wire to the radio rig and began troubleshooting. This took some time and was less entertaining than watching the big black man climb the tree. Some of the men, bored, began to wander off, shaking their heads as they went.

"It works!" thundered Corporal Howard.

The men hastened back and swarmed the equipment.

"We have an antenna! It's not just about the range, either. It's directional!"

Soon there was a clamor of boys with toys. "Let me try," said one. "It's my turn," shoved another.

"Do you read me? We got us a tin can antenna the Negro Howard made! How do you read me? Over."

A response crackled in from over the ridge, a hard day's hike away, "Read you loud and clear. Five-by-five. Read you five-by-five."

This marked Corporal Howard's last day as a wireman with the 24th.

The division mobilized for what would prove to be their final counteroffensive on the front lines. The men and their machines advanced north over rugged inland terrain toward Pyongyang, flanked on each side by divisions of the ROK South Korean army. The soldierly progress of the division's advance belied a pervasive apathy for yet another engagement. Combat veterans who had fought on the frontlines since the beginning had begun to rotate out of theater. The most experienced of men, battle-hardened warriors, had ridden a grisly seesaw up and down the peninsula, demoralizing retreat upon retreat, dehumanizing advance upon advance. Now, with an exit in their crosshairs, they wanted nothing more than to hear the sound of their name on that rotation roll call. The replacements fresh from boot camp read the story on the veterans' grim, gaunt faces. Nobody wanted to be the last man killed.

On the night they engaged the enemy, Young Nam accompanied his sergeant and Corporal Howard to the front to serve as an interpreter should communications with the flanking ROK divisions prove necessary. Night had fallen before their business was concluded. They hastily downed a can of c-rations and found refuge in slit trenches where the infantrymen had dug in for a few miserable hours of shut-eye. Like any exhausted teenager, the boy fell asleep instantly.

Sometime after midnight, the unnatural strains of a bugle wafted through the black of night. The boy was shocked awake by shouts: "The chinks! The chinks!" He scrambled out of the trench and blinked. In the moonless night, nothing was visible but the shadows of armed men flitting in every direction. In the distance, gunfire popped. Soon red and green tracers arced and crisscrossed overhead like a grotesquely resplendent fireworks display. Someone revved a nearby jeep shining a weak halo from its one working headlight.

Flares shot over the sky, illuminating a scene of controlled chaos. Men emerged from foxholes and charged up the ridge with their M-1s drawn. Other men dove for cover into the recently emptied holes. Jeeps and trucks gunned and rumbled. The gunfire was growing louder, denser, closer.

The boy sucked in a breath, eyeballs peeled, waiting for the next flare to light up the vicinity. Unarmed and disoriented, his best defense would be to locate the sergeant or corporal and attach himself to him. Floodlights flashed on, directed upward to reflect off the cloud ceiling, casting a sickly sepia light over the action. On the crest of the hill, a pair of soldiers shot rounds from a Browning automatic rifle on a bipod. A radio operator crouched nearby shouting into his mouthpiece. Korean litter bearers and army corpsmen sprinted forward into the combat zone. There was no sign of the sergeant or corporal.

Presently, white phosphorus blazed through sky like a murderous comet. The artillery unit had engaged in battle. Howitzers and heavy mortar pounded enemy positions over the hill. The explosions shook the earth. He smelled the burning. A terrible reality shot through him like a bullet: beneath the canopy of phantasmagorical sound and light, men were killing and being killed. And he could be one of them. He hurtled himself to the ground, low-crawled in a direction he judged to be away from the action, tumbled into a ditch, and covered the back of his head with his hands.

What if he should die in this ditch? Who would take care of Owlet? Oh, yes. Owlet was dead. He remembered this with a rush of relief and guilt. Then the vision of his mother stooped over Owlet's slight body, tears gushing like a waterfall over her high cheekbones soaking the little boy's bed clothes, came to him. What if he should die in this ditch? He was loath to inflict added pain on such a longsuffering and decent woman. In this desperate moment, he resorted to prayer.

Suddenly, two soldiers crashed his trench. One of the men was limp, his arm slung around the neck of the other, who exhorted, "Hang on, man. Stay with me." A flare shot up and lit the pair. The unconscious soldier was bathed in the blood of the man who supported him. The active soldier was oblivious to the appalling sight he presented. His helmet had been ripped through by shrapnel and a flap of his scalp had torn away, hanging over one eye like a beret of carved steak. The torso of his jacket was slick with blood, which continued to stream from his head. Heedless of his grisly condition, he asked the boy, "What's up, kid?" The boy stared agape, speechless. "Better get the hell outa' here, my friend." With that, the half-scalped soldier foisted his unconscious friend out of the ditch and carried him off.

Young Nam ventured to peer above grade and scan his surroundings. A semblance of organization appeared to have replaced the initial pandemonium. Bearers and corpsmen jogged to the rear with wounded on their litters. A fresh platoon of infantrymen advanced forward through the retreating wounded. Over the ridge, columns of fire and smoke rose from the valley and the opposite hillside.

Then he spied a tall black man. The man gimped along, dragging behind a mangled leg which was pointing in a cockamamie direction. He was hugging something precious to his chest, as a mother might clutch her baby in a lightning storm. The light of the next flare revealed this precious bundle to be his World War II radio, weighing nearly sixty pounds. This had to be Corporal Howard. The boy scampered from the trench and sprinted to the corporal, shouting with reckless abandon, "Corporal Howard! Corporal Howard!"

Just as the corporal looked up and recognized him, the boy was seized by the upper arm and flung into the back of a speeding jeep. He narrowly avoided landing atop a wounded soldier who was doubled over clutching the guts spilling from his eviscerated abdomen. Cocooned in his own agony, the soldier was oblivious to the loading of additional live cargo.

"Get down, kid!" the driver shouted.

"What the hell'd you do that for?" an officer growled from the passenger seat.

"He's just a kid," said the driver.

"You fuckin' idiot!"

By the time they reached camp, the wounded soldier in the back of the jeep was dead. The boy, slick with the soldier's blood, volunteered to unload the body. He was surprised to discover himself strong enough all on his own to carry the dead weight of a full grown man over his shoulder.

In the morning, when the fighting was over, more dead would be collected from the battlefield. Bodies were transported to a rear area behind the communications bunker where they were encased in black rubber body bags and stacked into a truck bound for Seoul.

A small crowd of men gathered, searching for fallen comrades. The boy came too. His sergeant would not, could not, be among the dead. No: Sarge was much too mean to die. After confirming this fact for himself quickly, he would get right back to work. But one glimpse of the corpses, dismembered and disemboweled, caked in blood and dirt, already foul smelling, was enough to jettison the boy back to his work area. He would find out about Sarge when the time came.

The shortage of fighting men was such that the walking wounded were stitched up and sent back to the front with bandages still seeping. It was in this condition that Corporal Howard returned, limping, with dressings on his forehead. This time, he rode in the cab of the truck. The driver jogged around to open his door and help him dismount. Men gathered around to welcome him, patting his back, shaking his hand. The boy waited until the end of the day when Corporal Howard was finally alone to approach him.

"Corporal Howard," he called.

"Well, hello, young man. I saw you out there, but before I could get to you, you hitched a ride. Smart move. Glad to see you made it back in one piece."

"Corporal Howard. Sarge?" asked the boy.

Howard drew a heavy breath and sighed. He shook his head. The boy understood.

"I am sorry," said the boy.

"Me too, Son. Me too," said Howard.

When the aftermath of the skirmish near Kumwha died down, a PFC Charles Smith sought out the Korean boy he had noticed could speak a little English and change a lot of tire, the same boy he had rescued from the shelling by heaving him into the back of his speeding jeep. Smith found him patching a tire on a three-quarter ton truck.

"How you makin' out there, kid?" Smith asked.

Young Nam recognized Smith at once and bowed several times.

"What's your name, kid?" Smith asked.

"Kim," the boy answered, bowing again.

"Could of seen that one coming," he laughed. "I'm Smith. Charles Smith. You can call me Chuck. So, kid, how is it you ended up with us? You an orphan? Ain't you got parents?"

"Father dead. Mother live farm with older brother. Home have small food. I work," the boy explained.

Smith sat on the running board, patted a spot beside him, lit a cigarette, and began, "Tell you what. When you get in the rear, a lot of the guys, officers mostly, grab themselves an orphan and ship it home to their wives. Sort of like a reverse care package. Women back home get a load of what their girlfriend got from the war, next thing you know, there's a run on Korean orphans. 'Course they prefer the little ones best, so you wouldn't stand a chance. Anyways, you ain't no orphan."

"No. I have mother." He felt a surge of pride saying the words. He might have bragged about her then, but he preferred to hear the American speak.

"Well, I been contemplating procuring one for my oldest sister when I get my rotation. Surprise her. Poor old sis is getting long in the tooth, and she ain't had any good luck in that area of life, if you get my drift. Christ. You can't believe the weeping that goes on. Believe it or not, I got a shitload of big sisters. I'm the baby of the family."

The boy started from a small revelation of his own and said, "I am! I'm the baby of the family."

"Now, ain't that a coincidence? We got us two babies here. Well, I always wanted to be a big brother. That was one thing I always wanted."

"I amma big brother," the boy blurted out.

"Now, wait a minute. You just said you was the baby of the family. Don't be going all inscrutable oriental on me."

"Ah! Young sister die. Young brother die. Another youngest brother die. *Now* I am 'baby of the family.'"

"Tough break. See that? Whenever I get to feeling sorry for myself, I just have to look around me to recognize my good fortune. I seen things here I never want to see again."

"I thank you save life," said the boy.

"Nah. That was nothing. That there what you saw was just a last spasm. War's winding down. I got a feeling we're going to call this one a draw and go on home."

"Not go on North Korea?" asked the boy. It was his first inkling that the reunification his countrymen had been yearning for, but were powerless to effect alone, might not be in the offing.

"Not if I had my way. I'm counting the days till rotation. I been here since just about the beginning. I been from way down in Pusan to way up where I could of pissed into the Yalu. I thought we won already. Then we fuckin' bugged out when the chinks swarmed us. We were asses and elbows way down south past Seoul. Now we made it back the way we come before. I bet I seen more of Korea than you. Mostly, I got no idea where the hell I am anymore."

"Korean give thanks America," said the boy. On the last word, his voice careened off course uncontrollably. Smith chuckled and patted his shoulder.

"That's okay, kid. You're becoming a man. I still remember when I went through that phase of life. Wasn't so long ago in reality. Seems like forever now. Funny thing is I wanted to kill myself. Now I'm in this shithole where I should want to die, all I want is to stay alive. At your age, I fantasized about death a lot. Even experimented with methods. Unsuccessfully, I might add. I had all the details of my own funeral worked out. Was it going to be some grand affair. All those females bawling their eyes out over my dead body. Ha ha! Bet you never think about stupid crap like that. I seen you working your ass off all the time. Kids like you, hard working good kids, make all this crap almost worthwhile. *Almost.*"

"Thank you."

"Kid," said Smith, gravely studying the boy's face, "Let me give you some very important advice."

"I welcome your word!" exclaimed the boy, leaning forward eagerly to receive the pearls of American wisdom.

"What you ought to do is put some mud on them pimples."

"Please?"

"On your face. It's covered with them big ugly pimples. Other than that, you'd be a real good looking kid. Just slap some mud on your face at night. Had the same problem myself. Kids at school called me pizza face. My mom was an Avon lady. Lady's makeup. She sold that crap to all the fancy ladies in town. Not that it did them a lick of good, mind you. She had this mud mask she gave me for zits. But you could just use some plentiful Korean goddamn monsoon mud. Makes 'em dry up. Understand what I'm sayin'?"

"Yes. I understand," replied the boy carefully.

How thoughtful this Mister Chuck was to concern himself at such a desperate time with a native country boy's facial blemishes. Only an American would exhibit such immense benevolence. Indeed, the boy had noticed his flaming facial eruptions in a jeep's side view mirrors with only a fleeting shadow of regret. He had been vaguely aware for some time that his body was changing. The pimples were of no consequence compared to other troubling developments, chiefly the insufferable itching of his crotch and armpits. Pain would have been preferable to the sheer torture of the itch which drove him to distraction. He would have excoriated his flesh with a ball of barbed wire given a chance. When he had finally snatched a private moment to inspect these regions, he discovered a new growth of black hair in which a riotous infestation of blood-engorged lice and mites were writhing.

At every rest camp, a delousing station would be established outside the tent showers. A sergeant stationed there brandishing a large flit can would bark at the assemblage, "Drop 'em! Peel it back and milk it down!" The exterminator would then drench the men's crotches with DDT. Some of them made a great show of rolling their eyes back and groaning in mock ecstasy as the poison drenched their private parts. The boy studiously avoided the delousing station with its largesse of American hose even more alarming than the great promontory of the American nose. But when his own infestation tortured his every waking and sleeping hour, he got in line behind the Americans and dropped his drawers with alacrity.

The following day, after chow time, Smith found the boy again and tossed him the GI's perennial favorite c-rations: canned peaches. Smith watched the boy suck it down and said, "Good, right? Now, don't eat too much all at once. You'll get the runs real bad. I know from firsthand experience. I won a whole stack of those in poker and ate them all in a sitting. Turns out, I only borrowed that meal. I had to keep my pants unzipped so I could make it to the latrine in time."

Young Nam could scarcely grasp his good fortune. As if the peaches were not gift enough, the American actually sought to converse again with a Korean laborer. Smith was a talker, as loquacious as Kim was reticent. Each gave the other something he wanted and needed. Smith waited till the boy licked the can clean and he had the full attention of the audience which made up for in rapt concentration what it lacked in number. He took out a well-worn piece of paper from his pocket and smoothed it on his lap. Cramped tally marks covered the paper.

"See this? I'm counting the days till rotation. I don't wanna' be the last man killed. You know what I mean?"

"Yes. I know what you mean," replied the boy carefully repeating the American's locution. "How Mister Chuck come Korea?"

"Well, kid, I'm glad you ask," began Smith, clearing his throat. He was gratified to note that the boy was moving his lips to imitate his speech and enunciated with extra care.

"I never heard of this place before in my entire life. First time I heard of Korea was at Fort Dix. Boot camp. That's where they train you to be a soldier. After we all got our heads shaved, this cracker DI lines us up – we're all starkers, dicks a-dangle, mind you – and says in his goddamn southern accent, 'All y'all are goin' to *Koooh*-rea.' I'm thinking to myself, 'what in the hell is a *Koooh*-rea?' I thought it sounded like some indigestion. Next thing I know, I'm on a military plane to Japan. Then we get shipped to Pusan. I bet you never been on a plane."

"No."

"Ever been on a ship?"

"No."

"You will, kid. Bide your time. You're going places. I can tell by the looks of you."

"A man, a medicine man, tell me thus long time past!"

"See? Great minds think alike. Anyways, like I was saying, the Pusan Perimeter was a bitch. The guys who'd been there since even before me, all they seen in Korea was two things: defeat and retreat. Never saw a sorrier, more depressed, bunch of guys in your life. It was not encouraging to the newcomer.

"One of the guys by the name of Joe tells me about the time he got separated from his platoon that gave themselves up. He was hiding in the woods and saw the whole thing that happened. The gooks – pardon my French – tied their hands behind their backs. Then they march down the line and bang, bang, bang shot them in the back of the head one after the other. Shot the whole platoon, including the officer who surrendered them, probably expecting to save their lives. This guy, Joe, who tells me this story says he vowed right then and there to fight to the death after seeing that shit. He kept a revolver with one bullet in his pocket to use on himself in case he was about to be captured. No way was he going to get executed like some kind of common criminal by a gook. Can you believe that?"

"Yes," the boy answered reluctantly, remembering the mass grave found near his home, the grave in which Doug had been buried alive.

"Why the hell do they do that?"

"I believe…evil…sin…all man can do."

"Horseshit!" said Smith.

"Mister Chuck first come Pusan," prompted the boy.

"Oh, right. Now where was I? Started off as a BAR man. That's what they make the new guys, on account of the freaking thing weighs as much as your mama. Try carrying that up and down these mountains. Plus, the enemy is on you like white on rice when you got the BAR. You may as well be painted with a damn bull's-eye. You can literally feel the bullets whizzing past your ears. It was a real bitch.

"We broke out of the Pusan Perimeter after the Marines landed at Inchon. Truth be told, I can't stand them. Them bastards are full of themselves. Your jarhead thinks the sun shines out his ass. If you got the best of everything from Uncle Sam, the best training, best weapons, best equipment, you'd do better than everyone else, wouldn't you? You could act like a goddamn superhero too if you got lavished with all the riches and shit. But I have to admit, things were in the crapper till the tide turned at Inchon.

"So we finally get our asses on the offensive, which I have to admit was actually an improvement to wallowing in defeat like a bunch of pussies in the nastiest rottenest stinkiest shithole you ever seen. Once I got my taste of fighting, I could see why we got ourselves so badly beat before that point. The commie gooks have a bunch of Russian T-34 tanks that roll right on through the line like you don't even exist. We had nothing could pierce them. So our commander gets all hot under the collar and decides to demonstrate we can beat the T-34. He jumps out of his hole and grabs a 2.36 bazooka and fires point blank at one. Fuckin' rocket bounces right off the side of the tank. The driver sees him and turns the damn tank and rolls right over him. You don't want to know what that looks like, all the guts and shit. Road kill, that's what it looks like.

"I tell you what. Them commies fight like hell. They don't care if they live or die. How they do it is they have the front guard comes at you with the rifles. Behind them in the rear they have goddamn spears and knives. Spears and knives, for Christ's sake. After you gun down the front gooks, the rear gooks run right on through the dead ones and pick up the dead guys' rifles and come straight at you, guns blazing. Sometimes they come riding freaking horses. So what you do is you shoot the horse first. That's a no-brainer.

"I got a good idea from the gooks, though. Next time I passed a dead soldier, I checked if his M-1 was any better than the World War II piece of shit I got issued. If it was, I swapped it. I remember to take the ammo since we kept on running out.

"Time we got to Chongju or Chonggodo or Chongchan or Chingchong, or wherever the hell, the shit hit the fan. Here's what happens. In the middle of the night, you hear a goddamn bugle. Then a bunch of commie chinks come swarming over the mountain like an exploded nest of fire ants. I'm not ashamed to say it. The sight of a million chinks coming at you with one purpose in mind, to kill you, is enough to make any man shit his pants. Every time a flare goes up, you see more of them crawling over the crest of the hill. They're covering the earth like a goddamn plague of Egypt. You shoot till your ammunition is all gone, which don't take long. You can see a bunch of them scattered dead all over the place. But more and more chinks just keep on coming and coming. There's a freaking endless supply of little killer chinks coming at you with their goddamn rice pots strapped to their backs just running right over the dead ones. When your ammo's gone, and you've thrown out your last grenade, all you can do is to dig into your foxhole. You just dig and pray, dig and pray.

I tell you what. Nobody expected China to shit on our parade. Not MacArthur. Not nobody. What the hell?"

The boy said, "Bunch of North Koreans fight in China during World War, help Commie in China. Now Commie help North Koreans."

"Ain't that a bitch. So later on, the Air Force would bomb them for us before we had to move in. Strafing was pretty helpful. Bombing was even better. But when they started using napalm it was the best thing since sliced bread far as I'm concerned. Napalm is a highly effective and excellent weapon, know what I'm saying? Of course you don't like to have to wade through all the black charred bodies with the red juice oozing out of them. Well, but you get used to it. It's them or us. The sight of them planes truly lift the spirit of the infantryman. Feels like the second coming of Christ, know what I mean?" asked Smith.

The death of his beloved baby brother welled like tears in the boy's consciousness. But he swallowed the hard lump in his throat and said, "I know what Mr. Chuck mean."

"Then we got the flamethrower. Each platoon got one. The flamethrower man shoots fire into every hole before we pass by. Sometimes we'd hear this blood curdling shriek from inside the hole. Even after all what I seen, that made me feel kind of sick to my stomach, to be honest. But it was necessary. You don't want them running out of their hole and shooting you in the back.

"Only one sound I hate more than the chink bugle. Three words: 'every man for himself.' Maybe that's four words. You hear them shout that when it's time to bug out. Means we been over-run by the goddamn horde of killer chinks. Them's the scariest and the loneliest words on earth.

"Tell you what. Felt like the rug got pulled out from under us when they sacked MacArthur. It was like finding out your dad got kicked out of the house and your mom takes up with some strange asshole you never seen before."

"Also Koreans understand this not. My country love MacArthur. We honor old man wisdom," said Young Nam.

"Well, I appreciate your appreciation. But anyways, this Ridgeway, he's the man. Stand or die. Know what I mean? That's how you win. Stand or die, he says. That's when we woke up and smelled the coffee. We realized we could push them chinks back all the way where they come from if we had a mind to. The question is: how much American blood do you want to spill? I hope to God there's some good reason for all this. All I know is, I'm outa' here soon. That's all I know."

"I hope Mister Chuck go home safe."

"That's mighty kind of you to say so. 'Cause I know you guys are stuck between a rock and a hard place."

Each visit, PFC Charles Smith made a point of bringing something for the boy. As winter was approaching, he brought a pair of woolen socks in a richly hued argyle pattern with reinforced toes and heels of double thickness. Smith's initials were lovingly embroidered in curlicued font on each cuff. Breathlessly, two hands outstretched, the boy accepted the gift.

"Like 'em? My ma made 'em."

"Mister Chuck mother wish her son wear such beautiful garment."

"She sent me a ton of socks."

"Mister Chuck name sewn here."

"I'd have to be a damn centipede to wear all the socks she makes. These are for you."

"Thank you!"

"No problem. Tell you what. Bunch of my buddies had a good old time at mail call laughing their asses off making fun of the care package my ma sent with my first batch of socks. At that time, it was hotter than hell. Then before you know it winter comes. First time one of the guys gets frostbite and loses a toe, wouldn't you know, the ones laughed hardest are at the front of the line with their grubby mitts out wanting a pair of ma's socks. Now she's got a knitting factory going with all the sisters and coffee klatch ladies needing to do something for us guys in Korea.

"All these guys, you talk to them, they're gonna' bitch about the winter. You get these blacks and Hispanics from the south ain't never seen a flake of snow, and they're scared shitless of Korean winter. Well, I know from winter. I'm from a place in America gets ten feet of snow. New York. Heard of New York?"

"New York!" said the boy with wide eyes. He had never heard of it.

"No, not New York City. You're not the only one thinks "New York" equals the city. It's a big state, New York. City's just a pimple on its butt. I'm from upstate. And upstate, we know from winter.

"But it still sucked pretty bad I have to admit. We come here in our summer uniforms and by the time winter came, we were still in our goddamn summer uniforms. Meantime, it's getting colder than a witch's tit. I was lucky I had my socks and long underwear from Ma. We made ourselves coats out of our summer sleeping bags by cutting out head holes and arm holes. They did manage to give us white ponchos for camouflage. Yeah, Uncle Sam really knows how to treat you good.

"One time at a rest camp, we come across some British uniforms and decide we're going to snag ourselves some warmer trousers. Talk about itchy! Them British wool pants are worse than a hairshirt. Thanks, but no thanks. Your Englishman is from a race of man which did not learn one thing from the American Revolution. You actually see them poor bastards marching close order drills in rest camp for Christ's sake. You can see how we defeated them back in 1776, know what I mean?"

"America defeat every enemy," said the boy, hopefully.

"Not them killer chinks. Too goddamn many of them. Like roaches. Can't get rid of them. Anyways, like I was saying, I ain't one of these pussies about winter. Tell you what I have a problem with. Your summers. Jesus, it's hotter than hell. The one and only time I was positive I was going to die in Korea was when we run out of water. We're up on a rock with no food and no water getting shot at so we can't get off and find stuff. I'd rather be in a lousy pizza oven. I don't know how long it was. Days. I swear to God, it gets to the point where I start to pray aloud for water. *For Christ's sake, send us some goddamn water*, I says. Then, I swear to God, right that moment, it rains. Believe that?"

Young Nam said, "God answer my prayer too sometime."

"You goddamn right he does."

"Sometimes not answer."

"Yeah, well. The guy's busy. Like I was saying, it only rains a bit, nothing but a pittle, but it was like goddamn manna from heaven. Except we got no way to collect it. So we spread out our blankets and collect the rain. We wring the water out and drink it all full of sweat and dirt and blood and woolly boogers. Most refreshing drink I ever drunk.

"Never forget my first Christmas here. We're dug into the bottom of a hill. Cook and his Koreans come with the kitchen truck and start making hot chow on the other side of the hill where it's safe. We're supposed to take turns eating in shifts of like ten, twelve guys. The guys that go first come back and tell us guys in the trench all about it: turkey with stuffing, mashed potato with gravy, cranberry sauce, and all kinds of tasty shit to eat. Fresh for a change, not canned. Well, don't we get all excited and start singing Christmas carols. Real quiet, though, because the enemy is in pissing distance. So there we are singing 'Deck the Halls' and crap and our mouths are watering like dogs waiting for our turn. But before my turn comes, wouldn't you know, the enemy sees the smoke from all the cooking activity and lets the artillery loose on our goddamn kitchen. They had to break it down and take cover. So I never got my turn."

The boy's brows gathered in a black storm over his glistening eyes, his face flushed red, and his lips pressed bloodlessly together. Smith, surprised, thumped the boy's back while he struggled to regain composure to no avail. Tears shot past his cheeks and spattered to the dirt. The boy sobbed, "Such...such sad story!"

Smith laughed and said, "Aw, shucks. Come on now, kid. It wasn't all *that* bad."

Their final conversation concerned a topic Kim Young Nam held most dear.

"Tell me, kid. What are you planning to do when the war is over? You can't work for us forever."

"I go school Seoul."

"Do that. That's the ticket. You should go to school. I am too. First, I'm getting my GED. That's high school. Then I'm doing college. It finally comes to me what I should do with my life in the hospital. It took a shot in the knee to get me to lay there with nothing to do but rub my two brain cells together and come up with the same plan you come up with on your own.

"It was real ironic how that happened. The worst injury that happened to me in combat was I fell off a cliff from real high up and got the wind knocked out of me. Scared the living b'jesus out of me. I thought I got shot to death. But after a while, I started to breathe again and I checked and didn't feel any blood. So I picked myself up, found my gun, and climbed back up and went right back to shooting. That was the worst thing happened to me in combat.

"So then after like six months or so, me and a few other guys get R&R in Japan. R&R stands for rest and recuperation. Except all of us call it I&I for intoxication and intercourse. Soon as we land in Yokohama, me and my buddy, this guy by the name of Joe, hook up with a Japanese lady who brings us to her house. There was this old geezer living with her who was real nice and polite to us. At first, we thought he was her father, but then we realized they slept in the same bed, so we reckoned he might of been her husband."

"Whole family sleep same room," explained the boy.

"Well, that's a bitch, ain't it? I was right the first time then. He was her father all right. She wasn't particularly attractive. Back home, I would have called her a two bagger. That means to do it with her you need to put one bag over her head and a second bag over your own head in case her bag falls off. Get it? Well, far as we were concerned at the time, she was plenty good looking. No bags necessary. Let's just put it this way. She taught me stuff I never done before. She made me a man so to speak. Girls back home, they don't let you do much. You're lucky to get to second base. You know, sucking face with some tongue if she's a real slut. So we were pretty grateful. We turned our pockets inside out into her little money pot, which was not that much, actually, but she didn't seem to mind.

"So then my buddy Joe decides he's in love with this lady and he wants to marry her. One night, he ties one on pretty good. He comes in on me and her and starts ranting and raving like a lunatic. We weren't supposed to have guns on us, but he snuck this revolver he kept on him to shoot himself if he ever got captured. So the crazy bastard pulls out his gun and says he's going to shoot my dick off. Only he's so goddamn drunk, he passes out in the act of pulling the trigger and only gets me in the knee.

"Tell you the truth, he did me a big favor. After that, I got pulled off the front and put in odd jobs, this and that, like kitchen duty. Then when the knee healed up good enough, they let me drive the officer's jeep. Pretty good gig. Except on infantry I was getting four points a month. Now I'm only getting three points. I'm okay with it. Six of one, half dozen of the other. At least now I'm out of shooting range most of the time. I'm almost up to thirty-six points. Thirty-six points equals the Big R. Means I get to rotate out of Korea.

"So anyways, after getting shot, I'm lying there on my hospital bed staring at the ceiling and it reminds me of something. Back home, when I was in high school, I just quit going to school for no particular reason. I lay in my bed with my thumb up my ass for days. I stared at this crack in the ceiling and fantasized about it opening up into a gigantic deep black hole that would suck me into it. Felt like a ten-ton weight was keeping me on that bed and I couldn't of gotten up for nothing or nobody.

"Weren't my sisters flying up my ass on their burning broomsticks? You haven't got sisters, so you can't imagine. They only made matters worse. Then they start bitching to my dad. Well, wouldn't you know, one day my old man just grabs me and stuffs me in the car and drives me over to where they have this army recruiting station set up. And the rest is history.

"It was like the same thing was happening in the army hospital. Only this time, I wasn't going there. So then it comes to me. I'm not making the same dumbass mistake twice. Damn if I'm not gonna' be the first one in my family to go to college. If I can survive this shithole, I can do anything. See, in my country we got the GI bill for soldiers. You can get money for college. When I get home, I'm going to take my fair share and go to school like I should of done in the first place."

"Mister Chuck be good student. Hardship in my country make thankful school."

"Damn right. I'm going to look into Syracuse University. Why not? Then I'm going to get me a good paying office job. I'm going to get me a pretty wife and a nice house with a picket fence, and a station wagon to cart all my offspring to church on Sundays. American dream, kid. American dream."

Smith smoothed his worn paper on his knee and performed his ritual counting of the tally marks. He returned the paper to his pocket and gave it a comforting pat. He took a deep breath and sighed, "I'm done. I'm ready to go home."

"I pray this wish come Mister Chuck."

"Why, thanks. I appreciate that. I sincerely do."

Finally one day, PFC Smith was on the roll call for the Big R. His injury-related job changes, and staff turnover resulting from the rotation policy, had diminished his circle of close army mates. But those who made rotation were minor celebrities, and a handful of men donated enough beer from their rations to render Smith plenty feted, splayed senseless, his helmet filled with thrown up beer beside his cot.

Smith felt wretched the following morning. Nevertheless, he made a special effort to bid his young Korean friend farewell. The troop transport truck screeched to a stop at the Korean laborer's encampment where the boy was slurping his bowl of breakfast rice gruel.

"Make it quick," shouted the driver as Smith jumped from the truck and approached the Young Nam.

"Kid, I'm leaving. They only give me one day's notice. Sorry about that. Here take this," he said handing him his talisman, the worn paper with thirty-six hard earned tally marks. "Turn it over. That's my mother's address on the back. That's how you can reach me. If you study real good, spiff up your English, I'll see about helping you get into Syracuse University."

"Thank you, Mister Chuck!"

"Listen. I want to send you something real special from America. Minute I get to Seoul, I'll wire Ma and have her send it to you so you don't have to wait. Plus, that way I'll know where to send it. You might of moved on by the time I make it back stateside. Tell me: what do you want more than anything from the good old U.S. of A.? Name it."

"Mister Chuck give me too much."

The truck driver leaned out the window and bellowed, "Come on, come on. I got a load of guys itching to get the hell outta' this shit hole!"

"One second," shouted Smith and turned to the boy. "Kid,

I wouldn't offer if I didn't want to. I *want* to give you something to remember me by because it will make my day, see? Make Mister Chuck happy. You name it. Anything you want. Anything at all."

"Please, Mister Chuck, if not too much, *Webster Dictionary?*"

Smith blinked twice and then laughed uproariously. "A dictionary? Not just any dictionary. A *Webster's Dictionary!* Wait till Ma hears this."

"Not cost too much?"

"Come on, man!" the driver shouted gunning the engine and pounding on his door with his open palm.

"Hold your horses! Christ!" said Smith and turned back to his young friend. "Kid, I ain't spent a dime here. Free food, free clothes, free car, free gas. I've been living like a king here. Ha ha! It's not too much."

"Thank you! *Komapsumnida!* Thank you!" exclaimed the boy with a bow, smiling broadly despite himself.

Smith thrust his hands deep into his pockets, looked at his boots, and kicked a pebble back and forth. The truck driver smacked his forehead, rolled his eyes, and groaned. Ignoring this display of exasperation, Smith confided to the boy, "Tell you what. I can't believe I'm saying this, but I hate to leave in a way. The fellas. You. I feel like I'm abandoning everyone."

"Mister Chuck good man leave great country of America. Mister Chuck fight long hard time in Korea. Good and right go home now. Time now take care Mother."

"You're a real good kid."

"Get in or I'm leaving your sorry ass behind," brayed the driver.

Smith said, "Listen. I want you should take real good care of yourself, little brother. You hear?"

"Yes, *Hyung.*"

Smith tousled the boy's hair then jogged to the back of the

truck and ducked inside. As the truck rumbled forward, the boy walked slowly into its cumulus of dust, waving one hand. The truck gained speed, and Smith leaned out the open back and gave the boy a smart two-fingered salute. The boy stopped walking, stood at attention, and returned the salute.

PFC Charles Smith was in the vanguard. Having suffered over ten thousand casualties, the 24th Division was pulled out of Korea and sent to Japan to rebuild. Without fanfare, without consecration, without hallowing, the 24th simply disappeared, one truckload at a time. The boy stayed on, reassigned to the 40th Division which took the place of its decimated predecessor, and continued to change tires for the US Army. The Armistice Agreement was signed in July of 1953.

Kim Young Nam weathered his adolescence performing hard labor on the front lines of his country's unresolved civil war. His body was sapped to the bone. Yet a fire still burned inside him. He knew that in his country, despite the bombs and the burning, the mutilation and the massacres, the terror and the heartbreak, on a morning the sun rose over a peaceful peninsula, the surviving scholars would crawl from their holes and begin teaching again. With this certitude, with his hard earned pay in his pocket, the young man, no longer a boy, headed for Seoul.

15

Lee Hana
South Korea
1953

At sunrise, a pair of women climbed a hillside dotted with scrubby pine trees. They shouldered A-frames upon which large woven baskets were strapped. Using handmade wooden pitch forks, they raked the soil, separated the wood from dust through the tines, and threw the twigs over their shoulders into their baskets. Then with bare hands, they scooped up the disturbed earth, sifted it through their fingers, plucked out the minutest shards of tinder, and added it to the load. They left the sparse growth of live seedlings, lifeblood of future generations, untouched. With care usually reserved for newborn infants, they cradled tiny saplings with one hand and scraped the dirt around them with the other. Moving methodically over the hillside, they left the earth around the trees swept as naked as paper flooring, not a cone or twig or even needle left behind. Firewood collection was laborious enough on the craggy mountainsides. But during the war, the bombing had scorched neighboring hillsides, driving peasants from miles around farther and farther in search of wood. To beat the traveling scavengers and collect every splinter that fell from the trees overnight, the women awoke before dawn and combed for newly fallen tinder until it was time to go home and cook breakfast.

One of the women observed to the other, "It is a good thing you were not the one who was shot. You are a hard worker. Like me."

"Sometimes...sometimes I wonder why I am alive," Hana replied.

"To work, of course! Why think so much? What good did it do our sister-in-law?"

Then a curious sight appeared over the horizon. A solitary bomber, silver and snub-nosed, flew north toward Pyongyang with surreal lassitude. Hana saw it first. She shrieked, "*Unni!*" In a flying leap, she shoved her sister-in-law to the ground, and threw herself on top of the shocked woman, A-frame and all. The plane buzzed on over the mountains like an immense metallic bumblebee.

The women separated, clothing torn, skin scratched, baskets spilled, and A-frames askew. Hana collapsed on the dirt clutching her heart, panting. Her sister-in-law sprang to a squatting position and hastened to repair the twisted A-frames and reload the scattered firewood while scolding her underling.

"What is wrong with you? You have undone all our hard work! Why are you so afraid all the time? When I am afraid, I control myself."

"I am sorry, *Unni.*"

"Never mind. It is not your fault. My husband does not beat me. I am not a frightened rabbit like you. It is my good luck that I can be stronger than you."

She had forgotten that Hana had arrived into the family in this damaged state and that her syndrome therefore had little to do with her husband or his fists. She went on.

"You are unlucky. That is all. And unlucky people keep having more and more bad luck till they die. Once you have bad luck, the bad luck multiplies itself. It is no fault of yours."

"Thank you, *Unni*," said Hana, and genuine gratitude warmed her heart.

"You are right to fear your husband. But do not fear the flying machines. They are harmless."

The ignorant farm woman could not know that a superpower beyond her ken was staging practice bomber runs for a nuclear strategy: to string Korea's throat at the Yalu River with a necklace of atom bombs. She could not know how right Hana was to be afraid. Neither woman knew of the battles being waged beyond their hillsides. They struggled on, surviving day by day, one twig at a time, in the valley of the shadow of death.

They only learned that the war was over when the second son returned home from the frontlines and told them it was so.

16

Kim Young Nam
Seoul
1954 to 1957

A young man strolled down the central corridor of the newly founded Seoul Bible College. He looked right and left into the open doorways for an empty classroom in which to study. Tucked behind his ear was a new ballpoint pen, under his left arm a stack of papers, in his right hand a book, which he lifted to his face to inhale as he walked.

During the war, the stench of gasoline, burnt rubber, overflowing latrine trenches, and putrid corpses had assailed his respiratory tract without a moment of respite. Now, the musty, woody scent of books summoned a delightful sensation of peace and possibility. With a ravenous urgency he devoured whatever books he could lay claim to, reading all day and deep into every night, till he fell asleep with an open volume covering his face.

He was lured from his walking reverie halfway down the hall by a resonant alto voice flooding the corridor. The young man stopped and lowered his book to listen to the familiar melody, a hymn he knew and loved. Periodically, the singing stopped and restarted a phrase or two back, like a tape reel rewound and replayed. The voice drew him to an empty room where he saw its mistress and knew who she must be. The singer was facing away from the doorway where he stood, toward an open window, but he instantly recognized that she must be the eldest daughter of the president of his college. On the small campus it was big news that Miss Kang Sun Hee was home on break from Ewha University. He had overheard some of the overblown gossip: that Miss Kang was preternaturally pale from being bathed in goat's milk as an infant, that she played the harmonica, that she could juggle five balls.

The young lady wore a simple rendition of the western fashion of the time, a white blouse with a Peter Pan collar, navy blue flared skirt, bobby socks, and saddle shoes. From her long hair wrestled into a thick black plait down her back and bound at the end with a navy ribbon, defiant waves and unruly sprigs sprang free. Her eyes were riveted to sheets of music propped against a stack of books on a desk. Her fingers played over a keyboard consisting of a plank of wood painted precisely with the ebony and ivory keys of a piano. When she hit the wrong note, discernible only to herself, she stopped singing, raised her hands above the plank, issued herself a reproachful *tsk tsk*, and, finding her spot, began again. Before the young man could tiptoe past, she suddenly wheeled around and pinned him with her eyes.

"Hello," she sang out.

"Hello."

He stood frozen in the doorway with nothing more to say.

"Can you play?" she asked, tilting her head to one side with a quizzical half-smile.

"No. You play piano very well."

"Ha ha! How can you possibly tell?" she demanded, lifting her keyboard in the air and flipping it back and forth for him to see that it was only a piece of wood. Of course, he had noticed straightaway that she did not have a real instrument, but he elected not to waste his breath on needless explanation which could only serve to dampen her triumph.

"You *sing* very well," he attempted.

"Humph. It is impossible to sing two parts. If you work very hard, you can make a chord by singing one note and whistling another," she said and whistle-sang a brief demonstration.

"I never heard such a thing before."

"Because it is a unique and absurd skill few trouble themselves to perfect. You can help me practice. I'll sing the melody while playing my splendid piano here and you sing the harmony, here, like this," she commanded, pointing out his intended part on her sheet of music.

"I do not know how," he demurred.

She huffed rather impatiently, "Then you must sing the melody. And I will sing the harmony. I know both parts. Ready?"

She hummed an introductory phrase while playing on her wooden board and nodded toward him at his cue to come in. What else could he do? He sang. He began with the croaking sound of desuetude which caused his accompanist's eyes to flash resentfully in his direction, but soon enough cleared his voice into a sonorously pleasing baritone. She came in with the harmony. Their voices met with ringing energy and youthful spirit. Despite instrumental accompaniment consisting only of a painted wooden board, they were in perfect tune.

But at the conclusion of their duet she declared, "You were flat."

"I am sorry."

"My father says you are his best student."

"I am honored," he said. (So she knew who he was!)

"Kim Young Nam, is it?"

"Yes." (She even knew his name!)

"So! Are you? Are you the smartest one here?" she asked.

"I could not say," he replied to be modest.

"Oh well. If my father says so, then it must be true," she sighed and shrugged as if vaguely disappointed.

He laughed politely for want of a ready reply.

"I must go type for my father soon. There is an enormous stack of his writing that builds up while I am away at university. So I must finish my piano practice now. Goodbye!" she said curtly and spun back to her sheet music and her painted plank to resume her practice.

Thus dismissed, the young man continued down the hall, more slowly this time, his ear turned toward the voice made all the more alluring for the discomfiting encounter.

Upon the signing of the Armistice Agreement, Kim had turned his resignation in to the 40th Division of the US Army and returned to Seoul. The city was like a smashed anthill, no sooner laid to waste, than teeming with workers rebuilding. In and around the dusty ruins, men gathered bricks and wood, women washed laundry in grey gutter water, and children peddled bits and pieces scavenged from the rubble. Kim had found his eldest brother's home, riddled with bullet holes but still standing. Of the million plus residents of Seoul, eldest brother numbered among less than ten percent who remained in the city throughout the war. A testament to the invincibility of life, he was now the father of two sons with a baby on the way. But the chaotic return of over a million refugees after the war strained resources to the limit. Kim had stayed at his eldest brother's house just long enough secure a job and a room.

Said job and room both were furnished by a doctor who, unburdened by any formal education, practiced his invented amalgam of western and eastern medicine from a makeshift clinic set up in his home. The doctor taught his apprentice to stitch wounds, set broken bones, concoct herbal remedies, and administer a form of acupuncture that required only the patient's hand. "So you do not have to touch their foul bodies," he explained.

Utilizing poorer patients for practice, the young apprentice had received instruction on the ancient art of acupuncture. The needles must be sterilized by running the tip over one's scalp thereby harnessing the disinfecting properties of static electricity. For stomach ailments, the thumbs must be plunged just above the thumbnail as deep as the needle could penetrate. If the patient did not scream in agony, the needle must be plunged deeper. The louder they screamed, the quicker they paid. For throat ailments, each fingertip must be punctured three times above and three times below the first crease. If he forgot which hand was which, he must stab both and remember to charge double.

The doctor's baseline revenue came from the prostitutes who populated the red light districts and alleyways outside the American military bases. A migraine cloud of garish perfume announced the arrival of such a patient before she tottered in on spiked heels, bedizened in a flimsy dress and noisily clicking beads, her face heavily plastered with makeup. These entertainers presented for treatment the occupational hazards of their industry: lacerations, broken noses, unwanted pregnancies, venereal disease. The young apprentice's scalp contracted into a cap of a thousand pin pricks whenever one of the painted ladies clattered through the door. He could scarcely suppress a shudder of shame and revulsion. That this should be the representation of Korean womanhood the Americans would know! It was unbearable. The good doctor, however, hustled from his office, elbowing his reluctant assistant aside, to greet the entertainers with a deep bow. He flattered them with compliments and pleased them with jokes. His accommodating reputation spread through the red lit streets. More and more came to avail themselves of his therapies, toting glossy patent leather purses stuffed with American dollars.

The young man proved to be an able practitioner of the makeshift healing arts. He bore himself with gravity beyond his years, and his phlegmatic manner in the face of any suppurating wound or virulent disease put patients at ease. The sick and suffering poured their hearts out to him. He was a lightning rod, conducting the violent discharge of misery into the ground. In this process, the patients usually diagnosed their own ailments and relieved the loneliness of their pain.

Soon the doctor had offered to put his promising apprentice through medical school and to elevate him to partner in his medical practice. A framed degree on the wall would legitimize the business. There was a crying need in the teeming city. Business would burgeon. Both would prosper.

Without hesitation, the young man had declined. He had his fill of dirty work and, in his view, medicine was no less dirty than changing the tire of a mud-splattered, gut-flecked military jeep on the front lines. No, he would work for the doctor only as long as necessary to put himself through school.

The war had changed everything. The country was razed and denuded. Society was in chaos. The caste system was scrambled. Now, it seemed, anything was possible. From the smoldering ashes the heartiest weeds made bold to climb for the sun. The young man passed his upper school entrance exams and put down his tuition in American dollars. But he was only one of a great exodus that would clog the city and overwhelm the educational system. Legions of country boys had migrated to Seoul seeking an education, hoping to improve the poor lot in life offered by subsistence farming.

Well into the high school education he had waited and worked for years to achieve, the young man's future had been abruptly uprooted. To hack the overgrowth of students down to a more cultivated and manageable crop, the government decreed that only students able to present documentation of their formal educational background would be eligible to continue in high school. The young man lacked any such papers. What little preparatory education he could claim had been snatched and pieced together in dribs and drabs, a patchwork of fleeting opportunities stolen from the farm work and from the war. He brought his case before his teachers who recommended him in the most glowing terms to the school leadership. The administrators, while sympathetic, could do nothing for him. It was a staggering blow.

On that day, the parade of patients who came to the doctor's office were treated by a stoic young man who heard their litany of complaints, lanced pustules, and sopped pus with his usual stolid patience and professionalism. No one, not even the doctor, had the slightest inkling that while the young man neatly and methodically stitched rent flesh together, his own innards were shredding with agitation; that while he absorbed confidences of deep dark sins concluding in burning urination, his mind was aflame over the disposition of his future.

There were no schools outside Seoul that could meet his needs. Even in Seoul, he had been earning the highest marks in his class. And it counted for nothing. How far would he need to backtrack to satisfy the government's requirement? He pictured himself with his knees crammed under a child's desk relearning addition and subtraction, reading and writing. It would not do. He felt himself growing old. The older he grew, the more he felt the passage of time, its inexorable acceleration, leaving him nowhere.

After work, alone in his room, he sat cross-legged on the floor with a great tome on his lap. He carefully opened the volume for which he had fashioned a protective cover of hemp cloth and rice glue. It was his beloved *Webster's New International Dictionary*, second edition, an enormous volume, gorgeous and golden, loaded with three columns of close-packed definitions on each of almost three thousand pages. From the biography on the facing page, upon laborious study of innumerable vocabulary words, the young man was able to glean that Noah Webster was born on a farm and grew to become a scholar and a churchman. This precious volume, sent as a gift toward the end of the war by Mrs. Betty Smith of the Village of Baldwinsville, New York, had provided the most steadily illuminating education of his staccato academic career. He had already skimmed the tome cover-to-cover and started over from the beginning for more detailed study. He opened the book to the section where his bookmark was tucked and ran the corrugated fingernail of this thick digit down the column of words till he found the place where he had left off.

The staggering English lexicon positively dwarfed the basic vocabulary of *Hangul.* The Korean language was traditionally augmented with Chinese for the expression of a formal, complex, or nuanced idea, a practice which, in his estimation, had stunted his native language. He turned to the front papers and gazed at the painting of the book's creator, the farmer turned scholar, whose three quarter profile was fascinatingly familiar. He felt that he had been sent an afflatus.

Returning to his high school one last time, he extracted from the office some prorated portion of his tuition money, declining his right to finish out the term. Then he proceeded to neighboring street stalls where he purchased a second-hand white dress shirt and black trousers with his refunded money. He was finished with his school uniform. He toyed with the notion of buying a necktie, but he did not want to spend too much and he was unsure of how to fashion the double Windsor he had seen on the city's businessmen.

Over the ensuing weeks, he had methodically canvassed the institutions of higher learning established in the city of Seoul. The opportunities for education ranged from a rude wooden shack where an ancient bearded scholar in a horsehair top hat presided over the memorization of Mandarin and classic poetry, to Seoul National University, the country's most prestigious institution, an ivory tower he could never dream of penetrating without wealth, connections, and formal upper school transcripts stamped with the highest marks. In his survey of colleges, Seoul Bible College had sparked his interest upon his discovery that its founder, Dr. Kang, had earned his Ph.D. in America.

In his boyhood, so long ago, a shaman had predicted that his future belonged in a great foreign land. The lunatic fantasy he dared not acknowledge, even to himself, began to crystallize into something: hope…ambition even. His American soldier friend, Mister Chuck, had promised to help him gain admittance into an American university. But after the war, his letters to Mister Chuck had gone unanswered.

Syngman Rhee had earned a Ph.D. at Princeton University, as all Koreans knew. But the former president of South Korea was as inaccessible and remote as the Ivy League university itself. The president of this small Christian college, were it to become *his* college, were he to excel and make himself known, would be a man he could actually meet. His subsequent discovery that the college tuition was the lowest of any of the institutions he had investigated thus far cemented his resolve.

The campus was nestled on the side of a mountain at the edge of the sprawling city of Seoul, a simple two-story building, rectangular, whitewashed, with a dozen classrooms lined up on either side of the long central corridor. The building overlooked a hardpan courtyard where ball games were played in clouds of dust. Farther up the mountain, at the top of a long steep flight of narrow concrete steps which wound into the wooded summit, lived President Kang and his family. He arranged for an interview with the dean of Seoul Bible College.

"Where are your transcripts?" the dean had demanded at the interview, eyeing the young man's costume of second hand black trousers, worn shiny at the knees, and ill-fitting white shirt, straining open at the buttons.

"I do not have any."

"Why do you come here to waste my time?"

But something in the young man's bearing, the proud set of the spine, the steady gaze of the eye, showed he was no ordinary country bumpkin.

"Sir, if you will only allow me to sit for the entrance exams, you will find that I have not wasted your time. I do not have any transcripts. I come before you with only my solemn promise that I will not disappoint you."

"Are you from a good family?"

"I am. We have a genealogy. And my mother is a deaconess of the Holiness Church."

With society in chaos, an orderly presentation of paperwork could hardly be expected. The young man was permitted to sit for the entrance exams. He scored the highest grade of all the applicants. The high school dropout became a college undergraduate.

On registration day, the young man was unexpectedly summoned to President Kang's office. As he followed the secretary down the hall, he rehearsed responses to the impending inquisition into the paucity of his preparatory education. He had been perfectly honest with the dean who had allowed him to sit for the entrance exams. His exam score should stand as proof of his abilities. He would willingly take the exams over to prove it was no fluke. Failing all else, he would plead for the right to complete just one term to prove his worth. They reached the president's office.

The door was open, and the president was in. He was writing with fierce concentration in a square of free desk space just large enough for a pad of paper, the entire perimeter of his large steel case desk being stacked with towers of books. The secretary tapped on the door and introduced the young man with a flurry of bowing before scurrying off. Dr. Kang looked up from his writing and put his pen down. The young man stood at attention, paused, and bowed with deep respect. An easy smile spread over Dr. Kang's face. The unexpected warmth of his elder's smile — something he must have picked up in America — dissipated the young man's anxiety. The president stood, returned his greeting with nod of his head, and extended his right hand over his book stacks and said, "And now let us shake hands in the American style."

The president inquired at some length about the young man's family, education, work history, and religious affiliations with sincere curiosity. He was cheered to learn that his new student's mother was a deaconess in her village church. He took a special interest in learning about the Communist occupation of their village during the war, particularly the disposition of worship services.

"Church was banned. We worshipped secretly at home," reported the young man.

"More than once, a godless people have attempted to subjugate us," the president commented as his eyes darkened behind his spectacles and the jagged keloid scar on his forehead, which everyone knew to be the mark of his imprisonment and torture during the Japanese occupation, filled with purple. "But it was not God's will. God's will be done."

The president confided that his wife had expected him to campaign for the presidency of the Republic of Korea. But he had answered a higher calling. He decided to found the Seoul Bible College to provide a Christian education for talented young men and women who could not otherwise afford higher learning. A flood of applicants had poured through the gates and twice the anticipated enrollment swelled the incoming freshman class.

"But I suspect they will be no competition for you. We have admitted as many as we can possibly handle in the service of Christ Jesus. But to tell the truth, few students even understood my essay questions on the entrance exam, and fewer still gave insightful answers. Today you take your first step on a lifelong journey. To choose the righteous path, you must know your destination before you begin. Young man, what are your goals for the future?"

"It is my goal to emulate your example and pursue graduate study in the United States," he replied, without realizing his impossible dream had already solidified into a goal.

"What I meant was, is it your intention to apply your education to serve the Lord Jesus Christ?" the president said, adjusting his glasses and scrutinizing the young man through its lenses as if examining a specimen.

It was evident that he had answered the wrong question altogether. Granted, he had professed his faith on the entrance forms, as required for admission, but Jesus Christ had not been on the forefront of his mind at the time...or at any time, except when he found himself in extremis. But, out of a sense of respect and duty, he automatically replied, "Yes. It is my intent."

The expansive smile returned to Dr. Kang's face, and he leaned back in his chair. He said, "Let us see if you fulfill the great promise you demonstrated on your entrance exam. If the Lord is willing, anything is possible."

Once admitted to college, the young man's studies had been uninterrupted by any claim on his attention...until the day of his musical encounter with Miss Kang. He spotted her a second time the very next day. It was late in the afternoon and she proceeded in long, quick strides across the dusty courtyard and out of the campus gates, carrying a small tote bag. He had the day off from the doctor's office and, without any conscious intent or purpose, in fact hardly aware of what he was about, he followed after her at sufficient distance to avoid notice. She walked down the mountainside and plunged herself into the crowded streets of Seoul, side-stepping piles of feces or leprous mendicants, without slowing her pace. On the streets, vendors hawked amidst war rubble, and everywhere was the commotion and dust cloud of reconstruction. Miss Kang strode right through. Despite her velocity, she was easy to track because her head projected well above the other pedestrians. She marched for well over an hour at a rapid, unabated clip.

Miss Kang reached the Sejongno region, where the Blue House presided in stately serenity, a cerulean mountain rising auspiciously in the backdrop. The US Embassy was situated in this area, and the Americans inhabited the gracious dwellings of the heavily guarded, immaculate environs. Turning toward one of these brick buildings, Miss Kang skipped up the steps with a swing of her tote bag and a flip of her braid. He approached an open window on the ground floor and heard the young lady warmly welcomed by an older American woman. The women conversed in English for a time. It was evident that Miss Kang had brought sweet rice cakes which needed to be fawned over, sampled, and deconstructed. After the tasting, piano music wafted out the window. The lesson was punctuated with jokes and easy laughter. "Wonderful!" the American woman exclaimed after every piece. He wondered if the piano teacher was aware that her pupil practiced on a wooden plank. After an hour, there came an exchange of parting pleasantries. The young man hastened away and took up a covert position on the street. He waited for her to gain some distance before trailing her back to her home. In another hour it would be dusk. Having followed her this far, he felt somehow responsible for her safe return.

On the way back, she proceeded at the same rapid pace, but her head turned side to side scanning the street vendor's wares. Her legs churned faster than her mind could process the sensory input so that when something caught her eye, she drew to a stop and back-stepped several steps. She rifled through piles of clothing, snapped apparel in the air, ran her fingers along every seam, and wrangled with the vendors. A great many offerings commanded her notice. And now he was hungry. Was it necessary to fondle every scrap of fabric that crossed her path? Shopping was an odious chore he avoided until faced with its absolute necessity whereupon he executed the required purchase without deliberation. His stomach groused audibly. Was it essential to wrest from each vendor their last won of profit? Bargaining was not in his nature. If he could not afford the asking price, which was usually the case, he simply went without.

By the time she returned to campus, Miss Kang's tote bag was bulging with a girl's yellow dress and four white dress shirts in an array of descending sizes. The young man watched her safe inside the campus gate and hurried toward home and supper, as evening's darkness descended around him.

The third time he saw Miss Kang, she was staggering behind the college building under the weight of an iron cauldron so enormous that her arms barely encircled its circumference. What in the world could she be up to now? Was there never a banal moment in her day? He hurried to her and relieved her of the burden. She seemed to take it as a matter of course that aid should materialize when she required it. She led him up a steep and narrow stairway of concrete steps that wound endless flights to the top of the mountain, stopping only to check that her pot was following her.

At the crest of the hill, the young man put down the iron pot and wiped his brow. Cacophonous barking drew his attention to a pair of snow-white dogs sporting extravagant manes. They strained at their leather collars which were attached by chains to two neat whitewashed dog houses. Placed before each of the dog houses were large ceramic bowls, one filled with water, the other with half-eaten meat.

A man in a hemp shirt and dusty trousers trudged to the dog houses and proceeded to shovel the dung that was scattered about. The animals bounded upon him in an unruly frenzy, streaking his shirt with paw prints as he worked. The young lady pointed to her dogs.

"They are purebred spitzes, imported from Japan. My father named this one, the male, Sodeka. What do you suppose that name means?"

"Something American?" he ventured.

"He is named after Socrates, Descartes, and Kant: So-de-ka!"

"Ah!"

"And the bitch is named Moneka."

"And what does it stand for?"

"Why, nothing!" she replied as if he had asked the most inane question imaginable. "It simply rhymes with Sodeka."

"They are splendid specimens."

"I am afraid of dogs. I was bitten as a child."

"A childhood experience has a lasting effect."

"True!"

The half-feral, half-tame pets of his own family sprang to mind, matted and dingy mutts, never fed by human hand, hunting and scavenging for their own food. There were no droppings to shovel because what was extruded from one animal was consumed, still steaming, by another. He thought of the mutt that had been butchered and served for supper to his starving older brothers when they returned from the Japanese labor camps.

Miss Kang led the young man into her house. It was a large house, a mix of western and eastern architecture, with electricity and running water. Her younger sister came skipping out from one of the back rooms wearing the yellow dress he recognized from the street vendor.

"*Unni*! What have you got?"

"A giant pot to boil enough water for your bath!"

"Hot baths!" cried the girl, jumping and clapping her hands.

"Shhhh! Settle down. It is a secret."

"Hot baths," the girl whispered, tapping her index fingers together soundlessly.

"You funny little fox," Miss Kang laughed. "Call the maid to take this to the kitchen. Hurry."

Miss Kang explained to her pot bearer, "We have no hot water because Mother eschews physical self-indulgence. She is a great admirer of the ancient Spartans. She emulates their ways to teach us to endure privation. But as a consequence, my little brothers and sister never bathe!"

Silently, he reflected that the avoidance of privation was a daily life and death struggle for his own mother, that the very notion of fabricating hardship where none existed organically for purposes of training one's offspring would be incomprehensible to the illiterate country woman. And they had never bathed in the house. They washed, rarely, in the stream that ran out back.

"Mother studied in Japan where she learned a great many interesting things. The Japanese know all about Western history and culture, unlike our provincial country."

Ruefully, he recalled his brothers' excursions to Japan, one conscripted to a metal working factory and another to a coal mine where they slaved in labor camps under subhuman conditions. He perceived the insurmountable chasm between his upbringing and that of Miss Kang. She continued.

"Mother would have sent us too, to get the best education, but my father would never allow it. Not after what they did to our country...and to him," she said pointing to the area of her forehead where her father's bore a scar.

With this simple gesture, a feeling of kinship welled in his heart. Finally, they stood on common ground. But he could not bring himself to mention his own mother's imprisonment during the occupation. The pain of the memory prevented its airing. Instead, he said, "I am glad that you stayed."

They were interrupted by the boisterous entry of two younger brothers sporting their new white-collared shirts.

"*Noonah*! You are here!" the boys shouted. "Look what we brought. Your juggling balls. Remember, you promised. Who is he?"

"He helped me carry something heavy up the stairs..."

"*Noonah*! You promised to teach us to juggle."

"Not now, boys."

"Please! You promised! Here are the balls!"

The boys' clamorous cajoling aside, the temptation to perform was irresistible. She took three balls from the boys and easily tossed a three ball cascade while the boys clapped. Then, on her cue, each little brother threw in a ball and soon she had a five balls suspended in a frenzied feat of levitation. The boys jumped up and down. A smile flashed enormous on her flushed face while she juggled. So those crazy rumors around campus were true. What an unusual female.

Then, abruptly, the boys fell silent. Their enlarged eyes stared beyond their sister at the prepossessing figure of their mother who loomed behind her back. Her every mental and physical fiber focused on the juggling, Miss Kang remained oblivious to the storm cloud of disapproval amassing at her back.

Until, like a clap of thunder, her mother shouted, "Stop this nonsense!"

Several balls fell from their orbit and bounced willy-nilly over the floor. Miss Kang whirled about to face her mother, hiding her hands behind her back, each clutching a salvaged ball. The boys scurried about picking up the remaining balls and hid behind their sister's skirts.

A stormy discharge of maternal reproach ensued. Sun Hee's mouth clamped shut. Her chin went down. Her eyes fixed upon her mother, but they were eyes flashing with defiance. As the tirade gathered momentum, the two little brothers sheepishly snuck off. No more notice was taken of the young man than the dung shoveler out by the dog houses might have commanded. It turned into an extended scolding.

Sun Hee must close her mouth when she smiled. Never show those big horse teeth. Stop wasting time on pointless pursuits. She should teach her brothers something useful. She should set a good example for them. She was a ridiculous girl engaged in incessant tomfoolery. Her disgraceful manners would render her unmarriageable.

"*Yuhbo!*"

President Kang entered the house bearing a heavy sheaf of papers. Sun Hee quickly put her head back down while he addressed his wife.

"Do you need Sun Hee right now? I have work for her. She needs to retype some pages of my manuscript and then it will be done at last."

"Take her then. I am done with her!"

A grateful daughter followed her father toward the study. As she passed her mother she muttered, "I am sorry, Mother. It will not happen again."

The young man ducked for the exit. But Dr. Kang suddenly whirled around and broke into his magnanimous smile. He extended an open palm in theatrical surprise.

"Why, look there! Imagine! Here is my best student. *Yuhbo*, this is Kim Young Nam. Perhaps he would care for refreshments."

Finally, Dr. Kang's wife took notice of the young man. She did not return his bow but looked him over in displeased puzzlement. Meanwhile, Sun Hee was uncharacteristically silent, gazing at the young man with bland curiosity, as if she had never laid eyes on him before. He excused himself and made haste for the door. Involuntarily, he stole a last glance over his shoulder at the discomfiting domestic scene. Beyond her mother's view, the young lady was smiling at him, perhaps even silently laughing at him, flashing those teeth she had been forbidden to show.

He hastened out the courtyard, past the yelping dogs, and half-way down the steps before slowing to his own lumbering pace to reflect upon his telling encounter with the Kang family. It was plain that the Dr. Kang favored his eldest daughter, perhaps unwittingly stoking the wrath of his wife against her. Regardless, mother-daughter conflict was inevitable. They could not be more opposite: one a would-be Spartan, the other a juggling pianist. Certainly, he had heard the campus gossip. President Kang's wife, hailing from Jejudo, island of mighty women, was the scion of one of the richest merchant families in Korea. It was she who had financed the college. On one occasion he had seen and heard her in the courtyard, fists on her hips, surrounded by a semi-circle of black suits, berating the businessmen in strident tones that ripped right throughout the campus. Rumors circulated that she was beset with the school's creditors whom she vigilantly isolated from her husband so he might devote himself to his scholarship and teaching. The fierceness of the president's wife bankrolled the magnanimity of the president.

The president had appeared genuinely pleased to see him. What did it mean? His wife, however, had been distinctly displeased. On that point there was no confusion. She was a formidable woman whose opinion mattered. He admitted to himself that he had to concur with the maternal criticism that Miss Kang's pursuits were frivolous. But should her silly antics and unladylike grin frighten away her potential suitors, well, so much the better. An unsettling realization gave him pause: she probably could not cook.

When Miss Kang returned to Ewha, drabness settled over the college like the pall after a party. The young man redoubled his studies with a passionate fervor. To distinguish himself academically was his only hope of advancement. He began to receive invitations to dinner at the president's home with faculty members. He remained silent at these dinners, focusing on his meal, unless drawn out by Dr. Kang to opine on a particular subject of theology or philosophy or history, whereupon he held forth with a natural pedagogic gift. He was the only student chosen to deliver opening prayers at the college church's Sunday service.

It was during midterm exams that Dr. Kang's two oldest sons, Chung Hee and Sang Hee, both high school students, sought Kim out with an intriguing invitation.

"*Hyung*!" Sang Hee said, addressing him familiarly now as an older brother. "Let us go see *Noonah* at Ewha."

"Miss Kang?"

"Yes. We are leaving right now. Come on!"

"Did she invite me?"

"Of course not."

"I am sorry I cannot go with you. I am studying for exams."

"She is in the college play. Everyone is talking about it," insisted Sang Hee, putting his arm around Kim's shoulder.

"A play?"

It certainly was tempting. But he had set himself the goal of achieving the highest marks in his class in midterm exams. It was his only chance. His workload at the doctor's office was ever growing. He could not afford time for a play, not even to see her.

"Father gave us permission. He gave us money. He said, 'Go and be sure to applaud loudly for your sister.'"

"Of course, you must see her performance. But I must study."

"Father told us to invite you," stated Chung Hee.

Kim went.

He had visited Seoul National University campus before, not to apply, but to admire. To lose himself deep into the halls of higher learning redolent of antiseptic, chalk, and musty tomes filled him with a sense of well-being tinged with bittersweet longing. He had never thought to visit Ewha before because it was a women's university. Nevertheless, he always looked forward to visiting any college and Ewha was no exception. When they arrived on campus, he found he was not alone. A full capacity audience, a sea of young men in slick new suits, laughed too loudly, pounded each other's backs with excess machismo, all but licked their chops. It was obvious they had not come to admire the books.

The playbill announced that the production would chronicle, from a rarely explored female point of view, one of the proudest moments in Korean history, the reign of King Sejong. The script was written by the undergraduate women. The young man was relieved to be spared yet another maudlin tearjerker about the Japanese occupation.

The curtain opened on a drawing room denoted in the program as Kyung Bok Palace. A colorful posy of ladies-in-waiting were scattered about the room. They wore rich silken *hanboks*, headdresses vibrating with spangles, and red lipstick. They sat on cushions at low tables, writing with brushes on parchment, while conversing meaningfully with each other. The ponderous intellectual dialogue, interspersed with Mandarin, gave the audience to know that were it not for the king's invention of the written language *Hangul*, the ladies' ignorant parents back home would be unable to read the letters they were writing.

"Which one do you think is the prettiest?" whispered Sang Hee to his guest.

Kim Young Nam shrugged. Their sister had not come on stage yet.

"I think the one in red is prettiest," said Sang Hee leaning over to fill in the blank.

"What? She is so fat. The green one is tolerable," pronounced Chung Hee.

"The green one has beady little eyes. She is all makeup!" complained Sang Hee.

The Kang brothers reached across their stoic companion to give each other a fraternal shove before settling down.

In the second scene, the queen, surrounded by the colorful ladies-in-waiting held an audience with a female supplicant whose husband had been convicted of a minor theft and sentenced to a flogging. The peasant woman knelt face down on the floor, pleading for mercy for her husband who would surely perish from such a draconian punishment. The queen was played by a real beauty, resplendent in her lush costume and crown shimmering with gold pieces. But her voice, a mere peep, could hardly be heard in the audience.

"She is the prettiest one so far," whispered Sang Hee.

"I cannot hear a word she is saying," criticized Chung Hee.

"Who cares? She is on stage to be looked at, obviously," laughed Sang Hee.

Then, from stage right, announced by drum fanfare, King Sejong the magnificent made a stirring entrance. Standing a head taller than anyone else on stage, he radiated majesty. Across the chest and broad shoulders of his crimson robes were embroidered circular medallions of golden dragons. His handsome jawline, aristocratic nose, pancake whiteness, and raven mustache and beard made a striking impression. All the women on stage, including his queen, collapsed in slow motion billows of silk, touching their foreheads to the floor in obeisance. The king raised his hand for all to rise.

The queen delivered a lengthy monologue in a miniscule voice as unintelligible as bird chirps. It could be surmised from the attitude of the weeping peasant that the queen was pleading for mercy on behalf of the sticky-fingered peasant husband. The audience murmured "What did she say?" and "Shhh!" After the strain of the queen's anemic voice, came the relief of King Sejong's sonorous tones which filled the auditorium with a resonance and cadence not unlike President Kang's Sunday sermons.

The king declared, "Pursuant to the entreaty of our beloved Queen, We deign to pardon your husband. But he must never again take from another man that which is not his own."

Then, turning to the furiously scribbling official at his side the king dictated his famously enlightened decree: "Whereas the practice of flogging upon the back and buttocks of a man endangers his very life, We do hereby outlaw this primitive practice, throughout the kingdom of Chosun, now and forever!"

Kim took stock of the young stud playing the king, doubtless a womanizing dandy imported from Seoul National. There could be only one motive for a young man to powder his face white and mount the stage of a women's college. The simpering demeanor of the females when he moved through their midst was an embarrassment. What a peacock!

Periodically, Kim was jostled by the Kang brothers elbowing his ribs. Even the eldest son, Chung Hee, dropped his dignity and nudged him repeatedly. The restless boys seemed intent on goading him into admiring one of the young maidens on stage. Perhaps they were conspiring to entrap him and tattle to their *Noonah*. Teenagers! He ignored their puerility and waited for their sister's entrance.

The next scene took place in a foundry where King Sejong personally oversaw the mechanization of book printing. A retinue of porters carrying food and wine for the workers filed in behind the ruler. The king raised his hand and a hush fell over the auditorium.

The king declared, "The language of our kingdom differs in sound and nuance from those of China and cannot be expressed readily in Mandarin characters. As a consequence, our ignorant subjects are unable to record their thoughts, simple though they may be, in the written form. Out of compassion for these, my people, We have devised a scientific system of writing using twenty-eight letters, symbolizing the sounds of our language, which can be mastered by the simplest mind and put to use in daily life."

A gaggle of second stringers, squatter and homelier coeds, played the wood carvers, metal workers, typesetters, and printers. When the king proceeded through their midst with his retinue, the workers careened about in comic disarray. The king commanded a presentation of their handiwork. In their eagerness to impress the king, the workers scattered printing plates, spilled molten copper on their feet, bumped heads, and bounced onto their bottoms, evoking paroxysms of laughter from the friendly audience.

The young man steadily ignored the prying eyes and poking elbows of the Kang brothers throughout the scene. He seemed to be the only stone-faced person in the audience, finding nothing funny about the slapstick humor, wishing the script had given more attention to the technical details of the printmaking process. Finally, intermission came.

Sang Hee asked him with a great grin and twinkling eyes, "So! What did you think of *Noonah*?"

This question confused him.

"Has she come on yet?"

The brothers looked at each other for a second before exploding into uproarious guffaws. In that moment, he realized that she had been on stage all along: King Sejong. The height, the porcelain complexion, the resonant voice, the regal bearing…it was all there.

How convincingly she had transformed herself into a man. It was, frankly, disturbing. He checked the program. Sure enough, he was she. But during the second half of the play, after he knew, King Sejong looked and sounded, reassuringly, all woman to him.

After the performance, a throng of well-wishers mobbed the cast. Kim stood apart while the Kang brothers thrust themselves into the crowd to wade toward King Sejong. A well-heeled university slicker reached her first and gave her a bouquet of flowers. She buried her face into the bouquet to smell and broke into a toothy smile. They conversed with easy familiarity. Then she broke off a blossom and stuck it into his lapel. As their conversation and laughter continued, the dandy caressed the *boutonnière* she had bestowed upon him.

Watching this scene from the periphery, to his dismay, heat rose to Kim's face. What had he been dreaming of? He would make himself forget all about her. He should have stayed at home to study. Perhaps he should turn back then and there. He might still have some dictionary time left. But neither his feet nor his eyes budged.

King Sejong suddenly heard her brothers calling to her. Her eyes popped with delight and the wattage of her smile amplified. She violently waved the bouquet up high and called to them, shedding petals over her admirer's head. Abruptly, she shoved the bouquet back into the hands of her crestfallen suitor, the better to plough her way through the crowd to reach her brothers. She reached out both hands and squeezed theirs. The brothers linked arms with her and led her to the outskirts of the crowd where the young man stood waiting. Afflicted by none of the cultural modesty of her counterparts, she milked her brothers for compliments while they walked arm in arm. Did you like my costume? Was I just like a real king? Did you cry during the sad parts? Then, she noticed the young man standing there.

"Did my brothers bring you here?" she asked in a surprised and vaguely displeased manner.

"Yes," he replied.

Turning to her brothers she asked, "Why on earth did you bring *him*?"

"*Noonah*, let us all go to a restaurant for dinner."

"Look at me. I have my mustache on!" she stage-whispered dramatically to her brothers.

"Father said we could. He gave us money."

"Peasant!" she spoke in her king voice, stroking her whiskers. "What do you say to the proposal of the crown prince?"

"Yes," he answered quickly.

"Yes, *your majesty!*" she corrected.

At that moment, the young man made up his mind. He knew he wanted, no, needed this woman who confused, embarrassed, and fascinated him. He returned to campus with renewed resolve to earn the highest marks and build his good will with President Kang. It was his only hope.

Before Kim Young Nam could achieve his goal, the Korean government instituted a mandatory draft requiring of all young men three years of service in the ROK army. After a life filled with tumult and setbacks, it should have come as no shock when a roadblock obstructed his path. Three years: an eternity! What about *her*? His thoughts flew to his *Webster's* dictionary. From his prior service with the US Army during the war, he knew it would be impossible to carry the dictionary with his gear. And what about *her*? In three years, she would certainly be married.

The campus was abuzz. Each young man with a draft notice burning in his pocket was acutely aware of the surplus of applicants, noses pressed against the windows, eager to take their place. Someone made inquiries and discovered that college students might reduce their service to one year if their school filed for an exemption for its matriculating students. The eldest Kang brother had confided that he had asked around and ascertained he would only serve one year since he was accepted to Seoul National University. With this knowledge, and the surety that he was a prize student, Kim Young Nam was appointed by his classmates to appeal to President Kang.

At the appointed time, the young man took his draft notice from his shirt pocket and passed it over Dr. Kang's stack of books.

"I have been drafted for three years in the army," he said. Then he sat and waited for Dr. Kang to read the document.

"This is a great disappointment."

"But I have learned that college students may qualify for a much reduced commitment if their institution files the necessary paperwork."

"Yes. I know this," said Dr. Kang passing the paper back to him.

"I hoped you would consider applying for such a status for the students of Seoul Bible College."

"I have considered it."

"May I ask what you decided?"

"I will not apply."

"May I ask why?"

"Trust in the Lord. Everything happens for a reason."

Carefully he said, "With all due respect and deference, I know that your son will only serve one year because Seoul National has already secured an exemption."

Blood filled the jagged scar on Dr. Kang's forehead. He replied in an uncharacteristically agitated manner, "Do you really expect me to cooperate with a corrupt administration?"

Actually, yes. It *had* been Kim's expectation and fondest hope. To answer truthfully would be disrespectful, so he sat in silence.

"We may not understand why trials and tribulations are set before us. But you must have faith. Trust in the Lord. The Lord will provide."

"I understand."

But he did not.

"Do not worry. I will personally see to it that you will not lose your place here."

The young man swallowed his frustration and disappointment. He rose, bowed, and turned to leave. As he reached the door, he heard President Kang's parting words.

"You will not lose her."

He turned around, startled. But Dr. Kang had picked up his pen and absorbed himself in his writing and did not look up again.

17

The rains came. The summer shower mounted monotonically to a downpour that would pound for days. The able-minded men of the household girded themselves and plunged barefoot into the monsoon to repair the dykes that washed out in the storm. They shouldered a five-man shovel, a man-sized wooden paddle, tied with two long ropes where the shaft met the shoulder. To move the heavy mud took five men, one to plant and guide the shovel, and two on each side to pull the ropes and heave sludge. But one shovel operator was missing.

In the house, the atmosphere weighed heavy and humid. Green and black slime molds spread over the walls. Lee Hana moved the laundry, damp too long and beginning to sour, to the kitchen before the fire. The fire threatened to fizzle out. She sorted through the sodden wood stack, found the driest pieces to throw on, and carefully stoked the dying embers.

Hana heard one of her little nieces squeal. She turned to find husband standing in the doorway, rainwater draining from his hair and clothing into a puddle on the threshold. He had a wild look in his eye.

"It is raining too hard," he said.

"*Yuboh*, please go back to your nap."

"No. I am not myself," he replied.

"Please, I beg you. Rest. Look, I have built the fire and I will make you hot tea. You can drink it and go back to sleep."

"Why are you here? Why do you speak to me? Something is wrong with me!"

He seized Hana, threw her to the floor, and struck her with his fists. The little girl ran screaming through the house calling for her aunt, *Komo! Komo!* Hana's sister-in-law raced to the kitchen.

"Stop! Stop! You are killing her," she screamed. Then she too ran off.

As the blows rained down, Hana went limp. She entered a disembodied state, as if observing a scene from a detached vantage point. She felt sorry for her little niece and her diligent sister-in-law; she had troubled their simple lives with her bad luck. After an interminable time, Hana perceived the heavy tread of men, but felt no sense of relief. The fire was dying. The rain poured and poured. Nothing seemed to matter anymore.

Four brothers charged into the house, dredged in mud from the knees down. They carried their five-man shovel, the ropes dragging two sludge tracks across the floor. The eldest son raised the shovel over his head and wacked his brother on the buttocks with all his might, splattering a fireworks of mud everywhere. The lunatic loosened his hold on Hana, and his brothers wrestled him to the ground. They tied him to the shovel with one of the attached ropes, carried it like a litter outside, and secured him upright to a post on the front porch with the other rope. The fourth son issued instructions to his wife: his brother was to be kept tied up till the sickness passed, he was to be spoon fed, he was to be equipped with a chamber pot. And then the men returned to the fields.

"It would be better for the family if he died," the fourth sister-in-law commented matter-of-factly while mopping up the mud. "But then what would *Uhmonim* do with you?"

But Hana did not wish her husband dead or even tied to a shovel. She did not hate or blame him. She was blameless; she understood this now. She was superior in mind to her husband, and she pitied him. When her sister-in-law hurried off to the chore from which she had been interrupted, Hana found a quiet corner of the house. She took out her compact which, with her, had survived so much. Slowly, deliberately, she caked the makeup thick on her face till the marks of the beating were concealed. When she finally returned to the kitchen, the fire was out.

She pawed through the wood pile, placing kindling on the vestigial embers of the fire. The wood fizzled, popped, and steamed. With the house, the walls, floor, bedding, laundry, kindling, everything damp, her efforts were futile. She waited by the stove to receive the old lady's wrath. She heard *Uhmonim* address her husband tied to the post.

"Not again! Why do you break my heart? Where is your wife?"

She knew what was coming next. Her mother-in-law entered the kitchen. Before *Uhmonim* could launch a tirade, Hana tried a diversion.

"The fire is out."

"Go outside and look for some wood, stupid girl!" spat her mother-in-law.

"But it is raining…"

"You had time to paint your face like a whore, but you cannot find time to gather wood!"

"Everything is wet."

"How can you be a good wife when you cannot even make a fire? I raised five sons. And what do you have to show for yourself? Stupid girl! Nobody wanted you. I took you in. I feed you. I clothe you. And what do I get in return for my sacrifice?"

At that particular moment, not much different from so many others, for some reason, perhaps the rain, Hana could not bear to hear that ripcord of a voice one more time. She was simply unlucky. One piece of terrible misfortune had caused another and another. She did not deserve her mother-in-law's ceaseless censure. It was not her fault. To her own horror and astonishment, a foreign voice from an unplumbed depth erupted into her mother-in-law's face.

"You did not raise five sons. You raised four sons and one maniac. You are a stupid old woman who gave birth to an insane son and does not even know it! I will do what you want! I will find kindling. In the river!"

She ran out of the house. She ran into the rain. She scarcely knew what she would do. Through the din of the rain, she heard the old lady screaming behind her. She looked over her shoulder and saw *Uhmonim* hobble toward her, drenched, her arms waving frantically. Hana sped up. Her light figure skimmed over the sucking mud. She could hear by the diminishing sound that the old lady was losing ground. It felt good.

Through the torrent, she discerned the roar of the Sap Kyo River and ran to it. The river had swollen to a turbid, roiling monster that could swallow her whole. The disrespect she had shown to her elder was unimaginable. Unforgivable. There could be no going back. What now? She paused at the bank and looked over her shoulder. In that blinding instant, the bank of the river gave way, and she was engulfed in violent waters.

The brown river slurry coursed into her mouth and nostrils and filled her stomach and lungs. The debris churning in the turbulent waters scourged her face and body. She could not swim. She had no recourse but to relinquish her body to the river. Soon she was hurtling through darkness with effortless acceleration. There was no pain and no sound. She experienced a sensation of black emptiness and final peace to which she abandoned herself.

When she awoke, she was laying on the bank of the river surrounded by a gaggle of in-laws shouting to be heard through the deluge. They surrounded a young soldier, lavishing him with praise and gratitude and invitations to eat with them in their home. Hana surmised that she was not dead, but had been rescued by this soldier. He was sturdily built, broad shouldered, and handsome, with a square set jaw and prominent cheekbones. Hana heard him introduce himself to her in-laws as Corporal Kim Young Nam. The soldier parted through the old lady and her sons and leaned over to gaze upon her countenance with pity and concern. Hana hated soldiers. Hana hated him.

She began to cry. The old lady scolded her.

The same courage – or recklessness – that inflamed her attack on her mother-in-law heated up inside her. Doubtless, this soldier was expecting her to kowtow to him. She would not do it. She had nothing to lose now. She would speak her mind. She raised her anguished face and looked him in the eye.

"You should have let me die!"

18

After three long years of conscripted service in the ROK Army, Kim Young Nam could no longer call himself a young man. Immediately upon his discharge, propelled by a welling of urgency, he hastened back to Seoul, taking only one moment to post letters to his brother on the family farm and his schoolmaster brother informing the family of his movements. His old employer, practitioner of medical quackery, immediately rehired him as an assistant. He was lodged in the same modest back room, unaltered since he left three years ago.

Kim reported to Seoul Bible College, his readmission letter in his pocket, determined to take on the maximum load physically and mentally possible, and to graduate early, making up for lost time. He arrived on campus to find he had an unexpected new classmate: Miss Kang was now an undergraduate at her father's school.

"*You* are here!" he exclaimed when he saw her in the hallway.

"Yes, I am here," she said tartly. "Expelled from Ewha!"

"What?" he gasped.

A sharp laugh escaped her. "I was joking. Father took me out of Ewha."

"Why?"

"He thought I was becoming too worldly," she said with unconcealed bitterness.

"But you have not yet graduated?"

"I must be very stupid!" she snapped.

"No! I only meant..."

"Father made me repeat a year. Or two. He said I was behind on theology because of my time wasted at a secular school. Additionally, I have to do all his typing."

"Is Chung Hee here too then?"

"Of course not! My little brother is at Seoul National. Somehow, *he* is not too worldly. He will finish before me at this rate," she said.

"It does not seem fair."

"What difference does it make? I am only a girl."

"You are unhappy."

"No. I am just acting spoiled. Father bought me a piano. Well, it is really for the church."

"It was for you. You...you are your father's favorite."

"Not true."

"Yes. It is quite obvious to the most casual observer. I think he needed you here beside him as a helpmate."

Suddenly, she brightened theatrically, and asked with mock wonder, "You really think so?"

Kim answered seriously, "It is lonely at the top. One would want...one would need...someone like you," he said earnestly.

"Well! You were his favorite student and you are now behind me. And that makes me feel better!"

Undoubtedly, a man needed education more than a woman. Nevertheless, Kim could scarcely believe that a scholar like President Kang would deny his daughter a prestigious university degree while sending his son to the elite Seoul National. After all, an educated woman could teach her children; it was never a complete waste. On the other hand, had she graduated from Ewha while he was in the army, she would have waltzed straight from graduation to wedding. Of this he had no doubt. With a tangle of emotions – hope and regret, relief and guilt – he recalled the president's parting words to him: *You will not lose her.*

One crisp spring day, they sat on burlap sacks sharing a picnic lunch. They had traveled in a caravan from campus to a parcel of mountainous territory near the DMZ. Far from picturesque, the mountainside was ravaged by firebombs and stripped by plundering peasants for firewood. Grit that coated them from head to toe fell onto their *kimbab*, rolls of rice wrapped in seaweed. Nevertheless, intending to bestow his highest compliment, Kim remarked, "This is delicious."

"Yes! We finally got a good cook," answered Miss Kang.

He knew it. She was no cook. No matter. That day, he had discovered that she could work as hard as any man.

They were at the summit of a thousand-acre parcel purchased by Dr. Kang, his mission to reforest the land denuded by the war. Over the course of the spring, students, faculty, patriotic volunteers, and hired hands would plant one hundred thousand native pine trees.

In the epicenter of the reforestation, Miss Kang had dug into the rocky soil with ferocity. The only breaks she had taken from her fiendish planting were to heckle the other college students.

"Make your hole bigger so the roots can stretch out! We are not Chinese. We do not bind their feet," she shouted. "Position the trunk plumb. Not perpendicular. Trees grow straight up to the sky!"

During the outing, Dr. Kang bounded up the hillside, trailed by a newspaper reporter and photographer. He waved his hand and shouted, "Hello! Here are my best student and my best child! Let this newsman take our photograph together."

They posed for photographs, resting their arms on shovels, beside a balled sapling poised with expectancy at the edge of a hole.

"Smile! Young man, smile!" shouted the photographer.

Kim glanced at Dr. and Miss Kang, noted the charisma of their toothy grins, and unsuccessfully attempted the same.

"Look happy, young man! Smile! Smile!" urged the photographer.

"Oh, stop it!" scolded Miss Kang impatiently through her smiling teeth. "He does not know how."

Kim felt understood. Before Dr. Kang had led the newsmen down the mountainside, he had urged the young people to take a lunch break.

As they ate their *kimbap*, Miss Kang remarked, "You must be an intimate of dirt. But as for me, I have not been this dirty since we crossed the DMZ when I was a girl."

"When you came from Manchuria?"

"Oh, you heard about it? Yes. During the occupation, the Japanese kept capturing my father and torturing him. I missed him so much when he was gone. I was always in trouble with Mother. Once he came back with his head split open and my mother had a terrible time finding someone to stitch it up. It got infected and it never did heal properly. I do not know what else they did to him. He never complained about the torture. The only thing he complained about was that they did not let him sleep. Sleep deprivation was unbearable, he said. You go temporarily insane.

"Then my father took to dressing in rags and hiding amongst the rabble in the city to avoid capture. He left home before the sun came up and returned late at night after everyone was asleep. Everyone but me. I waited up for him. I held my eyelids open with my fingertips for hours. When I heard his footsteps I would sneak to the door. I was little then. Father would pick me up and hug me, and I did not mind that he smelled like a sewer.

"So we had to move to Manchuria. They did not know us there, or else the Japanese were too busy with the Chinese and Russians to persecute us. Father founded churches in the Korean community. I remember being happy there. We were comfortable. We had a goat. I loved goat's milk, but my siblings did not. There was so much milk leftover that my mother bathed us in it. Everyone says that is why I have this white skin. Can you imagine using milk for bathing?"

"It does not seem Spartan."

"Ha ha! You are amusing despite yourself. I remember we lived next door to a beautiful Chinese lady. She looked like a porcelain doll. I loved to peek through a hole in the gate and watch her in the yard. She had the smallest bound feet imaginable. You never saw such a thing. When she walked, she swayed back and forth as if balancing on balls. She could not do anything for herself. Her maids had to do everything for her. She never left the yard unless a rickshaw or palanquin was brought in for her and she was loaded into it by her maids.

"But her husband! He was the most hideous troll you ever saw. He was fat and had beady eyes and great slimy liver lips. He was kind enough to her from what I saw, but it must be awful to have to be married to such a nasty looking man. Every day, she swayed like a sapling in the wind out into her courtyard and cried and cried for hours. It was as if her occupation in life was weeping. I vowed I would rather be a spinster than marry a man who brought me such unhappiness! Crying and crying!"

"Perhaps her feet hurt."

"Spoken like a typical man. I told you she married a troll. I was happy in Manchuria. But one day, my father came to me and said, 'Pack up your essentials. We are going home.' I was sad to leave because we had lived there for years. I thought China *was* my home. But my mother and father were filled with such anticipation that we children could not help but be caught up in the excitement.

My father would lead our entire congregation, hundreds of people on the journey. Little did I know what lay in store.

"I found a cloth belonging to the maid and packed my most prized possessions. A couple of old cracked teacups and plates. I played cooking and house with my broken china every day. They were so precious to me. My father came upon me carefully packing these items and he burst out laughing. I was so embarrassed! But I begged him to let me bring my beloved things. He was very kind and patient and explained why I could not bring toys. It would be a long journey at the end of which we would only own what we could carry."

"How old were you?" he asked.

"I was eight. Also, there were my brothers, Chung Hee and Sang Hee, and sister, Cho Hee. Is that it? At the time, there were...er...there were four of us. Yes, and each of us held one of our parent's hands. My father had all our belongings in a great big satchel on his back.

"All the Korean refugees were leaving China. There were thousands. We waited at train stations for weeks at a time and camped out wherever there was a spot to lay our heads. When a train finally came, my father had to herd hundreds of church members onto the boxcars while my mother took care of us. It was utter chaos. At one of these railroad stations, someone stole our bag. Then we had absolutely nothing. I was selfishly relieved that I had buried my old cracked china set it in the yard believing one day, when I was grown up, I would come back and reclaim it. That was the one time I saw my mother cry. The worst thing in the world is to see your mother cry."

"I agree," said Kim. He felt his heart constrict with the memory of the tears his mother shed on so many occasions. He forced himself to focus on Miss Kang's story. "What did you do?"

"What could we do? We boarded the train empty handed. We were the lucky ones. The boxcar was full, and many refugees got on top of the cars with their sacks of belongings and children and rode that way in the terrible cold through the night. I remember one little girl crying because she did not want to climb up. Her mother tied the girl to herself using the sash about her waist. Her mother kept saying, 'Cry on, child. Cry on. We must stay awake all night or we will surely die.' When we arrived and got off the train, I looked for the mother and her child. But they were gone. To this day, I wonder what happened to them. Do you think they must have fallen off? Do you think they must have died? I cannot bear to imagine it! What do you think happened?" she asked.

"It is possible to fall off a train and survive. They may well have lived," he said, though he knew it was untrue.

"How do you know?"

"I have jumped from a moving train."

"What? Why on earth would anyone be so stupid?"

"I was late for school."

"That figures."

"What happened next?"

"After that we walked. We walked for days. Wait. Somewhere in there I think we took a boat. It was a short boat trip. But the walking! The walking went on for an eternity. Everyone had holes in their shoes and bloody feet. At the end, we had to climb over mountains on our ragged feet and rubbery legs. I remember pinching my little sister on her bottom to make her keep on going. She was so exhausted that she did not squeal or tattle as she usually does.

"Then we reached the 38th parallel and my father left us. There was some old lady, a North Korean, whom Father hired for a guide. We followed her across the parallel. It was the black of night. But my father was the last to cross because he had to make sure the others were safe before he would come. I remember how excruciating it was to wait for him. I never felt so anxious in my life.

"When we crossed the border, what did I see? The most scary, astonishing, horrible, wonderful sight: Americans! I never saw such huge and ugly and fascinating creatures in my life. Such bulgy blue eyes and yellow hair! We could not stop staring at them. Yet, despite their frightening appearance, they were very kind to us. At the border, the first thing the soldiers did was soak every man, woman, and child with DDT from their big metal spray cans. Only then did I realize we were crawling from head to toe with lice and vermin. The Americans had hospital tents and food tents. We had warm food to eat. We could not decide if it was incredibly tasty or terribly disgusting, but we were so hungry that we ate like starving animals. The American food was very rich, and we all had belly aches and diarrhea. We visited the medical tent and got a checkup. I remember they gave us some shots, which we did not like, but then the children got candy, which we liked very much. Oh, was it delicious!"

He gave a short chuckle of agreement. His teeth ached remembering the US Army chocolate bars.

"The Americans put us on a train to Seoul. Then our congregation dispersed and everyone found their families here and there. I remember when we made it to my aunt's house, they were not pleased to see us at all. We looked like beggars, skinny and ragged and dirty and greasy. In fact, we *were* beggars. We had no possessions whatsoever since our bag was stolen."

"What did you do?"

"My father founded a church right away and also got some teaching work at some school. But my mother is the one who really knows how to raise money. She is a businesswoman. It is in her blood, and I see no shame in it. She knows how to organize a *keh*, and since she organizes the bank, she always takes first. Pretty soon, she bought us a nice house and we were able to move out of our aunt's place. I was so glad because our aunt's children were treating us like poor relations. Not to brag, but the fact is, our new house was much better than Auntie's.

"You have a way about you that makes people want to talk too much. And you sit there absorbing everything and revealing nothing. Why do I talk so much?"

"Your story is more interesting than whatever I could tell," he replied. The truth was, he was physically incapable of reminiscing about his past. All memories led to his beloved Owlet. It was too painful to speak of. Miss Kang continued.

"It gets even better. Just when everything was getting settled and back to normal, my mother woke us up in the middle of the night and told us we were fleeing Seoul. The war had broken out. Mother had to stay behind to settle some business. My father, he was doing something too, maybe readying the congregation to leave. My mother hired some man, a student of my father's, to take us out of Seoul.

"So we got to the country where we had relatives on my father's side. We waited and waited for my parents to come. Finally, they turned up along with hundreds of members of their congregation. We had to move on farther south because the war was right at our backs. My father's relatives refused to join us. They were stubborn country farmers. Like you. Where did you go?"

"We stayed on the farm."

"Exactly like my country bumpkin relatives. We fled all the way to the Pusan Perimeter on buses and trains and hired ox-drawn carts and by foot along with herds of other refugees. It felt like a nightmare was repeating itself.

"At least when we left Manchuria and reached Seoul, we were joyous. But when we left Seoul and reached the Pusan Perimeter, we were depressed. There never was a filthier, more crowded, miserable place on earth. The Americans were there too. But they were refugees themselves. Too many refugees. Not enough space or food or sanitation or anything.

"One of my jobs was to fetch water at the pump. I dreaded that chore so much. The people mobbing the water line were vicious.

247

I did not even want to be near them. They shoved and pushed, and I kept falling farther back in the line. Because I was young, I deferred to the older people. But I would sometimes stand in the water line all day long and when I finally got back to our encampment, Mother would be furious. Finally, one day, I decided I had enough. I realized that I was already bigger than most of the grownups, even though I was only thirteen. I stood up straight and made liberal use of my big mouth. Do you think I have a big mouth?"

"Uh…"

"Well, I know what you are thinking. And failing my big mouth, I used my elbows to keep my place in line. I did not care if the elder folk shouted and cursed at me. It felt good to stand my ground. After that, the only time I ran away was when a leper threatened me."

"Perhaps you might have been better off on the farm."

"Farm boy *chonnom*! As soon as we got settled in our camp, my mother left us to take care of things. She never told us what she was doing. My father was gone somewhere doing something or other too. I never knew where or what. Mother put me in charge. They were gone for days. We were running out of money, and I grew nervous. I saw the other refugees selling things… junk, clothing, tins of American soldier food. Everyone was busy selling whatnot or cooking and doing laundry for the Americans or whatever they could think of to do.

"I had the bright idea to set up a stall and sell some things. I lined up my siblings on either side of me and opened up our suitcase and displayed our wares. I had a few polished apples and this and that I scrounged up from our belongings. I was a tough bargainer too. We were doing a pretty brisk business. I was so proud of myself!

"But then, out of nowhere, my mother showed up and slapped me so hard I went flying! Mother was furious! Her face was absolutely purple with rage. She screamed at me, 'We are not common peddlers!' So ended my entrepreneurial career. But I do not blame my mother. Imagine having such a silly daughter and finding your children all lined up in a row selling your personal belongings to strangers."

"Some mothers would have been proud."

"Ha! Not mine. It turned out that Mother had found us a house in Pusan, and we were able to move out of the refugee camp till the war was over.

"But I talk too much. Tell me about yourself. What happened to you? What did your family do during the occupation and the war?"

There was a long pause. His mind raced chaotically. Then Kim cleared his throat and replied, "Nothing much."

At Sunday service Dr. Kang preached from the book of Exodus: Moses leading the children of God from Egypt, guided by a pillar of cloud by day and a pillar of fire by night. The pastor president went on to analogize the Jewish exodus to his own, providing dates and details that had been missing from his daughter's childhood recollections.

"From 1940 to 1945 I taught the word of God in Manchuria. I planted five Korean churches in that foreign land. But after World War II, the people of God could no longer live there. In the fall of 1945, leading 698 Korean refugees, I began our exodus from Kaiwen, Manchuria. I had five children, the oldest eight years of age, the youngest an infant."

From the dais where he sat in the honored role of liturgist, Kim glanced at Miss Kang seated at the piano. She was glaring at her hymnal and wringing her hands. Dr. Kang continued.

"All the material belongings I was able to carry were packed into a large sack which I carried on my back. I held my eldest daughter's hand in my right hand and my eldest son's hand in my left. My wife carried the baby on her back. She held our second daughter's hand in her right hand and our second son's hand in her left.

"We traveled to the center of Manchuria, where thousands of Korean refugees were gathered to return to our own promised land. However, there were no trains. We waited twenty days in the bitter cold November, in a foreign land, seeking shelter wherever we could find it.

"Finally, I paid 200,000 won to the railroad authorities for twenty box cars. There was great confusion and hysteria as I loaded my 698 refugees onto the box cars. I took responsibility for my refugees, and my wife had to care for our five young children alone. In the chaos, someone stole the sack which contained everything we owned. I will never forget the tears my wife shed when she asked me, 'How will we live?'

"God gave me the words to speak to her. 'Let us trust in the Lord. When we were born into this world, we came naked and empty-handed. God gave us everything we needed to come this far. God will continue to provide for his children.' My wife dried her tears, and we put our children on the last boxcar.

"We arrived at Antung where we crossed the Yalu River in boats, reaching the town of Sin Eun Ju, Korea. There we waited for a very long week for a train to come. We were exhausted and cold. Finally, a train arrived and we took it to Sariwon. That was the end of the line.

"The 38th parallel was within reach. But even a Korean could not cross because our country had been divided in two. The parallel was to us the sea that blocked the children of Israel from escaping the Pharoah's armies.

"The word of God says, 'And Moses stretched out his hand over the sea; and the Lord caused the sea to go back by a strong east wind all that night, and made the sea dry land, and the waters were divided. And the children of Israel went into the midst of the sea upon the dry ground: and the waters were a wall unto them on their right hand, and on their left.'

"Our sea was the mountainous terrain and the demilitarized zone of barbed wire and land mines. By the grace of God, we would cross it. I grouped my refugees into three parties. We traveled for three nights through the cold mountains for one hundred miles, evading capture. The white of our women's *hanboks* was our pillar of fire in the night as we scrambled up and down the deadly terrain. After all my refugees crossed the border, I was the last to cross, alone.

"At Songdo, South Korea, the American army intercepted us. They fed us and administered medical attention. They treated us with astonishing kindness. They provided us with a train to Seoul, free of charge.

"It took us one month and four days to travel from Manchuria to our homeland. We arrived with nothing: no books, no clothing, no food, no money, no house. My family is safe only by the grace of God. He who claims miracles no longer happen, has not opened his eyes and looked around him.

"Alas, the journey was too long and hazardous for my youngest child. There was no medical attention of any kind. Our baby did not survive. God looked upon her distress and took mercy on His child. God called my youngest child home."

The congregation was noisily bawling. Even the president's wife was openly weeping. Behind the piano, Miss Kang's face was riven with anguish. But she continued to stare at her sheet music and did not shed tears with the others. Dr. Kang concluded.

"It is not for us to understand the way of the Almighty. God gave me another child and then another. Let us trust in the Lord. Let us give thanks to the Lord. John 12:24 says, 'Verily, verily, I say unto you, except a corn of wheat fall into the ground and die, it abideth alone: but if it die, it bringeth forth much fruit.'"

During the fellowship hour after church, Miss Kang refused to socialize or eat. Her siblings and friends hovered around her, solicitously offering her food, attempting in vain to coax her out of her uncharacteristic reticence. Sunday was incomplete without her. She steadfastly refused all overtures and eventually retreated to the hallway outside the kitchen. Kim found her there.

"You did not tell me everything about your journey from Manchuria."

"Yes I did."

"Not everything."

"I suppose you are referring to my baby sister who died."

"Yes."

"I did not mention it because it is none of your business!"

"I am sorry."

"Just go away. Leave me alone."

He swallowed hard and managed to say, "My two younger brothers and my younger sister died."

"I do not care! I said go away!" she snapped.

Then she crumbled. Tears coursed from her eyes. He longed to escape but could not. He longed to put his arms around her but could not. He longed to tell her of Owlet. But he could not. After gathering himself, Kim spoke slowly, deliberately.

"You were only a child yourself."

"I know," she cried.

"There was nothing you could do."

"Why are you telling me this?"

"It was not your fault."

Miss Kang dried her tears and spoke.

"One time, years after the war, my youngest brother fell sick. It was so scary. He was delirious with a high fever. We put cold compresses on his forehead and fed him broth one drip at a time. It went on twenty-four hours a day. It was me, my mother, and the maid. We were exhausted. But after a few days, he seemed to get better and everyone breathed a sigh of relief.

"Then one night, he cried and cried all night long. In the morning, we found he had lesions on his face and hands. We removed his clothing and saw the sores were covering his entire body. Of course, that was the reason he cried so pitifully all night. We knew right away he had smallpox. It was terrible. Father was away. Mother left to find a doctor. But I thought that nobody would come. She had to find a doctor who was immune to small-pox. She was gone for a long time. We had to quarantine my brother.

"I did not care if I caught it. I had the maid tie him to my back with a blanket. I walked for miles to soothe his cries. I sang to him. I made up stories to tell him. I continued until I was nauseated with fatigue. But then suddenly I realized that he was rubbing his face on my neck. I knew he would become horribly disfigured if he continued to do this.

"I had the maid turn him around, facing outward, so he could not rub his face on me, and bind his limbs tight against my back. In this position, he was very difficult to carry because he could not hold onto my neck and waist with his arms and legs. I could no longer stoop over to hold his weight because he would scream from discomfort of being bent backwards. I had to walk upright. He was two years old and very heavy.

"It was excruciating. My back and legs felt like they would disintegrate from the pain. But I walked him all over the house and yard and woods, all day and all night, till he fell asleep. Whenever I felt I could not go on, I remembered my baby sister who died on the trek from Manchuria and asked myself if I could ever forgive myself if my brother died on account of my laziness. That thought... no...that fear gave me strength. The only time I put him down was when he was sound asleep. The moment he stirred, I put him right on my back. When my brother finally got better, he had only minor scars on his face. He was not hideous like the other smallpox victims. You can see for yourself, he has grown up to be a very handsome boy."

"Your brother was lucky to have such a big sister."

"If I had done this for my baby sister, if I had tried my best to help instead of pining for the cracked china cups I left in Manchuria, would my baby sister have survived?"

If he had done this for Owlet, would his brother have survived? He swallowed hard.

"It had nothing to do with you or any being. Only the fittest could survive such circumstances."

She narrowed her eyes and remarked, "Well! That does not sound particularly religious. I was sure you would say it was God's will."

"I may not know everything about God. But I know this: you will be a great mother one day."

Sun Hee was taken aback for a moment, staring at him with wide eyes. Then, uncharacteristically, she blushed, cast her eyes downward and said, "Ha!"

* * *

Faithfully every new year, *Webster's* at the ready, Kim wrote a letter to his American friend, Charles Smith of Baldwinsville, New York. He apprised Mister Chuck of his latest whereabouts and reaffirmed his goal of one day attending an American college. Each time, he thanked Mr. Chuck and his mother, Mrs. Betty Smith, for the fine dictionary which furnished the vocabulary populating his letter. He had never forgotten the promise Smith had made him during the war. So in his last year at Seoul Bible College, Kim importuned his American friend to sponsor him for an international student visa and advise him on how one would apply to Syracuse University. Charles Smith never wrote back.

Not without misgiving, he turned to Dr. Kang.

The president was waiting. Already, he had devised a plan for his prize student. He was in communication with his colleagues from Bob Jones University who had founded a new theological seminary in San Francisco. These Americans had facilitated his fundraising efforts for the Seoul Bible College, and it was the president's desire to return the favor by furnishing them with his top student. Dr. Kang had already secured a spot for Kim. The paperwork was a mere formality. The president was certain his student would represent his college and his country with honor.

It was now or never. Kim dared to admit, "Dr. Kang, I am not decided about my field of study."

The president's eyebrows shot up over his glasses. He asked, "Have you not received your calling?"

"Is it…a voice?"

"It is much more than a voice."

"I simply do not know."

"But you are my top student. I was certain you received your calling."

"Perhaps I will not be one of the called."

Dr. Kang leaned forward and said, "Sometimes it is not a voice. It is a whisper. You must receive it, not with your ears, not with your brain, but with your heart."

"I was thinking of studying the science of politics."

"You excel in theology. In philosophy. Political science is a secular field of study. Where did you get this idea?"

"Syngman Rhee."

Dr. Kang shook his head. "Poor example. How many lives did Syngman Rhee save aside from his own? A man who does the work of God is worth a thousand Syngman Rhees. You must pray to God. Ask Him to show you the way."

"Thank you. Yes. I will think about it."

"No. Do not think. Thinking does not work. You must pray. Pray!"

"Yes. I will pray."

"And when you have accepted the will of God, I will get you to America."

Back in his room, he knelt to pray before beginning his work in the doctor's office. But, inevitably, the *Webster's* drew his eye. He took up the beloved volume, opened it with reverence, and began to study. Before long, he heard the doctor call.

Kim looked about and found no patients waiting for him. The old doctor entered. He carried an airmail envelope which he displayed in front of his chest like a placard. It was from America. When he was assured that his assistant's curiosity was stirred, he opened the envelope and, shoving some soiled rags aside, spread the contents onto the examination table. There was a letter and several photographs.

He pointed to the first photo which pictured a Korean man, his wife, and a daughter, perhaps two years old, clutching her mother's leg with one arm and a stuffed animal in the other.

The doctor explained, "This is the assistant I hired while you were in the army. He was almost through medical school when his family disowned him for marrying this woman beneath his station. You are a medical man, so I can tell you why. She was pregnant. He came to me for work. I put him through the remainder of medical school. Medical doctors can get visas to the United States easily. Also, scientists and engineers. You want to go to America, don't you?"

"How did you know?"

"That's what all the smart young men want nowadays. What do you suppose this one is?" he asked, pointing to the second photograph showing an aqua mass of indeterminate shape.

"I do not know."

"It is a swimming pool in the shape of a grand piano! The rascal was able to buy such a luxurious item. Now, look at this one. This is their house. Not a house. A mansion. Look at the car in the driveway. Mercedes. Expensive German car. In America, doctors are rich. They are considered the aristocracy of society. Imagine it!"

"It is hard to imagine."

"Now read the letter."

Kim read the letter, a thank you note to the old quack for making him rich. The doctor then reached inside the envelope and extracted a one-hundred-dollar bill which he waved in his apprentice's face.

"He sent this. One. Hundred. Dollars. He sends me a gift every quarter! It is nothing to him."

In light of this enticing precedent, the doctor reiterated the offer that had been summarily rejected years ago. He would put his apprentice through medical school and then make him a partner. The pedigree would legitimize his business and save him the bribe money he had to pay government officials. They would find another bright country boy to put through school. When the new doctor was ready to join the practice, Kim would be free to go to America.

"Do not answer now. Think about it. You are a smart young man. Use your brain. It is an offer you cannot refuse."

Their conference was interrupted by the entry of a customer. The click clack of high heels announced that it was a woman of ill repute. A grin hoisted the doctor's face.

"You do not care for them. When you have a diploma, we will no longer welcome them in our practice. But for now..." he said, hurrying out to greet her.

She was different from the other prostitutes. She wore the typical slatternly red dress, stockings, and high heels and carried a cheap patent leather purse. But she lacked the slutty bravado of her ilk. Her demeanor was hesitant and shy, ashamed even. She did not giggle when the doctor bowed at the waist to her, but returned the civility in similar fashion. Beneath the mask of makeup, she was a country beauty. The woman glanced at Kim. She did a double take before casting her eyes to the floor. Before the doctor could usher her into the exam room, she turned and flew out the door.

As night fell, Kim resisted the temptation to pore over *Webster's* and knelt to pray. It felt, as usual, like a unilateral conversation. He had read that saints heard the voice of God. It seemed that Dr. Kang was also privy to such direct communication. Even his mother, a simple farm woman, seemed to be transported in her faith. In the absence of any such inspiration, his thoughts wandered.

Miss Kang. Would she rather be the wife of a doctor with a piano-shaped swimming pool or the wife of a theology professor with little more than a collection of books to his name?

America. It would be at least five years, maybe more, if he took the doctor's offer. He could go this year if he entered the seminary Dr. Kang had selected for him.

A memory intruded upon his deliberations. When he was in the army, he had saved a woman from drowning in the Sap Kyo River during a monsoon. For a month after the rescue, now and again, he had idly wondered what had become of that foolish woman he had risked his life for. How ungrateful she was! Soon the memory had subsided, and eventually disappeared altogether. He had not thought of the incident in years. Though he never reveled in his heroism or even told a soul about it, the fact remained: he had saved a life. The *I-Ching* predicted that a man who rescues someone from certain death will experience a profound change of fortune.

He decided to go to San Francisco.

He was hardly in a position to propose to Miss Kang. But he grew determined to extract some assurance that she would wait for him to establish himself in America. The task proved daunting. Lately, she avoided him as if he were a leper. Should they be forced together by circumstances, she studiously ignored him or cloaked herself within a coterie of girlfriends. Graduation day passed without the exchange of a single civility.

The day of Kim's departure dawned. Still, he had been unable to speak to Miss Kang. His thick hair was tamed with grease, his second hand suit was donned, and his modest bag was packed with one change of clothing and his *Webster's*. The president, his wife, two oldest sons, and several members of the faculty had boarded the school van to escort the first graduate of Seoul Bible College to study abroad. The president waited in the front seat with his hands folded on his lap.

"Where is *Noonah*?" asked Chung Hee.

"I could not find her," said Kim.

"Start the car! Go on without her!" ordered the president's wife. The driver put his hand to the keys in the ignition.

"We will wait a few more minutes," said the president calmly. The driver dropped his hand to his lap and put his head down.

"We will be late. Put your bag in the back and get in. We are leaving. Quick!" commanded the president's wife.

"Can we wait for *Noonah*?" importuned the brothers.

"Start the car!"

The driver looked helplessly at Dr. Kang.

"I will find her," said Kim.

Dr. Kang chuckled and said, "You had better hurry. Do not miss your plane because of a woman!"

Kim raced up the hundreds of winding steps to the Kang home at the top of the mountain. The startled maid explained that her mistress had not returned home since slipping out of the house at dawn. He flew back down the stairs and sprinted to the college building. Panting, sweating, he searched every room of the academic building.

Finally, he found her in the same room where they had first met, the day he had come upon her singing and practicing piano on her makeshift, painted keyboard. She sat gazing blankly out the window with her hands uncharacteristically idle on her lap.

"Miss Kang! I must hurry to Kimpo. My plane leaves soon. We have been waiting by the van. I have been searching for you everywhere."

"So you found me," she said, fixedly staring out the window.

"Before I leave, I wanted to ask you something."

"I am only an ignorant woman. What could I possibly know that you do not know?" she replied, refusing to look at him.

"You know your heart."

"I know nothing!"

"I have to catch my plane. May we discuss a matter of importance?"

"I am not in the mood for talk. My big mouth is shut today."

"I really must leave now. I was hoping we might have an important discussion."

"There can be nothing to discuss."

"Then may I write to you?" he asked miserably.

"It is your decision. You are leaving. And I am stuck here. You know the address."

"Will you read my letters? Will you write back to me?"

"I would have to be faced with the situation."

"I will write to you as soon as I am established."

"Do as you like. Goodbye!" And she stormed out, slamming the door behind her.

After outlasting the Japanese and then the Communists, after surviving poverty, hunger, and war, after striving and overcoming all odds, at long last, his impossible dream, the fulfillment of a destiny foretold in his childhood, was within his grasp. It took a woman to darken his blue skies. That old proverb was true: *woman was born three days before the devil.*

His gloom did not lift until, boarded and buckled, he spied the airline safety literature, printed in Korean, Japanese, and English. He read the English first, then the Korean. He read the English again. It was happening. This penniless boy from third world Korea, son of a hardscrabble subsistence farmer, erstwhile child laborer, was bound for America. He pressed his hand against the window to make sure it was not a dream.

Between his thick fingers, he saw another passenger plane taxi down a runway. Though inured to the roar of military aircraft carving up Korean skies, Kim had never before witnessed a take-off. As the aircraft gained speed down the tarmac, he thought: if that hunk of metal can fly, anything can happen. Biblical miracles paled in comparison to the incredible sight of the mass of steel, row upon row of faces peering from its windows, slipping the grip of the blacktop, flouting gravity, lifting gracefully into the invisible air.

Soon enough, it was his turn to soar. Liftoff was different from his childhood flying dreams. The lurch of his stomach, the pressure in his ears, the vibration of the engine, the stale cabin air were not at all what he had imagined flying to be. But when cruising altitude was reached, and coffee was graciously served, he reflected silently that he had just survived the most exhilarating moment of his life.

Somewhere over the Pacific, the novelty wore off, and a pall settled upon him. He could not read. He could not converse. He stared out the window in miserable silence. At the airport, Chung Hee had given him kindly words of advice. "When *Noonah* is angry with us, which is not infrequent, we just give her some space. Time and space."

Kim gazed out the window. His homeland was out of sight. Whitecaps flashed and disappeared on the green ocean stretching to an infinite horizon where water met sky. So this was the climax he had waited and worked and risked his life for. Rather gloomily for one fulfilling a lifetime dream, he said aloud, "I guess this should be enough space."

19

Lee Hana was returned to her natal home a widow. Her husband, on one of his lunatic rampages, had been clubbed to death by a mob of angry villagers who left his broken body in the street. There were no repercussions for the murder; it was regarded as a merciful act of public service.

The old lady had gone wild with grief. When the shock abated, and the grief subsided, resentment had set in. Fault needed finding. It had to be Hana. She had not served her intended purpose. She had brought bad luck to their household. Worst of all, she had been unforgivably insolent and reckless. The old lady returned her to her senders.

Hana returned home to find that her mother and father had died. Her brother had married and had been blessed with a doll-faced daughter. The toddler girl took an immediate shine to her pretty aunt, and followed her like an imprinted duckling. When the two were together, their striking resemblance could not be denied. One day a visitor mistook Hana for the little girl's mother. The confusion was intolerable to both new parents. The attachment had to be severed without delay.

At the earliest opportunity, Hana was escorted on a day-long journey by cart and bus and train to the only place where she could be made to disappear: Seoul. Her brother deposited her at the train station with an allotment of money he considered generous and hurried back to his purified family. On the ride home he reflected that, though his ex-sister had been irreproachably passive and cooperative, life would have been much less troublesome had she died during the war.

It was not long before Hana found her purse penniless and her belly hollow. A solitary female, unmoored from any decent family referral, she could not find work, even as a scullery maid. She reminded herself that it was not her fault, that she was simply unlucky. When her money ran out, when the owner of her rooming house put her on the street, when she spent a fearful night in an alley infested with cockroaches, rats, and feral dogs, when the hunger gnawing at her innards grew unbearable, she found a lonely spot to crouch in, took out her compact, and with her fingernail dug out from the edges the last remaining bit of makeup to cover the dirt smears on her face. Thus armored, she proceeded to the red light district of Itaewon and entered the Paradise Club.

Her eyes stung as the vapor of cigarette smoke and hard liquor wrapped about her face. The club was raucous with revelers. There were American GIs pounding back shots at the bar. More soldiers sat around small tables with women on their laps. The women, in slippery dresses, crimson lipstick, and curled hair, laughed aloud and drank whisky and flirted brazenly with the men. Hana stood in her white *hanbok* like a pillar of salt haunting Sodom and Gomorrah.

The bartender was the only one who noticed her at first. He shook his head vehemently and, while pouring shots into his lineup of glasses, waved the back of his free hand toward her as if shooing out a pesky fly. The GI at the bar then noticed the object of the barkeep's irritation and let out a long wolf whistle. Another soldier joined in. Then the entire clientele of the Paradise was ogling the country woman in their midst, and a groundswell of sucking and hooting noises of every lewd nature arose from the mob. Suddenly, Hana was no longer afraid. These foreign soldiers, giant and wildly variegated though they may be, were to her no different from the Japanese soldiers she had serviced as a child. She boldly approached the Korean bartender and addressed him. After a brief conversation, she was directed to the owner's back office.

The proprietor of the Paradise Club, a corpulent Korean in his middle age, was seated behind a folding table with an open metal cash box. Glossy posters of blonde pinups in various stages of undress were tacked to the wall behind him. His eyes were closed as he fanned a wad of bills into his flared nostrils. Hana discreetly cleared her throat. His eyes popped open, and he started at the white clad apparition standing before him.

"What do you want?" he grunted, clutching the bills to his chest.

"I want to work. Please. I am hungry. I am quite desperate," cried Hana.

"This is not the place for you. Go back to the farm," he snorted, stashing his bills to his money box and slamming the lid.

"I have nowhere to go," she pleaded.

"Do you have any relatives?" he asked.

"None!"

"Do you have any friends?"

"None!"

He took stock of her again, stroking the wispy tendrils on his chin. Then, abruptly, he shook his head and said, "Sorry. You will make too much trouble. You do not understand. Go away. Goodbye!"

"Please, I do understand. I…I…"

"Come on, out with it. I don't have all night. I am a busy man."

"I was kidnapped!"

"So? Too bad. What do I care?"

"During the Japanese occupation, I was in the Women's Voluntary Service Corp."

"Is that so!" he exclaimed rubbing his money box and surveying her from head to toe. "Yes, yes! I have other girls like you. But my customers sometimes complain about your kind. They say you girls are no better than a warm corpse. If I hire you, you had better take care that I do not hear such complaints. I am a busy man. One complaint and you will be shown the door."

"There will be no complaints."

"Work hard and show a little gratitude. Act alive when you do it. Humph. Good thing you have a pretty face. The Americans like that. They are simple animals who do not know filth when they see it. The rule is the customers pay me. You get one quarter. You keep tips and gifts."

He rifled through a soiled cardboard box and pulled out a filmy red dress which he handed to her saying, "I will take this out of your pay. Change over there." He watched her while she disrobed, without a shadow of lasciviousness, rather objectively, as one might study livestock at the market. He said, "It is lucky you do not have bayonet scars like some of the others. I have to discount damaged goods sometimes."

He led her to a rectangular annex crudely constructed of plywood, partitioned into narrow stalls, much like a stable, in fact, much like the Japanese comfort station, except that these stations were decorated with pinup posters of naked white women. Hana stared at the well-fed nudes, proudly displaying their erupting breasts, smiling innocently as if they were schoolgirls who simply forgot to put on clothes. He pushed open the door of the last stall. There was a narrow cot and a small table with a vase of plastic flowers. Every surface of the stall was covered with graffiti, some crudely rendered, some expertly drawn in painstaking anatomical detail, of naked women, couples in coitus, and disembodied genitalia.

"Here is your workplace," announced Hana's boss.

Compared to her experience with the Japanese military, the Paradise was easy work. Most of the men paid for a full night. Some only paid for an hour but fell asleep after doing their business. She was not to awaken them, and in the morning they were required to pay for their time. Many GIs were generous with food, tips, and gifts. Beatings, though inevitable, were rare and broken up quickly by the Paradise bartender.

But in other ways, her work was more shameful. As a comfort woman, she had been kidnapped and enslaved. In wartime, everyone around her had been in dire straits of one kind or other with no capacity for the casting of judgment. Now, there was a large respectable population outside of the red light district. At best, the decent men and women of Seoul would turn away from her or cross the street in revulsion. At worst, they would curse and throw rocks at her. She avoided leaving her neighborhood. If a foray into the real world was unavoidable, she kept her head down lest a decent pedestrian read vice scrawled across her face.

Years passed. They were years she did not keep track of. But the day she was summoned into the Paradise Club office, Hana knew what was coming. The more seniority she gained at the club, the more standing she lost. A supply of nubile young girls, impoverished and hungry, came from the country, from the city, from farms, from factories, to stand before the folding desk and importune the Paradise proprietor for work. They needed to buy medicine for their ailing parents or they needed to feed their hungry siblings. One by one, the older women were fired to make room for fresher flesh.

"How old are you? Thirty? Forty?" asked the owner of Paradise.

"Not forty!" she replied. She was not certain how old she was anymore. But she could not be forty, and he knew it.

"You are getting too old for this work. You should find a better job," he said, stubbing out his cigarette. He opened his money box and gazed inside. He counted out some bills and pushed them to her over the desktop. "Go find a better job." He did not look at her. He knew very well there were no other jobs for women like her. And she knew very well it was pointless to plead for mercy.

She was cast out on the streets. Rent was due. Her stomach demanded feeding. Therefore, she hustled. It was against her nature to accost men and flaunt her wares in the slatternly fashion of some of the others. She shambled about the alleys outside the bars, avoiding her more territorial competitors, and waited for a GI, usually drunk, to grab her by the waist. This passive strategy took a long time, and she was lucky if she got one paying customer a night. But she could pocket the entire proceeds of her sale and the riskier sole proprietorship proved nearly as profitable as employment at the club.

She rented a room in a slum of iniquity designated for the bottom feeders of her ilk. The flophouse denizens shared a common kitchen and eating area and a semi-detached outhouse. The public bath was a short walk down the street. During the years she was employed at the club, despite the close quarters, she had managed to keep largely to herself. But as a streetwalker who needed to bring her work home, she grew familiar with the other women in her building, in particular a reclusive next door neighbor whom she met quite by chance.

One day there came a sharp rapping on her door. She opened it to find a lady with a round girlish face and short straight bob, wearing a smart navy blazer and plaid skirt, carrying a briefcase.

"Lee Hana, I presume?" asked the smart young lady.

"Yes."

"I am Mrs. Park. May I come in?"

The lady entered briskly without waiting for an answer. She looked about the room and, finding no seating, sat herself on the floor, opened her briefcase, took out a clipboard and a pen, and patted a spot next to herself saying, "Sit!"

"Lee Hana. Now! How far along are you?" asked Mrs. Park.

"I…I am not sure," answered Hana. In fact, she was completely baffled and frightened. Mrs. Park reached out and squeezed her hand gently.

"Do not be afraid," she said in a gentler tone. "You are doing the right thing. You have made a very wise decision."

"I think…excuse me…I believe there has been a mistake."

"No, no, no! Please do not doubt yourself. You are a wise woman. You made the right decision. Trust me. Now, I need to ask you some questions and you need to answer in complete honestly. I am not here to judge you. I am here to help you. Do you understand?"

"No. I do not understand. I…"

"All you need to know is that I am here to help you. You are doing the right thing. Remember that! Never doubt yourself. If you wait too long, it will be too late. I have seen those cases. Those women are always sorry.

"First thing: we need to know what race the baby will be. Well? Let me help you. We have the following classifications: Korean-Caucasian, Korean-Negro, Korean-Filipino, Korean-Turkish. If you are not sure, we will have to wait till the baby is born and make our best guess based on its appearance. But for placement purposes, it does help to have an idea beforehand."

"Baby?"

"Are you not Lee Hana?" asked Mrs. Park.

"Yes. But I am not having a baby."

"You did not contact International Social Services?"

"No."

Mrs. Park rifled through her briefcase. She found the file on Lee Hana. She studied Hana's flat stomach with a trace of reproach. Then, rather resourcefully, she inquired, "Is anyone else in your building pregnant?"

"I do not know."

But as Mrs. Park packed up her briefcase and straightened her skirt, Hana thought of her next door neighbor. She was a pretty, younger girl who had a steady American GI boyfriend. But her boyfriend had disappeared in recent weeks, and, through the thin walls, her pitiful weeping could be heard all night. Of late, on the rare occasions the girl emerged, she wore a *hanbok*. Perhaps it was to hide a pregnancy. Hana led Mrs. Park, whom she now understood to be a social worker, to her young neighbor's door. Mrs. Park stopped her from returning to her own apartment.

"Wait. I may need your help," she commanded.

A shivering, watery-eyed young girl cracked her door open and the social worker asked, "Are you Lee Hana?"

The girl nodded and glanced fearfully from the imposing lady to the woman she recognized as her neighbor. She cried, "I am sorry. Please forgive a stupid girl. I changed my mind."

The determined social worker stopped the door from closing with a strong hand.

"Can you believe it? Ha ha! Your neighbor is also Lee Hana! I went to her apartment by mistake," said Mrs. Park in a high-pitched voice as if talking to a small child.

Name duplication was common enough for Koreans; nevertheless, it had a reassuring effect on the young girl. She opened the door. She was wearing an old-fashioned, white *hanbok*.

She cried, "My husband will come back. When he finds out what I have done, he will be terribly angry."

Mrs. Park said gently, "Your so-called husband is not coming back. He is never coming back. He is gone. But *I* am here to help you. Let me in. We will talk."

"How do you know?" cried the girl.

"I know. I have seen this a hundred times. Trust me. I know. Please let me in. You did the right thing when you called us. You made a wise choice. Had you waited too long, it would have been too late. I have seen it too many times. I am here to help you."

The young girl reached across the threshold and linked arms with Hana. "Only if *Unni* can stay with me," she said.

"Of course!"

They learned that the younger Hana had a highly desirable exclusive contract with an American GI, which had kept her off the streets. He had promised to marry her. The couple called each other "husband" and "wife." But when she became pregnant and her belly began to expand, her "husband" vanished, leaving on his pillow a sum of money which was now nearly expended. The women admired a photograph of the baby's father, a sturdily built blond man of medium height, posing before a Howitzer, arms akimbo. Mrs. Park wrote K-C on her form and drew an emphatic underline as well as a circle around the acronym.

"I should not tell you this," said Mrs. Park in a conspiratorial manner. "But there will be a great demand for a healthy Korean-Caucasian infant. Off the record, I can report that it will be a good looking child. Word-of-mouth will travel to the American adoption agency. You will be in a position to make demands. Not for yourself, of course. But for the baby."

The younger Hana drew a sharp breath and her hands flew to her stomach. A shy smile tickled her lips and her eyes, shimmering with nascent tears, opened wide.

"What sort of demands?"

"That would be your choice."

"But I do not know what I could ask for."

"For example, some women request that the adoptive parents have a college education."

"Really? *I* could ask for this?" gasped the young girl, rubbing her stomach. She sat up a little straighter.

Mrs. Park held up two fingers and said, "*Both* parents. Many American women have a college education. And such parents

271

would be more likely to attend to the education of their children."

"*My* child could go to college in America!" Her chin rose a little higher.

"You have the right to ask for this. I will put down 'entertainer' for your occupation. The Americans do not need to know – in point of fact, they do not *want* to know – otherwise. Never say I gave you the idea. I could lose my job. So! Think about it. Is there anything *you* want to request?"

The necessary forms were completed, stipulating that the adoptive parents must provide proof of their college degrees. The younger Hana was illiterate and possessed no chop or signature seal. So Mrs. Park produced an ink pad and executed the contracts with the girl's thumb print. She gave the girl money for food and medical care and scheduled a follow-up visit the following week. On her way out, Mrs. Park turned to the elder Hana and said, "If you ever need me, call!"

But after the adoption, neither of the Hanas needed Mrs. Park. The younger Hana, still dewy and blooming, perhaps more so after her baby was snapped up with blinding rapidity by a wealthy college-educated American couple, met another soldier, became pregnant again, married her baby's father, and moved to America an honest woman. The elder Hana, irreparably damaged in her childhood, would remain barren.

20

Kim Young Nam
California
1961 to 1962

A Korean graduate student deplaned at the San Francisco International Airport. He descended the metal stairs, stepped onto American tarmac, and filled his lungs with the California air. It smelled crisp and fresh to the young man from Seoul, and the strains of petroleum and asphalt only added to its bracing quality. He strode past the gaggle of Asian families gathered to welcome their relatives and entered the terminal building.

The international terminal in the sixties comprised little more than a few tables manned by a couple of customs officials. One of the officials peered over his newspaper and nudged his partner awake as the young man approached with his passport and visa ready.

Past customs, at the end of the corridor awaited a lanky, sandy-haired gentleman in a suit and tie holding a placard that read "Young Nam Kim." He was Dr. Kang's colleague, a founding professor from the new seminary. Kim approached the professor and bowed, a reflex it would take months to rid himself of. Professor

Jardine chuckled and reciprocated the young man's gesture but with his hands clasped in front of him as he had seen on television. Then they shook hands. The professor held his hand in his firm grip and patted his shoulder with his free hand. He steered his charge with a broad palm on the back which he periodically thumped in congenial encouragement. For a Korean adult who barely made physical contact with even the closest family members, it was discomfiting yet touching to be welcomed so intimately.

Professor Jardine ushered Kim to the parking lot. Along the way, the new immigrant could not help himself; he examined the sidewalk. The poured concrete pavement was littered with cigarette butts and squashed black splotches of chewing gum. Nothing more. Not a speck of gold could be discerned. Of course, Kim knew all along that "streets paved with gold" was just a myth; he was only making sure.

In the parking lot, a vast and sparkling Buick convertible coupe awaited its owner. Kim's humble suitcase vanished into the cavernous trunk. The professor put the top down and, with something of a flourish, opened the passenger door for his protégé. Behind the wheel, he grinned with undisguised pride and stroked the dashboard.

"I bought this baby when we moved to California. Mint condition. Only two thousand sixteen miles. You can put the top down and enjoy the sunshine year round here. She's a beauty, eh?"

"Yes, indeed," said Kim.

A Korean would have apologized for the inadequacy of his rattletrap, especially if said vehicle was a newly purchased, prized possession. Americans said what they meant. Their candor was almost childlike.

"Mrs. Jardine is slow cooking a beef pot roast, so we have a little time. Shall we take a short driving tour of the city before dinner? Are you too tired?" asked Professor Jardine as they pulled out of the lot and merged onto the highway.

"I am not tired. Thank you very much," replied Kim, swallowing the saliva that spurted in his mouth upon mention of beef.

Exiting the freeway, they drove inland, proceeding to a hilly residential neighborhood of fairy tale charm. The perfume of forever blooming flowers wafted over Kim's broad brown face. Never had he breathed air so clean, so delicately infused with nectar. The professor pointed out the row upon row of pastel hued Victorian houses aligned hip to hip like showgirls in a musical revue. From curlicue corbels to ornately turned balusters to trellises bursting with morning glories, the painted ladies displayed the pampering of masters with prosperity and leisure time to spare.

They approached the crest of a hill from which an extravagant panorama of the city and bay spread below. "Look down," said the professor. A road wound in improbable hairpin turns down the hill, flanked on each side by picture perfect homes, their parabolic front yards lush with a controlled riot of succulents and blooms. The professor applied his wingtips to the breaks and they began the slow descent behind a backup of tourist automobiles.

"Lombard Street. Crookedest street in the world," explained the professor. "This hill is so steep they put in these switchbacks for safety. Is this steep enough for you?"

"Yes," replied Kim respectfully. He knew about steep. The climb to Miss Kang's home was steeper than this.

Then they proceeded northwest through a less developed territory. On the right, the land sloped down to a rocky beach where the green grey waters of the bay lapped ashore. On the left, stands of palm and pine trees gave way to glimpses of white stucco buildings with red tile roofs configured in soldierly geometry.

"Presidio on the left there. That's a US Army base. Most desirable tour of duty in the world," said Professor Jardine.

"US Army? What division is here?" asked Kim, leaning forward and peering intensely past Jardine as if he might glimpse a long lost friend loitering under the faraway palm trees.

"What's that? What division? Well, frankly, I have no idea."

"Is it possible to find particular American soldier there?"

"Oh, sure! I bet there's some sort of locator. We can look up the base number in the phone book when we get home. Why? Know someone?"

"Yes. I have friend."

He omitted mention of the circumstances leading to his acquaintance with American soldiers. It was not a good time to talk of war. It never was. Luckily, the professor was distracted with his driving and did not ask questions. He only laughed and said offhand, "It's a big outfit. Might be hard. But you sure can give it a try."

As they drove on, Jardine gestured in the southerly direction over his shoulder saying, "Down that way is Golden Gate Park. Mrs. Jardine's favorite is the Japanese Tea Garden. Beautiful! Make sure you visit soon as you're settled in. It'll make you feel right at home."

Kim cringed inside. But he did not correct the good professor's misconception.

A graceful gargantuan, the flame-colored marvel of a bridge spanning an impossible distance loomed ahead.

"Here you go! The Golden Gate Bridge. World's longest suspension bridge. This side, San Francisco Bay. That side, Pacific Ocean," announced the professor proudly.

"I have seen photographs of this Golden Gate Bridge. But to behold with one's own eyes is entirely different experience," remarked Kim.

"She's a beauty all right!"

He could scarcely believe he was about to traverse one of the greatest engineering structures on earth. But as they merged into the bridge traffic, and he looked across the bay, a vision of the last steel suspension bridge he had encountered welled before him: the explosion that shook the earth and threw him to the ground, the inferno, the collapse of decks loaded with humanity into the black waters of the Han River, vehicles plummeting, people jumping, the billowing white *hanboks* of the women with babies on their backs, the shrieks of the doomed and dying. This was unacceptable. Not here. Not now. He forcibly quelled the unwelcome flashback. He steadied his mind. He compelled himself to gaze across the bay with equilibrium.

"I understand you have a field of expertise in eschatology?" he asked the professor, initiating a conversation that took them all the way across the bridge, through the waterfront town of Sausalito, and into a slant-roofed carport attached to a compact stucco ranch house.

"Here we are! *Mi casa, su casa.* That's welcome in Spanish," said the professor.

"This house possesses excellent construction utilizing inflammable material," observed Kim. "It will not burn easily."

"I never thought of that before. Well, I'm certainly going to sleep easier tonight," chuckled the professor.

The professor led his graduate student across the stepping stones to the front door, past a mob of glossy bushes and ceramic pots disgorging vibrant overgrowth. The little front yard was dominated by a stubby palm tree against which a red bicycle was casually propped. Two folding lawn chairs of woven webbing flanked this palm, one holding a rubber ball, the other a stunning blonde doll in a fabulous gown. Taking in this scene – the inedible plantings, the lackadaisical storage of valuables – the visitor sensed the good fortune, the comfort, the security afforded to the Jardine children, and was glad.

Kim removed his shoes on the front steps and entered in his stocking feet. The professor said, "Oh, yes. Leave the shoes there. Fine, fine. Whatever makes you comfortable."

In the foyer hung a painting of Jesus with shoulder-length, tawny hair and sky blue eyes, poised to knock at a large wooden door. "Mrs. Jardine painted this," said the professor. "She takes oil painting lessons with a group of ladies from church."

"An excellent depiction," said the guest.

Mrs. Jardine bustled from the kitchen, wiping her hands on her apron. She was a robust woman, rosy from turning her roast in the oven, crowned with yellow curls, sheathed in a pink checked dress, shod in matching pink pumps. When she spoke, it sounded like singing rather than talking, imparting a celebratory impression. She called her children to display to the guest: Lisa, a flaxen facsimile of her mother, and Michael, a chubbier, freckled version of his father.

"Doesn't he have any shoes?" asked Michael, who was only seven.

"Mike!" chided Mrs. Jardine.

"In my country, we take shoes off before we come inside house. Keep house clean," explained Kim.

"Can I?" the little boy asked, flinging the oxfords off his feet into the air.

The house was padded with domestic comfort: couches and armchairs upholstered in harvest gold moiré, olive and orange accent pillows, walls decorated with glossy photographs of Lisa and Michael from birth to their present age, Mrs. Jardine's multiplicity of oil paintings, and macramé tapestries interwoven with sectioned walnut shells and wooden beads. Even the bathroom, he would soon find, was adorned with a painting of the seaside and seashells filled with potpourri, as if to deny the terrestrial body functions occurring therein.

The guest may not have specifically observed that the tablecloth, napkins, dinner plates, glasses, and even the curtains were a matching set, wheat-colored and edged with a scroll of verdant leafy pattern, but the ambiance of decorative orderliness could not fail to create an impression of security and prosperity. Then came the pot roast, deep brown within its cloud of meaty steam, surrounded by carrots, potatoes, and celery, ensconced in a pool of gravy.

The professor asked his guest to do the honor of saying grace. Kim complied: "Gracious Heavenly Father, thank you for the blessings bestowed upon us. Bless the Jardine family. Bless this food so we may gain our physical nourishment. Amen."

The children, hands still clasped in prayer, peered from their squinted eyes at their father. Every other grace said at their dinner table was tantamount to a sermon, and the children had hunkered down for a long haul. This foreigner had said a prayer of unprecedented brevity.

Why turn mealtime into a performance? Why belabor the point? Kim was hungry, and the food would get cold.

"Well? Let's eat," sang their mother. The children were beginning to like this Korean stranger.

Mrs. Jardine poured milk for the children and then offered her guest a drink. He requested milk too, which she poured into his red wine glass. He added two teaspoons of sugar to the milk and stirred it with the serving spoon from the sugar bowl. The Jardine clan stared in surprise.

"Mommy, we want sugar in our milk too!" shouted Michael.

"Well…just this once," said Mrs. Jardine, hardly able to deny the request without embarrassing her guest.

"Me too!" chimed Lisa. The children liked the Korean man even more.

He made a pleasing impression on Mrs. Jardine too. Compliments to the chef would be superfluous. Her dinner guest's dedication to his meal, eager acceptance of her offer of second and even third helpings, and dinner plate polished clean, not a smear of gravy nor skin of a pea left behind, were beyond gratifying. Conversely, on the children's plates remained forests of salad and outcroppings of meat. When Mrs. Jardine collected their plates, the toroid of peas the children had stuffed underneath rolled about the tablecloth. She scraped their plates into the garbage pail before piling the dishes in the sink. Kim's eyes followed each plateful from table to trash. Though he maintained a phlegmatic demeanor, each thud of meat hitting waste can pained him.

The dinner party moved to the living room where Mrs. Jardine announced that Lisa and Michael would play the piano for their guest. Immediately, the children balked. Wails of protest arose from the children. No amount of coaxing or bribing could persuade them to perform. Mrs. Jardine scolded that to disappoint their guest would be very rude.

"I understand if the children prefer relaxation after such bountiful meal," said Kim.

But Mrs. Jardine was determined not to lose this battle. Not with a foreigner observing. She need not have worried about his impression, if any, of her parenting skills. He was still mulling over the wasted beef, all richness and tenderness, sitting at the bottom of the kitchen garbage pail, and recalling the garbage dumps outside the American military establishments where the Koreans would scavenge.

"Mr. Jardine! Are you going to say something?"

"What would you like me to say, dear?"

"Tell the children they must play the piano for our guest. They are being very naughty and selfish!"

"Oh, I dare say our guest has no taste for piano music."

Kim spoke up.

"As it happens, back in Korea, I know a young lady who loved to play piano. However, she did not possess such superior instrument as you have here. So she painted piece of wood, this wide, this long, black and white, to look like piano keyboard. And this young lady practiced on this painted wood piece for years until the church bought her a piano."

"See, children? Did you hear that? Do you know how fortunate you are? You are so blessed to have a real piano to play!

In Mr. Nam's country, they have to practice on a piece of wood. Why, I'll bet Mr. Nam would give his right arm to be able to play like you!"

"If he gave his right arm, he'd never be able to play piano!" said Lisa.

"Don't be fresh!"

But Mrs. Jardine laughed. And her daughter, perhaps softened by her mother's laughter, perhaps touched by the foreigner's story, sat at the piano and hammered out a sonatina. Not to be outdone, Michael plunked through a little ditty too.

"Real piano makes difference," said Kim, clapping.

Mrs. Jardine was pleased, not with the piano performance per se, but that she had gotten their children to obey.

At the end of his thirty-six-hour day, Kim was driven back to downtown San Francisco where lodgings had been arranged for him in a little white church on Geary Street. In the youth group room of the church basement, the newest graduate student of the San Francisco Seminary lay on a narrow rollaway cot which barely contained his broad shoulders. His swollen stomach rumbled with indigestion. He felt like a wealthy man.

Before he fell into the dreamless sleep of traveler's exhaustion, he told himself to purchase airmail stationery the next morning, first thing. He must have the necessary materials on hand when the time came to fulfill a promise he had made. It was not long before he was able to make use of the airmail.

Dear Miss Kang,

Before I came to America, I half-believed what Koreans say... that the streets are paved with gold. But I find the natural beauty of California to be even more astonishing than gold-paved streets. There are flowers of every shape and hue bursting everywhere filling the air with their sweet scent.

There are majestic cliffs that plunge to the ocean. There are redwood forests that seem to reach the heavens. The weather is balmy and always comfortable, quite the opposite of the punishing extremes characteristic of our native country. Indeed, San Francisco is the land of endless springtime.

My seminary has no campus and operates out of a Presbyterian church in downtown San Francisco where I am also living. There are forty-two students, all male. Initially, I was discouraged that I had traveled so far to find myself in this tiny school that is less established than Seoul Bible College. But I settled down and put my mind to learning everything I can. I have been surprised to discover the depth and breadth of knowledge and the academic rigor of the professors who founded this school. When I have earned my master of divinity here, I intend to apply to the top theological seminaries in the United States so that I can pursue a Th.D., the goal which your father has established for me.

There are many Asian immigrants here. They wash dishes or scrub toilets. But I went with some American seminary students to take an exam at the Bank of America. I passed and was hired in data processing. All the Bank of America branches collect checks, which are sent to the central location where I work. We take pictures of every check and log and reconcile the information in a computer. There are countless boxes of computer punch cards. The information is processed during the night and then sent back to the branches in the morning. It is the best job an immigrant of no connections could hope for. I moved out of the basement and rented the upstairs apartment directly below the church belfry, the most auspicious location one could imagine. I also take care of the church grounds for additional income. I now make enough to support two, after sending money to my mother.

The purpose of my letter is to request your hand in marriage. I have already received the permission of your estimable father. I hope you will look kindly upon my proposal.

You are the only woman I have ever met who meets each criterion I have established for my partner in life:

1 You come from a good family,

2 You are healthy,

3 You are tall,

4 You are intelligent,

5 You are a good Christian with strong moral character.

I am aware that you cannot cook, but I will teach you how. I recognize that I am but a poor student with nothing to offer but my pledge of eternal faithfulness and devotion. I humbly request your consideration of my proposal.

Respectfully,
Kim Young Nam

After mailing his proposal, Kim opened his mailbox each day and reached his thick hand inside to sweep out the dust of emptiness, preparing the receptacle for the receipt of her letter. At last one day, he found a slender blue airmail envelope in his mailbox. He rushed to his room with the precious mail and opened it immediately. He could practically hear her voice.

Dear Mr. Kim,

What a very lucky female I am to meet your stringent criteria! To think that a humble homebody such as I could receive a marriage proposal from a traveling scholar such as you.

I have discovered that my father has been harboring the notion for quite some time that I ought to marry you. He has developed a particular liking for you. Unbeknownst to anyone, my father hired an agent to conduct a background check on your family. He was triumphant to discover your scholarly lineage and made me sit and look at all the silly documentation. But I do not care about such things.

The fact is, Father must be eager to marry me off because I am getting too old. So you really want to marry an old lady? Since my father wishes it, I have no choice but to give the matter its due consideration.

Kindly await my decision.

Sincerely,
Kang Sun Hee

Per instructions, he waited patiently, stoically. While he struggled with his English, his curriculum with its laboriously intensive writing component, and long late night hours at his job, at all times, a part of his mind was thinking of her.

Yet it did not occur to him to plead his case any further. He had made his offer. She had instructed him to wait for an answer. He would wait. He could only hope that she did not fall in love with some other suitor in his absence. Luckily, she was under the watchful eye of her father, the one person she was anxious to please. Several weeks later, he received a second airmail.

Dear Mr. Kim,

May I inquire why you have not responded to my letter? A man should write to the woman he wants to marry on a daily basis. Do you still want to marry me? I have no idea. Thus, I am forced to send this letter in blind faith that your proposal still stands.

I have been terribly busy at Father's school. I am teaching Introduction to English, handling mounds of paperwork, and fighting constantly with troublesome people wanting money from us. Father keeps finding more and more work for me to do.

Remember our mountain? Sorry to say, our pine trees will never become a proper forest. The peasants strip all the pine cones off. They use the pine nuts to make wine. We have no hope of any lumber. But the national press attention we get is inspiring more reforestation initiatives. Chung Hee and Sang Hee started a reforestation campaign at Seoul National. It has become the patriotic thing to do. The funny thing is, these photographers come and take pictures of us all day long, but then they always print the same old headshot of my father in the newspaper. After I fixed my hair so nicely for them!

Perhaps you have read about all the student protests in the news. Do they care about small Korea at all over there? My sister ended up in jail! Cho Hee was not one of the protestors, but she was hiding behind a food cart and watching a police-man club a student. Cho Hee ran to him and grabbed his arm and screamed at him not to beat his fellow countryman. She was dragged off, and we had no idea where she was. It took a long time and a lot of money for my mother and father to find her and bail her out of jail. Her head was injured, but she seems to be recovering. Mother plans to send her Japan to study pharmaceutical science and keep her out of trouble.

But I am more worried than ever. After this happened, my brothers began to lead student protests against the govern-ment. I am frightened of what might happen to them. They are men and may not get off as easily as my sister did.

From my office window, all I can see is a mountain, burned and scarred, rising up like a prison wall before me. If I stand outside in the courtyard, and turn around in a circle, I see more mountains and the patches of little woods struggling to grow. I feel claustrophobic. Sometimes I lie on my back outside and look up to the sky. The sky rises higher and higher to infinity. I feel like I could be free if I went up there.

I have made my decision. Though you are the most inconsiderate man on earth, I accept your proposal of marriage.

Sincerely,
Kang Sun Hee

With a soaring heart, Kim splurged on a trolley ride to a charity thrift store where an extravagant diamond jewelry set had caught his eye. He could scarcely believe his good fortune. The replicas of Queen Elizabeth's necklace, clip-on earrings, and bracelet, stunning to his eyes, were still on display. He purchased the lot for five dollars and enclosed it with a quickly dashed letter to his fiancée. He would write her a letter a day until she became his wife. He was eager to be a married man. But he could not afford the time or money to come to Korea for a wedding. Therefore, he wrote a second letter to Dr. Kang asking permission to be married in the United States. He did not have to wait long. A telegram came from Seoul.

I will come alone STOP Plan simple wedding STOP Arrive February 1 on JAL 350 STOP

Kang Sun Hee

Kim Young Nam, Professor and Mrs. Jardine, and several graduate students and their wives, in their suits and Sunday dresses, formed the greeting party for Miss Kang at the airport. Kim hardly blinked as he watched her plane land and taxi to their gate. A mother herding four children deplaned first. The two older daughters dismounted, followed by their frazzled mother. She carried a wailing baby boy in one arm and held the hand of a disoriented toddler girl in the other. The oldest girl reached the foot of the stairs and promptly vomited. The stewardesses, in their well-heeled efficiency, covered the mess with a blanket and ushered the green-gilled child away. The next daughter was reluctant to step onto the blanket. Passengers were piling up behind them. "Keep walking!" scolded her mother. Suddenly, the father breached the velvet ropes, ignoring the protests of the ground crew, and hurried toward his family to sweep his baby son from his wife's arms.

"*Three* daughters!" thought Kim pityingly.

After all the families with young children had deplaned, Miss Kang finally emerged. She came to a foreign country alone, with no dowry, no guardian, nothing but a small bag of clothing and a box of cookies. Her waist-long braid had been chopped off and her short hair curled into a modern, wavy bob. She glanced at her fiancé and stifled a smile. But then she noticed Professor Jardine snapping her picture with his camera. She turned to the camera, broke into an enormous smile, and waved. As the young lady strode toward her welcoming party, all strangers to her except for her fiancé, swinging her small carryon like a schoolgirl, smiling and waving as she approached, the professor remarked, "Well, Young Nam, I can see right off the bat why you like her. She's just like her father. She's just right for a man like you."

They were married right away. The bride wore white, the workaday color of the Korean people, to honor the traditions of her host country. But her *hanbok* was a rich silk embossed with symbols of good fortune and white gloves covered the long, elegant fingers wrapped around a bouquet of field daisies.

All the students and professors of the seminary were in attendance. The wives in blue eye shadow and orange lipstick, cinched into peach and turquoise cap-sleeved dresses, sumptuous rolls of well-fed flesh erupting over the top, giggled and fussed over the bride. In Korea, Miss Kang was a giantess. Here, encircled by these great shiny Amazons, she was petite, as dainty as the flowers she clutched.

Professor Jardine performed the wedding ceremony. Kim had been debriefed beforehand, and he was prepared when Jardine pronounced, "You may kiss the bride."

It was their first kiss.

Outside the church, the professor took more pictures. "Smile!" shouted the professor. Smiles on her wedding day were supposed to bring bad luck; apparently she did not give a damn. She made no attempt to suppress her joyful smile. The groom could hardly reprimand her for audacious behavior on her own wedding day and in front of all these strange people.

"Smile, Young Nam. You're a married man now!" urged his professor.

He felt the discomfort of a sheepish grin crack open his face.

21

Time passed. The gloss corroded from Lee Hana's wares. Her bone structure, elastic skin, and girlish physique remained intact. But her weariness was palpable, and customers waned with every passing year. Some nights, Hana might hobble up and down the alleys on throbbing feet from midnight till morning without hooking a john.

On one such hardscrabble night, she wanted nothing more than to retreat to her own humble home, the tiny room which any day now might be lost for want of rent money. She limped along for what seemed an eternity in her cheap heels. As she neared her building, the thoughts of her bed, of abandoning her troubles to sleep, sped her, faster and faster, till she was flying on her tip toes, a red flower petal blowing down the fetid alley. Perhaps the appearance of vitality attracted notice, because a young American soldier emerging from a bar ran after and caught up with her.

"Hey, baby! Where you running off to so fast?" he asked.

While she barely understood his words, his intent was perfectly clear. She slipped her arm through his and turned him toward her apartment. She calculated pay day in her head. She had just about enough to make her rent. If this customer proved generous, she would be able to pay her rent and have a little left over for food.

As they neared her building, a pubescent girl wearing a blonde wig and a hypothetical dress that barely covered her parts sashayed toward them. The young vixen raised a slender arm jangling with bangles and wagged her painted nails at Hana's customer.

"Herro, handsome!" she chirped in English.

"Well, hello there! What's your name?" answered the soldier stopping short. The blonde hair and the sound of his native tongue, thick accent notwithstanding, were irresistible to a homesick soldier.

"Mariryn Monroe!" giggled the girl.

"No kidding! I seen you sing at the USO concert," he said. He dropped his arm from Hana's and encircled the younger girl's waist. "You look like a helluva lot more fun."

A Korean man materialized from somewhere in the alley and addressed the American in broken English. A deal was struck and money was paid.

"So rong, *ahjummah!*" the adolescent called over her shoulder as she strutted off with Hana's meal ticket.

Once upon a time, Hana had been even younger than this saucy, wigged creature. She had been a country girl in a long white *hanbok* dress, clutching a satchel of burned rice crackers, running for her life, hunted like prey. To her surprise and dismay, a pain she had not felt in years pierced her heart. Her throat constricted. Tears stung her eyes. She fought back the emotion and hardened herself. She turned around. She would not go home yet. She had almost tasted success. She would not be defeated. She walked on.

Hana found herself outside a bar which was known to host a largely black clientele. But as she pushed open the door, an entertainer who lived in her building caught her arm.

"What are you doing?" her housemate demanded.

"Working," replied Hana.

"Do not go in there. If you do it once with a black, the whites will never touch you again. They all find out."

"Then I will work for the blacks."

"There are not enough of them to live on. And the blacks will never marry you. They will never give you an exclusive arrangement! They never even come back a second time."

"Nobody comes back for me. It makes no difference anymore."

She shook her arm free, pushed the door open, and entered. The stench of urine and vomit, tobacco and liquor, sweat and cheap perfume surrounded her. The seedy remains of the night's revelry were illuminated by a shaft of dusty morning sunlight. A vast immovable drunk was slumped over the bar, oblivious to the houseboy who mopped up the ooze spilling from his open gob. At a table, another drunk bounced a squealing girl on his lap, his hand snaking up her skirt. The bartender, sweeping up broken glass from under the feet of the lascivious pair, shook his head and muttered curses under his breath.

In a back corner of the bar, behind a grease and dust coated bamboo floor screen, a small group of black soldiers was celebrating the discharge of one of their platoon mates. Hana approached and stood by the partition. The men looked up at her with a sort of neutral curiosity. The multiplicity of dark faces and white eyes frightened her. She realized she ought to show the men that she was available. She bravely attempted a smile. It felt as if her face might shatter into a million brittle shards. One of the blacks, the youngest fellow, bobbed his head politely and said, "Ma'am." Then, with a scraping of chairs to turn their backs to the intruder, they closed ranks and resumed their drinking and conversation.

To her dismay, Hana erupted into tears. Powerless against the onslaught of hysteria, her entire slender frame was racked with uncontrollable violent sobs. The black men looked at her in surprise, and expressions of consternation rose from them. There was a hurried exchange among the men as to who ought to deal with the disturbance. The ranking sergeant nominated the youngest soldier saying, "Yo, Washington. It's on you, man. Get rid of her before she makes trouble."

Washington stood and approached Hana. He put a friendly hand on her shoulder and said smoothly, "Now, now. Calm down little lady." She stood to his chest in her stilettos. Her olive complexion paled against the dark hand on her shoulder. He led her to the bar and asked, "Drink?"

He ordered her a Coca-Cola. She had seen but never before tasted the American beverage which looked like a curvaceous bottle of soy sauce.

"Coke," explained Washington.

"Coh-kuh," she repeated between sobs.

"That's right. Coke. It's good. Try it," he urged.

She was famished and parched. She took an exploratory sip. It was the sweetest substance that had ever hit her taste buds, and the carbonation was reminiscent of kimchi gone sour ready to be made into a stew with a bit of sautéed pork. She encircled her painted lips around the bottle and guzzled.

"Whoa, there. Slow down, little lady," laughed Washington.

She did not slow down. She had nothing to lose, and she gulped with abandon. But halfway through the beverage, a panicky feeling overwhelmed her. The carbonation seared her throat and exploded her stomach. The vacuum sucked the bottle into her mouth. She made a drowning sound into the black liquid. Washington gaped in amused disbelief. She grasped the bottle with two hands and forcibly pulled it out of her mouth a loud pop. Soda fizz shot out of the bottle and drenched her face and the front of her dress. She gasped. Washington shook with laughter. He reached over the bar and took a towel, which he handed to her to mop herself up with.

The sergeant, on his way out, admonished over his shoulder, "Son, I told you to get rid of her. Not make love to her."

In fact, Washington had no romantic intent of any kind. He was merely following orders. But when the sergeant mentioned love making, he could not help but notice that his damsel in distress, prostitute though she might be, had a lovely face and a winsome manner, quite unlike the wanton wretches who accosted him after dark.

He walked her home. He had not touched a woman since his deployment, although the opportunities had been plenty. He had forgotten how pleasant a pretty woman on his arm could be. He remembered his grandmother's parting admonition when she packed his duffel bag for boot camp: *Baby, don't be dippin' yo' wick into no nasty places. You gonna' go blind.* No, he was only helping, nothing more. He would deposit her at her home and return to base and forget all about the brief episode.

At the door of her building he took his leave. Shyly, Hana tugged on his sleeve and lifted a beseeching expression to him. He shook his head and said gently, "Gotta' go, little lady. Take care now. You be good." Tears quivered in her eyes. A gaseous yowl rumbled in her soda-filled belly and rose into her throat. She stifled it with both hands and turned to flee inside.

Washington caught her by the upper arm. He dug into his field jacket and took out some bills which he pressed into her hands. She looked at the money and then at him. She cracked a painful smile, shook her head, and gave the money back to him. She would not become a beggar. Again, Washington tried to impress the money upon her. Trembling violently, she threw the money at his chest and ran inside.

There was nothing left to do. There was nowhere left to go. She was old and finished. She lay on the floor, spread eagle, and stared at the ceiling. A plan came to her. She knew how to end the misery. Long ago, in Tianjin, China, twin sisters had taught her the way. She should have done it then. Mother was always right.

She ransacked a neat stack of belongings in one corner of the room, and found several scarves which she tied together. It was not long enough for the job. She ripped off the long ties of her yellowing *hanbok* jacket and added these two lengths to the scarves. She fashioned a noose, tested it on her forearm, and, satisfied with its proper construction, placed it loosely around her neck. On tiptoe, she reached up to tie the free end to the socket of the electric light bulb fixture in the center of the room. She heard laughter outside her door. She rotated on mincing tiptoes toward the door, to face the living, as suicides will do. She steadied herself. Then, with grim determination, she lifted her feet behind her and grasped her ankles. The homemade noose tightened around her neck. She gagged in hideous torment yet willed her body motionless. It took a merciless eternity for the noose to strangle the life from her. She closed her eyes. A sensation of déjà vu greeted her like an old friend. She had been here before, through this dark, swift, soundless, painless hole. She could allow herself to hasten weightlessly to its end.

Somewhere a door smashed. A man swore. Then she was being lifted by strong arms wrapped about her waist. Fingers raked at her throat. A hand reached overhead and ripped the light fixture from the ceiling. The socket and bulb crashed to the floor and shattered. The fingers clawed her throat again, loosening the noose, opening her airway. A man fell to his knees, still holding her. He slapped her cheeks crying, "Oh God, no!" She opened her eyes and saw the alarmed black face and whites of the eyes of Private Washington. "What de hell's wrong wid' choo, woman?" he screamed, several unnatural pitches higher than his normal smooth bass. A groan of utter despair escaped her. Not this again. But he enfolded her in his arms, tucked her head under his chin, stroked her hair, and rocked back and forth. "Thank you, Jesus. Thank you, Jesus," he said as ceiling debris showered on his bowed head.

The landlord, wielding an iron rebar, approached Hana's room to investigate the disturbance. He saw the broken door. He saw shattered glass and plaster littering the floor. He saw a giant black American tenderly kissing his Korean tenant. He saw her hand reach up and clasp the dark neck. The landlord propped Hana's door shut and, fuming, stalked back to his apartment. He made the decision to evict her the very next day. After all, his establishment had standards to uphold.

Under no circumstances had Private Washington planned to entangle with a Korean prostitute more than a decade his senior. But having helped her once, he felt responsible for her. And that sense of responsibility impelled him to help her again and again. When she was evicted from her room, he found a new rooming house for her in a pocket of the city that was friendly to blacks. Watching as she prepared for the move, folding her few belongings into a large scarf, he snatched up a corroded metal compact.

"Woman, don't be bringing no chunks of rust to our new place," he said, and flung it into the garbage.

He brought her groceries and gave her a weekly allowance. Eventually, ignoring the ribbing and scolding of his superiors, he ingratiated himself with the mess hall staff till he was able to land her a job washing dishes.

She worked harder than anyone. She was a good cook. She was eager to learn English and sat at his feet like a lapdog during lessons. She was still a beauty. And when he held her in his arms at night, when she wrapped her slender arms around his neck and satiny legs around his waist, when in ecstasy he knew in his heart to be genuine she gasped the words he had taught her – "I love you" – he could make himself forget that he was placing himself where innumerable men had been before. She belonged to him now, only him, and that, he made himself believe, was all that mattered. Somewhere at the intersection of lust and pity, he found love.

Washington extended his tour of duty to stay with her. In the little base chapel, he converted her to Christianity. Hers was an easy soul to save; a void wants filling and she was more than anxious to please him. Finally, when he was required to return stateside, he brought Hana to the base chaplain and married her. Then Washington brought his bride to America.

22

Kim Young Nam
Northern Virginia
1980

Y our daddy saved someone's life."
There was one beat of silence. Then, a pitched clamor rose up around the dinner table: *Tell us the story, Daddy!* The Reverend Dr. Young Nam Kim surveyed his four daughters. His daughters were tall, taller than their mother, almost as tall as he. His daughters were straight-A students, something he demanded and they delivered. Twice annually, he inspected their report cards and, before his heart could burst at the sight of all those A's, he deadpanned, "Where are the pluses?" His daughters were healthy, as attested to by the collection of perfect school attendance blue ribbons, which he thumbtacked to the living room mantel, much to the girls' everlasting embarrassment. To survey their salubrious abundance never failed to tinge his heart with regret. Why four daughters? Why not at least one son?

Tell us the story, Daddy! Tell us, tell us!

The story. What could his wife be speaking of?

"You mean Miss Han?"

In fact, his entire adult life consisted of saving people. As the founder and president of a Christian college and seminary, as the pastor of a Korean congregation in Northern Virginia, he was called upon with more incessant urgency than an emergency room physician. With a growing congregation came the incessant jangling of the telephone and the parade of parishioners at the door. Rarely were the Kims without house guests in their one-bathroom home: would-be immigrants, F-1 visa students, children of warring parents, any Korean in want of succor. Every church member had received help of one form or another from their pastor and his wife.

Just this morning, he had responded to a frantic summons from Miss Han, a church member committed to a psychiatric hospital on grounds of hysteria by her American boyfriend. Miss Han, unburdened by English comprehension, had signed the commitment papers herself. A morning of negotiations later, Dr. Kim secured her release under his guardianship.

"No, not Miss Han," said his wife. "Don't you remember?"

He dug deeper.

"You mean Mr. Shin?"

Earlier that same week, another church member, Mr. Shin, had called from his mom-and-pop green grocery store. Feeling threatened by a customer, Mr. Shin had shot himself like a missile from behind his cash register and knocked his customer flat out with a Taekwondo head butt. Rather than call 911, Mr. Shin called his pastor. By the time Dr. Kim reached the green grocer's, the customer had regained consciousness and was stirring himself into a fury. Dr. Kim negotiated a peace agreement between Mr. Shin and the customer who walked away mollified by an apology, a one-hundred-dollar cash settlement, and a sack of polished apples.

"No, no, not Mr. Shin. In Korea long time ago. You remember. The river? The monsoon? That woman?"

Their daughters' eyes glittered. This was going to be good.

The river? The monsoon? The woman? Tell us the story!

A rusted-shut sluice gate cracked open. A memory flooded in: the day he had risked his life to save an unknown country woman from drowning in a monsoon-swollen river. For some years after the adventure, now and again, he had wondered whatever had become of that woman. But it had been decades since he had thought of it.

He was well aware that, behind his back, his daughters called him the Easter Island Head. To such cheerful chatterboxes, he certainly would seem a monolith of stoniness. Neither idle banter nor affectionate words cluttered his lexicon. His native tongue was unsheathed only to chisel his children into the image of his own monumental stoic dignity. "Silence your racket" or "stop acting up" were his most frequent fatherly utterances. He never spoke of his past. He often heard fellow immigrants harangue their children with their tales of wartime woe. He took a different view. What was the point of casting a shadow upon his girls' carefree lives? If his children felt entitled, so much the better. Even if he felt compelled to teach them a lesson, it was not in his nature to wallow in past history.

But on this occasion, his daughters wheedled with the relentless determination of their gender. *Tell us the story!* His wife added, "Oh, just tell them, *Yuboh*!" Dr. Kim found himself recounting the story of the day he saved a woman's life during a monsoon in Korea. The rapt attention of his audience held him at first, but soon he forgot he was speaking, and felt he was reliving. He could almost smell the muddy water. He could almost feel the turbulence and the debris. One false step and he would have drowned. Sun Hee would have married another man. His four children would never have been born. When he concluded his story, he looked upon his daughters' faces, illuminated with awe. As much as children might yearn to please their father, a father can scarcely suppress his satisfaction upon earning the admiration of his children. Spontaneously, they clapped. Dr. Kim adjusted his glasses and shrugged.

Then his girls began their talk show style post-mortem. Would *they* risk their lives to save a stranger? Might the same individual act courageously one day but shrink from danger the next? Faced with such a life and death moment, would it make a difference if you had a headache? Shooting diarrhea pains? During this, the girls grazed on the broccoli tray, dipping the florets in hot bean paste, nibbling off the flowery heads, and arranging the stalks like denuded trees on hills of uneaten rice.

Their fussy appetites had, at one time, infuriated him. In San Francisco, his daughters, Candace and Chloe, barely out of diapers, had proved the most finicky eaters imaginable. On one occasion, Candace, his firstborn, had refused to eat the fish because it had been served whole, head, fins, and tail intact. She whined about the baleful eyes staring at her. His wife carved the choicest morsels from the mackerel and placed them on her daughter's plate.

In his mind's eye had arisen the vision of his own mother picking off the good meat for her sons while she extracted every molecule of nutrition from the meager leftovers. The deaconess would excavate and devour the head's bits of flesh and brain, vacuum the fins down to a diaphanous fan of cartilage, suck the marrow and spinal cord from the vertebrae, and pop the eyes into her mouth, all the while smacking her lips gratefully.

"Eat it!"

But Candace had sealed her mouth into a white line. Her mother forked a succulent piece and coaxed it into her mouth. The child gagged. At that moment, Kim had exploded in uncontrolled fury. He stood and pounded the table with both fists, causing a glass to fall over and shatter. He bellowed at his three-year-old daughter, "*Get out of this house and never come back!*"

Little Candace burst into tears and ran out the door of the apartment. Chloe then burst into tears and hid under the table.

His wife screamed *Yuboh!* and chased after their daughter. She returned carrying the weeping child, and put her to bed.

His eyes burned two holes into the uneaten food growing cold on his daughter's plates. When his wife returned to the table, Chloe scrambled from under the table into her lap and clung on fiercely. He did not know to whom his wife was speaking when, in a warm soothing voice, she said, "It is fine. Do not worry. It is fine."

And now the garbage disposal would soon be grinding up his girls' uneaten and toyed with food, that metal-on-meat racket he abhorred. Candace had formed a river bank of her leftover rice and placed a broccoli spear bitten into vaguely human form into the river bed. The girls continued to hound him for details of particular interest to the feminine race about the woman he had saved.

How old was she?

Was she pretty?

Did her makeup include lipstick?

Dr. Kim lapsed into silence. What good was it in the end? She was not the one he should have saved. Yet that stranger had lived, while another, more deserving, had died. What if he had exerted himself to his utmost, risking his life, to save the one? What might that child have become?

He arose from his chair.

"I should have let her drown."

Then he stalked off to his room before his wife and daughters could see the tears welling his eyes.

23

Lee Hana
Greater Washington DC
1978 to 1980

Mr. and Mrs. Noah Washington had moved into his grandmother's apartment in the Anacostia neighborhood of southeast District of Columbia. Everyone in the neighborhood was black. Hana Washington found herself lonelier than she imagined possible. The women shunned Hana; a good man had been wasted on her. The men could be kindly enough, but she could never befriend a man.

All the qualities in his wife that Washington had held most dear in a foreign land, grew increasingly irksome in his hometown. Hana's selfless devotion suffocated him. Her incessant industry itched like a cocklebur. Her oriental face and light skin were motes in his eyes. Where she had once served as his translator, he now served as hers. His grandmother, the woman who had raised him, who had poured the best of herself into him, loathed the Korean woman.

Nighttime in Anacostia brought gunfire and sirens, fights and screams. Hana, soaked in a cold sweat, fought to control the panic that attacked her, to suppress the urge to crawl under the bed.

She clung to the bulwark of her husband's vast frame. Her husband remained unperturbed by the violence outside his window, the familiar backdrop of his upbringing. He would mutter in his sleep, roll over, turning his back to his wife, and fall back to sleep.

Washington had drifted through a series of dead end jobs until his grandmother prevailed upon him to matriculate to Howard University on the GI Bill. The chasm between him and his foreign wife widened. Washington left the apartment in the morning and returned late at night. He ate the dinner Hana warmed up for him with one hand and held a textbook with the other. He came to bed late. Some nights he would not come home at all.

Early on, Washington had brought his wife to his grandmother's church. Hana barely understood the sermon and found herself unable to participate in the joyful celebration. Amidst the swaying and clapping, singing and shouting, Hana had been paralyzed with self-consciousness. She would cringe if another churchgoer's glance fell her way. Soon, Washington stopped bringing Hana to church. She missed church, not for the sermon or the singing, but for her husband's arm around her shoulder and whispered explanations in her ear.

Then one day, unexpectedly, Noah Washington instructed his wife to fix her hair and don her Sunday dress. At Union Station, they met up with Bill Johnson, a Howard University student, and Bernice, his wife. The party boarded a chartered bus headed to Baltimore for a Billy Graham crusade. Hana's unlikely inclusion in the outing was occasioned by the insistence of Bill Johnson. He was just as curious to meet his new friend's Korean wife as he was to find out firsthand what these big crusades were all about. On the long bus ride, the men sat together engrossed in discussion of religion, politics, and sports.

Hana sat beside Bernice and did her best to answer her polite questions. Did she know who Billy Graham was? *No.* Are there buses in Korea? *Yes.* How did she and Noah happen to meet? *Korea.* She was relieved when the awkward bus trip was over.

The stadium was packed with more people than Hana had seen congregated together in her life. Stands encircled the ball field and rose to the heavens. Behind second base was erected a large wooden dais and pulpit against the backdrop of the scoreboard blazing with the message: *Jesus said: I am the way, the truth, and the life.* The air hummed with the excitement of over thirty thousand excited worshippers. Hana ascertained that this Billy Graham must be a very famous man.

The audience was predominantly white. Hana felt her husband's side stiffen beside her. Their small colored party fell reticent in the vast canvas of whiteness. When the opening ceremonies began, they did not sing with joyful gusto nor raise their hands in righteous celebration. They did not shout "amen" along with the white Christians who belonged there. She understood the anxiety; she experienced it on a daily basis in her all-black neighborhood. She slipped her hand through her husband's unresponsive arm and hoped it would be over soon. Then something astonishing occurred.

From behind a partition, a Korean man lumbered to the podium. He was stocky with massive shoulders and a solid belly under a navy suit. He wore large gold-rimmed glasses and a great mass of black hair was slicked back over his large square head. Hana's eyes popped. He was introduced as the Reverend Dr. Young Nam Kim.

The Korean man took the microphone with an easy confidence that did not lack an aura of gravitas. He proceeded to deliver the opening benediction in what sounded to her ears like perfect English. While the Americans bowed their heads, closed their eyes, and murmured "amen" at key junctures in the prayer, Hana's wide open eyes were riveted to the sight of the Korean minister. She yanked her husband's binoculars from around his neck and took a closer look. She recognized his face, the square set of the jaw, the high cheekbones. Then she bounced like a baby in her seat and swatted Washington's arm.

"I know him!" she whispered.

"No you don't," hissed Washington, his head still bowed and his eyes still shut.

"I know him Korea," she insisted.

"Quiet, woman. All your people look the same. You don't know him."

"I know him! I know him!"

"You was a heathen till I saved you. You can't know him. He's a preacher!"

"I know him. Not in church. In river. He soldier. He save me time I drown in Sap Kyo River. I know face. I never forget man save my life!"

Noah Washington lifted his head and opened his eyes. He took the binoculars from her and peered at the Korean man as if he could thereby ascertain the truth of his wife's assertions.

After the English prayer, the minister prayed in the Korean language. Hana's hands flew to her mouth. She held her breath so as not to miss a syllable of her native tongue. All these Americans, tens of thousands of them, bowed their heads to hear this Korean man, a man she knew, pray to their God in Korean. Great tears filled her eyes and coursed over her face and hands. Her sides heaved in and out, but she did not make a sound or take a breath. The Korean minister then resumed in English to conclude his benediction. Hana then covered her face and let out the loud sobs she had been forcibly stifling.

Bernice leaned over and patted her shoulder and asked, "Did you say you know that Chinese man?"

"Yes! He Korean!" she replied triumphantly.

"Sugar, Noah's wife knows that Korean minister. Isn't that wonderful?" Bernice said to her husband.

The binoculars were passed around so that everyone could have a good look at this Korean minister, known to Hana Washington. He was now seated, along with the other crusade dignitaries, behind the podium. He sat like a statue, motionless, phlegmatic, as if aware he was being scrutinized under high powered magnification.

The white audience members seated near the colored party overheard the conversation. The wives craned about to confirm that, indeed, the Korean minister seated at the right hand of Billy Graham was an acquaintance of the lady sitting right beside them. The wives excitedly informed their husbands who stole a curious glance at Hana before training their eyes back on the stage. One of the white women handed Hana a tissue for her tears. Another pressed her hand and said in a congratulatory way, "Why, God bless you, dear!"

Hana sat up taller and prouder. She had neither interest in nor understanding of Billy Graham's sermon. She was absorbed in staring at the Korean minister, marveling at the fixity of his posture and facial expression. She was not the only keen observer of the Korean minister. Washington studied him through the binoculars and then looked at Hana with an odd expression. She felt his eyes upon her and smiled at her husband. Washington quickly turned away.

He found the Korean minister's name in the program: Dr. Young Nam Kim, Founder and President, Washington Bible College & Seminary. He carefully folded the program and secured it in his breast pocket. Periodically, he took out the program and studied the name again and returned the document to his pocket. When the crusade ended, as the stadium emptied, Noah Washington took his wife's arm in one hand, patted his breast pocket with the other, and exited.

24

Kim Young Nam
Northern Virginia
1980

Noah Washington stood at the threshold of a two-story brick building in Falls Church, Virginia. He checked the placard on the front wall and glanced at the printed tract in his hand. He turned around as if to leave, but suddenly turned back, opened the door, and charged inside. He did not stop at the receptionist's desk, but stalked straight to the office marked with a brass nameplate announcing "Office of the President."

"Dr. Kim in meeting!" the receptionist squealed, bounding out from behind her desk. But the stranger took no notice of her. She scurried after the intruder. A meeting in progress was visible through the glass panel. Ignoring this, he opened the door. The receptionist gesticulated behind the vast back now blocking the president's doorway.

"He barged in," she said in Korean. "I tried to stop him, but he would not listen. I am sorry. Should I call for help?"

"We were finished. Come in," said Dr. Kim.

The graduate student in the office, whose meeting was thus summarily concluded, packed up his briefcase and bowed his way out the door, though not before casting a resentful glance upon the intruder. The stranger entered, closing the door behind him. He paced in the narrow gauntlet between stacks of books and papers until Dr. Kim motioned to a seat. Trapped in the caved recess of the overused guest chair, the man shifted about, rubbed his face, and ironed the tops of his trousers with his palms. He craned to scrutinize the diplomas on the wall.

"Reverend Dr. Young Nam Kim!" he declared.

"Yes."

"We saw you give the opening benediction at the Billy Graham crusade. We were there. Orioles' stadium," he said, spreading the pamphlet from the event on the desk and pointing to the spot where Dr. Kim was listed on the program.

"Is that so?" replied Dr. Kim.

"Me and my wife were there. My wife. You know her. She recognized you. From Korea. That's why I'm here."

"Is that so?" replied Dr. Kim with increased interest.

"Her name is…was… Hana Lee. Uh…Lee Hana as y'all say it," said the visitor leaning forward with electric expectancy.

Dr. Kim's eyes unfocused while he attempted to recall a person attached to this name. His uninvited guest grew visibly agitated. Dr. Kim came up empty and cleared his throat.

"I meet many people. On occasion, regrettably, I find I am unable to recall a name."

"You knew her in Korea. You fished her out of a river. She was drowning," said the man.

"What?"

"That's what she said. Blast the woman! Didn't you save a Hana Lee from a river in Korea during a monsoon? She was drowning."

It was not unusual for Koreans from Dr. Kim's past to track him down. He was frequently featured in the Korean newspapers. He hosted a Korean language radio program that was syndicated in cities with Korean American populations across the country. It seemed a weekly occurrence that a long lost acquaintance sent a letter or turned up unannounced at his home, and such meetings ceased to surprise him. This occasion felt different. Only days ago his wife had unearthed the monsoon story after decades of silence on the subject. It felt more like fate.

"The Sap Kyo River? Oh, twenty some years ago?"

"Yes! That's it. Must be. We saw you at the Billy Graham crusade. She said she was positive it was you. She looked at you through my binoculars. Didn't matter if Billy Graham was preaching. She stared at you sitting on that stage the whole time. When you prayed that part of the benediction in Korean, woman cried and cried through the whole thing. She made a real connection. She was positive. She knows you."

"I did not know her per se. But I saved a woman from drowning so long ago I had forgotten all about it till…till my wife brought it up just the other day. For years, I used to wonder what became of her."

"I married her."

"I see."

"She was a prostitute."

"I know."

"How?"

"Women of my generation would not intermarry otherwise."

"I made a big mistake. My wife doesn't know I came to see you. I never meant to marry her. I was young and stupid. Noah Washington. That's my name. I met her when I was stationed in Seoul. I'm a student at Howard University now. On the GI bill. I'm making real good grades. I have a future. Professors all tell me that. I'm gonna' get a good job in the federal government. Know where I'm coming from?

"Far as Hana, I did my best. Know what? I saved her life too. Just like you, Reverend. She was trying to kill herself. I saved her.

She was a heathen. I saved her soul too while I'm at it. I can't do any more. I'm done. I don't know where to turn to. I need someone to help me. I can't take it any more. I made a big mistake."

"She is your wife. You took a vow before God."

"You gotta' understand. Look around. You in America but this whole building is full of Koreans. When I walked in here, felt just like I was back in Seoul. My grandma, she raised me. Grandma cried for days when I brought a Korean wife home. Grandma, my aunts, my whole family…nobody wants her around. She doesn't talk hardly. She doesn't fit in. She has no friends. It's all on me. I can't take it no more… anymore. My church…even they don't want her there. I'm meeting people at Howard, you know what I'm sayin'? Folks like me. Folks I can talk to. There's somebody else. A girl. A black girl. I can relate to her. I can talk to her about anything: politics, music…anything. She understands me. Don't get me wrong. I been one hundred percent faithful to my wife. But when I met this girl is when I realized what a terrible mistake I made."

"I see," said Dr. Kim.

"Reverend, you gotta' help me. You're the only person in the world she knows. She hasn't got a single soul. I made a mistake I never meant to in the first place. You don't understand what it's like when you're in a foreign country and you're lonely."

"I do understand."

"It was all a mistake."

"You wanted a partner. You chose her."

"Reverend. Listen. I'm still a young man. I'm getting a college degree. Bottom line: I want to have a family. She can't have a baby. I didn't know that when I married her. She's a lot older than me. She might be as old as you. I don't know. It's hard to tell. She doesn't even know her own age. Like I said, I was a young, stupid kid then. But now I'm getting older. When I met this young lady at Howard is when I got this awful realization that I'll never be a father. How would you feel?"

Washington put his head in his hands. Dr. Kim considered wordlessly, staring at the top of Washington's head. Usually, he discussed important matters with his wife. In this case, no discussion was necessary. He knew his wife would disapprove. Lee Hana, Mrs. Washington, could not be hidden. He would not lie about her past. The faculty, staff, and students of the college and seminary he had painstakingly built from scratch would become agitated. The congregation of the church, his church, one he had founded and grown from a one-member family to hundreds, would be incensed. Indeed, he himself could hardly relish the contamination of his meticulously tended society at its righteous crest.

Finally, Washington looked up. He placed his open palms on the edge of the desk and said, "I'm done, man. You gotta' help me."

Dr. Kim cleared his throat. His decision was made.

"You are a good man. You could have left her on the street. But you did not. She is not your kind, yet you took her in."

"Thank you, Reverend. Thank you for saying that. I'm a good Christian, same as you. I mean to do right. I do. God knows, I do," he cried.

"You have done your part. Bring her here for Sunday service at 10 a.m."

"Thank you, Reverend. Thank you!"

"Thank you for your service in Korea."

"You're welcome, Reverend. Thank you, Reverend. Thank you. Reverend...I'm concerned. When I bring her here, do I have to take her back? If I take her back home, I won't be able to get rid of her. Woman clings like white on rice. She'll be onto me. Know what I'm saying?"

"Send her belongings to my office. Serve divorce papers to my office. Also, send some money. You are a student, so you cannot send much. But send as much as you can. You owe your wife this consideration. Then you may start life anew with a clean conscience."

Washington stood and grasped Dr. Kim's hand as if it were a lifeline. "Thank you, Reverend. Thank you. Thank you!"

"One more thing," said Dr. Kim.

"Anything. Anything. I wanna' do the right thing. God knows I do."

"Study hard."

From his ministry of a burgeoning flock, Dr. Kim was all too familiar with marriage in crisis. It came in all colors and flavors. The most incendiary marital explosions were ignited by extramarital affairs, yet these flash fires were the easiest to quell. Other marriages ratcheted loose, joint by joint, by sickness, money shortage, problem children. Then there were marriages that slowly but inexorably decayed from love to apathy to contempt to revulsion for no specific reason other than familiarity.

Dr. and Mrs. Kim devoted vast tracts of time saving marriages in distress. They logged untold hours counseling couples, answered distress calls in the middle of the night, cooked meals, took in children for weekends, vacations, and summers, found jobs, and gave loans, which invariably turned out to be grants, from their own modest coffers. Few of the couples taken under their wing divorced.

The case of Mr. and Mrs. Washington was hopeless. He concluded this, not because they were different races with nothing in common, not because the Washington family might not accept a Korean in their midst, not because of the woman's sordid past, not even because Washington had met another woman. Washington wanted to be a father, and Mrs. Washington would never be a mother. Their marriage was doomed.

Kim Young Nam had always prided himself on his ability to integrate into American society. In Korea, he had walked across the peninsula to work for the US Army. His dearest friend had been an American enlisted man. That the Bank of America had been his first employer upon immigrating felt, to him, symbolic. The voice of God never did speak to him, yet he embraced theology because he loved its fringe benefits: philosophy, history, exotic ancient languages like Hebrew, Greek, Latin, Aramaic. He crisscrossed the country beginning in San Francisco, then Dallas, then New York, his ever burgeoning family by his side, to earn his advanced degrees at increasingly reputable institutes of higher learning, until at last his wife cried *enough*! He landed his first professorships at American colleges and eked out a scholar's living for many years.

Yet even transplanted on the opposite end of the earth and assimilated into American academia, his own countrymen pulled him in with the inexorability of a gravitational field. Many Korean immigrants made much greater fortunes than he with all his degrees. They left behind prestigious positions in Korea to come to America where they began as menial laborers, worked hard, saved, helped each other, and became prosperous business owners. One such Korean, self-made millionaire Mr. Pak, after years of entreaty and promises of funding, finally persuaded Dr. Kim to found a bilingual Christian college and seminary. The burgeoning Korean American community in greater Washington and beyond provided the critical mass Dr. Kim needed to earn enough money to put four children through college.

Dr. Kim was no entrepreneur, but his wife would take care of the business side. He possessed the knowledge and, equally important, the pedigree so sought after by the immigrant community. Once the decision was made, he tendered his resignation, sold the house, moved his family, founded the college and seminary, and planted a church.

The nucleus of spiritual and social life for Korean immigrants in America was the church. For the Korean man of a certain age, who had made his fortune in small business and packed his progeny off to the Ivy Leagues, there was no happier ending to his American dream than to become the minister of his own Korean congregation. Dr. Kim provided the education such aspirants required. Korean men, and a handful of women, traveled to Northern Virginia from all over the United States and even from Korea to study under Dr. Kim. Armed with doctorates of divinity, the newly minted ministers fanned out over the country, dotting the landscape with Korean churches.

Noah Washington could not know that he had planted a landmine under an edifice that had taken years to build.

What with afternoon visitation, a late evening graduate seminar, incessant phone calls, and an editor's deadline on his latest manuscript, Dr. Kim had no chance to tell his wife about his surprise visitor until midnight, when she awoke him by lifting *The History of the Peloponnesian War* from his face. She marked his place with a paper napkin, and, seeing that he had awakened enough, downloaded a nightly update on their daughters: Candace had an A- on her English term paper (why a minus? why not a plus?), Chloe made the track team (expensive running shoes needed), Claudia had a stomachache (check in the morning to see if she needs acupuncture), Christine lost her last molar (tooth fairy already came).

Dr. Kim waited till his wife was finished. Then he told her about Lee Hana, Mrs. Washington. He told her she must expect Hana at church on Sunday.

His wife sprang from the bed and cried, "It will not do! You have four young daughters! You cannot bring her here!"

"It is already done."

"You did not ask my opinion. I am the one who will have to take care of her. She will become my burden. If you must help such a lowly creature, why bring her to our church? This will destroy everything we have worked so hard to build!"

Dr. Kim lifted Thucydides from the nightstand and laid it on his chest like a shield, his thick hands folded on top. His wife had devoted her life to his, typing and editing thousands of pages of manuscript, auditing his courses and turning her notes into publications in his name, slogging tirelessly to visitations, securing the donations and loans that bankrolled his seminary, then managing its administration. She was owed the courtesy of his attentiveness. But the diatribe flamed on until their youngest daughter was heard crying outside their bedroom door. His wife stormed out of the room and swept her daughter up in a fierce embrace that did nothing to calm the child's anxiety.

That Sunday, Mrs. Washington came to church. She was late, however, and the eldest Kim daughter, Candace, was stationed outside to wait for her and usher her in to service. Dr. Kim was already at the pulpit, delivering more of a lecture than a sermon, from a half page of scribbled notes upon which he never glanced.

"Where in the Bible does it say you have to be happy?" he queried rhetorically. Man's right to pursue happiness, he lectured, was merely an invention of the 17th century philosopher, John Locke, and assuredly not God's will.

He saw his oldest, Candace, enter, leading a slim Korean woman in a ruffled blouse and mismatched peasant skirt. Candace slid into the back pew and patted the seat beside herself, flashing her orthodontically perfected smile. Hana darted into the indicated spot, put her head down, and glanced up infrequently. His daughter leaned over and whispered something to her, and Hana covered her mouth to smother a shy giggle. Although Dr. Kim observed keenly, his sermon continued without a hiccup. He knew his wife must be watching from the choir loft and seething.

After service, the congregation mustered in the church basement for fellowship hour of coffee, rice cakes, and donuts. As was his wont, Dr. Kim ensconced himself at the head of the most prominent table to receive the parade of parishioners who would flank his right and his left to seek advice, schedule wedding, funeral, and visitation dates, and solicit prayers. The church members viewed Mrs. Washington with wary curiosity, but, engaged in socializing, did not immediately approach her. Candace and Chloe had taken a fancy to the newcomer in their outgoing American way. Hana appeared flattered by their attention and plainly admired the girls. Her moist eyes clung to them with a wistful sort of longing.

In the role of minister's wife, *Samonim*, she seemed born to play, his wife worked the room, smoothing strife, formulating marital matches, finding jobs for the unemployed, flattering, scolding, and keeping her small society in ship shape. She was the director, the church her stage, the church members her cast. She seemed completely absorbed in her production. But the instant a busybody church lady approached Hana and her girls, she swooped in and snatched the woman off. Hana, shoulders hunched, head bowed, shuffling in mincing steps behind *Samonim*, obeyed her commands to gather paper plates or straighten chairs, and shrank whenever a church member approached.

Dr. Kim saw what was happening. Despite her initial objections, his wife could not resist a challenge; she would make this godforsaken woman into one of her projects. His wife relished problem solving and Hana was an immense problem. She cottoned to followers and Hana was as good as a shadow. She needed to mold and Hana was malleable clay. Inevitably, the church ladies would grow jealous. Lee Hana would be found out. A rift would cleave the church and threaten the school. Yet, instead of proper dread, he felt a curious sense of fatality, even relief. Let it come. He had survived worse than this. There must be a purpose. At the end of fellowship hour, a hundred inquisitive eyes watched as their pastor and his family took Hana Washington home for dinner.

Though middle-aged, Hana was still striking. Her silky skin, high cheekbones, and chiseled jawline defied the pull of time. A small, straight nose and a heart-shaped mouth adorned her symmetrical face. Her dark eyes were drawn to the Kim daughters but darted away nervously when they met her gaze. She did not dare look upon Dr. Kim and he, in turn, ignored her presence at his dinner table. She shyly complimented *Samonim* on her daughters' heights and lucky features. *Samonim* could not help herself: "Candace and Chloe were taller than I by the time they were twelve! And all my girls get straight A's!" Hana clucked and bobbed her head.

Dr. Kim applied himself to his meal with his usual steadfast concentration. He had taught himself to disregard his children during mealtime. As usual, the girls nattered on like magpies, tucked their sea cucumber under their plates, separated and spooned the mushrooms into the shape of a question mark. Today, their antics seemed of no consequence with the disaster seated before him.

The moment Dr. Kim polished his plate, Hana sprang silently from her chair to clear it. She managed to move faster and get more work done than four girls put together. She urged the girls, "Read book. I help Mommy." She intercepted Candace between the kitchen and dining room and snatched the dishes out of her hands. She whisked the sponge from Chloe and washed the dishes. She wrestled the broom from Claudia and swept the floor. After cleanup, they did not regroup in the living room for coffee and counseling as they normally would. "You girls finish your homework now," said Dr. and Mrs. Kim before they drove off with their mystery guest.

In the neighboring town of South Arlington lived a Korean widow who rented rooms in her duplex house to seminary students. Dr. Kim parked at the curb and idled the engine. He turned around and cleared his throat. But his wife interrupted, "*Yuhboh,* please go inside and settle the account. I had better tell her."

Sitting in the station wagon under the wan light of a street lamp, *Samonim* informed Mrs. Washington that her marriage was over, and she would not be going home. Hana received the news in absolute silence. Then the women entered the house and proceeded upstairs to what appeared to be a storage closet converted into a tiny bedroom.

"Mr. Washington has placed you in our care. He sent money for one month's rent."

"I want to call my husband," whispered Hana.

"Look over there," *Samonim* said, pointing to a box of belongings at the foot of the bed. "Do you see that? Mr. Washington dropped off all your things. He never wants to see you again. Your mistake was marrying him in the first place."

Hana lifted a garment from the jumbled mess in the open cardboard box, a red sweater, festooned with jingle bells and tiny bows. It was a gift from her husband, given last Christmas. She lowered herself to the bed and sat with the sweater clutched to her chest. *Samonim* rattled off instructions.

"Do not try to be friendly with other renters. Keep to yourself. Do not tell them about Mr. Washington. Then they will know about you. You are allowed to use the kitchen. But wait till it is empty. We will come for you in the morning. We will give you a temporary job at the school, but you must find your own work as soon as possible. Do not go anywhere or do anything without my permission. We must not receive any complaints."

Samonim's voice was a faraway echo. She thought of her husband. Her lifeline. Her true love. Since their move to America, she knew he was slipping away. And now he was gone altogether. For a woman intimate with unspeakable suffering, such a commonplace pain as heartbreak might have been borne stoically. Yet tears threatened to erupt. She pressed her trembling lips together. *Samonim* heaved a great sigh and sat beside her.

"Go ahead and cry. You deserve it."

This startled her. Nobody had ever given her permission to cry before. Tears filled her eyes and coursed down her cheeks.

She buried her face in the red sweater and sobbed. *Samonim* sat beside her charge on the bed and sighed again, more dramatically, in a demonstration of sympathy.

"A woman's life is hard," she said.

"I am an unlucky woman."

"Unlucky? *Unlucky?* For shame! Think of where you came from. Think of where you are now. I would say you are one of the luckiest women on earth. Here. Take this. It is for you."

Hana accepted a leather-bound book, respectfully, with two hands. Her tears splashed onto the cover. She wiped the drops away with the Christmas sweater sleeve and noticed the gold *Hangul* embossed on the cover. Opening the book from the back, she recognized she was holding a Korean language Bible, her first.

"Let me find a good passage," said *Samonim*, swiping the book out of her hands and flipping back and forth busily.

"Genesis, no. Exodus, no. Here comes the talking ass. No. The begats. How boring. My father made us read every word of it and make genealogy charts. Can you believe it? Oh, Mary and Martha. Mary always made me so angry. Lazy good-for-nothing that Mary. You would agree with me. Revelations. Definitely not. Let's go back. Here. You read this tonight. We recite it with the children every night. Our girls had it memorized before they could talk. Dr. Kim's favorite part is: *Thou preparest a table before me in the presence of mine enemies.* How perfect. He says the Jews do not believe in forgiveness. I admit it. Sometimes, I wish I could be Jewish in that regard. Now is one of those times. Men!"

She handed back the open Bible and stood up.

"Thank you, *Samonim*."

"Keep it. It is yours. Of course, you will be very sad. Cry as much as you can. Then you will survive. In your darkest moments, put your trust in the Lord. It works. It makes you feel better. So you may as well, particularly when you have no alternative. And go to sleep early. You must be very tired. We will come for you at eight o'clock."

After Mrs. Kim closed the door, Hana took up the Korean Bible and read the Psalms. How straightforward it was in her native tongue. How simple, like truth. Eagerly, she paged forward to Genesis and started at the beginning. She read swiftly, voraciously. The stories that had befuddled her suddenly became clear as water. She had struggled to get through the King James version to please the Washingtons and strained to understand the words of her husband's pastor. Despite her desire and effort, American Christianity remained foreign and convoluted and unreal, a ritual she submitted herself to for her husband and his grandmother. Reading the Bible in Korean felt like coming home. Here it all was, just as her husband had tried to teach her, written in the graphic blocks of *Hangul*.

She did not cry. She read herself to sleep.

25

Greater Washington DC
1981 to 1982

From the oversized steel case desk crammed into his small bedroom, Dr. Kim overheard his daughters ambushing their mother. Who was Mrs. Washington? Who was Mr. Washington? Where was he? Did they have children? Why did she come to our church? Where did they take her? How old was she? Did Mother think she was beautiful?

"She is not beautiful at all! She looks *chonnom*! Country bumpkin. Like your father."

Mrs. Washington, *chonnom* or not, was a striking woman, and therefore a source of fascination to the young Kim females. That a woman of their parents' generation had married a non-Korean only added to the mystery.

Hana was to be the object of drastic modification. Mrs. Kim made Hana cut her glossy curtain of raven hair and inflicted upon her a home permanent. Hana instantly aged a decade. Mrs. Kim took her clothes shopping at Dress Barn for double knit plaid sans-a-belt pant suits, and a variegated flower-blasted Sunday dress. Mrs. Kim enrolled her into an ESL class. Mrs. Kim hired her as an office assistant at the seminary. And despite all the time they were spending together at their work and at their home, Mrs. Kim managed to keep Hana an arm's length from her inquiring daughters.

One evening, after they had dropped Mrs. Washington off at her apartment, Dr. Kim overheard his wife delivering a unique rendition of the birds and the bees lecture to the girls. It began with a shrill admonition to abstain from premarital sex at all costs. When a man wants to have sex, she explained, the urge is overwhelming, precisely like the urge to release a massive excrement. In this condition of pressing need, a man would do or say anything to get sex, just as he would do or say anything to relieve his bowels. When a man has sex with a woman who is not his wife, that woman is like the toilet he unloads his feces into. A woman who grants premarital sex, therefore, is no better than a toilet, and will be and should be treated as such.

There followed an interactive unit on self-defense. She detailed methods of crippling a would-be rapist by assault upon his gonads: kicking, kneeing, squeezing with both hands, bashing with a hard object. "Hard as you can," she hissed. "Hard as you can!" Should an exposed penis have the misfortune of presenting itself, the girls were to wring it and yank it right off. At this, peals of laughter rang out.

Undeterred, the ferocious mother issued her girls instruction on a technique for gouging out the rapist's eyes with their thumbnails. He did not need to be in the room to visualize the scene: his wife's teeth bared and black eyes glittering, his teenagers, Candace and Chloe, snickering, and his younger girls, Claudia and Christine, wide-eyed and gape-mouthed.

Dr. Kim sighed and bent his head to his manuscript. Why four daughters? Why not four sons?

Hana performed odd jobs at the seminary, photocopying, brewing coffee, serving and cleaning up after luncheon conferences. But the longer she lingered, the more inquisitive the other Korean office ladies grew. Continued evasion grew ever more harrowing. *Samonim* decided that the time was past due to find Mrs. Washington new employment. Mrs. Kim hatched the plot, perfectly audacious, as most of her ideas were, that her assiduous protégé would make an excellent small business owner. She could never be fired, even if she were found out. She could join the hordes of Korean immigrants who, lacking a medical, science, or engineering background and finding themselves jobless in American society, resorted to opening mom-and-pop establishments. *Samonim* organized a *keh*, a private lending club of her ten most trusted women friends. In what amounted to an egregious breech of etiquette, which she granted herself permission not to fret over, she neglected to disclose her intentions for the pot when her turn came to take it.

The Kims purchased, in Hana's name, the only business available for the ten thousand dollar *keh* pot, a laundromat in the Anacostia ghetto of southeast District of Columbia. As Jackson, the elderly black businessman who sold them Jackson's Coin Op, handed over the keys, he advised the Koreans to invest in a gun. He explained that all the business owners in the neighborhood packed heat, especially the Koreans. He offered to sell them a handgun from his collection. As the pastor and his wife watched in surprise, Hana accepted the gun, hefted it in her palm, loaded rounds into the chamber with a practiced hand, and deposited the weapon into her handbag.

"Looks like you're going to make out just fine here, young lady," Mr. Jackson laughed.

Then Dr. and Mrs. Kim accompanied Hana to visit the businesses on her corner, all Korean owned, all purchased with *keh* money, no doubt. Crossing the street to the Kentucky Fried Chicken, where a goateed Colonel grinned over the storefront of bulletproof glass and stainless steel pass-through, they stood before the order window.

"Remember," said Mrs. Kim. "You are Lee Hana. Spinster."

"What you having?" asked the fried chicken purveyor without looking up.

"I am Reverend Dr. Kim Young Nam of Washington Bible College & Seminary," Dr. Kim announced into the speaker in Korean.

The Korean behind the bulletproof glass jumped, cried *Aigo!* and bowed repeatedly in quick succession. The fried chicken vendor had no idea who this man was, but the mention of title and college was enough. He scurried to the side door, unlocked the battery of dead bolts, and ushered the party inside. Dr. Kim introduced Miss Hana Lee, new owner of the laundromat. The owner of Kentucky Fried Chicken promised to look out for the new owner of Jackson's Coin Op. They departed with three buckets of complimentary Extra Crispy.

A cluster of neighborhood residents had congregated on the corner. Mrs. Kim muttered something in Korean to her husband and grasped Hana by the elbow. But Hana seemed unperturbed. Her poodle *pahmah* and her hausfrau outfit eliminated the wolf whistles and cat calls that used to make her suffer. She was at ease in this neighborhood. One of the men approached them.

"You buy old man Jackson's laundry?"

"Yes," replied Dr. Kim.

"How come you Japs own all the stores and shit? Why the government help y'all and leave us twistin'?"

"Contrary to popular belief, there exists no government assistance for Asians," said Dr. Kim.

"*Yuhboh*, let us go," said his wife in Korean.

"Damn conspiracy is what it is. It's a goddamn government plot to kill us off. We get the goddamn shaft time after time. How else you go and buy up all this shit around here? What the fuck?"

"In answer to your question, we help each other buy businesses…"

"Bull*shit*! That's a load of bullshit is what it is. You really gonna' work in my hood? Fancy Chinaman all dressed up in that goddamn suit?"

Dr. Kim glanced at Hana and deliberated momentarily, a gap swiftly spackled by his wife.

"Oh, yes," she exclaimed. "Dr. Kim will work here every day. He will be in back room. Miss Lee will be in store. Hope to see you soon. Bring lots and lots of dirty laundry. Bring all your quarters. Empty out piggy bank and come. You be the first customer. Miss Lee will give you big price break. So nice to meet you. So sorry we have to run now. Goodbye!"

As they crossed the street, she said to Hana in Korean, "Let them think there is a man in the store."

They proceeded into the liquor store located kitty-corner to the laundry. The Korean proprietor greeted them with the abundance of the respect due a minister and his party. He too promised to keep a watchful eye on the laundromat and Miss Lee. From a back room where she had been eavesdropping, the storekeeper's wife and appeared bearing a tower of fruit, chocolates, and nuts, wrapped in iridescent cellophane, topped with a pink gift bow, which she gave to Mrs. Kim. There was a hole in the side of the wrapping from which, presumably, a bottle of booze, deemed inappropriate to gift a man of God, had been extracted.

Then the liquor store owner launched into a disquisition regarding the source of their livelihood, soon to be their mutual patrons.

"You may as well know how things will be around here," he said. "I will tell you. Welfare check day is pandemonium. First, they come to my liquor store. They form a line that stretches all the way down and around the block. By midday, fights break out. By nightfall, drunks collapse in the gutter. What can I do? It's not my fault. I cannot refuse to sell to anyone.

"Their second stop is the Kentucky Fried Chicken. You see these welfare mothers gobbling fried chicken and guzzling sodas while their hungry children hang off them, begging for a crumb or a sip of soda. When one of them has a baby, you think their first question is 'Did you have a boy or a girl?' No. Their first question is 'Did you get your check?'"

Hana stiffened. Mrs. Kim gripped her elbow and gave her a warning glance. The liquor store took no notice of the women's discomfiture but continued on.

"The last station on their welfare train will be your laundromat. They will go through great lengths to shortchange you. They carve perfect quarters out of wood, plastic, linoleum, whatever, and even whittle in the serrated edge. Mr. Jackson showed me some of them. He collected them in a shoebox. If they had time to carve a perfect quarter, why don't they just find a job instead?

"After welfare check day, business slows down. It doesn't pick up again till the next welfare check. The men make a baby and then leave. They don't even know which baby is their baby. These people are hopeless. There is not a good man among them."

Hana cast her gaze to the ground. She knew there were good men here; she had been married to one of them. But she kept her mouth shut. Once outside, Mrs. Kim said, "You did right to say nothing. You need him on your side. Anyway, he was not speaking of your husband. Your ex-husband, I should say."

Back in Jackson's Coin Op, the Kims and Hana took a look around. Mr. Jackson had grown too decrepit to handle upkeep of the premises. The linoleum floor was filthy. Half the machines had a hand-scrawled "out of order" sign taped onto their doors. Graffiti covered the walls top to bottom. The ceiling was coated with grime and dust.

"Look up," said Dr. Kim, pointing at the ceiling. "Under that dirt, there are antique tin tiles. They are beautiful works of art."

And indeed, upon closer inspection, they discerned under the coating of neglect the elaborate filigree and floral pattern of intricately pressed metal. Each tile was a stand-alone picture, yet the tiles fitted together into a pattern that expanded and replicated into a greater whole. It *was* beautiful. Lee Hana began to fall in love her place of business.

The liquor store Korean burst in, flush with excitement.

"I just had an idea. I have an old man working for me loading and stocking. He is a hard worker but too old for the job. I have to do most of it myself. Just now, after you left, he dropped a crate. Every single bottle broke. He just cost me hundreds of dollars in lost profit. While I was helping him sweep up, I had an idea. Maybe you can hire the old man. My son is old enough to help me in the store after school now. The old man is happy to work for minimum wage. You can trust him with your life. As a matter of fact, one time he saved my life. A gang of hoodlums were threatening me with guns and the old man talked them into leaving my store. Just like that. Saved me from having to shoot someone. That is why I cannot just fire him."

"Is he Korean?" asked Mrs. Kim.

"Of course not. He's black. Everyone here is black. That is what makes him so useful. He is respected on the block. Gramps. That's what they call him. Nobody would bother you with Gramps here. Your work would be easy enough for him. Sit in a chair and watch out for troublemakers. Help someone when they get a coin stuck in the machine. Escort you to the car when you are carrying the coins. No heavy lifting required. This job is perfect for Gramps. Minimum wage. He is a good man. An excellent man!"

Hana looked at *Samonim* who looked at Dr. Kim.

"Miss Lee will hire him," he said.

Overnight, Hana became a business owner and employer. During the entire drive to her rooming house, *Samonim* dispensed advice, though the closest she had come to running a retail business was a child refugee's makeshift version of a lemonade stand at the Pusan perimeter. When they pulled into the car port of Hana's rooming house, she wound up her lecture saying, "You must work very hard. Remember I will owe the *keh* one thousand dollars by the first of the month."

"I will do it," Hana promised.

And she did. She welcomed hard work; it freed her from the demons in her mind. She stationed Gramps on an easy chair to mind the store. She scrubbed with mad fervor. She kept the place spotless, right down to the holes in the dryers, which she cleaned individually with cotton swabs. She opened seven days a week and doubled the hours of operation. She started a wash and fold service. She took in mending. She leased a soda machine, then a snack machine. People from neighboring areas traveled extra distances, lugging their bulging laundry bags, to enjoy the cleanliness of Lee's Coin Op. One quarter at a time, she earned her independence.

Soon after her initiation as an entrepreneur, Hana pulled into the Kim's driveway ensconced in the passenger seat of a great golden Cadillac with a middle-aged white gentleman at the wheel. The Cadillac filled the weedy driveway with its vast four-door girth, whitewall tires, stylishly sloped trunk, and endless hood, punctuated with the trademark ornament which glinted like a newly minted silver piece in the sun.

The driver sprang from the car clutching a jar of pennies under one arm. He tossed the ring of keys up in the air, caught them, and then dangled the ring from his index finger to Hana smiling, "She's all yours!" Then, all but clicking his heels, he strutted down the street whistling "Ticket to Ride."

Hana raised the key ring in the air on her outstretched palm with a look of fearful glee. "Need car drive to laundry," she explained sheepishly. She handed the title to Mrs. Kim who handed it to her husband to inspect for authenticity.

"Was *that* Mr. Washington?" asked Candace.

Hana was taken aback for a moment. Then she covered her mouth and smothered a laugh. No, that was not Mr. Washington.

She had answered a classified ad for a mint-condition Cadillac for sale by owner for the price of one dollar. The owner was ecstatic to receive her call. Learning that his potential buyer had no transportation and no driver's license, the gentleman drove the Cadillac to her place, whereupon the sale was finalized. He spied a jar filled with pennies on the kitchen counter and encouraged her to pay with that. Not knowing what to do next, Hana asked him if he would drive her in her new Cadillac over to her pastor's house. He was more than happy to oblige. On the way, he confided to Hana that he had recently finalized a bitter divorce. As a part of the divorce settlement, the judge had ordered him to sell his new car and turn over the proceeds of the sale to his ex-wife. He would be damned if he gave her a penny over one dollar. Hana was the only person who answered his advertisement.

Hana said, "Rich American have husband problem. Not only me!"

The day Hana got her driver's license, Mrs. Kim insisted that the car must be caked with mud to deter theft in Southeast DC. The Cadillac, mud and all, served her well. She was able to drive to and from the laundromat at all hours of the day and night. She visibly puffed with pride when chauffeuring Mrs. Kim about town. She discovered discount stores and Korean groceries in the greater Washington area and introduced her benefactress to a whole new world of the bargain hunting Dr. Kim had no patience for. Eventually, Mrs. Kim even called upon her to drive her daughters to their meets and rehearsals and play dates, providing Dr. Kim hours of extra time for his writing.

Should unrest of one kind or another foment in the church, Dr. Kim could be counted upon to disregard it. The jealousy, petty bickering and power plays that inevitably bubbled up in their community, if ignored, usually resolved themselves. The case of Lee Hana was different. The unease among the righteous when she came in their midst did not abate despite Dr. Kim's benign neglect.

When Mr. Pak, ruling elder of the church's session, chairman of the seminary's board of trustees, self-made grocery store millionaire, and primary benefactor paid an unannounced visit, the gravity of the unrest became evident.

Mr. Pak began in a conciliatory spirit. The women, his wife included, were jealous of the attention the *Samonim* was paying this Lee Hana. Though Mr. Pak himself found Miss Lee's absence of family connections disturbing, he was able to set his concerns aside. However, when other elders of the church called the validity of her church membership into question, he had no choice but to conduct an investigation. He learned that Miss Lee was once married to a black man named Noah Washington. It followed that she must have been a woman of ill repute in Korea. Of course, Dr. Kim must have been deceived regarding her background or else he would not let such a woman join the church, much less get so close to his own wife and daughters.

"I knew," replied Dr. Kim. He also knew this day would come.

Mr. Pak blanched. He continued in a more offended tone. The dishonor such a church member would bring upon the community could not be borne. Their sons and daughters would be unable to make an advantageous match given their association with such a lowly person. They appreciated the fact that she was no longer working at the seminary. But, in addition, she must be expelled from the church.

"No."

Mr. Pak reminded the founder and leader of the church that the session had the power to hire and fire the ministers. Furthermore, the board of directors of the College & Seminary had the power to terminate the president and nominate a new candidate. These powers of the session and of the board were set down in the church and seminary bylaws.

"I know," said Dr. Kim. "I wrote the bylaws."

Mr. Pak continued. Session had held a meeting. Mr. Pak himself did not want to meet behind the pastor's back, but the others insisted upon it. In an informal vote, it was unanimously agreed that they would have no choice but to part with their respected pastor rather than brook the presence of a prostitute in the most holy of memberships. Several of these church elders were also on the board of directors of the College & Seminary. The ministry and the school were so intertwined that the presidency would also be in jeopardy.

"Do as you must."

Mr. Pak launched his final desperate salvo. His own wife had participated in the *keh* that the *Samonim* organized. His own wife figured out where her money went. So beloved was *Samonim* that his own wife repeatedly covered up for her. His own wife, the most honest of women, lied to the suspicious lending club members that the money was used to pay off credit card debt. The situation could be easily remedied. There were dozens of Korean churches in greater DC that Miss Lee could join. Her secret would be safe. Why sacrifice his ministry for a harlot?

"It is not our place to banish a believer from the house of God."

With a leaden heart and downcast eyes, Mr. Pak left his pastor, confidante, and friend's home for what he knew would be the final time.

Within the month, with six mouths to feed, one daughter applying to college, a balloon mortgage coming due, and the minimum balance in the bank, the Reverend Dr. Young Nam Kim found himself unemployed.

26

Washington DC
Upstate New York
1985

One morning, Gramps escorted surprise visitors into Lucky Lee Coin Op to see Hana.

"Hey," said Noah Washington. He held a little boy in one arm.

Lee Hana gasped. Her hands flew to her flushed cheeks. At her ankles, a miniature dog of indeterminate breed, fawn colored with a black mask, cocked his head quizzically, observing his mistress's unusual demeanor.

"Miss Hana, I believe you are acquainted with Noah Washington," said Gramps.

"You got a new hairdo," said Washington. "Looks nice."

Hana could not speak. Washington had run out of pleasantries.

Gramps said, "Now if Miss Hana ain't the prettiest, nicest boss I ever had I'll eat my hat. And hard working? You never met a harder working lady. Look how clean our place is. Place so shiny it hurts my eyes. You could eat off our floors. Folks come to our laundromat from miles around. Miss Hana give me two raises already. This here young lady, she's a keeper."

As it happened, Gramps knew someone who knew someone who knew Washington's grandmother. Word traveled.
Washington had come to see for himself if the rumors about his
ex-wife were true. He surveyed the premises and let out a low,
slow whistle, which incited the little dog to howl. Hana scooped
up the little animal and held him up so that the child could pet
him.

"This dog gift from Gramps. I say, no dog. Too busy. Gramps
say I need dog. Most time, I listen to Gramps. He right most
time."

The little dog licked her face in agreement.

"What's his name?" asked Washington.

"Goliath."

Washington threw his head back and laughed.

"I ask Dr. Kim name him. He say dog who look like only
slipper need giant name. Make think big."

"Well, looks like you thought pretty big yourself. Want to
show us around?"

Hana took her visitors on a tour of the establishment. At
the storefront a small cubby was partitioned by a half wall. A
sewing machine stood at one end, and a small desk at the other.
Atop the desk was a framed photograph of Dr. and Mrs. Kim
and a vase of artificial flowers. Hana opened the desk drawer and
took out the candy jar hidden there for the children. She offered
Washington's son a lollipop and he squealed with glee. In the
main area, a double row of washing machines stood back-to-
back, twenty strong, gleaming. Along the opposite walls, equal
numbers of dryers faced their matching partners. At the rear of
the store, the storage room was stocked with cleaning supplies
and tools, neatly sorted. The tour was over.

Washington set his little son on the lid of a washing machine
balancing his hands under the boys' armpits.

"He very very handsome. Look like you," said Hana.

"Nah. Looks just like his ma. Lucky for him."

"How old?"

"Eighteen months."

"Big boy for age."

"Yup. Smart too. Just like his ma."

"Thank you visit me. I appreciate lot."

"I just had to see it for myself. We moved to Baltimore. I don't come as much as I should. We're planning to move Nana in with us. Then I'll come back even less. She doesn't want to move, but she's getting too old to live alone."

"I wish her health and happy fortune."

"You still live around here?"

"Oh, no. I live Arlington."

"With Dr. Kim's family?"

"Oh, no. Dr. Kim say I need to buy house. I cannot afford so soon. He say take renter. So I buy small townhouse and take renter. She American woman. Very nice lady. I join her American church. We cook for youth group every Sunday lots and lots food. She teach me cook American. Macaroni plus cheese. Tuna casserole. Apple pie. I get very fat."

Washington laughed again and said, "You're about as fat as that dog is a giant."

He took another look around, smiled, and nodded.

"Guess everything turned out right."

He picked up his son and tucked him in the crook of his elbow, extending his free hand to his ex-wife. Hana slipped her hand, rough as the webbing on a cheap lawn chair, into his warm, satin palm.

"Congratulations, darlin'. I am real proud of you."

Hana accompanied the Washingtons to the doorway and stood on the sidewalk to watch them depart. Over his father's broad shoulder, the little boy waved his lollipop and smiled at her. When the Washingtons were out of sight, she darted back inside, ran into the storage room, and locked the door. Sliding down to the floor with the door against her back, she squatted on her haunches. She covered her face with her hands to stifle the wild sounds erupting from within. Goliath put his forepaws on her legs and whimpered until she picked him up and buried her face in his fur. Outside the storage room door, his ear pressed against it, Gramps could not tell if his boss was laughing or crying. Inside the door, neither could Lee Hana.

* * *

After his ouster from the helm of the church and school he had founded and built in America, Dr. Kim found himself unexpectedly content. He had immediately been engaged by his successor as a full professor at a higher salary than he had allotted to himself when he was the president. What with fewer Koreans with American doctorates in theology than fingers on a hand, his pedigree was an invaluable asset. With his name still headlining the faculty roster, Korean divinity students continued to come from all over the country to study the bilingual curriculum offered at the seminary and earn an accredited degree. He found he enjoyed the simple life of teaching, scholarship, and writing, free from administrative and fiscal duties, disentangled from the endless turmoil and insatiable neediness of his church flock. He was comfortable. He owned a small ranch home in a good school district. In every room, his homemade floor-to-ceiling bookshelves creaked and bowed beneath the weight of his beloved book collection. It was his American dream realized in satisfactory proportions. His children could not speak a word of Korean, a product, not of neglect, but of design. He had expected to settle forever in this great land. He had intended his offspring to become masters of the English language.

Unexpectedly, from his sick bed across the Pacific, Dr. Kang summoned his son-in-law to take the helm of Seoul Bible College.

Offices for both Dr. and Mrs. Kim as well as a fully furnished apartment were already set up. Candace would be away at college. The younger girls could attend American school in Seoul. All necessary arrangements were in place. Most of all, Dr. Kang yearned to spend his final months in the company of his firstborn daughter. The call was impossible to refuse.

Before returning to Korea, the last miles were eked out of Dr. Kim's rattletrap station wagon paying visits to family and friends across the United States, carsick family in tow. For their final visitation, the Kim family drove seven hours from Northern Virginia to the Village of Baldwinsville in upstate New York. There, Dr. Kim met Mrs. Betty Smith, mother of PFC Charles Smith, whom he had known during the Korean War as Mister Chuck.

Betty Smith's grown up daughters, curious to meet the Korean boy their brother had written of so long ago, traveled to their mother's home from neighboring towns, bearing brownies and cupcakes and potted plants. The Smith women fawned over Dr. Kim's four daughters, snapping photos with various combinations of Kims and Smiths. They remembered how Chuck had written about the cute Korean kids and even promised to bring one home with him. The plastic covers were removed from the best parlor furniture, coffee poured, and baked goodies set out. All the while, Betty Smith never removed her ravenous eyes from Dr. Kim's face. Abruptly, she interrupted the snacking and friendly banter.

"How was he in Korea?" she demanded.

But before her guest could reply, she unburdened her mind.

Her son had returned from Korea an altered man. Not at first. At first, he had seemed the same as always, happy and relieved to be home. A big welcome home barbecue was thrown for him. Everyone was invited. Everyone was having a great time. Chuck was telling funny war stories. He talked about his young friend, Kim, about how bright the young Korean boy was.

Then something went wrong. Chuck opened the lid of the barbecue to find the hot dogs had burned to a crisp. He stood transfixed by the sight of the blackened meat with juice hissing out of the cracks. An awful sound, the sound of a wounded animal, came out of him. The sound frightened everyone. Then Chuck vomited all over the deck. He fled to his bedroom, hid under his bed, and cried like a baby. Nobody could get him out from under the bed. The guests cleared out in a hurry.

After that, Chuck became withdrawn. During the day, he lay on the couch and watched soap operas or cartoons on television, hour after hour. It did not seem to matter what was on the tube. At night, he often slept under his bed. Loud noises, like a siren or the slamming of a car door, startled him out of his skin. He trembled and sweated.

Chuck started drinking. He stood outside the pub doors before they opened and stayed at the bar till closing time. He rode his motorcycle all around town, drunk, singing a Korean folk song *Arirang* at the top of his lungs.

For a long time, the neighbors were sympathetic. They kept the peace. But Chuck's public disturbances grew intolerable. The police would often come knocking on the door. One night, he left a one-line note: *I'm sorry everyone.* He rode his motorcycle into the Seneca River, went through the locks, and drowned.

There was a moment of silence. A familiar rush of sorrow flooded the hole punched in Dr. Kim's heart, belied by his impassive exterior.

"How was he in Korea?" Betty Smith asked again.

He swallowed the lump in his throat and answered.

"Charles was a brave, good man. He was well respected by all the men. He was very kind to me. He was generous. I admired him very much."

"He was brave!" repeated Mrs. Smith.

"He helped me during a battle. I was running from a firefight.

He picked me up and put me in his jeep and drove to safety. If he had not rescued me, I might have died. In this and many ways, I know he was a brave soldier and a good man."

"There were other boys from our town who came back from Korea. One of them is our mayor now. Not all the men were… were like him," said Betty Smith.

"The Korean War was a terrible time. Napalm, an incendiary gel, was used. There were guns that shot flames. Everything was burned: villages, trees, livestock, people…everything. Your son was on the frontlines. He endured the worst of it. No man can witness such atrocities and remain unaltered."

Samonim leaned over and prompted her husband under her breath in Korean. Dr. Kim spoke up, "Charles spoke of you in Korea."

"Did he? What did he say?" gasped Mrs. Smith as tears filled her eyes.

"He said you were an accomplished businesswoman. He spoke of your successful enterprise involving beauty products. Your handmade woolen socks brought joy and comfort and relieved much suffering. Many of the men lost toes from frostbite and there was a terrific demand for the socks you produced. Even I received a pair of these ingenious socks. They keep one's feet cool in the summer and warm in the winter. He spoke of you with the greatest respect."

"Did he talk about us?" asked one of the daughters.

"Yes. He said you always encouraged him to make something of himself. He spoke of you with the deep fondness of a loving brother."

"And his father? What did he say of his father?"

"He said his father taught him to be a man. He was proud of his father as a son should be."

"Oh, I wish my husband were here right now. You hear that up there?" said Betty Smith. She clasped her hands together and looked up to the ceiling. Then she crossed herself.

A troubled shadow crossed Mrs. Smith's face. She took a deep breath and glanced anxiously at her daughters. She had to ask it.

"You are a reverend. You will know the answer."

"No, Mama," warned her daughter.

"You have studied the scripture," she continued.

"Mama, don't."

"I'm not talking to you," she snapped and turned to Dr. Kim. "Reverend, did my son go to heaven? Can you…can someone do that to himself and still go to heaven?"

Dr. Kim deliberated for a moment and then cleared his throat. "Your son was not a suicide," he said. "He was a casualty of war."

A strangling sound escaped Mrs. Smith. Then she sobbed openly. Her daughters came to her and knelt in a circle around her. The Smith women held onto each other in a huddle of tears. While their parents bowed their heads in silence, the four Kim girls wept. All the cocktail napkins were soaked. Once they regained a semblance of composure, Mrs. Smith motioned to her daughter. "Get the box from Chuckie's room."

A worn shoebox was produced. Dr. Kim carefully opened the lid and took out an airmail envelope. It was one of the letters he had written to Smith from Korea after the war.

"Chuck saved every letter you wrote to him," said Mrs. Smith.

"Is that so?"

"Did you save his letters? Did he ever write back?" asked Mrs. Smith.

"No. I am afraid he did not write back."

"Well, if he could've, he surely would've."

"I know he would have," he said, returning the unanswered letter to the box.

"Look at the bottom of the stack," urged one of the Smith daughters. "Chuck took and saved the thank you note you wrote for the dictionary Mama sent you. It has lots of big words in it.

We showed everyone. Everyone loved it. We all needed to get out a dictionary ourselves to look up half the words. Read it!"

Dr. Kim read the letter aloud.

Honorable Mrs. Betty Smith:

I offer enormous gratitude magnanimous gift *Webster's New International Dictionary*, Second Edition, Unabridged. I learn plethora definition in capacious tome. I study each and every day excellent dictionary.

I pray Mister Smith and family maintain salubrious condition health and welfare. Korean people thank you citizens America for courage and sacrifice. God bless America.

Sincerely,
Kim Young Nam

"SAT words!" said Candace with a hoot, though she knew very well she was to remain silent during this, and any, visitation.

"I kept that dictionary you gave me all these many years. It has been my most treasured material possession."

"God bless you!" cried Mrs. Smith.

* * *

The following morning, Lee Hana, along with a church member, arrived to drive the Kim family to the airport. For the honor, Hana rolled hours early into the driveway in her freshly washed and waxed Cadillac, wearing a smart new double-knit suit, with her hair poodle-tightened in a fresh *pahmah*. Even Goliath, peering out of her tote bag, was freshly groomed and coiffed with a bow tie around his neck for the occasion. She bestowed farewell gifts upon the girls, a cashmere sweater for Candace, a gold pendant for Chloe, a leather-bound journal for Claudia, a cloisonné pin for Christine.

"Do not waste money!" scolded Mrs. Kim.

While the girls played with Goliath, Hana received last minute instructions from *Samonim* regarding the incoming renters and took possession of the house keys. When the church member, their second driver, arrived, the family organized into two groups, and Dr. Kim announced, "I will ride with Miss Lee."

To their surprise, at the airport, a sending party was gathered at their terminal. It included some dozen professors, graduate students, and faithful church members. Many of them were already in tears.

"Oh, no! Why did you come? Wasting gas! So much trouble!" protested Mrs. Kim. But she was visibly pleased.

Swarmed, Dr. and Mrs. Kim shook hands, returned bows, posed for photographs, and delivered blessings for the hour before boarding. The Kim girls received more gifts: boxes of candy, games, and books.

Then it was boarding time. Their rows were called. Dr. Kim abruptly left the boarding line, parted his way through the entourage, and approached Lee Hana, who had been hovering anonymously at the periphery. He extended his hand to her. She took in a sharp breath. She looked down at the floor and thrust her slender hand forward. Dr. Kim shook it and patted the back of her hand gently. It was the first time he had made physical contact with her since he saved her life in the Sap Kyo River. Tears fell from her bowed head and splashed onto his broad hands.

"Thank you for bringing me here," he said.

27

Kim Young Nam
Seoul
1985

A s Kim Young Nam shepherded his family through the immaculately renovated terminal of Gimpo International Airport, the precise diction of his native tongue over the loudspeakers and the *Hangul* on every board and poster fit him like a favorite old cardigan. At baggage claim, a large welcome committee of Koreans, dressed in their best gabardine suits and silk dresses, greeted his family, exchanged many bows, and enfolded them into their midst.

Seoul was unrecognizable. He had left Korea a third world country, still in partial ruins. He had returned to find a rising and sprawling metropolis. In every direction, complexes of high-rise buildings, densely packed towers of grey uniformity, ascended into the yellow smog. Korean-made automobiles crawled along the choked highway, like a black armored phalanx. With a start, Dr. Kim recognized that their caravan was crossing a new bridge over the Han River. Then, he saw additional new bridges flanking theirs to the east and west. Beyond the adjacent bridge, he could just discern the smudged outlines of yet another bridge.

"I swam across this river once," he said.

"You mean waded?" asked Candace.

He looked over the bridge and saw patches of exposed river bed rocks jutting here and there where the water ran dry. But the dry season had only just begun; the explosion of industry and population growth must be pushing water consumption to limit. Even the rivers were altered beyond recognition. On the horizon, the mountains anchored the vista, blue and immutable, the only visible reminder of the old Korea.

He had never told his daughters about the bombing of the Hangang Bridge. As he looked out over the dry riverbed, the memory played out in his mind: the explosion, the fire, people falling like white rags in the darkness. He now understood that the South Korean military had ordered the bombing of a bridge, loaded beyond capacity with their own people, in a futile attempt to delay the advance of the Communists. He thought he should tell his daughters the story. But he remained silent.

From a country of wretched poverty, razed to rubble and rotting corpses, his people had constructed a modern civilization. The very traffic jam in which they waited at a stock standstill, the infinite lineup of mirror-shiny black sedans, made Manhattan's worst rush hour look anemic. Though he had been an expatriate during the Miracle on the Han, though he was as patriotic as any naturalized American citizen, he could not help himself. An immense surge of pride and joy swelled in his heart.

"What a big mess!" said his wife.

Over a thousand people congregated to witness the installation of the Reverend Dr. Kim Young Nam as the second president of the Seoul Bible College in South Korea. The overflow spilled into the aisles and jam-packed the lobby where the ceremony was broadcast on monitors. This was the first college that had opened its doors to him, the son of an illiterate widow, poor country boy, and child laborer. Without contacts, transcripts, or credentials, despite smoking maws blown in his preparatory education by poverty and war, he had been granted an opportunity that would alter his life. Here he had been taken under the president's wing. Here he had fallen in love with the woman who would become his wife and the mother of his four children. Here, in the end, he felt compelled to return and to serve.

As he assumed the mantle of the presidency of the Seoul Bible College, as he gazed out over the sea of rapt Korean faces, as he resolved in that moment that his personal legacy would be to elevate this, his first alma mater, from a college to a university, he realized something. He was very hungry.

After the installation ceremony, a banquet was laid out in the cafeteria, buffet style. The feast announced itself from outside the building with a pungent aroma of sesame oil and garlic, promising to ooze from the diner's pores for days to come. Like any good Korean, Dr. Kim loved a buffet, the variety, the plenitude it represented. But he was ushered to the dais where he sat before the microphone at the right hand of Dr. Kang. His mouth watered as he waited to be served. From this inferior vantage point, he admired the feast.

There were marinated bean sprouts, savory spinach, fried tofu, roasted seaweed, battered and fried summer squash, pickled daikon, stir fried bellflower root, and fiddle heads. There was beef sliced razor thin, marinated overnight in soy sauce, rice wine, sesame oil, garlic, ginger, sugar, and scallions, and barbecued till the edges crisped. There were steamed flying fish, basted squid, prawn tempura, abalone, baby octopus, and jelly fish salad. There were pots of rice, glutinous and steaming in decadent pure whiteness.

There were varieties of kimchi, the Korean cook's pièce de résistance, red hot sinus-clearing pickled cabbage and radishes. In ancient times, kimchi was prepared at harvest, packed in waist-high earthen jars, and buried in the earth below the frost-line to be preserved for consumption throughout the year. Kimchi juice could counteract carbon monoxide poisoning from a leaky *ondol* floor. Kimchi kept the Koreans alive through the long bleak winters of the mountainous peninsula. Nowadays, there were special temperature-controlled kimchi refrigerators; every prosperous Korean owned one.

A separate dessert table before the dais presented gleaming pyramids of oranges, apples, Korean pears, persimmons, and chestnuts. Trays of rice cakes dyed pastel pink, green, and yellow adorned the glorious bounty.

Dr. Kim watched as ladies prepared plates for the dignitaries on the dais. As was his wont, Dr. Kim ate with focused intensity, swiftly, first, second, and third helpings, until his stomach was filled beyond capacity and a dull pain halted further consumption. Then he sat back in stoic silence and allowed the familiar guilt to set in.

* * *

The monsoon raged. The heavens broke asunder spilling black across the firmament. Relentless rain pounded the earth. The paddies flooded. The river swelled. Water was everywhere.

A young boy walked along the riverbank, barefoot, his soaked clothing plastered to his skin. The sludge sucked at his feet and ankles. He needed to get somewhere. He ploughed forth against the hammering rain. He needed to do something.

The boy spied a young girl, with a baby strapped to her back, walking in the adjacent field. But the baby was strapped on backwards, facing outward. The baby was squalling pitifully. He wanted to stop and talk to the girl with the baby. But a sense of urgency prevented it. There was something he had to get done. The girl would take care of herself and the baby too. He knew that.

He was nearly blinded by the sheets of water. The rain hammered him deeper into the sodden earth. The roar of the river drowned his ears.

Farther downstream, he saw a woman standing on the bank of the river. Then she was in the river. She floated peacefully, face down. He knew that a grown man, a soldier, would soon come along and save her. The boy need not stop for this woman. He pulled his feet out of the mud and struggled on.

Now, he knew what to do. He slid on his backside into the river. Eels swarmed about feeding on the worms in the exposed bank where the flood had scoured away the cover. He caught one and stuffed it into his pants. More eels slithered out of the bank and swam to him, surrounding him. He had only to open the sash tied around his waist and let them swim inside. His pants filled up. He crawled on his hands and knees onto the bank, his clothing alive with eels.

Now he was home. He boiled the eels into a slurry of thick, brown stew. He carried a steaming bowl to the sick room where a child lay still and small on his bedding. The invalid turned his head weakly. The boy knelt on the floor beside him. He fed the sick child a spoonful. The child's eyes glistened and a pink flush rose in his cheeks. The child raised himself on one elbow and whispered, "More."

The boy fed the entire bowlful to the sick child. He could barely spoon fast enough. Euphoria buoyed his soul. Suddenly, the child lifted his blankets away and levitated with weightless ease. His limbs were chubby and clean and glossy. He stretched his arms toward the boy.

He cried, "*Hyung*, you saved me!"

ACKNOWLEDGEMENTS

I am deeply indebted to my first reader, Sissy, who gave me the courage to put ink on paper, and went on to critique innumerable drafts of *Tiger Pelt*. Her trenchant insight made this novel come to life. My brilliant and generous sister and brother, Adrienne and Teddy, provided an infinite wellspring of advice, editing, and support. Many thanks to my children for their encouragement and enthusiasm. To my husband, who believes in me and supports my every endeavor, I owe endless gratitude. Most of all, I am grateful to my parents without whom this story could never have been told.

Annabelle Kim's debut novel, *Tiger Pelt*, was named to *Kirkus Reviews'* Best Books of 2015. She studied in the MIT Writing Program. She lives with her husband, four children, and Bouvier des Flandres in New Jersey: Exit 8.